INDIAN RESERVATION

PONCA IND.

SANTEE
SANTEE IND. RESERV.

Keya Paha • South Side
Grand Rapids
Dustin
Cleveland • Lavinia
Belknap
Chelsea
Clifton Grove
Greeley • Turner
Paddock
Red Bird
Pishelyville
Dukeville
Niobrara
Twing • Celia
Saratoga
Blackbird
cottville
Omaret
Armstrong
Richmond
Ray
Leanie
Mineola
Knoxville
Star
Pine
Verdigris Valley
Plan

SIOUX
Stuart
CITY
&
Atkinson
PACIFIC
Emmet
RAIL
O'Neil
ROAD
Agee
Parker
Middle Branch
Hainesville
Walnut Grove
Arthur
Verdigris Bridge
Bazil
Creig

K N O C

HOLT
Inman
Elkhorn
River
Lambert
Veras
Millerborough
Jessup
Glenalpin
Royal
Clear Spr.
NIOBRARA

Orchard
Chicago

S. Branch of Elkhorn R.
Chambers
Ferndale
Cr.
Vickroy
Ewing
Ford
Frenchtown
Willowdale
Slough

ANTELOPE

Swan L.
Conley
Little
Cache
Cache Creek
Clearwater
Cedar Cr.
Neligh

16   15   14   13   12   Walker   11   10   Deloit   9   8   7   6   5

Francis
Thompson
Oakdale
Burnett
Dry Creek

Erina
Buffalo
Cumminsville
Mentorville
Wheeler

GARFIELD
WHEELER
Reilly
Arden
Raeville
Cla

Harrington
Beaver Cr.
Olnes

The Forks
Garner
Coon Prairie

Willow Springs
Middleport
Moran
Akron

Ida
Calamus
Cedar   Cr.
Spaulding
B O O N E
San

Sedlow
Parnell
Troy
Dublin
Rosebna
Albion
Lo

Geranium
Ord
Floss.
Lee Valley
Council
St. Edwards
Bo

Manderson
North   Loup
VALLEY   GREELEY
Enfield
Mosside
Cedar Rapids
Neoma

Vinton
O'Connor City
Belgrade
1st. Guide Meridian

Mira Creek
North Loup
River
Scotia
Ellsworth
Chase
Red Way
Tekonsha

Yale
Scotia
Scotia Junc.
Glasgow
N A N C

Arcadia
Summit
Glenwood
Fullerton
Lone Tree
LOUP

Lee Park
Balsora
Dannevirke
Calesville
Cascade

THE
ROAD
HOME

THE
ROAD
HOME

Jim Harrison

Atlantic Monthly Press
New York

Endpaper map of Nebraska from the Official State Atlas of Nebraska, 1885, used by permission of the Nebraska State Historical Society.

Published simultaneously in Canada
Printed in the United States of America

FIRST EDITION

Library of Congress Cataloging-in-Publication Data
Harrison, Jim, 1937–
The road home / Jim Harrison.
p. cm.
ISBN 0–87113–724–0
ISBN 0–87113–729–1 (Limited Edition)
I. Title.
PS3558.A67R63 1998   98–8391
813'.54—dc21   CIP

Design by Laura Hammond Hough

Atlantic Monthly Press
841 Broadway
New York, NY 10003

98 99 00 01   10 9 8 7 6 5 4 3 2 1

To Peter and Molly Phinny

The Northridge Family

Aase ••••••• John Wesley = = = = = Small Bird •••••••••
            Northridge   (Margaret)

                    John Wesley = = = = =
                    Northridge II
                                    ••••••

Rachel   Naomi ───────────

Duane Stone Horse •••••••••••••• Dalva

                    Nelse

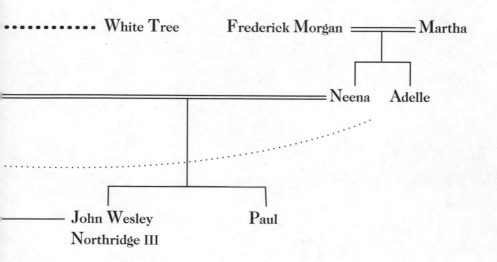

•••••••••••• White Tree   Frederick Morgan ══════ Martha

══════════════════════ Neena   Adelle

John Wesley   Paul
Northridge III

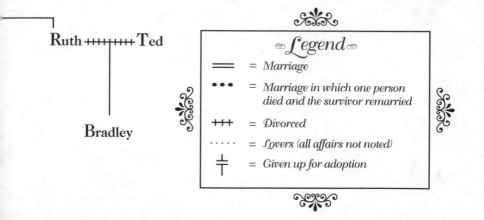

Ruth ++++++++ Ted

Bradley

	Legend
══	= Marriage
•••	= Marriage in which one person died and the survivor remarried
+++	= Divorced
·····	= Lovers (all affairs not noted)
⊥	= Given up for adoption

THE
ROAD
HOME

1

JOHN WESLEY NORTHRIDGE II

October 21st, 1952

It is easy to forget that in the main we die only seven times more slowly than our dogs. The simplicity of this law of proportion came to me early in life, growing up as I did so remotely that dogs were my closest childhood friends. It is for this reason I've always been a slow talker, though if my vocal cords had been otherwise constructed I may have done well at a growl or bark or howl at scented but unseen dangers beyond the light we think surrounds us, but more often enshrouds us. My mother was an Oglala Sioux (they call themselves Lakota), my father was an orphan from the East, grayish white like March snow, under which you don't count on spring, intermittently mad as he was over a life largely spent on helping the Natives accommodate themselves to their conquerors. After his release from the Civil War (sic!) until December of 1890 he burned up body and soul in these efforts, fixing on botany as the tool of liberation and this is in an area, the Great Plains, that is ill disposed to the cultivation of fruit-bearing trees, or berry-bearing bushes of an Eastern nature. The fact that he failed utterly in his life's mission only increases my reverence for him, though he was much easier to live with dead than alive, so powerful were the spates of irrationality that came upon him in the last twenty years of his life.

I have always collected my thoughts on Sunday, a habit enforced in my childhood when my father gave up on the church and turned to my own education with an energy that must be called unpleasant. He had gradually come over to the Native religious view that every day should be Sunday in terms of piety, and the lack of an immediate target for religious impulses made me the likeliest of prey. What young boy would truly wish to have Emerson on "Self-Reliance" read to him on long winter evenings before the fire, or in summer when the last light comes late, to sit there listening when one could still be in the hills on the far side of the Niobrara River looking for arrowheads with the dogs? One female Airedale, Kate, even supposed she could find them herself, when not looking for something to kill and eat, barking insistently at any peculiar, small sharp-edged stone. And each Sunday evening I was seated at the kitchen table to make sense of the preceding week, the very first slate-blue-covered notebook reading, in infantile scrawl, "I dont wan be hear."

Yesterday morning when I began this I had been startled from sleep thinking I heard my son John Wesley's car coming up the long two-track to the house, but then he's been dead two years and it was only the milk truck rattling on the section road a mile to the east. Nonetheless, I had rolled from my bed, my heart thumping with hope, before his face in the photo on the dresser spoke more loudly than he had ever in life. Panmunjom. But his daughter, my granddaughter, had asked me the day before why my parents had died within three days of each other back in February in 1910. Dalva is a scant eleven years of age and was curious I suppose because an October storm had threshed off the leaves of the lilac grove wherein we had our family cemetery, and she became mindful again of those buried including her father though there is no body there, the remains of which still rest on a snowy mountain hillside in South Korea. In any event, when I thrust myself out of bed so violently, my heart became tremulous, literally shaking in its sac, and I had the direst sense of mortality I have ever experienced, short of my youthful scrapes with physical violence in Arizona, Mexico and France, not to speak of two drunken louts I pitched into the East River in New York back in 1913 after a nasty struggle. Brushes with death are so memorable you can still see the pores in the face of the immediate enemy decades later.

Now, no one asks a more serious question than an eleven-year-old, and they deserve to be answered in kind, inasmuch as they are attentive to a painful degree, waiting for an answer rather than mentally concocting their next question. Usually she asked the same or similar questions about the horses of the past, liking familiar stories: how in 1934 did Lundquist and I feed up a Belgian stallion until he weighed twenty-eight hundred pounds, purportedly the largest in the country, if not the world at that time. But why my parents died within three days of each other could not be answered with, "Because they were sick and heartbroken with age and illness." The event had to be encapsulated in a story and not a simple one at that; at eleven she was already reading Dickens and the Brontë sisters and a reality painted in careless pastels would not be sufficient.

Another event, albeit strange, had occurred the week before and deeply unsettled me. Lundquist and I had made a three-hour drive to the west and north to hunt my remaining English setter, Tess, very likely the last bird hunt for both of us, she being twelve, and my knowing for a year that when Tess was gone this game would be over in this life. We had left before dawn and reached our first spot near Parmelee across the border in South Dakota, from whence we intended to travel onward to Gordon to visit some coverts where the dog had had her best day many years before. Bird dogs are fond of revisiting scenes of early happiness just as we are. Lundquist grumbled about the Parmelee area as expected; three members of his family, or so he maintained, had lost their lives in the New Ulm Massacre in Minnesota nearly a hundred years before and he was fearful of the Lakota. Tess pointed a sharp-tailed grouse that I flushed, shot but only crippled, and then we floundered in sedge and spike rush for a half hour, damning Lundquist who had wandered off as if following a distant star at midmorning. Tess repointed the wounded bird, unwilling to dispose of it, so gentle was her disposition. I grasped it by the neck and broke it, feeling the fragile vertebrae crush beneath my thumb. For some reason I kissed the bird, then dizzied and stooped to my haunches long enough to concern the dog. An old man half-kneeling in a bog saying good-bye to the hunt after a half century is a melancholy portrait indeed. Bringing the bird back to life was a casual and sentimental impulse, not the less absurd for being so heartfelt. In this grim world there is more sentimentality about killing than motherhood.

When I stood up and headed back to the car the day that had begun sunny and warmish for mid-October had turned gray and cool with the wind beginning to bluster out of the northwest. My heart that had been so eager for this last hunt now labored to get me back to the car which seemed to grow more distant, and the legs that had carried me as far as thirty miles in a single day now stumbled over blades of short-stemmed grama, tripped over dead flowers. I reminded myself that I had made love with a specific vigor only a week before, but that was thin fuel to get me to the car which had become a shiny dot on a far hillock. In this sea of grass you always park on a hillock for visibility so that you don't lose your way in the sere and undulating landscape, a color painters used to call "burnt sienna."

I had two stiff gulps from the whiskey bottle to the disapproval of Lundquist who had the heater running and was eating a peanut butter, onion and mustard sandwich, an enthusiasm, I daresay, he shared only with himself. He had worked for me since 1919, and his life was organized into peculiar rites. He always drank his water before the whiskey. We never quarreled but, as is usual of old friends, commented on each other's beliefs and habits in the most sidelong manner. "You're drinking the whiskey first?" No matter that I had done so hundreds of times in his company.

I dozed while Lundquist drove off for home, abandoning our plan for a full day's hunt. I awoke when the car stopped and Lundquist got out, sensing that we hadn't gone all that far. The engine was still running, the windshield wipers were on, my shins too hot from the heater. He was fumbling in the trunk and my eyes opened to watch him walk off with a gunny sack, perhaps fifty yards, where perhaps two dozen or so men, women and children were picking potatoes in a mixture of light rain and sleet. Most of them were Lakota, both pure and mixed breed. Three little boys, impervious to the weather, were having a fine potato fight. In my youth I had picked a lot of potatoes in nasty weather and checked myself short of sympathy: it was work and in this case, it was what one did to keep alive. Neihardt, the scholar and poet, had told me that even the legendary Lakota medicine man Black Elk picked potatoes in the fall, though with a great deal more humor than anyone else but the children.

It was then that my attention was caught by an old man in especially ragged clothing who had a stiff left arm that made him pick more slowly than the others. Even at a distance I caught the peculiar and pronounced hook in the bridge of his nose, the sag in a cheekbone, that had been caused by a cow's kick when we were scarcely ten years old. There was no doubt that it was Smith, a name adopted in humor because so many white men were named Smith and the name offered the ultimate in gentle concealment. He was from the family of Samuel American Horse and though I knew his real name I could not bring myself to utter his secret over fifty years later. I had bid him good-bye in 1906 when we were both about eighteen and he was off to Europe as a trick rider with a troupe of cowboys and warriors, one of the last of the touring Wild West shows.

I fairly bolted from the car, stumbling in the ditch, but my legs regained their strength as I made my way toward him. When I was only halfway there and still thirty yards away he turned and recognized me, then looked away blankly which gave me some anxiety but I continued on, calling out his name and saying, "It's good to see you" in my pidgin Lakota, cursing that my father had kept me as far as possible from the language. His own voice was soft and firm as ever, lacking the slightest of quavers I had begun to discover in my own. I wanted to embrace him but his words were utterly punishing: it was good to see that I was alive and he thanked me for the kindness that my family had shown him so long ago, kindness that had ill prepared him for the life ahead which had been brutal. He was a *wicasan wanka* now, a medicine man, and he no longer spoke to white people, and though I was half Lakota I lived as a white man and that's what mattered. Now he wished that I would go away, but said that he would visit me in the last year of my life when he had risen above all the differences his life had caused. He bowed slightly and returned to his potato picking. There was a childish, perhaps natural, urge to ask him just when the last year of my life would be, but I knew it to be wrong so I left, my legs slow again with the thought that this was the man I had considered to be the best friend of my life.

This morning when I woke at the first, faint light, merely a blur, I could see that my world was covered by a thick frost. I had slept fitfully, driving myself half daft with Dalva's question about my parents' death. My desire for a wise answer kept dissembling with memories in the darkness so that I kept turning on the lights to return myself to what we think of as the actual world, a pleasant enough fiction. I put on my wool robe but forgot my slippers, passing through the den where the Airedales lay sprawled on a buffalo robe. Only the smallish female, Sonia, got up to greet me. The others settled for a collective rumble at this interruption of schedule when no danger was sensed. I stubbed my toe, catching myself by hand against the door jamb, fearing that my fingers wouldn't miss a Maynard Dixon painting, a small one I cherished from his last years.

Sonia stayed on the porch steps as I wandered out on the bright frozen grass. The cold quickly penetrated my feet and I hopped a bit but not very high. I got close enough to the lilac grove to see the gravestones, then turned back, noting with delight how my feet had partially melted the frost, the choreography of my hops, remembering the hopscotch we played before I was withdrawn permanently from school. It was awkward to precisely retrace my steps but I did so, hopping right and left on numb feet until I laughed at my clumsiness, my wobbling frost dance.

I soaked my feet in a big dutch oven full of hot water, drinking my coffee and watching the frost slowly disappear in the none too strong October sun. Paul, the elder of my two sons, had traveled to South America several winters. His training was in geology though I suspect his main intent was for longer days. As a boy he told me he preferred it to be summer solstice every day if that could be arranged. He would travel with his mother to Arizona in the winters while John

Wesley would stay on the farm with me. It's certainly more ranch than farm but I like the latter out of habit so engrained is the popular misunderstanding of rancher. I once told a churlish woman in Kentucky that I operated a spa for cows to gain weight. That was at the 1947 Derby when I was staying with some hardboot horse friends and I sensed this woman wishing I were a captain of industry rather than a failed painter with a modest knack for land. Greed has always struck me as one of the most readily identifiable human vices and I'd spent far too long as its victim. My father, to whom God was more real than the milk cow in the barnyard, was also guilty on this count, though more excusably as he saw the Lakota suffer horribly for want of good land. Even that arch-enemy of the Natives, General Philip Sheridan, admitted that "a reservation is a worthless piece of land surrounded by scoundrels." Very late in his life my father was delighted with Henry Adams's radically low opinion of the "Western movement" while I found the book (*The Education of Henry Adams*) too long on the ironies and short on the primary colors that life can offer to those who are energetically curious. I suppose poor Adams never recovered from the suicide of his wife, though it is arguable whether anyone ever truly recovers from anything. I still twitch at ancient rifle shots, and an errant memory of Adelle, dead now forty-one years, can still make my body rigid with anguish. But then at other times, mostly when I am walking, her voice can become as musical as the May warblers in the thickets along the Niobrara. The dead do not offer themselves up as a consoling study when we loved them so.

Naomi has called from the country school where she teaches to see if Dalva can come for dinner. Naomi has to take Ruth to her piano recital, an event that Dalva loathes because they keep playing the same pieces over and over. This child is not sharp for the grace of repetition, nor was I, though there are penalties for this restlessness. I will cook myself as my housekeeper, Lundquist's wife, is off at a Lutheran conference down in the capital, Lincoln. This woman is forever in a state of spiritual high dudgeon, and a list of her dislikes is as long as the Omaha phone book. She is called Frieda and has given her daughter the same name though Lundquist told me he wished it otherwise, preferring Victoria for reasons of his own. Frieda has the conformation of a Hampshire sow and speaks in an irritatingly wee voice, and despite all of this, is on rare occasions endearing, being a master flower gardener, and I love flowers.

I judge that there's time to thaw last week's lone sharp-tailed grouse as Dalva likes what she calls "Indian food," which she doesn't get at her home, what with Naomi being a devout amateur naturalist who doesn't want wild things in her kitchen. I've asked her teasingly if her God loves deer over cows, but she is so truehearted that I'm gentle on the subject. At one time I raised the best beef in the state and I would be unwilling to give up either. A few years back Dalva came running into the house from Lundquist's pickup with the heart and liver of a deer in a small bloody paper sack. "It's just like our own and now we can eat it for lunch," she fairly screeched. Lundquist would pick her up on weekends on his way to work and at least once or twice a year would discover a fresh road kill in a ditch, the product of some late-night speeding drunk out on the country road who would outdrive his headlights and hit a deer.

Not very far back in my mind I am now begging the question of the day, the ends of my parents' lives. She knows the end of her father's story and wishes to know the end of mine. It won't be comfortable dinner talk but children lack interest in these distinctions.

It is now lunchtime and I have skipped breakfast watching the frost thaw. I'm still wearing my old wool navy blue robe, the hem tattered where Sonia used to pull on it as a puppy, then hang there to be dragged from bedroom to kitchen for morning coffee, a habit that sent Frieda into a dither of spleen. I can't very well sit here watching a sharp-tailed grouse thaw, though it's tempting as if I were some Chinese ancient in *Jade Mountain*. I have come very late to the pleasure of sitting still with little or nothing on my mind.

In the den, from the safe behind the bookcase with its difficult combination—1–2–3—I draw out the appropriate notebook.
On the way out of the room I pause at a Burchfield and a Charley
Russell, both bought for songs when my world was young and so
was theirs. With age I need not make judgments about their com-
parative merits, having lost the impulse to be right. One is one, and
the other is another. With age one loses all sense of the supposed
inevitability of art and life. Vivid moments are no longer strung
together by imagined fate. The sense of proportion in good and bad
experience loses its appeal. Bad is bad and you let it go. Good you
cherish as it whizzes by. Mental struggles become lucid and muted
with particular visual images attached to them, somewhat irrationally or beyond ordinary logic. Money shrinks to money. Fear is
always recognizable rather than generalized. It is sharp and its aim
is very good indeed. If there is wisdom as such, it is boiled down by
fatigue. On the very rare occasion that I check out an old notebook
as I am doing now, the sweat rises in my hair roots and I wonder,
What is this fool going to do next? There is a double melancholy
in my notebooks up until I entered World War I at the comparatively ripe age of thirty-one. Until that time the notebooks are thick
with sketches, nearly every page in fact, more drawings than prose,
the world as seen rather than thought. It would be nearly pleasant
to think that the war made me abandon what I thought was my
calling to be an artist, but the truth is that my talent wasn't strong
or obsessive enough to overcome my disappointments. My soul was
frozen for a long time and when it regathered its heat I was otherwise occupied.

Feb. 7, 1910—Coming up from well south of Magdalena in
Sonora and headed for Nogales. At twilight it turned damna-
bly cold so I used the horse blanket over the bed roll, having
gathered a cushion of grass for underneath. Firewood scarce near
the road so went well up a canyon & managed three sketches
before sunset. I will leave this horse with regret as in a lifetime

of horses this is the most intelligent I've owned. A roan gelding, he looks over my shoulder as I sketch and he chews his grass.
I judge that he could be trained to fetch firewood but my security is in his hobbles. He did not shy at the troop of coatimundi
(called "chulos" down here) that scurried off a side canyon as
we approached. Odd creatures as if crossbred between an otter
and a raccoon. Stopped at a hacienda around noon to replen-
ish my water and met an interesting young Mexican rancher
about my age who had been at University of Kansas for two
years. He tells me it is a good time to leave Mexico as the re-
fusal of Diaz to leave office will mean trouble, if not revolution.
He admires my horse and is startled to hear that I have traveled on him all the way up from Mazatlan since September. I
cannot give him a good answer other than to say I wander and
sketch when it's cool, and paint and trade horses during the hot
summer months. There is enough of a far-off look in his eye for
me to know he'd like to ride over the horizon from his big
hacienda. Both his parents and wife live in Hermosillo, preferring society life to that of a ranch. He beckons a servant girl to
bring me something to eat, and then embarrasses himself to
admit that when he was a boy he wished to be a poet. The servant girl had put her baby down on a pillow in the shade, the
days have been as warm as the nights are cold, and I glance over
at it, itching to make a sketch. The baby begins to cry and I get
up to tend it but he holds my arm. He tells me that the baby's
deformed and the girl thinks this is so because it was born out
of wedlock. The girl comes back and she is of surpassing loveli-
ness. She gives me lemonade and a bowl of stew, then moves
over to tend the baby and in a brief glimpse I see that the baby's
face is twisted askew. He senses that I know his secret and looks
away. Now the girl is looking at me rather boldly and I hold
out my arms. She carries the baby over and places it in my arms
and I hold it to my breast. We are all lost in the silence until
she asks him a question in Spanish and he turns to me saying

she wishes I would sing it a lucky song. I can think of nothing appropriate, then remember the Stevenson my Lakota mother read to me, which was her favorite:

> *"Whenever the moon and stars are set,*
> *whenever the wind is high,*
> *All night long in the dark and wet,*
> *a man goes riding by."*

I put the notebook down and got dressed for equilibrium. In 1921 when I was again in the area I found the hacienda but it was in ruin, its stucco pocked with bullet holes. I wandered around Hermosillo a bit, thinking I might run into them, but it was not to be. I had no names to work with but it seemed that afternoon when they had asked me to stay I should have done so. We think of life as a solid and are haunted when time tells us it is a fluid. Old Heraclitus couldn't have stepped in the same river once, let alone twice.

Feb. 10, 1910—I am in the Moctezuma Hotel in Nogales, Arizona, where I stepped off into this other world five months before. There are a number of doleful letters from home including too much money, then a telegram from Walgren, our neighbor, one of the original Swede carpenters who built our house and later had become a lawyer to the large immigrant community in the area. He was a grumpy, stern old bastard who could never resist an occasion for an homily. My parents are quite ill and I note the telegram is over a month old, having been sent shortly after the New Year. I make the short walk to the train station to book my passage, looking back across the border with regret to the distant hillside farm where I left my horse. I paid a year's board and told them to ride it which delighted a boy of about ten years who was already brushing the horse down. If there's a revolution what's to become of my horse? Neither Walgren or my parents have a phone, they being rare in our area. I send

both Walgren and the county sheriff, who dislikes me, a wire
saying that I am on my way home.

Back at the hotel I sort and pack my sketches, then have
my first hot bath in a month. There's a lump in my throat and
beneath my breastbone over my parents, but also a troubling
image of a girl I saw that morning mounting a horse Apache
style in one fluid leap. She smiled at me as I watched, then
reined off at a good speed, her hair flowing out in the wind,
toward the top of a hill where she decidedly did not turn around
for another glance. One is enough. Dying parents and the specter
of sex. My father somewhat opposed my art obsession especially
early on, while happy with my evident talent as a horse, also a
land trader, from which I've made a livelihood since fourteen.
The two, art and money, didn't go together in his mind. When
I was but a snooping boy and he was gone I looked at his locked
up papers concerning his tree nursery business he began after
the Civil War. The key was under the rug beneath his chair,
and he was forever secretive perhaps thinking business was a
bad mix with his devoutness. Since I was early set in my ways
in ambition to be an artist he made it his mission to comment
from the peripheries about "graven images," Edison's possible
blasphemy in recreating the human voice, the deceptiveness
of the photographic arts, the error in the attempt to make "moving" pictures, and the profound dangers of the auto itself which
was radically changing the sense of time, which before had
depended so much on distance. Or so he insisted . . .

I chop an onion and put it in a pan with butter, then pluck a
few leaves of fresh sage from Frieda's herb pots in the window. She
also churns the butter, the likes of which you can't get in Chicago or
New York, but must travel to far-off Normandy. I mince the bird's
gizzard in the pan with the onion, then tear some bread in pieces.
Dalva likes the dressing roasted, not "gummy" from inside the bird.
She will only eat rutabaga if it's mashed with the potatoes, and brus-
sels sprouts are out of the question unless halved and fried in butter

rather than boiled. There is little in her life that lacks her full attention. She has Sonia swimming in the Niobrara while I have trouble getting her to cross a creek. Lundquist carried Sonia around too much as a puppy, to protect her from the barnyard geese. When she grew she killed a single goose in vengeance. My thoughts turn to my friend Davis who was an excellent camp cook but died on my first trip to Mexico in 1909. He was from Omaha and much more talented at his sketchbook than I, but utterly foolhardy and captious. We were near El Salto west of Durango, camped in a canyon near precipitous mountains, two flatlanders but I was long on caution and he wasn't. It was late spring and there were too many rattlers to make exploring comfortable except in the cool of the morning. In the noon heat I was sketching and Davis swigging tequila for a toothache when he said he was going to climb a mountain to catch the breeze. This irritated me and I said, "Go ahead you fool, you'll break your neck" and he did, and more than that. He called out from a cliff a half mile up, or so I thought, and I looked up to see him teeter then teeter forward, shooting and pitching down a "couloir." Oddly, there was a large snake near his body, which was fairly peeled with remnants of his clothing in blood-soaked tatters. He said no last words so crushed was his face but his eyes still moved for a moment or two after I reached him.

Feb. 25, 1910—Back home for a week now, the last seventeen miles in an ugly blizzard on a borrowed horse, but then late in the afternoon, when I could see all the trees we planted perhaps three miles distant, the wind turned suddenly around to the south as if to ask me why all the concern, with the temperature rising from twenty to over forty.

They are both dead and I have buried them myself, making myself quite ill from exhaustion and the terror of attempting to keep them alive when they wished not to be. It was transparent that they were holding on for my arrival and I was ashamed and begged forgiveness but he hushed me, making a biblical joke, "Let the dead bury the dead but you will have to

do it." It struck me that neither had eaten in several days though
the larder was full. They drank quantities of Lakota tea which
made them a bit dreamy but did nothing to still my father's pain.
I was always made to call my mother Margaret though he used
her Lakota name, "Small Bird." It occurred to me that though
she was a full twenty years younger than his seventy-five she
did not intend to be with us much longer after he went, so I
vowed to keep a close watch on her. Other than Walgren his
only friend in the area was the youngish doctor, an amateur
scholar of Indian affairs, who had left pain medicine father refused, wanting to be "fully conscious" when he entered "the
kingdom." I don't know if this was courageous or foolhardy. It
went with the extremities the man had reached in his life. I got
him to take a glass of whiskey which helped and at the same
time made him more ill. He was to become a ghost before my
eyes that evening. He said that though he knew I would take
care of myself, I was well taken care of, and that the sin of his
life was greed. I assured him that certainly this was not notice-
able to anyone else, that though the house and property were
fine and solid we had lived simply. He would have none of this
and wept. We prayed before the fireplace with Margaret between us. It was plain that there was no time to summon any of
his old friends from up on the Reservation, the dozens who had
stopped by over the years in their secretive wanderings. He fell
asleep during his prayer and I caught him before he could fall
into the fire and carried him into his bed. Afterwards Margaret
gave me a stone in a small leather pouch. We sat up late so she
could hear about Mexico and look at my sketchbook. It was all
quite peaceful until she shook me at dawn and cried out, pointing out the window where my father was dancing around the
barnyard in his long underwear. I rushed out in my own and he
was all howling, bloody and incontinent, having danced a circle
in the snow. I could barely restrain him at first then by gesture,
also by cries through his bloody beard, I understood he wanted
me to dance around the circle which I did once before I hauled

him indoors, startled at how light he was and still how brutally strong. I forced some medicine down him then held his nose so he swallowed involuntarily. I rode only a few miles toward Walgren's before I was met by the doctor and Walgren coming toward me. By the time we got back home he was laying back out in the snow, quite dead, his head in Small Bird's lap. The doctor couldn't help but asked me what she was singing and I said I didn't know. I was a white man, whatever the hell that was.

I laid my journal aside, the repressed tears a poor preparation for dinner. My image of my father had become so strange that when I thought of him I also saw in my mind's eye a mountain goat up on a ledge down in the Pinacates. His blood was cold and Davis's warm, growing warmer in the afternoon heat as I carried him to the horse, then packed him into El Salto.

I poured myself my daily drink of Canadian whiskey, stared at it long and hard, then dumped it out in the sink and opened a bottle of good red wine. Ducru-Beaucaillou, bought in Chicago because I liked the sound of the name though it was more than palatable. My father made godawful rhubarb wine which put me off the beverage for years.

Walgren had tried to help me dig the grave but was arthritic and the temperature had dropped well below freezing. The ground had frozen before the snow came so I had to use a pick-ax for the first foot or two, with Walgren admiring the quality of the topsoil through chattering teeth until I sent him inside. The doctor came for the burial, the four of us standing there in the blustery twilight. They looked to me to say something but I was unable so we merely bowed. Walgren went inside and Margaret stood there singing in her native tongue while the doctor and I filled the grave.

Two nights later after tucking me into bed as if I were still a child she slipped out of the house after I fell asleep. At first light I tracked her the three miles to a spring beside a creek that flows into the Niobrara. She sat upright against a tree in a thicket, thinly dressed and quite dead. There was a bit of humor on her part in this as when

I was a boy I bothered her incessantly to go here, our favorite camping spot, and now she was leading me where I wanted to go. We kept a tipi in this place until I was about eighteen and some trespassing hunters desecrated it. My father was quick to forgive everyone except the U.S. Government, but I searched them out in a country tavern and they paid dearly for their crime.

I put the grouse in the oven, now eager for the arrival of my granddaughter. Out the kitchen window, in the cool autumn breeze between where I sat and our family burial ground, I felt for an instant I could see time moving in the air. I knew I was being foolish but it struck me as odd that time never went backward except in the fragile structure of memory. Everyone wanted to "get on with it," whatever that meant, other than a distaste for what they had already done. At the "time" that I buried my parents I would have given anything, a meaningless gesture as we have nothing to propitiate these gods, to be an artist or even a writer, but I was to be neither, perhaps caught in the netherworld between the two, the space itself creating a hopelessly restive spirit. For a brief period I sought to blame it on the mixed genes of white and Native, but that configuration meant nothing to the living touch, except to fall through the thin ice of its making into a comic bath of self-pity, certainly the most destructive of human emotions.

The doctor helped me begin to dig my mother's grave, though he was a poor shovel man and couldn't help but ask questions that were inappropriate to what we were doing. Could he read the journals my father mentioned keeping? Shouldn't the collection of artifacts be given to a museum? That sort of thing. It has always amazed me how people dither away the most sacred occasions. I sent him home in a huff, and before I tossed out the last shovelful, Walgren stopped by to ask when we might discuss my father's will and he too was dismissed. Thus it was that I buried my mother alone and far from her own people, though with full knowledge that her spirit would wish to visit them had it not already done so.

I had barely made it back into the house just before dark after kneeling on the fresh earth and once again caught short of anything to say when an illness struck which was later determined to be a form of malaria I had caught well down into Mexico. I was half delirious for several days and my mind and dreams took such odd turns that twice I tried to sketch the visions. Smith's young sister whom I had loved a great deal when we were both fourteen kept visiting me. She was called Willow and her parents were traditional people, our fathers close friends for many years. They discovered our affection and she was sent over to Manderson, some two hundred miles away, to live with an aunt, or so they said. When I went off to look I found no trace. That was in the late spring of 1900 and I didn't speak to my parents until winter, building my own quarters out beside the barn and taking up horse-trading in earnest for my support. It was the first mortal blow of my life. Her parents did not wish me near her because I was half white, and later on, another set of parents with equal determination would cast me out because I was half "savage," a word they mouthed with enthusiastic terror.

FEB. 27, 1910—Odd sights, quite frightening, as if I could ever paint, or anyone could, the landscape of this fever. Inside the thresher. First the cow guts were pulled at in tug-of-war up on the reservation when I was three or four when they butchered the allotment. Men ate raw slices of heart. The women took the guts away from us after the dogs dragged us, holding onto the intestines. Waking I drink water that seems hot though I know it's cold because the house is freezing with no fire. I'm too hot for a fire I think, breaking the ice in the pail. Now I am half-way up Harney Peak when I was ten where father hoped to show me a bear which we only saw through his glass far off at the edge of the meadow and forest. Willow wakes me by the spring. We are naked, having swum. The sand is hot at mid-day with ten million cicadas droning in the air. She said I heard them say they are taking me away to Manderson. I fall down the stairs to catch her and wake at the bottom wet and finally cold . . .

Dalva arrives in the yard on her dun gelding, greeted in a uproar by the dogs. I had dozed at the bottom of my ancient stairs and
thought for an instant it might be Willow in the same yard fifty years
before. At Dalva's insistence Lundquist had built a tether rail in front
of the porch. She bursts in and we embrace and I ask what happened
to the school bus which she doesn't answer, but announces she's
spending the night. What she thinks so becomes so, which stops a
bit short of fibbing. She races back out to put her horse away, fetching her satchel on hearing I'm not up for a ride in the cold October
wind.

Last evening I got my comeuppance halfway through dinner where
she ate far more than I did. She asked, "When you tell me stories about
your life why do you always pretend you were such a nice person?
Naomi says you weren't. Everyone in town says you were the scariest
man in the county. Old people at church say you were even worse
than your father. They say you're not even a Christian person. So I
wish you wouldn't just tell the good parts about yourself. I'm not some
little kid, I'm eleven."

This struck me as more interesting than upsetting. Have I ever
met a man who didn't wish his daughter or granddaughter would stay
unspoiled by the likes of us and a substantially evil world? But what
is behind this wish aside from hoping that a living being will stay a
porcelain figurine of our mind which she bears no resemblance to
except in our minds, and in societal deceit in the first place? I've yet
to know a woman who carries any true resemblance to what society
seems to wish her to be. They are not constructed thusly, any more
than we are.

Instead of telling her of the deaths of my parents, her original
question, I painted a tale of the aftermath of Willow being taken from
me. I shot my father's best bull as it drank from the Niobrara. It trusted
me and let me come close and I put my Iver Johnson revolver to its
ear, shooting three times before the bull dropped to its knees in the
water, then floundered further into the river, roaring and bawling,

shooting gouts of blood from its nose and mouth before it tipped sideways and floated off.

I plotted the deaths of Willow's father and my own but what stopped me, sensibly enough, is that I'd never find her if I was in prison. It took me but five days to ride to Manderson and when her relatives would tell me nothing I again drew my revolver but was subdued by an old man and he and several other ancient Lakota warriors bound me hand and foot and took me home. Among them was He Dog, a friend of both Crazy Horse and my father. These were not tame souls but bore the full weight of battles from Little Bighorn to Twin Buttes. To say that they frightened me was the mildest of euphemisms. One of them who was Willow's uncle said that if he saw me again in Manderson he'd feed my balls to the crows. He waved a knife the others said had taken a hundred cavalry scalps. He became so overwrought in his threats that he leapt from his horse, though I judged him to be seventy, and danced madly around my own, howling and yelping so I nearly peed my trousers. These were not Methodist Indians but warriors with a lineage that owed nothing to the white man. We did not live upon the same earth that they did and we flatter ourselves when we think we understand them. To pity these men is to pity the gods.

The group of old warriors, I seemed to remember there were five, stayed three days. Like others before them they gave my father parcels wrapped in deer hide for safekeeping. They camped out in the barnyard, doubtless giving my father counsel on my behavior, also discussing the old days after Wounded Knee when my father had suffered a nervous disorder and was encamped with these friends up in the Badlands. To my later regret I stayed well clear of the others, sulking out at the spring but reappearing at dinner for fear they would track me down which was their sure intention. To my further regret my father had been out on a ride that day and had heard the shots and had seen the floating bull, dragging it out of the river with our Belgian draft horse Tom. He never pointed the finger at me but the last evening when we feasted on the meat Willow's uncle thanked me for being a good shot, following the comment with wild laughter.

After they left I set about building my shack, part of which is now one end of the bunkhouse. Smith tried to help but had even less talent for carpentry than myself. He wisely suggested bringing up my parents' tipi from the spring but I wanted nothing from them. I'd have to filch some of last year's potatoes, cabbage, and rutabagas from the root cellar but other than that I'd live on game that I shot. Smith brought up the question of heat but since it was late spring I said I'd worry about it when the first snowflakes fell. It rained hard for a week and we struggled in the mud with our inept carpentry, studying from the pages of a shed booklet I'd ordered from *Nebraska Farmer,* a magazine guaranteed to fill an adventuresome lad with the direst boredom possible. I horribly missed the pies my mother made from dried fruit and when the wind was right from the east I could smell their odor wafting across from the farmhouse a hundred yards in the distance. Smith missed the pies, too, and suggested with Native wisdom that my mother had probably had nothing to do with the decision over Willow and I could forgive her by asking for pie. Smith soon abandoned our mutual tipi camp in favor of his parents' shack on a far corner of our land on the banks of the Niobrara. There was a grace note in a good dinner every evening, though he'd arrive at dawn punctually with a wedge of cornbread for me.

One June morning when my miserable shack was nearly erect Smith had arrived with what he thought was a solid clue to Willow's location. He had left his place at dawn then returned having forgotten my cornbread and had overheard his parents talking about a mixed-breed cousin who worked far to the east in an iron mine in Ishpeming, Michigan. This was Chippewa country (*anishinabe*, they called themselves) so the cousin could scarcely admit that he was part Lakota because of ancient enmity. He was a daring fellow, Smith said, and had once bought them a milk cow on a visit, and had married a white woman from Finland.

I straightaway rode to town to get some tar paper for my roof, but also to check out the location of Ishpeming. It was certainly too far for horseback and anyway my prolonged disappearance might alert Smith's parents and my own that I was again on the track of Willow.

I must strike quick, I thought, while checking the atlas and train schedule at the county library. I judged that I'd have to sell three of the eleven horses I'd accumulated to afford the journey, a trifling price for a young Romeo hell-bent for his lost love.

At this point it was Dalva's bedtime and I stopped my woeful tale. She was teary and dabbed her eyes with a handkerchief I gave her. Her first comment was, "It all makes you want to be a dog." She knelt on the rug and kissed the Airedales good night, then was startled by her own thoughts. "If you had married Willow when you were fourteen then I wouldn't exist," she said. I had noted before that young people were struck by the fragility of their existence but this seemed premature for a little girl. "It is always good to know how the story ends," I teased her, but she was already off on another tangent. "Why wouldn't your father let you love an Indian girl? He was married to one." I told her I'd think that one over, although all my thinking on the matter had long since finished itself by exhaustion. I sent her upstairs to her grandmother's bedroom which she adored for its ornate dollhouse qualities, so unlike the rest of the house. My long since departed wife hadn't slept there the last ten years of her life, having left me for Omaha and Chicago in 1930. "You'll be much happier," she had said. "You've been a bachelor since you were a child."

I had a Hine cognac and listened to the scratchy and plaintive strains of "You Can't Be True, Dear" ("There's nothing more to say"), through the den's ceiling, picking up a phrase now and then that I already knew. Dalva always played the song on an old crank-up Victrola before going to bed because it was "romantic," unlike her mother's steady diet of Brahms and Dvořák since losing her husband, my beloved son John Wesley. How irreparably changed the world becomes when the loves of one's life are dead. It is always the last day of Indian summer. We are caught out in the cold and there's no door to get back in.

I chided myself for my sentiment, remembering the great ladles of Dickens my father would pass my way to ensure that I developed a proper compassion. My captious nostrum for Copperfield and Cratchit was to shoot their tormentors or beat them into the ground, an idea that made no headway with my father. The last draught of cognac sent me coughing and I considered something so adventuresome as a visit to the doctor, feeling my heart wobbling, but then I remembered Maynard Dixon and his courageous wheezing. I had also noted in others that life largely passes while they are still making grand plans for it. I had certainly committed no sins of omission but this was less virtue than obsession. I could not help myself. My mother liked to stare at the map while I described the specifics of places I'd been on my early sketching trips, and then I'd wait for her soft questions. What did they eat? What kind of horse did they ride? Were there Indians and were they treated well? With the latter I didn't want to be honest, but was so out of obligation to her own lucid, albeit limited, sense of history of other people: Seri, Tarahumara, the Yaqui sold into slavery from their native southern Sonora down into the Yucatán where they died of the weather; the greatest proportion of the Seri (thousands) butchered by vaqueros and the Mexican army over a cattle-stealing incident. The Tarahumara seemed safe in their mountain fastness but one doubted this to be a permanent arrangement. I remember the three of us sitting at the kitchen table before the atlas and her wondering why the invaders of our own country had bothered crossing a dangerous ocean, when we could have traveled east to the vast bare stretches her brown finger pointed out in Russian Siberia. I was perhaps ten at the time and my father looked to me for help, a unique gesture on his part. I piped in that people liked to ride on boats to which she disagreed. At the grand Trans-Mississippi Exposition in 1897 in Omaha we had gone to as a family she had felt unpleasant on a Missouri steamer, and crossing the bridge into Iowa for my boyish sake had been nightmarish for her. She wouldn't get in the small johnboat we used when we wanted to float or cross the Niobrara, but she did take pleasure in swimming across in late summer, whereupon she'd call out childishly, "I'm on the other side."

The most poignant moment for her at the grandiose Exposition had been a meal at a Chinese restaurant where she didn't eat the food but thought the Chinese resembled the Cheyenne. My father kept her clear of the mock battles being performed by the gathering of tribes for fear of further strengthening the melancholy of her nature. The trip had been for my own benefit so I could see what was to become of the modern world in order that I might adjust to the change, but what had impressed me most as a bumpkin was not the immense absurdity of the filigreed architecture, but the sight at the French exhibition of a lovely Frenchwoman speaking French. She looked exactly like a woman in a Courbet reproduction some thirty feet from where she was speaking. I drew close enough to the platform from which she spoke to scent her lilac odor and admire her skin and trim figure, which even a ten-year-old notices. For less than a second she glanced down at me and smiled, and thus by happenstance began my obsession with art.

I was awakened early by the sound of Dalva in the kitchen, thankful again that Frieda was still in Lincoln on her religious binge. Dalva had a single breakfast recipe wherein she'd cut a round hole in a piece of toast, then fry the bread in butter with an egg in the hole. She was pleased to make this for me before our Saturday morning rides, though she didn't eat it herself, preferring cereal. I had heard Lundquist's pick-up arrive before daylight for chores, then turned on the radio out of habit for the livestock report, shutting it off quickly before the political inanities could begin. I was thankful that the air out the window was still and that there was the sun. An old rider is far less resilient on a shying horse, and a strong wind makes all creatures nervous. That thought turned me again to Willow who sat a horse better than anyone I've ever known, including jockeys. It was a mixture of temperament and athleticism, a removal of any distance between her and the animal. And she left Smith and myself far behind in the breaking of young horses. Far later it occurred to me this was because she had no "will to power," but rather a marriage of her intentions and the horse's. Her loudest voice with an animal was a crisp whisper, and dogs were also quick to co-operate, while they would shun the manly shouting

of Smith and me, doubtless thinking it resembled the angry bark of
one of their compatriots.

Willow's mother must have given her some herbal concoction
against pregnancy because we made love whenever the impulse
seized us, which was often, beginning with the aftermath of a Fourth
of July celebration, through the rest of the summer and winter,
whenever possible, on into spring when we were parted by force.
On the Fourth we had ridden toward town in the evening of a big
moon, stopping at the outskirts near the park. Both Willow and
Smith were forbidden by their parents to go to town so we sat there
well out in a dark field listening to the distant band music and
watching the fireworks, the music broken intermittently by the
explosions. Willow snuggled close to me, finding the music rather
than the explosions frightening. Smith was of an irritable bent that
evening and snuck off with his coup stick, feather attached, to mock-
destroy some *wasichu* on the edge of the gathering. With her brother
gone Willow kissed me one long kiss until I noted the moon had
moved a foot or two across the sky in our mating, and we had to
light matches to find our clothing. We didn't know any better,
because there wasn't any. And when it was truncated my youthful
emotions aimed themselves for bear.

When we reached the barn Lundquist had us all saddled up, a relief
as I was still feeling a tad quaky. I called my "thank you" up into the
mow door but he was over in the shop at the far end of the stanchions
from when we kept a few milk cows. I had been irritated that I couldn't
get good cheddar like they made in England so we set off on our cheese
project which turned out to be far too labor intensive. Lundquist's
diminutive mutt, Shirley, barked from the work bench at the Airedales thinking herself at that height to be their equal. Lundquist was
busy saddle-soaping a set of show harnesses we hadn't used since before
World War II. He was a bit worried about Frieda's stay in sinful Lincoln and I again reassured him that it was unlikely she'd be molested.

We made our habitual two-hour ride upstream on a ridge along the Niobrara, cutting well inland after three miles along the property border, bearing left along our favorite shelterbelt to the forty-acre thicket with its spring and creek, the home of the tipi so many years before. My sons, Paul and John Wesley, began to excavate a mound here when they were young, possibly a Pawnee or Ponca gravesite, but ceased when I told them they were bound to release a few ghosts. This digging of the graves of others for sport or science has always struck me as wretched, another more peculiar form of greed than the usual.

We rested here and Dalva brought out two blueberry muffins and lemonade while we watched the Airedales thrash around in a cold pond trying to catch any of a family of muskrats that lived there. Well out of their element in the water the dogs swam until mournfully exhausted, then flopped near us on the bank for a snooze, except for their ringleader Sonia who sat ever watchful at the water's edge, continuing her alertness even as she ate the half muffin that Dalva gave her.

In summer we'd unsaddle the horses and let them have a swim but now they too seemed autumnal, stirring the lid of yellow cottonwood leaves on the pond for a drink. I glanced at my granddaughter wondering for the thousandth time how poor a substitute I made as a father. Naomi disagreed with this, insisting I was doubtless better with Dalva than I had been with my sons. She could be sharp-tongued indeed and offered little comfort when honesty was at stake. She was a handsome woman and I had imagined that over the years hundreds of farm boys she had taught at country school had become infatuated with her.

At odd moments life will take an abrupt bite out of the heart. Dalva sitting there in the clear October sun on the sand bank had a look on her face similar to Willow's when she was in a state of contemplation. She wasn't trying to overcome life, only to get along with it, to blend with processes she could scarcely understand in a world that had permitted her no solid ground. After profound and nearly uni-

versal violence we settle back into business, Willow without a homeland, and Dalva without a father.

She asked then when it was that I found Willow, and said it
seemed a shame that she had been sent to Michigan, so far from home.
Well, she wasn't sent there after all, I said, that was Smith trying to
be helpful, and only a fourteen-year-old boy would tear off on a journey on so little evidence. I did sneak into the house and leave a note
for my mother, perceiving that Smith was being sensible when he
said she had no part in the decision. My father slept soundly but I
was sure my mother heard me pack a satchel with clean clothes, a
skinning knife and a revolver. I left the note under a pie tin, having
cut a large wedge of blackberry pie for my breakfast.

The train ride as far as Minneapolis was uneventful though I
saw altogether too many cornfields, and was confident that some
of the shifty-eyed fellow passengers might be intent on stealing my
satchel. My money was dispersed in my pockets and left boot, the
latter giving me a limp so I wouldn't wear the money out. I was
somewhat ashamed when a saucy young married woman with an
urchin in tow caught my eye. Here I was bent on finding Willow
but having unhallowed thoughts about a married woman who rubbed
my neck as her child slept. That was as far as it went, though she
gave me a peck on the cheek after I helped her with her trunk in
Minneapolis. I quickly caught the wrong train northeast out of
Minneapolis on purpose—one traveling across northern Wisconsin was a shorter route—because I had noted on the library map that
Duluth was on Lake Superior and I had not yet seen a large body of
water. Right away the train was coursing along amid trees so densely
situated that a few square miles of them could have replaced all of
the trees in western Nebraska. The sight was wondrous to me, even
in the large areas where all the trees had been cut for lumber, which
gave some relief to the landscape. I questioned my seat mate, a somewhat prissy middle-aged man who had earlier announced himself
to a be a "Duluth businessman," as if this in itself carried a special
virtue, on how one would learn to find one's way amid such a forest. He said it was death without a compass unless one were a "red-

skin." I doubted to myself that my half-breed nature would keep me from getting lost in such a forest. It was easy, though, to understand that the locals could survive the bitter climate with this endless supply of firewood.

My own misshapen and rebellious nature was drawn to these trees because they were so unplanned and haphazard, so utterly wild compared to my father's shelterbelts that had taken so much of our time, virtually since I began remembering in the ten years since we were off the reservation area. I began helping with a child's shovel but soon graduated to an adult one by the time I left the country school, now Naomi's, at age nine. My father's grand plan for this succession of windbreaks to grid three thousand acres was to protect enclosed pastures and tilled fields from the violence of Great Plains weather, to retain moisture, and later to amend the local shortage of firewood and lumber. While also raising cattle and my own growing collection of horses, and row crops of corn, wheat and oats, we spent just short of ten years planting staggered and mixed rows of bull pine and ponderosa, caragana, buffaloberry, Russian olive, wild cherry, Juneberry, wild plum, thornapple, and willow, with sturdier inside rows of the larger green ash, white elm, silver maple, black walnut, European larch, hackberry, and wild black cherry. I never questioned when we picked up the huge bundles of rootstock at the train station, with their discreet and formal labeling of Northridge Nurseries from different locations in Illinois, Iowa, and New York State. My father said they came from our cousin and it was years before I questioned the idea of the cousin when my father had insisted he was alone in the world. The idea that he felt shamed by his business acumen was tied to the fact that he had mortgaged his life for a grubstake in this world, taking another's place in the Civil War for pay. Anyone but a cretin knows that nearly all men mortgage their lives for survival or profit, but such was my father's fidelity toward what he thought was the truth of the Gospels that his own activities made him miserable with guilt. His essentially orphaned youth and his later efforts with the landless and penniless Lakota certainly gave him adequate motive.

All of this was but a moment's thought when I told Dalva about
my first wild forest, a forest presumably devised by some god with a
level of genius incomprehensible to us, who need not bother design-
ing ordered rows or digging a hundred thousand holes in the ground,
or constructing hydraulic rams for irrigation water. But then we loved
this marsh, spring and creek for its true wildness that we had no part
in making. Now, fifty years later, when these endless shelterbelts
present themselves to strangers as owning the beauty of a forest, I am
grudging to admit they are beautiful indeed, but a portion of my heart
belonged to the grand woodlands of northern Minnesota, Wisconsin and Michigan. If I had not been a dreamy and cantankerous youth
I would have noticed those forests were doomed by the gathering and
enormous fields and hills covered with giant stumps, but back then
the remnants of the virgin forest herself seemed endless.

I played the fool in a number of not very unique ways in Duluth.
The harbor and Lake Superior, the hilly city herself seemed gorgeous,
so why did I lose half my money playing cards in a saloon? I was served
a piece of beef at a dockside restaurant that no one in Nebraska would
consent to eat, paid for the uneaten meal, then strolled down the
street and saw a saloon that offered free Lake Superior trout and perch
as long as you kept buying drinks. I had no experience with alcohol
short of my father's homemade wine, the taste of which encouraged
moderation, but I was bold enough to order a shot and a beer, and
was given a basket of fried fish on the side. I was fully grown and strong
from work at fourteen but my capacity far exceeded my talent for
booze. I was shortly quite drunk, chock full of fish, and losing at a
poker game until a Norwegian logger guided me back to my cheap
hotel. A very big lady on the street tried to wrest me away but the
Norwegian got me safely to my room. In the middle of the night I
vomited on myself, an experience that kept me away from both alcohol and fish for quite some time. And at dawn I was wakened by a
bellowing and cursing group of loggers fist-fighting in the street, the
group evidently having failed to go to bed at all. I was suddenly quite
homesick for my horses and mother, though I stopped short of any

fond memories of my dad. I drank a whole pitcher of water, was sick again, then left the hotel in a nauseous rush, eager for the open air.

This questionable dawn was further compromised when I opted for steamer passage from Duluth to Marquette near Ishpeming, rather than take the train. The muggy weather had dissipated and there was a fresh cool breeze out of the northwest, rare indeed for a Nebraska summer, but commonplace in Duluth, or so I was told. What I wasn't told was the effect this bracing wind had on Lake Superior, and straightaway out of Duluth harbor our ship began being pounded by waves that I found uncomfortable. These waves, which no one else thought worthy of notice, continued on throughout the day and evening, and grew even more fearsome when we passed the Apostle Islands and received the full brunt of the sea. My misery continued through the night until the steamer came around the Keweenaw Peninsula and we received a full lee, traveling south to Houghton for a brief stop before heading on another hundred miles or so to Marquette. Much as I loved Willow I was in the deepest state of regret over this trip. A sympathetic sailor had given me salt crackers which helped a bit and said we'd be in Marquette by nightfall. I bolted the ship, however, in Houghton, resolving to crawl to Ishpeming if I had to, any measure that would get me off the water. Once the world stopped rocking, I stumbled into town and tried to buy a cheap horse but couldn't find anything I could afford except draft horses in miserable health from overwork. On the advice of a drunken lout I jumped a logging train, sharing a flat car with a group of men in far worse shape than myself, it being a Sunday night after a day off and a night of pleasure. The train sped by Ishpeming before dawn, and I got off in Marquette and walked a dozen or so miles in the early morning back to Ishpeming where I had no difficulty finding Smith's "cousin" by asking a policeman who first advised me that they were hiring at the mine. This did not tempt me as I had no more wish to spend a life underground than I did at sea.

I bought two chickens and a bottle of whiskey, not wanting to arrive empty-handed. Smith's cousin called himself Jake and was an enormous fellow, a mixed breed in whom there was a definite trace of a Buffalo soldier (black). His hand was wrapped from two crushed fingers but he hoped to get back to work in a few days. He immediately opened the whiskey and I heartily declined a drink. His wife was a very large Finnish woman who set about frying the chickens and drawing me a bath. Quite naturally they hadn't heard a thing about Willow, but after a few drinks Jake supposed she must be up near Mobridge, South Dakota, with the Standing Rock people. Her mother had a sister up there somewhere, he thought, adding that I should give up my quest before I got "my ass kicked real good." After dinner we went out to the town dump and watched bears pick over the garbage, a melancholy sight indeed.

I made my uneventful way home and finally spoke to my mother who wept at my new intentions. I sold another horse for a grubstake, saddled up, taking a string of two more, and rode way up to Watauga, west of Mobridge, with my loaded Iver Johnson at my belt and my rifle in a scabbard. It was a five-day ride, all day and half of each summer night. I saw Willow only for a few moments at the door of a shack, and then was asked to leave by a gathering of men. When I strongly resisted I took a beating that I still remember clearly, and one of my horses was seized for good measure. I made my way back south but fainted from pain outside Pierre where a doctor wrapped my broken ribs and pulled two busted teeth. It took me a full ten days to make it home as my taped-up chest didn't greatly reduce the pain in my ribs, and riding was difficult. Despite all of this I enjoyed the countryside as much as I had on my trip to Ishpeming. The young are resilient and I had done as much as I could to retrieve my lost love. When I got home I presented myself at the front door, was embraced by my parents, went to bed for twenty-four hours and ate a half of an apricot pie on arising.

Dalva was inconsolable over my story having read *Wuthering Heights* several times to the neglect of her schoolwork. Naomi had brought over dinner but was a great deal less sympathetic over my beating when she caught the tail end of the story. I then admitted that I had pressed the attack, sensing that it was "all or nothing," an attitude I got from dime novels rather than the large stack of classic literature my father gathered for me. Dalva was pleased to learn that I had started the fight, adding, "That's what I meant when I said you pretended you were always nice. The worst case of this is our minister." She was referring to the Methodist minister up the road who had been there a couple of years, and it had recently come to light that he beat both his wife and children regularly. I was a great deal less amazed than his parishioners, not being a church-goer myself. Lundquist as a devout Lutheran was sure that if the minister would only read Swedenborg he would behave, while Frieda thought he should be lynched.

Naomi sighed and got up for a deck of cards for our gin rummy game which Dalva always won out of a superior level of attention. She loathed the minister and was merely baiting her mother with the sorest of subjects. Naomi didn't want to have the minister run out of the area which would only leave the wife and children in a further lurch. She had even indicated that I as a total outsider might speak to the minister though I'd met him only a few times in passing. I viewed the man as a vicious pest, and told Naomi that since she had lots of money she'd never get around to spending why not intercede herself? She could give the woman and two children a new start in life far from this pious lout. Naomi was currently getting up the courage to do so.

The long ride made me doze through the rummy game and I played badly. During the badinage of the game Dalva admitted she hadn't spent a moment with her homework, and was sent upstairs to pack her suitcase, rather than being allowed to spend another night. Despite my sleepiness I remained curious about the peripheral way the female argues, so unlike the quarrels between father and son. With Dalva out of earshot Naomi asked me not to tell the story of Adelle for a few more years and I nodded in assent. I was startled because I had never heard her mention the name, but then presumed John Wesley had told her the story. When we die we are only stories in

the minds of others, I thought, then dismissed the notion as Dalva
kissed me good night, saying, "I love you," always splendid words.

There was the slightest hope in her face that I might interfere
in the idea of her going home to catch up on schoolwork but I
wouldn't think of doing so. My having left school at age nine had
always intrigued her, even when she knew my father had tripled the
learning load. At the encouragement of some older boys, I didn't need
much, I had set fire to the country school outhouse during recess, then
as the enormity of the act had registered on everyone I had escaped
for home on horseback, hiding out in the haymow of the barn. The
teacher was in hot pursuit but on a slower horse. I peeked out through
the slats of the barn as he banged and hollered at our back door, still
carrying his whipping stick. When my mother was not able to offer
up the culprit the teacher, a pompous young man from Hastings,
called her a "damnable squaw," which my father heard from the den.
He rushed out and flung the teacher off the porch into an icy March
puddle. "Damnable squaw" was not a wise choice of words to use
within the hearing of a man who had spent twenty-five years with
the Lakota and had lost so many dear friends at the massacre at
Wounded Knee.

When I walked Naomi and Dalva to the door I stood out in the
moonlight until I shuddered from the cold air, watching their tail
lights bobbing out the long bumpy driveway and down the gravel road,
the stones rattling under the fenders. The moon on the trees stung
my memory. My mother had been married to White Tree (because
he dreamed of birches though he had never seen one), an adoptive
brother of my father's, and when White Tree died in the mid-1880s
my father felt called upon to take his place. She was the quietest of
women but with a fine sense of amusement and an implacable will.
My father had not thought the world worthy of raising children and
my existence had been my mother's idea. Her affections were tender
and boundless as long as I was obedient, which I was with her because she was never unreasonable. Previous to the last trip to Mexico
before their death, my father and I had both been reading William
James's *Principles of Psychology*, which had enlightened me to some

of the subtleties of her behavior. For instance, we could sit on the banks of the Niobrara for hours on a summer morning simply watching and listening to the nature of nature, or whatever one calls all that happens without immediate human intervention, and not speak a word to each other but I would be left with the feeling we had communicated perfectly. I've read this is true of people who have been married a long time and still love each other. I doubt if there's anything mystical in this matter but that people have never been taught to be truly attentive except to the banalities. When I was a child she'd announce her brother was coming for a visit often days before he would appear. Despite my father's deeply religious nature such experiences were not in his tenets and they mystified him to the point of irritation. To the white people, among whom I helplessly number myself, life is a very long and high set of stairs, but to my mother life was a river, a slow and stately wind across the sky, an endless sea of grass.

When I had finally gotten settled after my pair of doomed trips to find Willow I had to sit down and fill in the whole canvas of the trip for my mother like the pointillist Seurat. Nothing could be left out. She picked the bears in the Ishpeming dump, and the profusion of white birches I had seen from the log-train flat car shimmering in the moonlight, to dwell on. Of course this was because her first husband was White Tree and if he hadn't died he certainly would have traveled to this area. To her, the saddest thing about Native dispossession is that the people weren't able to live out the cues from their dreams. She told me that when she was a child she was with a small group of Lakota who had traveled to the south and east to trade buffalo meat and tanned hides to the Pawnee for corn, of which the Pawnee are said to have developed fourteen kinds. What my mother remembered was the delight of her grandmother on the trip, who had dreamt she would meet the Pawnee and now she was doing so.

Long after she died my mother had kept one of my legs ever so slightly in her world, despite my father's active insistence that the future of the world was grievously white. She was so utterly ordinary she was as real as the moon to me after she had been dead forty years.

I stood there, an old fool shivering on a cold October night, and could still hear her soft but bell-clear voice offering me the names of birds in Lakota, none of which I remember though the voice is clearer than my own, or Sonia's bark down near our graveyard. Sonia allows none of the other dogs in front of her when they are let out to pee before bedtime, though the two males pretend they are defending her from the rear and her daughter strays just behind her flank. I suddenly remembered that my mother talked to the dogs in Lakota which they seemed to understand clearly. And to Smith, whose departure at eighteen she mourned because she had dreamt he'd have a difficult life. When I called the dogs to go back inside I thought perhaps she wasn't dead in any meaningful sense. This gave me a further shiver that my nightcap glass of brandy did not dispel.

In the den a twinge behind my left kneecap forced a smile. After my extended pratfall in the search for Willow my character took on a melancholy bent, and Smith had made some effort to cheer me up, as did my father who had failed terribly by telling me of the loss to tuberculosis of his beloved first wife, Aase, shortly after they had been married. This increased my desperation, rather than healing it, as it hadn't occurred to me that anyone I loved could die.

Smith had come up with a plan to make money by capturing an unbranded and wild longhorn bull his father had seen in a big thicket along the Niobrara some twenty miles upriver from our place. The bull was a remnant of the herd Texans drove north for the thick pasturage of the Sandhills. There was a Norwegian farmer in the area who had offered Smith's father ten dollars for the death of this beast that had become a fence-breaking nuisance provoking a reign of terror among more civilized cattle. The local cowboys had given up trying to catch or kill it, which should have offered a tip to us that the project was over our heads. If we could somehow haul or lead the creature to the cattle sale over in Bassett we would clear a hundred dollars, a fortune in those days. There also was the added incentive in that the young men in the dime novels I had begun to lose interest in often became cowboys or desperadoes after losing in love. It had been suggested in print that if a fair lass had offered Billy the Kid some female tenderness he might not have started, or once started might have ceased his murderous ways. A dull-witted beast, no matter that he weighed a wild ton, was no match for two bright young men. Smith was even a distant relative of Crazy Horse, though it might have occurred to us that the bull was ignorant of this fact. Our main, nearly fatal error was in confusing longhorns with other cattle breeds, all of which are dull indeed compared to this fabled Texas beast who had had none of the difficult brilliance bred out of him.

We took a pack horse loaded down with hammers, saw, wire, an ax and a few days' grub. My father, who was worried sick about the project, loaned us his third-best cowdog, a half-feral pooch named Buck, who I once caught trying to mate a calf. Smith was riding an Indian pony he claimed came from an old buffalo-hunting line, surely a match for any white man's bull which, of course, a longhorn wasn't. I rode my best cow horse, a claybank dun gelding who didn't seem to know he was gelded. His idea of what to do with a difficult cow was to punish it. Our aim was to build a trap pen at the end of a small canyon leading down to the river, drive the bull into it, de-horn it for safety, tie its nuts to a hind leg with a leather thong to hobble it, a Mexican trick I had read about in a letter to the editor from El Paso in a stock magazine. Battle weary, we'd then lead the beast way over to Bassett and collect our money, and not incidentally, become renowned. I suspect the renown was foremost in our minds as money had not yet become the widespread motive for all activity in those days. The country itself was still a bit of a teenager. Smith could scarcely read and my father would not allow a newspaper into our home, but we'd seen and heard enough of them to think that our imminent heroism might catch the public attention. Two years before at age twelve we had both felt embittered that the Spanish-American War had taken place without us. It was clearly the right moment for a daring feat to be followed by wide admiration.

We were only a few miles upriver when I discovered I'd left my spare ammunition at home and only had two bullets for the rifle and three for the Iver Johnson. Smith made a lame joke about my previous bull-killing expertise that I let pass, feeling my whole body blush with shame. I meant someday to replace that expensive bull but the wherewithal was beyond my reach. It had mostly English Hereford blood with improbably thickish quarters and was meant to add meat to our rawboned herd.

We made camp in the bull's vicinity after a hard day's ride, and decided to forgo a camp deer to save ammunition and also not to warn the bull of our presence by rifle shot. The pie my mother sent along for our victory celebration had become a bit mashed in the pack horse's trepanniers so we scooped it up with our fingers as best we could. The loaf of bread was an unattractive idea without roasted venison, the heart of which we had intended to eat raw for strength and bravery, which Smith insisted his people used to do.

By dark we were being tortured by mosquitoes and thought of moving our campsite away from the river bottom to a distant hill but had become too lazy to do so. We added bunches of green grass to the fire for smudge which only helped with the mosquitoes if our bed rolls were right next to the fire. Unfortunately it was an overwarm night and it came down to death and discomfort by roasting smoke or mosquitoes. Smith had filched a bottle of his father's plum wine which I at first refused, still smarting from my Duluth binge, but in the end took a couple of pulls in order to sleep. We talked for a few minutes about the blond immigrant Norwegian girl who had moved with her family into a deserted homestead choked with nettles a half dozen miles down the road from our homeplace. The father doubtless bought the worthless property by mail and there was a month's work in clearing the nettles. We resolved to help when he was nearly finished to get a closer look at the girl. The talk of the Norwegian girl did nothing toward making us sleepy. Smith asked where the hell Norway was and if they were against Indians there. I said I didn't know but I bet the girl couldn't ride a horse and perhaps we could teach her. Certain stories my father told me about longhorns in an attempt to dissuade us from the mission drifted into my mind. There was a somewhat famous attack of longhorn bulls on a cavalry contingent and this cheered Smith. Another lone bull had gored two mules, one man, and had tipped over a loaded chuck wagon before being killed. We took several more pulls of the plum wine while thinking this over, then finally slept to the crackle of the fire and drone of mosquitoes.

An hour before dawn there were vast and powerful explosions, a violent thunderstorm, and us without a tarp because the weather had looked assuredly fair. Buck, the fierce cowdog, began howling and crawled under my sodden blanket with me. I finally jumped up and got my horse blanket for extra protection, the dried horse sweat on the blanket offering some waterproofing. During a flash of lightning I thought I had a brief glimpse of an animal bigger than God pretty close to our campsite, so I kept the rifle clutched in my hands. I could not believe that Smith snored through the entire storm, though he had had the lion's share of the plum wine.

At first light Smith was off at the edge of our small clearing examining the ground. He came back and turned over a large damp fire log, stirring some coals to life for coffee. He announced gravely that the critter had visited us during the night and we were lucky to be alive. I went off and tended the hobbled horses, noting their restlessness and the fact that they were staring into the densest thicket, about forty acres in size, that was on a horseshoe bend in the Niobrara. That was where the tracks of our nighttime visitor had emerged and returned to the thicket.

While we drank coffee Buck ate one of our loaves of bread and buried his nose deep in the jam jar. A poor camper, Buck, but then he looked up, stared into the thicket and growled a rather timid growl. I passed Smith the revolver so we'd both be armed. We mounted up carrying our tools and leaving the pack horse hobbled.

There was a hoped-for gully at the top end of the horseshoe bend and we set about to make our trap pen and makeshift corral out of the ample supply of cottonwood saplings. The morning had turned quite windy and we thought we'd heard an awful noise from our encampment but hurried through our chores before checking. Our plan was to follow the tracks through the thicket, driving the unwary bull before us until he trotted down the gully and into our trap near the river.

We returned to the campsite to find our pack horse terribly gored, a line of entrails strung out behind him, with a large patch of brush torn up by the struggle which had obviously been one-sided. While Buck began to feed on the carnage both our courage and sense of humor dissipated. We stayed mounted for safety and I fired the rifle in the air to signal our serious intent. Smith mentioned that he'd heard a longhorn could run faster than a buffalo which did not increase our sense of security. We both desperately wished to be elsewhere, and I made a halfhearted joke that it might be difficult to thread a leather throng through this bull's nuts, and Smith could busy himself with the project while I sawed off the horns like a merry barber. In response Smith laughed, then let off a blood-curdling war cry, heading for the thicket at a full gallop. I added my own howling as we thrashed into the dense thicket on the bull's track, not pausing as we heard the bull crashing through the brush well ahead of us.

As luck would have it the thicket became sparser and we could see the bull's immense ass disappearing over the lip of the gully straight toward our trap. We increased the volume of our screams and speed of our horses, reaching the gully's edge in time to see the bull blast through our enclosure as if it were built of twigs. Up on the bank we were still about forty feet higher than the bull, but even that far up a tree would not have given me comfort from this creature. We had a clear view of its massive brindle-and-black shape standing in the river, its widespread horns still red from the pack horse's blood. It turned to us and bellowed, the sound reverberating up and down the river. Then in the arrogance of its position it paused to take a deep drink of water. We never quite got over that gesture, but at this point Smith whispered, "Shoot the son-of-a-bitch before he kills us." I raised the rifle but in a trice the bull was out of the river and charging up the bank toward us. My horse reared and took off without my urging. I went one way and Smith the other. It was several hours before we found each other on the far side of the river. I assumed the bull had chased him because in a three-mile run looking over my shoulder and crossing the river I never saw it. Smith said he'd had no control over his horse which after a hundred-yard run had floundered across the river. He glanced back then and the bull was up on the bank where I'd drawn out my rifle. The bull was grazing. We sat there on our horses thinking this over when Buck trotted up with a red muzzle and a distended gut full of horse meat. We rode a few more miles toward home for absolute safety, then stopped for a swim and a snooze, arriving back at the farm at the end of a long summer twilight.

It is accurate and fair to say that the longhorn experience knocked the cowboy out of me for quite some time, and my Willow melancholy took a new turn. My father had threatened to send me over to the Indian school in Genoa, Nebraska, if I didn't settle down to my studies. The young folks there were virtual captives, and I replied that I'd shoot my way out. This errant comment occasioned a lecture and a bribe. He knew of my sidelong interest in art that had scarcely been sated by our single book of Gustave Doré reproductions, and all that I could find in our 1895 *Britannica,* which wasn't that much. The Frenchwoman at the Omaha exposition kept coming to mind and I'd look at the map of France in the atlas studiously trying to figure out where she might live.

My father's bribe was that he'd order a raft of art books for me, plus a subscription to *Scribner's* magazine, if I'd settle down to my prescribed studies in mathematics, natural history and literature. The *Scribner's* was quite a concession on his part to modern times, as he was intent on not only protecting me from his own obsession with the Lakota but from the whole world at large, an effort he must have begun to sense that summer as hopeless. Of course *Scribner's* was laughably sedate but I had seen it in the town library and had begun to feel a poignant curiosity about the outside world. I was such a late child, my father was in his fifties at the time, that my shenanigans must have exhausted him into realizing there was no way of protecting me. Our only magazine at that time was the *Philosophical Specula-*

tor which contained alarming (to my father) disquisitions by William James on the nature of psychology. I found them intriguing, but then as a wild young man of fourteen I had no cultural or religious territory to defend. The only subject I knew very well was horses and it was already being bandied about that horses would pass from our existence with the advent of the motor car.

Most of the contents of my studies were onerous and generally too far advanced for my capabilities. Mathematics was relatively easy, biology painfully difficult with our antique microscope revealing nothing of interest to me. Anthropology was in its heyday as a new science and was fascinating to me, from the drama of the Egyptologists to the obsessions of Boas. I liked Keats well enough, though I read Willow's name between many lines, but found Pope and Wordsworth dreary. Shelley was flimsy indeed compared to the glories of Lord Byron whom I strongly admired and envied right down to his efforts to be buried with his dog. I thought Tennyson a hopeless windbag and could never quite get the hang of Dickens. Shakespeare was quite beyond me, though I liked the music of the language that my father had told me must be read aloud. Lucretius was soporific but Virgil's *Georgics* of sharp interest as I could see his concerns in the country around me. Emerson was pounded into me, while I only pretended to read Hawthorne. After all of my father's years with the Lakota our household was neither puritanical or Victorian, and I could not fathom or sympathize with people under such repression. My father viewed Walt Whitman and Melville as "curiosities" but I was drawn to both. Melville had fallen well out of literary favor but I noted the copy of *Moby-Dick* was dog-eared and much underlined. The Natives were my father's own white whale and he was given to delivering eccentric lectures on their fate at any time from dawn to dark.

Amid this whirl of mental activity which took place in the heat of the day and in the late evening I was bold and ignorant enough to try to write poems to Willow which mainly served to increase my respect for Keats. In my notebooks, more important, I tried to draw pictures of her and deeply regretted that no photo of her had ever been taken. Her odor was warm sand and plums, her voice mostly soft except while laughing, her body beige and supple and deceptively strong. She could climb trees much faster than Smith and I with our more bulky musculature. How could it be that there was not a single photo of her slender beauty? Nowadays it is unthinkable that there is someone unphotographed. Whether this is good or bad I'm not sure, but it is a struggle for me to recapture her image except in the rare dream, or just on waking while still in a half-sleeping state when perhaps the truer content of our lives begins to dissipate. In any event, my first clumsy drawings failed to capture her; in one perhaps an eye would be correct, in another, the lips, or part of the neck, the arm jaunty against a fence post.

My life was to change quite abruptly at the 1900 version of the Nebraska State Fair late that summer. Back then it was almost totally an agricultural event with countless exhibits of produce and livestock, an elaborate meeting of ranchers and farmers and their families and a grand respite from the year's labor.

My mother had urged Smith to go with us because he was in a dour mood, having been driven at gunpoint from the Norwegian's yard after stopping by to help clean the nettles. He had said hello to the blond girl as she pumped water and she began to scream, whereupon her father ran from the house with his shotgun, not a promising beginning to a courtship. I had been in a Keatsian fever that day and had thankfully not gone along, though Smith's idea of burning down their house and scalping them seemed reasonable. Smith had settled for riding past their house while standing on his horse and baring his bottom at them as they sat in their miserable yard. Even my father smiled at this story though he had brooded about the family, what with their having arrived too late to plant crops, and what would they eat in the winter?

At the fair we felt thrilled to see Peerless Big-Boned Bob, a boar of over a thousand pounds and said to be the largest pig in creation. Bob failed to show any signs of life until we tossed him a piece of

sausage which he was glad to eat, proving himself a cannibal according to a gleeful Smith. Bob's keeper told us to move along which we
ignored, and this precipitated a scrape with some young men from
Lincoln, thuggish city kids, during which we acquitted ourselves quite
well. I pitched one over the fence and he landed near Bob which put
the boar in an ugly mood. We ran for it after a crowd gathered, drawing up to catch our breath in front of an exhibit that advertised "the
only living Eskimo family in the United States." A man, woman and
child sat there in and on furs in a hot tent surrounded by blocks of
ice. They were sweating profusely and the scene was dismal indeed.
Smith and I discussed setting them free but then we weren't sure they
were captured or simply there of their own free will, far from their
Arctic wasteland. One of the furs they sat upon was a polar bear so
unimaginably large that we were confident it was a fake. The tent
was crowded with folks jostling to see these poor sweating creatures
from the great North, and Smith could no longer contain himself,
bellowing, "What a goddamn shame!" Immediately a group of burly
farmers advanced on us: "Get out of here you son-of-a-bitching
redskins." And we did.

Smith took off on a several-mile walk to downtown Lincoln,
wanting to see the state capital, while I continued to drift with less-
ening enthusiasm around the crowded midway. I thought of checking the bull and cow barns to see the best of the year but was stopped
again by Keats. All I would hear there was the usual "nice and thick
through the crops and chine, remarkable spring of rib and built right
on the ground." I was all cowed out and even the horse show sched-
uled for late that afternoon failed to stir my interest. I stood there in
the crowded dust murmuring rather strangely to myself, "What can
ail thee, wretched wight, alone and palely loitering; the sedge is
wither'd from the lake, and no birds sing, etc." That sort of thing,
the memory of which brings embarrassed blood to my ears. Then, by
happenstance, I spied the arts and crafts tent well off the side, and
was drawn there by fatal luck, passing from the brassy sunlight into
the dim tent loaded with painted china, elaborate hot pads, a cow
sculpted out of glued-together corncobs with black river stones for

eyes, certainly nothing that approached my vaunted notion of the art calling. At that moment the word "arts" meant as much to me as the name "Jesus" does to a cloistered nun, with the actual object of adoration the same distance away.

Down at the far end of the tent in the least favorable location sat a gaggle of Sunday painters displaying their sunsets, vases of flowers, mountain ranges, and a few ill-proportioned horses, children and house pets. Further off to the side stood a tall thin young man in a smock and blue beret surrounded by a half dozen young ladies, whom he was sketching deftly in turn on a large pad, charging them a quarter apiece. I stood well back, gradually coming closer, until I could hear his badinage clearly. I was instantly jealous of his abilities which would have allowed me to draw Willow in a memorable fashion. After finishing each sketch he would shout "Voilà!" which I took to be a French word because he wore a beret. One ditzy girl wanted a full-length drawing and he sharply accentuated the size of her breasts to the merriment of the others. This seemed utterly daring to me, so much so that I joined the group as he was telling the big-breasted girl to "stick around" and he'd buy her a soda, whereupon she blushed with pleasure and pride. He noticed me standing there and asked if a "son of the soil" would like his picture drawn, and I said, "No thank you." I added that I greatly admired his skill as an artist, and this embarrassed him a trifle. He attempted to make me a butt of the general fun and asked me to name my favorite artists other than Rembrandt and Michelangelo, perhaps hoping to catch me at a loss. I mentioned the English landscapist I'd read about in the *Britannica*, Joseph Mallord William Turner, using his full name. He raised an eyebrow, and asked "Who else?" I struggled and came up with Courbet, pronouncing it "Corbett." This gave him an angle and he yelled " 'Coorbay,' you bumpkin. It's pronounced 'Coorbay.' " I blushed deeply and found myself saying, "A shit-heel like you could get thrown through the side of this tent." He and the tittering girls became silent, and I felt further shame in threatening the first real artist I'd ever met. Then he asked, now serious, "Do you draw?" and I answered, "Not very well."

He took a break then and we went off for sodas with the girl in tow, proudly holding her mawkish drawing. She said she was pleased to have met two real artists which made me feel terribly awkward. He dismissed her, telling her to come back before dinner for a free roll in the hay, at which she nodded and left. I was astounded at his cheekiness but assumed it must be the way actual artists talked.

His name was Theodore Davis and he came from Omaha where his father was a railroad executive, a "benighted capitalist," Davis called him. Davis could never utter a sentence without a flourish of hyperbole. I took him to be older but he was eighteen and was headed off in a few weeks to the Chicago Art Institute. His beret was a bit of fakery to help prove to his father that an artist could make money. He was pleased with himself, jingling his pocketful of quarters, "the fruits of my labor" as he called them. Before we parted company he gave me a large sketch pad and some drawing pencils, promising to keep in touch. I had fibbed and said I was sixteen and he suggested I quit high school and join him when I could at the Art Institute. I admitted that I had left school at age nine, telling him the story in brief which he found "preposterously marvelous." I walked off with my brain in a storm of possibilities, totally ignorant that I was making the first step into an upheaval that would be with me the rest of my life. It is largely misunderstood that the first forays of a young man or young woman into the world of arts and literature, the making of them, are utterly comic and full of misadventures, rather than most of the dour and melancholy renditions that are made public.

My feeling of being baptized maintained itself when I got back to our campsite at the edge of the fairground, though there had been a momentary urge to track Smith to downtown Lincoln. I had overheard some farm boys talking about a saloon on the far side of the city where girls danced without their clothing, a fascinating prospect, but possibly not serious enough for someone who had just had his sacred calling reaffirmed. If only that Frenchwoman had been there to guide me, I thought.

I had been at the campsite only a little while when my parents appeared, well out of my own mood of ethereal scornfulness for those in the other rows of tents who were obviously unaware of a higher sort of being in their midst. My father was as happy as I had ever seen him. The Hereford bulls we had rented out to other farmers and ranchers had proved spectacular, and their progeny had won many prizes at the cattle show. He fairly danced around the little fire where my mother was brewing coffee. I hadn't the heart to play out my newfound artistic mood of high purpose because I could not recall seeing him this happy. There was also the thought that the bull I had shot in late spring might have been even more valuable than previously supposed as he was out of the same sire as the others. We had a nip of whiskey in our coffee, my first with him, and then my mother noted my large sketch pad which I had been careless enough not to conceal. In a rush I told them all of my ambitions, including going off to Chicago, and they became quiet and ruminative, with my mother staring off to the west as if discovering a new meaning there.

It took a while, right up through dinner, in fact, for us to strike a bargain. I would be allowed to go to art school in a year and a half when I became sixteen, if I promised to try Cornell College, my father's alma mater, the following year. To pass their entrance exams I would have to bear down miserably hard on my studies and abandon my wild and irascible habits. I nodded in agreement to everything that would facilitate my going off to art school at sixteen. After fixing us a simple dinner my mother had leafed through each empty page of the sketch book as if imagining what belonged on it. She said, "Get kahnah" which meant birds in Lakota and I was obliged to draw her a meadowlark from memory at which point she did an imitation of the song of the meadowlark which startled those lounging in front of the tent nearest us. Well off in the distance, in the late summer twilight, we could hear the calliope music which seemed as beautiful to me then as Mozart's Jupiter Symphony does now.

I think of it as the best evening of our lives together. It was a specific moment of relief and leisure—for my parents from the extended Lakota "Götterdämmerung," and for me, the subsiding of anxiety over telling them I wished to be an artist, certainly an uncommon ambition for one from my background. There was none of the strident middle-class reaction against the fey and wayward son one reads about, but then, despite his avowed sin of greed and her homely preoccupations, they were scarcely bourgeois. They were their own peculiar class.

Later that evening we joined a group of Swedes and a growing crowd at a dance down at the end of the rows of tents. There were fiddles and concertinas and some young men had made a grand fire out of pilfered railroad ties. There were all manner of immigrant farmer groups including Bohemian, German, a full Scandinavian mix, and plain white, stolid Nebraska farmers and ranchers, though not the most prosperous sort who favored the downtown hotels during State Fair. My father had been always treated with some suspicion for being on the wrong side of the "Indian Question" though there was the usual respect given to the prosperous, and he rarely if ever got to mix in with ordinary folk as he did that evening. Everyone drank from barrels of beer and danced to the polka music until they were dense with sweat and exhaustion. I heard the last of the music at dawn from our tent. I didn't know how to dance but had done so with every one from the old and fat to the young and fetching. The mood of the gathering seems so distant from our present day when ranchers and farmers make parodies of their virtues for the public sentiment. There was still a raw and unforgiving exuberance then in a place that had only been a state for thirty-three years.

I was disturbed from my maunderings by Lundquist's knock. He had been making sure that the barn plumbing was well wrapped in anticipation of a predicted freeze that was to be especially bitter for October. He brought in a kettle of his "stew" from the pick-up, a mixture of dried salt cod, potatoes and onions, and I regretted telling him that Frieda had called to say that she would be another full day down in Lincoln, the Holy Ghost himself having visited their church gathering which was requiring an extra day to discuss the incident.

"That Frieda takes her religion to the nethermost," he said, slumping at my bidding into a chair. Though he had been working for me and we had been friends since soon after Armistice in 1919 he would not dream of sitting down in the house without being asked to. I poured him a stiff whiskey and he went to the kitchen for his requisite water so as not to insult what he called his "stomach juices." I called out to have him bring Shirley, his little dog, inside out of the cold which he did gladly. Shirley got along well with the Airedales who rolled her around with their noses, the kind of peculiar game dogs make up on their own.

While Lundquist was washing up I put his stew on to heat, adding some garlic and hot pepper. He knew I did this but chose to ignore it, announcing invariably that his "momma's" recipe always tasted better at my house. He would also never accept a glass of red wine without a brief comment on the idea that the beverage was "papist," usually followed by grumbling that the atomic bomb had changed the weather for the worse, and that all politicians bore the Mark of the Beast, the latter contention not difficult to agree with. On all things agricultural, however, he was absolutely knowledgeable and current, his life's biggest announced disappointment being that I had lost interest in both the subject and its practice, having essentially put our place to rest after John Wesley's death.

It is difficult indeed for us to accept others and ourselves at the level of our intentions without noting the disparity between them and the way we actually live. Lundquist seemed an exception; his innermost and outermost thoughts were the same, full of a quirky originality of perception. He would begin a sentence railing against war profiteering and finish it by naming a half a dozen different birds' nests he had located for Naomi. Though his formal schooling was as brief as mine, he was especially pleased that Linnaeus had been a Swede. In a somewhat unkind trick I had once loaned him Strindberg's memoirs which troubled him. "That fellow had himself confused with God," Lundquist had muttered, not an inaccurate assessment of tormented Strindberg. His only vaguely immodest gesture was his ability to run up the side of the barn using a rope hanging from the mow door, an improbable feat for a man past fifty, and one he'd only perform when Dalva and Ruth teased him into it. He early startled me by saying of both my Marsden Hartley and Stuart Davis paintings, "He's got it just right," while he found nothing of particular interest in Thomas Hart Benton or Charley Russell. We quarreled over Benton and it turned out that Lundquist felt he was overly familiar with much of Benton's material and preferred paintings that "rattle my gourd." Despite his Christian faith he saw nudes as "the glory of God," a matter over which he and Frieda disagreed.

What I mean to say was that Lundquist was always what he intended to be, but unlike so many matter-of-fact people, he had intense empathy for the more troubled in mind. I had overheard through the porch window his explanation to Dalva about whether animals went to heaven, a matter which had been bothering her. He told her simply that he had dreamt of seeing cows, horses, snakes, chickens, coyotes, lions and tigers, all up in heaven drinking sweet fresh milk from the same huge golden bowl. That was proof enough for him and he hoped it would be for her.

Looking at him across the dinner table while he rocked and cooed at his mutt Shirley, I was struck again by the evils of primogeniture, the manner in which farm property in the old days was transferred to the oldest son to keep the results of the hard work intact, leaving the other sons to wander through life as hired hands or shop clerks. It was partly the source of the Populist unrest, this large population of the disaffected. Lundquist was a brilliant farmer destined to never own a farm, just as the most capable "top hands," cowboys, ranch managers will never themselves own a ranch. It was my own father's almost errant providence that "blessed" me as the religionists say, so that even in the worst days of the Great Depression I could readily buy land, or travel to the Kentucky Derby, the Dublin Horse Show, or lay in the best Bordeaux. My older son, Paul, who is somewhat estranged from me, accepted his mother's money which turned out to be considerable, and John Wesley was to receive this farm and my own other holdings. I left off my spending ways when John Wesley enlisted in World War II. I kept the farm going for the war effort though it was more Lundquist but I lost heart so great was my fear for my namesake's safety, only to have him die in Korea. Thousands of times I've cursed the day I took him for a ride in a barnstormer's plane in the late twenties. I lost my beloved son to machines, but then we are in deepest error when we think our children are truly our own. We may have problems forgiving others, or ourselves, because life herself has never forgiven anyone a single minute's time. I think of my blood brother—yes, we performed that childish rite—standing there in the cold potato field.

I am chastened to discover that my forays into wisdom are less interesting than Lundquist's new batch of home-smoked bacon. He stopped by this morning with a slab, disturbed to find me out in the bunkhouse without a fire, sitting at the desk and thinking about this, my first studio, and the pathetic sign that once hung on the door. ART STUDIO NO ENTRANCE.

We tested the bacon with a critical palate as others do at wine tastings. Lundquist had also brought over a jar of his fresh-grated horseradish root he mixed with a bit of vinegar and heavy Jersey cream. We also had eggs and his eyes were red with tears from the dollop of horseradish. We decided a beer was appropriate though it was only midmorning. He was pleased when I announced the bacon to be one of the best batches ever. He had added extra applewood to the hickory to give it a fruity zing, totally unlike the bacon available to the public trough.

This was a breakfast fit for an active farmer so we saddled up two peaceful mares for a chilly ride to avoid falling asleep in our chairs. We headed across our southwest pasture, known as Smith's pasture because that's where he badly fractured his nose in a rough game we played as children. You sprint up to a heifer, grab her tail and give a jerk, seeing how long you can hold on as you're dragged hither and yon at a gallop. You grab the tail as far back as possible to avoid the flailing hoofs. A wise cow had refused to run, and backed up with a kick, making a mess of Smith's nose which gave it the appearance of the Indian on the nickel. My father set the bone, first giving Smith a dose of opium that he rather liked.

The late autumn fields reminded me of Millet, a banal painter but that's what the fields helplessly looked like. We joggled along, half asleep in the saddle. Lundquist had Shirley nestled just behind the pommel where she liked to ride, barking occasionally at the Airedales coursing out in front of us. They had been chasing after the same female coyote for years and I had supposed they meant to kill her, but then out the kitchen window in September I had seen Sonia hunting mice with this coyote in the newly mown alfalfa.

I reflected that from this same saddle had hung a soft leather bag kept spread by alder stays that carried my first sketch book on my rides. My father gave it to me for that purpose when we had come home from the State Fair. He said it had been made from elk skin that a Lakota woman had traded for with a Cheyenne during one of their peaceful intervals when they were collectively angry with the Crows and Blackfoot after Little Bighorn. My father had kept botanical specimens in this bag and I was astounded when he showed me his notebook drawings of plants right down to their root hairs, as fragile as spider webs. I asked him if he had ever drawn a human, and he said no, but that he wished he had drawn his first wife, Aase, whom he'd been married to only briefly before she died of tuberculosis, then he could still look upon her face on occasion. I said nothing of my similar wishes for Willow, but I remembered that at the time he became less a towering and remote adult than a fellow creature. We scarcely think much that our fathers loved as much as we.

If only Willow would send me a letter, I thought at the time, but then I'd never seen her read or write and doubted she was up to a letter. Of course I had vowed never to love again if it were to be the source of so much pain, unmindful that a scant ten years ahead a love would come along that made my sorrow over Willow look idyllic. On a cold spring day one ached for summer, and on a hot summer afternoon, one ached again for the first chill norther of autumn. I had begun to think it was central to my character and number of years to ache. I hoped it would be useful for my art, but had grave doubts about how one would get this ache into a sketch or painting, the latter being beyond my possible dreams at the time.

I only gradually became conscious that Lundquist was talking and my horse was drinking water at the spring. I said that the watercress was dead for the year, hoping it an adequate response as Lundquist took umbrage when not listened to carefully.

"Don't be in such a hurry to be off in the clouds. You'll get there soon enough." He was immediately fond of this witticism and repeated it. It was less amusing for me what with the recent tremors of my heart. He then gave me the gist of what he was talking about which was a paragraph in a recent *Nebraska Farmer* by a research veterinarian to the effect that if all the dogs on earth were left in free concourse, soon enough all dogs would be medium-sized and brown.

I looked at Shirley and the Airedales and too readily agreed for Lundquist's taste because I saw this contention leading us into the type of sump that I found tiresome. Any cattle- or horseman has elaborate notions of breeding programs that would drive a layman daffy with boredom. I had bred all too many fast and pretty horses that would kick their way out of a trailer, bite barn cats, become frantic in the full moon and jump sky high at a bird shadow. Gene programs required good sense rather than romantic greed. Man o' War was a conditioned plan that also managed to breed a thousand unlike himself and relatively worthless.

There was a recent fire ring up the creek bank that caught my eye and Lundquist followed my glance. It wasn't trespassers he said but that Dalva got a rare A on a test and Naomi had asked him to bring her out here to roast frankfurters over a fire, her desired reward. Lundquist then said her behavior frightened him and he prayed she'd become a more ordinary girl. This irritated me and I said we had quite enough of those, whatever they are. I could fairly see his mind clicking off her somewhat troubled genealogy, including myself, my father, her father all wild-eyed for the machineries of war.

I studied relentlessly hard all that winter with cold mornings devoted to the books, chores and sketching off horseback in the afternoons, and more studies in the evening. Often, rather than my prescribed work, I'd ready my *Scribner's* or the little art books on Rodin, William Morris, or Millet my father had ordered by mail. Nearly everything was disappointing and incomprehensible to me, especially John Ruskin and Henry James. With my meager background all of the attenuations of emotion in Henry James meant no more than a pond at the back of our property that Smith and I had viewed as bottomless. I had the gravest of doubts about whether I was up to snuff and turned for solace to his relative William James, and a piece he wrote called "The Consciousness of Self." I liked the part about the "Empirical Me" and how the self may preserve its integrity. That was close enough to home to be understandable. Any nascent artist must pump up their ego so they can function in an area that no one feels comfortable in until later years. You have selected yourself to be someone extraordinary and you must manufacture enough mental fuel to carry you along, which for one so young and unlettered and unpracticed as myself could be a grim chore. My confusion was further added to by the article on art in the 1895 *Britannica* where many quotes were in Latin, and an idea of Shakespeare had been noted to the effect that "art was nature, too." How the hell was I supposed to make nature, something that I actually knew about in all of its grand permutations in that my father taught me about every weed, flower, type of grass, tree, shrub and all of the habits of the creature world in our area?

I simply had no gift for abstract thought at the time and what saved me were the countless afternoons of sketching which was a visceral act, along with guiding the horse through snowbanks or through slush puddles, or finding a sunny canyon out of the chill wind to sit down and study the appearances of things.

I had received a brief but jubilant note from Davis on the glories and temptations of the Art Institute and Chicago that ended with "Where are the sketches?" referring to my promise to send my work for criticism. Oddly, I suppose, this was the first piece of truly personal mail I had received in my life. I fearfully sent him a batch, adding with a scarcely felt braggadocio that I was sure I was ready to start painting. It was a full three weeks before the reply came, by which time I was a moping chunk of raw meat. He pronounced my draw-ings as *mostly average* with a few that showed *promise*, adding, "You must sketch years before you begin to paint. The eye and brain know the appearances of things whilst the hand doesn't. The hand must be trained to follow our most fantastical notions of all the varieties of what we see in the world." He also said that he was living with a beautiful woman of twenty-five years which meant I couldn't share the letter with my parents though I certainly read them the part about my showing *promise*.

After another set of sketches had been sent off and a reply had been sent back that my efforts were becoming *too pinched*, I became quite depressed only to be saved by an experience that some might think of as transcendental. I had taken a long ride on a horse not fully broke, too sodden in spirit to pack along my sketch book. The night before there had been an ice storm that covered the snow of which there was still a fair amount in some places, and the horse hated the deeper drifts, finding the footing unsure as it broke through the crust. The sun had come out, and the temperature that I judged to be high in the thirties would, I hoped, melt the ice enough to pacify the horse who normally had no problem with simple snow.

There was a two-hour struggle with hard reining and an ample use of the crop before I finally reached my destination, a smallish canyon containing a spring that led down and emptied out into the Niobrara. I had intended to watch the chunks of ice float by on the river until my mind cooled off enough to function as an *artist* again. Making our way up the sun-dazzled, icy canyon a forehoof broke through the spring's ice into soft muck and the horse became a buck-ing bronc. After a few radical leaps and twirls I was thrown clear, cracking my head against a rock and twisting my left arm. As I lost consciousness I remember thinking that at least it wasn't my sketch-ing arm.

I must have been passed out for at least an hour, I was a pretty good judge of the sun's movement, when I rolled against the injured arm and the pain brought me awake. I sat up slowly and noted that a group of crows were watching me from up on the canyon's edge. I squawked at them and they squawked back which lifted my spirits. The horse had long since headed for home and I had a good five-mile hike ahead of me. I checked my arm and judged it to be sprained rather than broken, then ate my fried venison sandwich that contained mustard and a particularly strong onion. When not chewing I whistled, quite happy for the time being to be alive. The canyon mouth narrowed the view, and a grand piece of ice floated by with a crow standing upon it. We exchanged glances for a moment and then I wished I had brought along my sketch book. When Davis had said my drawings were too pinched he had added that I had to do it *all at once* rather than starting off in the lower left-hand corner trying to make it perfect.

I sat there so long my ass fairly froze to the ground. I noted that my right hand was cold in the shadow of the canyon wall, but just above my wrist the sun was warmish on my arm. I watched the shadow moving up my arm as the sun descended, as if I were seeing time herself. I did not move except for my eyes which looked up and found the earth quite eerily unrecognizable, both outside and inside my brain. Everything seemed held together by the fragilest connections—rocks, trees, birds, deer, horses and most of all people. Blue sky. Brown mother. Black crow. White father. And the language my brain kept muttering to itself was supposedly the glue that bound it all together. Only it didn't, at least during that hour or so it failed, and I was struck by the immutable presence of the nameless.

I was not far into my long walk home when my father appeared with a spare horse, my favorite buckskin. He had naturally guessed what happened when the other came vaulting into the barnyard, lathered and still mad as a hatter. When spring came I sold this horse to a pious and unsuspecting farmer who would be surprised indeed when snow fell and the first ice storm came along.

By the stupidity of coincidence I slipped while going downstairs to fetch some wine. I was inattentive, thinking of the treasures of Native artifacts my father had hidden away and I had not examined for many years because one corner of the hidden room contained some unpleasant skeletons with their clothes still on. A fully dressed skeleton is a poignant reminder of mortality and I had enough of that in my living body. I gave myself quite a thumping in the fall down the steps, but there was no consequent numinous experience, or at least it didn't glow like my other one in the canyon. My agreement with my own peculiar world of spirits was to try to stay alive until my granddaughters, Dalva and Ruth, graduated from high school, and my fall struck me as a prelude to failure.

I stretched out against the bottom step feeling pained and lumpish. I then remembered reading a speculation in *Scientific American* on how rarely mammals, except for man, simply stumble and fall down, barring very youthful incidents. The notion was that other mammals are less double-minded and perhaps incapable of thinking of the specifics of one thing while doing another. My neck was sore enough from striking the ridge of stairs that I suddenly wasn't sure whether I had actually read this article or my mind was making it up and putting it beneath a cover story of a galaxy that had been recently discovered at the nether edge of the cosmos. I had never had a peek through a powerful telescope and was unsettled by the idea that there are stars beyond those which we see in a dense floss on a cold, clear winter night.

A throbbing in my left arm returned me quickly from sidereal reality to that of the coolish basement floor. This was the body that once jumped a horse off a thirty-foot cliff into a deep pool of the Niobrara on a fifty-cent bet with Smith. We had to do it on a dead run and the horse never trusted me again. There was an urge to try to get up but my ass felt numb from its skid down the last few steps. I could hear Frieda far above me vacuuming rooms that no one had slept in for over a decade, save Dalva in my wife's room. Frieda had returned from Lincoln, a triumphant Amazon with what she supposed an aura of the Holy Ghost round about her, but her eyes were a shallow pool of insensitivity to all but her own immediate concerns. In short, I did not want to elicit her help, doubting anyway that my voice at full yell could transcend that of the vacuum cleaner.

For irrational reasons I began to think of the women in my life, and the women in their own lives when I hadn't been around. There had been no great number compared to the scorecards of Lotharios I had known for the simple fact I had difficulty liking people no matter how attractive. A Mexican woman with two children near Los Mochis comes to mind. I had sketched her for three full days to the disgust of Smith who stayed in a hotel downtown with a fair *conchita*. My own was rather homely and "Indio" but she had a bowl full of wildflowers on her wood table in the small adobe with a dirt floor. Her son, about five years, carried around an old brindle cat missing one paw. I bought her a dozen laying hens and a fine nanny goat from her neighbor. I took her seven-year-old daughter for a ride on my horse and wanted to buy her a pony but the mother said it would be a burden to feed. I was in my earliest twenties, still full of obtuse piss and vinegar, and asked her how she supported herself when I shouldn't have pried. Her husband was in prison for reasons she wouldn't say, and a shopkeeper gave her a little money in exchange for her affections. He had kindly stepped aside, perhaps to save his pesos, when she had caught my eye. This upset and embarrassed me because I was quite stupid, and I left, throwing her some money which she threw back. After I saddled up I tucked the money in the little boy's pocket and his cat gave me an ugly scratch on the hand which became moderately infected. I had a lump in my throat as I waved toward the door but she wasn't standing there.

A Spanish poet, whose name I don't recall, wrote that we leave small pieces of our hearts here and there until there is not enough left to give away and stay alive. Sitting there at the bottom of the steps with the sense that a nail had been driven into my elbow I doubted this was true. When I was in love it filled me up, and when I recovered, there was more to give away. Assuming that our energies are sufficient, love is interminable. Here I sprawled, a lonely geezer with memories that now caused an erection in my trousers. When the woman from Los Mochis had sponged off her strong brown body in the candlelight I'd felt my ears would pop off.

I moved around and drew myself to my knees, cursing the inat-
tentiveness that had caused this pratfall. On my knees I was a child's
height, and looking up the stairs, I was a child again smelling the wood
when it was newly sawn pine. Once again, as when I had been pitched
from the horse in the canyon so long ago, the world lost its normal
and inferior coherence. I was in an attitude of prayer to the incomprehensible—the abyss between the woman from Los Mochis and the
present which is time, the face of my first horse which I owned from
age seven to age thirty-one when I went off to World War I, Willow
naked by the creek singing a song she'd heard hiding in a lilac thicket
outside the Methodist Church, a song about Jerusalem. How far is it
from Standing Rock to Jerusalem? Three clouds I had drawn down
in the Pinacates floated through my mind, and I heard the plaintive,
insane voice of a Norwegian girl who hid in her room during the
largest phase of the moon, and whenever some distant dust storm
turned the rising or setting sun red. Now Sonia appeared in the square
of light at the top of the stairs, and scenting trouble, began to bay
and bark which brought Frieda to my temporary rescue.

Lundquist drove me to town where the doctor diagnosed a simple
fracture of the radial bone in my left arm, and a mass of decidedly
nonfatal bruises on my back and bottom. The arm could not be put
in a cast or I would lose its mobility, so he gave me a simple elbow
pad and told me to treat the limb lightly for a couple of months. He
then questioned me and checked my heart at some length, full of false
concern. The doctor was nearly my own age and was sure that his
wife and I had made love one summer night thirty years before and
neither of us had ever bothered disabusing him of his suspicions which
were untrue. He also thought me a wicked Democrat when I was simply contrary. His politeness came from the fact that I had given the
town its hospital, really only a twelve-bed infirmary, on John Wesley's
safe return from World War II. He announced that I suffered from
"tachycardia," which need not be fatal, charged me for a bottle of

pills as the nearest pharmacy is seventy miles distant, and we nodded our good-byes. His wife had left him for a professor down in Lincoln years ago and he struck me as lonely with his big portrait of
Eisenhower in the examining room.

We stopped at the butcher's for a bone for Shirley who sat between us on county roads but had her forepaws on the dashboard to
protect us from any oncoming traffic. At the far edge of town we, after
some pause, stopped at a country tavern for lunch and a few whiskeys that are the dubious reward for a broken bone and a trip to the
doctor. We anyway could not stop at the cafe which is owned and
operated by my girlfriend, a woman in her thirties who had fled
Chicago with her husband and daughter after World War II, bought
the cafe from a cousin only to see the loutish husband return to
Chicago. The affair had been going on at a sedate pace of twice a
month for several years. Lundquist had been quite embarrassed one
morning in the yard when he had pointed out a strange set of tire
tracks and I admitted I had a lady friend. We might have gone to the
cafe but then no whiskey was served there, the Rotary Club was having its weekly luncheon, and I had always been somewhat estranged,
to put it in its mildest form, from the county's business leaders.

The tavern owner, Byrnes by name, had got hold of a fine side
of beef which we inspected in the kitchen. We used to hunt together
now and then but he had lost a lower leg to diabetes, and gave away
his bird dogs to a son-in-law who mistreated them, a fact which caused
him some pain. We had several whiskeys and a T-bone steak which,
to my embarrassment, Lundquist had to cut up for me because of my
painful arm.

When we got home Frieda had a dishpan full of ice and water
for me to soak the elbow. She quickly achieved a state of outrage
over us being a tad drunk but did so out of my earshot, or so she
thought as she upbraided Lundquist out in the barnyard. I watched
out the kitchen window as she tried to make Lundquist pray with
her while Shirley barked, which she did when people were upset.
This aroused the Airedales, all of which I let out to join the fun.
Frieda drove off weeping and yelling and Lundquist fled to his shop

in the barn to play the fiddle which he favored when Frieda came down on him hard. He played poorly but "good enough for me," as he liked to say.

There was a particular song he played, a Swedish barn-dance polka, that reminded me of those played by the *norteño* musicians of Sonora. Davis could dance like a madman to this music and his easy ways made us liked among the Mexicans. Lacking enough rope I had to tie his broken body over the saddle with barbed wire. When I led the horse into El Salto the locals at first thought I was bringing in a bad hombre I had shot. I telegrammed his parents in Omaha and received word from his father to "bury him there," which I achieved with some difficulty by bribing a German Protestant missionary. Later, when I visited his parents to deliver his personal items, the mother was bereft to hysteria but the father and the sullen and prosperous brothers had avowed that they knew Davis would come to a "bad end." When I asked what had become of his work, I was told it was none of my business. His mother showed me to the door, kissed my hand and said she prayed I would continue in my art, then looked furtively over her shoulder toward the bourgeois monsters in the interior of the house. So far as I know the only three Davis paintings extant hang in my bedroom. I doubt if he ever sold a thing aside from the quarter sketches of the girls at the State Fair. He was just getting started when he tumbled from the cliff with his toothache, a flask of tequila in his back pocket. The paintings aren't all that good, though far superior to my own efforts. I mourned him that year before my parents died, and then was off on my nearly fatal misadventure with the main love of my existence.

I awoke with a strange cluster of sensations, having gone to bed quite drunk and letting cold wind blow through a wide-open window. I must have made odd noises in the night from rolling against my fractured bone because both my setter Tess and Sonia were on the bed with me at first light and they usually stayed clear of each other. My temples seemed to pound in unison with my arm and I reflected that

that was quite enough whiskey for this life. I had heard Lundquist
rise from the den couch about an hour before, sleeping off our long
drunken talk about cattle, horses and, very late, life herself. I wondered if I was happy because Dalva was coming for the weekend, but
then it was only Thursday and she wouldn't arrive until tomorrow.
It is in the obvious nature of overdrinking to become quite stupid,
and I finally realized that the dawn breeze coming through the window
was warming and that we might have a spate of Indian summer. I
turned on the radio for the stock report, not Dow Jones but cattle,
and caught the end of the weather which guaranteed at least three
fine days to end October.

I got up quickly, wanting to have coffee and a bite before Frieda
could arrive and cloud the day, wincing as I saw two empty wine
bottles, one nearly empty whiskey bottle, a half-full cognac next to
the coffee pot I warmed up. I wrapped bread around a piece of venison congealed on the platter, cutting the rest up and tossing it to the
eager dogs.

I was out the door with my day pack and halfway to the barn
when Frieda swerved into the yard in front of me with tear-red eyes
and quaking jowls. "I'm praying for you, sir," she said, to which I replied, "If you do so in the future, keep it to yourself." That was a bit
nasty but I had to cut it short. Unfortunately, when I was in the barn
and reached for my saddle it occurred to me that lifting the saddle
and reining a horse were out of the question with my injured arm. I
did not pause for a moment but set off north toward the river, breathing in the springish air that owned the toast flavors of its true season,
autumn. The dogs were quizzical about my not being on a horse, then
slowed their usual pace.

I admit I was not half a mile into the two miles to the river when
I damned myself for not bringing my doughboy canteen of water. I
couldn't take a chance on the river but made my way further upstream,
gasping with effort, to the small canyon with the spring. I could not
see the rock my head had struck because my elder son, Paul, had made
it a month's effort as a boy to dig out this spring to increase the flow
after I had warned him and John Wesley about Pawnee graves at the

other spring. Typically, Paul found he liked the spring better in its original form and filled in the excavation, though the rock my head struck still lay concealed.

I knelt and drank too deeply from the icy water, bringing on another slight attack of what the doctor had called "tachycardia," certainly a homely word. I lay there in the thick grass watching the dogs flounder and roll in the mud below the spring where my horse's hooves had broken through the ice. The narrowed view of the river beyond the dogs was similar but I did not long for my sketch pad. As my heart stuttered along I reflected that the madness brought on by my art doubtless came from the fact that my ambition far exceeded my limited talent. Perhaps deep within myself I knew that early, and could not bear it, imagining that those truly gifted created their art with the grace and ease of taking an afternoon nap. I don't mean those unquestionable gods like Caravaggio, Turner or Gauguin, but those of a lesser level, still unreachable to the millions who sensed what it was but failed to reach it: even such ignored Americans as Glackens, Piazzoni, Bellows, Dixon and Sloan were in the ageless guild hall of which the rest of us could only peek in windows.

Against the backdrop of the river in the manner of a slide show I reviewed their paintings but then let them drop away. There was a tinge of the feeling of how utterly enlivened I felt on my trip to New York City museums in 1913, but that also dropped away and I had dried white campion, side oats grama, a little wild rye, dead bloodroot, and a patch of buffaloberry before my eyes. In this part of the West one also had to paint invisible ghosts to inhabit the canvas, to thicken the texture of what could be seen. I forced a smile, remembering Smith's contention that cows struck him as a poor substitute for buffalo. That was after my father told us the story of being treed by a herd of buffalo so vast he at first thought it the shadow of a storm in which the thunder was emerging from the earth.

I could not help but think again that those countable years obsessed with art, seventeen in all, were the most fractious preparation for a life which, after all, could not be lived. My elder son, Paul, came home from a lengthy trip to Brazil the year before John Wesley left for World War II. He had a record we played on our old Victrola, the music coming softly through the window and visiting us on the front porch before which the lilacs bloomed in the wildest profusion. One of the songs, "Estrella Dalva," gave my future granddaughter her name, with John Wesley and Naomi dancing on the evening porch as if the rest of us, even the world, did not exist. We were drinking wine and Paul told me that there was a word in Portuguese called *saudade* that appeared to represent our farm and lives, a homesickness or longing for something vital that had been irretrievably lost and only the dream of it could be recovered, as if for a brief period you had loved a woman with every ounce of body and soul and then, quite suddenly, she had died. He fell dumb and stricken, then said, "Oh my God, Father, I am sorry," and rushed away. I sat there until well past midnight, watching a yellow moon turn white as it rose above the lilacs and cottonwoods.

Paul was that rare young man whose essential melancholy was equal to his great energies. Apart from physical resemblance it would be impossible for an outsider to think of him and John Wesley as brothers. He was a scant sixteen, his brain as old as the hills, when he confronted me with the question of why, since I was an artist when his mother and her sister first met me, did I give up so noble a calling to become a monster. It was outside the pumpshed near the back door and I knocked him to the ground. John Wesley saw it and came running from the barn, and said, "Goddamn you, Dad, don't be such a goddamn bully!" I drove off then for a month without so much as packing a suitcase, but it was two years away on a hunting trip before I had the stomach to apologize. This was an unpardonable act for one who pretended to so despise the utter, unerasable primitiveness of man in matters of war and greed, race and religion. The adequate response was to cut off the hand that hit him.

I lifted the hand high and looked at it against the backdrop of a single memorable cloud that was pushed along quickly by a stiff wind not present on the ground. It was a hand doubtless more gifted for reining horses, branding cows, picking potatoes than its higher aspiration. I smiled as Sonia abruptly nuzzled me with her muddy snout.

She was pleased with her dense coat of fresh mud and seemed to want my approval. In reverse of the usual order of dogs she was the youngest, but had taken over control of the pack, and the others waited rather impatiently for their turns to be petted.

My breath and heart had returned to normal so I made my way down to the river and began throwing sticks in for the dogs to fetch and cleanse themselves. Sonia was stubborn so I used the nonironical voice that made Dalva so successful with the dogs, and Sonia jumped in the river and out in a trice, much of the mud still clinging to her. When we got back home I'd have to brush her out which she also loathed, her black eyes sparkling in anger. Anyone with frilly notions of the feminine, as opposed to masculine, ought to study the sex characteristics in canines to be drawn up short.

In that beginning year of my art obsession Smith made a number of efforts to draw me out, and we made brief forays into the world of the heroic by getting into fistfights with other young men on trips to town. Smith had quarreled with his parents and left home so my father had taken him on as a ranch hand since my art had made me a great deal less useful. We had plenty of room but Smith refused to live in the house despite my mother's wishes. He bunked in my art studio to my dismay, but then my father had our distant neighbor, the Norwegian, expand these quarters. The Norwegian was a shy and frightened man but an amazing carpenter, helped by his ten-year-old son who was as withdrawn as the father. Smith took pity on the boy and rather laboriously taught him to ride our worst horse, an old plug we kept out of sentiment. Throughout the winter my father had been taking the family food, having seen quite enough starvation among the Lakota. The man had begged Smith's forgiveness for firing the shotgun but he had thought a wild Indian was attacking his daughter. Smith was merry at this and told him he was "right on the money" which the man didn't understand.

By midsummer we were involved in a rather shameful business that we were too insensitive to quite understand. While riding our border fence to look for breaks Smith had snuck up on the Norwegian girl while she bathed in a pond well behind their farmhouse.

He figured she did so on warm summer mornings and invited me along. We drew two days of blanks, then were rewarded by a vision without equal in feminine shape. It was especially comic since I had been reading William James again in an effort to keep my head from whirling off my trunk and this nude girl reminded me of James's chapter on "the strongness and weakness of sensations." In this vision "lust" was a euphemism. The breath drew short and blood drummed.

This went on a number of mornings and I took to sketching my first nudes from memory as we had to lay too flat in the grass for me to draw directly from life and that was certainly what we were looking at. On separate mornings we were disturbed by a king snake and a rattler, either of which would normally have startled us. After a week or so we were betrayed by my very loud sneeze with a result we least expected. Though we only knew her well enough to nod hello she waved us over to join her swim. She made love to us that and every other morning for a month or so until her little brother discovered us and we fled.

The word "craven" comes to mind for our actions because what I first perceived as mysterious and winsome in her behavior soon appeared to me as merely daft. We were simply taking advantage of a retarded girl, and this spooked Smith as much as me, though we still continued on until we were discovered. Parents visited parents and my mother made a Lakota herbal concoction to ensure that the girl miscarried should she be pregnant. Naturally I never knew this until later. My mother in her matter-of-fact way wasn't disposed to be angry with me, while my father upbraided me with the fact that the retarded were children. I said I didn't know this at first, and he said but you continued when you did. At his insistence I ended up trading my five best horses for a team of Belgian mares because the Norwegian badly needed a pair of draft horses for his farming. I walked the horses over in a good set of harness, presented them, bowed and walked home, my face deeply reddened by the laughter of the girl behind the screen door.

* * *

Dalva called before school on Friday morning to check on the health of my arm and to request foreign food for dinner by which she meant steak and spaghetti, the latter with olive oil, parsley and garlic. This would, as always, be accompanied by my tales of my trip to France and Italy the year after my parents died. We had worked our way slowly to this point in my life and I was careful to avoid the slightest mention of the young woman I had so loved at this time. Naomi needn't have warned me of that, but I had understood her concern, so great were the dire consequences of that period of my life.

In preparation I checked my journals for that European trip and was amazed at their banality, as if a literate chimpanzee had been taken on its first trip to the zoo. None of the emotions, the feelings, the moods, as it were, had any interest, while descriptions of buildings, crowds, meals, and paintings still held a tinge of fascination. The latter were textural concretia while the former were romantic filigree that required a Tu Fu or a James Joyce to give substance. A young man wandering in Europe in 1911 caressing his moods was an embarrassment, as if it were unique to see a life swallowed up by an obsession. I met Edward Curtis once down in Arizona, and then again in Mexico, and the litany of his complaints, mostly about marriage and money, were silly indeed in the light of the splendor of his work. Of course, I was guilty of the musings but not the first-rate work. I might better have painted a nun's goiter than the bridge over Pont Neuf or a far corner of a Medici garden. My heart favored the remote corners of Mexico, and Europe was an obligation I could not begin to comprehend until older when, quite sickened by the cant that we do everything better over here, I saw the glories of Paris anew. There was the disturbing thought of how Davis had teased me for trying to read Henry James before the campfire where we were roasting the smallest of *cabrito*, which he was basting with garlic and hot chiles. I admitted I had been strenuously on the same page for days.

Quite comically Dalva was concerned with communism over dinner rather than my European travels. She ate the Florentine steak and spaghetti with gusto but I sensed something was wrong, and she said she had expected the spaghetti and meatballs I had made for her

Labor Day weekend. I felt apologetically senile and said she could help me make the dish tomorrow. The communism fear had arisen again that morning when the county school superintendent had stopped by to warn the children about the world threat. Dalva couldn't remember a "b" word and I suggested "bastion" at which she nodded with pleasure. According to this nitwit, Nebraska was one of the last bastions against godless communism. After the man left the children were quite frightened and it took some time for Naomi to calm them down. A 4-H girl was crying because the Russians were going to drop an A-bomb on her pet heifer.

It was hard to allay this fear in a simple fashion when, what with my bad arm, I was unable to strangle it at its source. The prairie and Great Plains could generate a quality of bumpkin idiocy that would quickly die elsewhere under intelligent scrutiny, the exception being the Deep South where the shenanigans of such men as Huey Long had always provided shock and amusement for the literate. This particular man had been hired partly because he had advertised himself as "God fearing" and bore a Ph.D. from a Bible college that I viewed as doubtless bogus. It all made one yawn with a bone-deep despair, recalling how my own two sons received their true education from my den library.

After I had assured Dalva that the Russian attack was unlikely at the moment we looked at horse and cattle scrapbooks from the twenties and thirties, and then I helped her with her history lessons so that she wouldn't need to be dragged off home by Naomi after Saturday-night dinner. She had always been fond of the photos of the polo games up at Fort Robinson before World War I, when the fort was a remount station for the U.S. Cavalry, a force that became a pleasant illusion when it met the horror of modern armament in France. Dalva's history lesson seemed quite complicated but then her teacher was Naomi. Who would you have voted for, Theodore Roosevelt or William Jennings Bryan, and I could scarcely offer the young lady my answer of "neither."

I struggled to give her some sense of history beyond memorizing a few details from the textbook. She loved our canyon so I reminded her that when you sat well up in it, the walls narrowed the view of the river but the movement was the same. Whether it was Bryan or Roosevelt, or Heathcliff and Catherine in her favorite novel, you could imagine them with the passage of the river taking place in a segment of time that then went onward. No matter that historical phenomena disappear, they are still a part of the substance of the river and continue to affect what we are. Roosevelt and Bryan might have immediately less to do with her life now than the passions of Emily Brontë, but they were very much part of the structure of what our country had become, and since this country was her home, it was best to know about them.

She was very much in agreement with my fatiguing attempt to explain history, but I could see her mind had drifted elsewhere, her eyes beginning to tear as they always did when they thought of her father, John Wesley. She stopped herself, and smiled at me, dismissing where John Wesley might fit in my worn-out metaphor of the river.

"You sound like Professor Rosenthal," she said, and I agreed. We'd met Rosenthal two springs before, shortly after the news came of John Wesley. We were riding down the tail end of the county road to the Niobrara when we saw an old man in a suit and tie sitting under a cottonwood tree with a picnic hamper, and an open bottle of wine on its lid, and reading a book. It was Saturday afternoon and the radio in his parked car was playing the opera. I am normally stern with the very few trespassers we get, usually hunters, but this man represented a unique and extraordinary sight, his tailoring similar to the suits men wore in London back in the thirties. He stood to bid us good day, gesturing at his wife well down the riverbank, saying that she was a *lepidopterist*, continuing at our puzzled looks to explain that this meant a student of butterflies. He added that the opera on the car radio was Mozart's *Così fan tutte* and that was the limit of his knowledge of his immediate surroundings. He was an émigré scholar at our state university in Lincoln, via Germany, Cambridge and the Warburg Institute in London. I commented that there was no trace of German in his accent and he replied that that was something he had worked to get rid of; for obvious reasons. He then asked us if he could pet our horses, announcing that he had never actually touched a horse before. This startled both Dalva and myself, but she was the first to respond, jumping off her mare and leading it under the tree. Dalva said, "Go slow" because her mare was skittish and this man, Rosenthal by name, slid his hand ever so softly along her flank, then laughed and said, "Amazing."

His wife made a muddy appearance, a jolly woman with the paraphernalia of her trade, and called Dalva "Rapunzel" for her long hair. Dalva was so pleased she asked me if they could come for tea and I readily agreed, though I am worse than a Frenchman about whom I let in my home. Dalva assured the woman, Sarah, that Lundquist knew every butterfly in the book and Sarah said she'd like to meet this creature. Dalva was only eight at the time and paused at the word "creature," chiming in that Lundquist was actually a Swede.

I was lucky enough to spend the afternoon with this man while Dalva and Sarah, guided by Lundquist, were off looking at a fresh assortment of butterflies, after Lundquist in the barnyard had assured the woman that butterflies were the direct cousins of birds. Rosenthal was curious about the paintings and the books in my den but we only touched lightly on our separate backgrounds. His area of interest he referred to as the "history of ideas" which was sometimes as hard to track as the history of rain. He was altogether willing to sacrifice the most profound thing he said to an apt witticism, and I was delighted at the lightness of his mind, and the way he was able to deliver his ponderous knowledge as if he were commenting on a fascinating dinner menu. I had never met the like of him and I recalled that even the brightest men I had met early in the arts world were basically sunk in the emotional content of any day, while this man flitted and skittered in the history of world cultures to pluck out what he needed to prove a point or fuel the conversation.

He was curious about the Natives that had lived in the area, the Pawnee with the Lakota on the western edge, though I sensed he knew the answers to most of his questions before he asked. We prodded each other with questions and I was eager to be the student when he began talking about the *idea* of land. The Jews, blacks, and Natives had had a far more tribal notion of land than the dominant Anglo-Saxon or northern European cultures. The Jews, blacks, and Natives tended to be shunted aside or oppressed partly for this reason of specific land ownership. If you want someone's wealth, or the area in which they live, or their bodies themselves in the case of the blacks, your motives are basically economic but you attack them on religious grounds, portraying them as godless savages, the Antichrist, or worse yet, having no discernible religion at all because it had become gradually lost when they were uprooted from their homeland. And after the utter and complete defeat of the enemy you want nothing more from them, they have nothing more to give, except that the remnant behave themselves. You only give reparations or rebuild in the economies of the like-minded as in the case of Germany and Japan.

I cracked a bit here, admitting that I was half Lakota though it showed in my appearance only lightly, and that I later perceived my father had tried to make me a gentleman to escape the pain he had witnessed among the landless who had been forced aside into the country described by Sheridan, the reservations themselves, as "worthless pieces of land surrounded by scoundrels." I also admitted that I had bought a great deal of land in western Nebraska when the agricultural depression hit early in the mid-twenties, and then bought a great deal more throughout the West during the Great Depression of the thirties, only to sell nearly all of it after my son had died in Korea.

I felt a bit embarrassed as I rattled on and when I finished he put me at ease by saying that in this country the very perception of reality is economic. Artists and poets get away from that but not their collectors, he joked. He exempted me from the latter when on questioning I said I had never sold one of my collection of paintings and had no idea of their worth, nor was I curious. There was a slightly raw moment when he asked how long I had painted myself, but then we were interrupted by the butterfly collectors.

The Rosenthals visited again in August, this time staying the night, and we had a grand time including a picnic way back at the spring. The professor had ridden his first horse and butterflies were abundant. I planned on taking Dalva down to Lincoln to visit them in the fall, but around Labor Day we received the alarming news by letter that they had made a rather sudden decision to move to Cambridge in England. There was a slight reference to the fact that foreign-born intellectuals were particularly vulnerable during the current *red scare*. I immediately called our governor, not a bad fellow and a long-time acquaintance, and he had looked into the matter, the upshot being that Rosenthal was under some suspicion, but would have managed to keep his job had he not *flown the coop*. I felt melancholy indeed though I still managed to exchange a few letters a year with them in England where he is doing quite well, though Sarah terribly misses our butterflies.

I was strangely full of anxiety after Naomi and Ruth picked up Dalva for church on Sunday morning. They had also come over for our spaghetti and meatball dinner the evening before. The meatballs somehow disintegrated in the sauce, Naomi said because we had forgotten the egg to bind the meat, and Dalva said it was on purpose because she didn't like eggs because they came from a chicken's butt, a simple enough dislike. We went out twice during dinner in the twilight to watch great numbers of wild geese flying over us on their way south. There was a severe cold front heading slowly down toward us from Canada and North Dakota but it would be another full day for it to reach us.

Over dinner I once again wished that my wife and myself had managed at least one daughter. Daughters would have made me more human while my sons had tended to pull me apart in the daily struggle of wills. I suspect I was romanticizing a bit because the girls were a considerable chore for Naomi, with each going in a willfully opposite direction on every matter. Naomi had spent the day outside and there was a fine flush on her skin and for a moment I envied my dead son his wife, so gracefully accepting compared to my departed own

who never awoke on a single morning without implicitly questioning her existence on earth.

In the middle of a restless night with a still-warm wind billow-
ing the curtains I awoke thinking I heard the door open, a noise certain to put the dogs in an uproar. I got up and checked to find Dalva
sitting on the porch steps with the dogs around her, and this at three
a.m. Rather than being upset I sat down beside her and we stared
wordlessly at a big yellow harvest moon, the breeze rattling the last
of the yard's maple leaves. There were even more geese than at dinner time, and we were lucky enough to see a skein of them fly across
the moon, at which point Dalva gripped my hand tightly and we went
inside.

I have no idea why I was so upset the next morning, or I didn't
understand when I first thought about it standing there in the yard
with a knot in my stomach as they drove off to church. Even the dogs
lay in a depressed clump near the edge of the bare lilacs, but then
they were always sullen when Dalva went home. It was a selfish
thought but it occurred to me that the two daughters and the mother
in the car were my only anchors to earth, and I wandered the yard all
hollow and trembling, averting my eyes from the graves in the lilacs
where I would one day join my parents, my wife and my son. I certainly hoped to beat the rest of the family there, even my other son,
Paul, whom I hadn't seen since John Wesley's funeral three years ago
last spring. Then I was quite suddenly disturbed by the word "my,"
as if I had somehow owned these beloved kin, when each in their own
universe were joined in fragile contiguity without owning the others,
much less their own fate.

It is at such rare and somewhat unpleasant times that we visit
the part of ourselves that is incomprehensible. My incomprehension,
in fact, was palpable to my skin, and I looked around at the forested
shelterbelts that surrounded me, perhaps further then I could walk
at my age, and felt a flash of anger that I had been so immovably stuck
to the location, bound and tied here by not totally familiar parts of
soul and mind. And this is improperly rational for the surge of plea-

sure and dread I felt for this place at that moment. It was a maddening struggle with ghosts, the ghosts of others, and the ghosts of my former selves that could not leave for more than a few months, excepting for the First World War, this trap my father had built, and I continued building, for body and spirit. I tried to breathe deeply and couldn't. I looked at my hands and didn't quite recognize them.

I turned to the house, at last recognizing the seizure that had begun to take place. I went from room to room, avoiding the mirrors. I put on my boots and emptied a bottle of Canadian whiskey into my canteen. I sliced a large raw steak in pieces for the dogs and drank nearly a quart of cold water. My temples were drumming and I still couldn't quite catch my breath. I felt cold from the water and shuddered, then strode into the den, threw some books aside and opened the safe. I uncovered the folder that contained a single photo of her, also a thickish group of drawings I had made when she was riding, of her sitting on the leather couch I knelt by to spread the drawings out, nude except for the towel around her waist, another with only a scarf around her neck, another sitting in the spring up to her waist, another leaning against a tree. There's nothing so nude as a girl eating an apple in an orchard. I gathered them together because I couldn't properly see, and stumbled against the desks when I put them away. There was still part of me that was ashamed that I hadn't killed her father. I passed the stairs I had fallen down when I'd dreamt of Willow in my delirium after my parents died. How strange it seemed to me now not to have known then that there would be another Willow, implacably more damaging, so that one went through life carrying an invisible gravestone that would disappear, then return with leaden fury, which, when dissipated, would arrange itself in the lucid and melancholy paintings the mind constructs of love.

I went out the door thinking that I hadn't made this walk since John Wesley died but this time I headed north to cover the path counterclockwise, doubting as I crossed the barnyard with the jubilant dogs that I could make the whole walk but caring less. If I failed I could always stumble, crawl, even sleep like those tired cowdogs after roundup who make their way back on sore and bloody pads. If that threatened northern front arrived I could happily freeze to death in a thicket like my mother.

When I had sufficiently recovered from my illness in 1910 I rode out of the yard one early April morning past the raw earth graves of my parents, pausing down the road at Walgren's drive where he joined me on his fat sorrel. We made town in a short three hours, left our horses and mud dusters at the livery, and boarded the east-bound train for Omaha, arriving in the early evening and checking into, as per the instructions Walgren held dearly, the Paxton Hotel. We were shy at the place's extravagance, but arrangements had been made for us by a law firm in Omaha that was an extension of one in Chicago which managed my father's affairs, saving those of a local nature that Walgren dealt with. Elegantly dressed ladies and gents passed by in the lobby and I peeked into the dining room with chagrin at its opulence, figuring despite our fatigue that we might have to head down the street for supper. We were shown to two bedrooms joined in the middle by a living room in which there were vases of fresh flowers, and a small bar containing wine and whiskey. An assistant manager and bellhop stood there looking at us, then the former showed us a menu in case we wished supper in our rooms. Walgren grumbled at the prices and the man said the law firm was being billed for our stay. When the meal arrived Walgren scraped off the strange sauce that covered the meat, and further complained that there was no way to save the excess food. He then determined the dollar amount that it would take to bribe him into eating the plate of oysters that had been set before me.

After an unsettled night we were taken to the law offices a few blocks away by an officious young man in a well-cut suit who whined relentlessly that the sidewalk hadn't been salted against a thin coat of ice. I was delighted when he fell down and amazed when he pretended he hadn't. I had spent enough time at the Art Institute in Chicago to recognize a fop when I saw one, including in Mexico where some young cowboys are foppish. Besides I was an artist, somewhat a bohemian, and I had no intention of being swept away by a pack of bourgeois lawyers. I meant to get business over with quickly

and head up to Duluth in Minnesota and paint the break-up of the
ice on Lake Superior with a friend, an artist from Sweden who lived
there because it reminded him of home.

    We were led into a corner office that resembled a rich man's den,
and were greeted by the chief partner, Frederick Morgan, a stern and
hard-edged man, but with a specific twinkle in his eye, who read the
will. My father had told me most of the information the summer
before, but I was quite surprised at the amounts involved in the sale
of a half dozen tree nurseries in the northern Midwest. A goodly piece
of property immediately north of Chicago would be held onto as it
seemed to be in the path of "progress," a word I already loathed at
twenty-four. I was not to have full control of my holdings for another
eleven years, until I reached thirty-five, but could draw on a yearly
amount that was about ten times what I was used to spending in the
pursuit of my art. Walgren was to look after the farm for the time
being, including the hiring of his cousin as a farm manager as I was
frequently elsewhere and otherwise occupied. There was also a pro-
vision for several thousand dollars each for Willow and Smith, and
it was Walgren's duty to track them down. Everything was to be ad-
ministered by the law firm in conjunction with a bank in Chicago.

    It was so hot in the room that my eyes became rheumy and I
yawned. There was a very high quality portrait of two young ladies
behind Morgan and I wanted to study the painting more closely. He
then dismissed Walgren and I also got up to leave but learned that I
had to stay for the day to go over investment procedures. I felt trapped
in a hothouse and when he showed Walgren to the door I studied
the painting at close range. By the time I turned he had a large folder
spread upon his desk. "My daughters," he said. "We'll have dinner
with them tonight." He then said I was very fortunate indeed to have
such a grand start in life. I couldn't think of a proper reply but suggested we take a walk while we discussed finances as I was far too warm
to think. He opened the office windows wide and put on his over-
coat, then sat back down at the desk. Everything with this man was
a battle of wills. He thought of himself as a benign autocrat but could
imagine no reality fully except his own.

Later, at dinner at his home which I viewed as a huge Victorian monstrosity, I studied the deference offered to him by his wife and two daughters that he readily mistook as sincerity.

But then let me stop and take a gun and knife to this nonsense, this garden toad hopping in short hops, and he will never get out of the well pit he's fallen into by dint of will, and that he has begun to think of as his universe. I am both walking to the west along the Niobrara and remembering that dinner in terms of a reality I no longer believe in. It was a series of jolts only a little muted by wine. I was not so much confused but that I had lost my "self" soon after sitting down. Frederick Morgan's wife was named Martha and hailed from Rhode Island, bright and more genteel than any woman I had ever met. First Neena entered, rather sweet and grave but one could never quite know what she was thinking right up to the day she died. She was the younger, sixteen years of age, deeply handsome like her mother rather than pretty, and one sensed iron in the spine of that girl. Then came Adelle and my stomach hollowed, both handsome and pretty, a year older than Neena, but captious, late for dinner, a falsely felt curtsy and a peck for her father's face, but also a slight tweak to an ear at which he reddened a trace. She was the dancer, a lover of music while Neena read, and in reverse of the normal order Adelle, the older, was youngest in behavior. She stared at me critically too long for comfort as if I were an absolutely new creature brought to market. Her mother had been forewarned and she asked me if my art was thriving and I said I thought so. I was going to travel to Duluth in the morning and when I returned home in a week I hope to begin a series of paintings based on my last Mexican trip before my parents had died.

We all seemed to like each other, at least for the time being. The family had made three summer trips to Europe and I hadn't been at all which amazed them. How could a burgeoning artist not travel to Europe, the living source of art? There was an odd urge to tell them, as Davis would have, that they were fuller of shit than Christmas geese, but I held my tongue. Adelle then asked teasingly how I knew if I was any good, which angered her father at the impertinence of the question. I said that I didn't, of course, know at this point, and quoted the Bible, "Many are called, but few are chosen," and said it would likely come to nothing, but that it was my calling and I had to live out my life within its strictures. "Which are?" she asked. "Hard work and absolute freedom." Her father then interrupted with the predictable inanity that wealth in itself was a great responsibility in that it required itself to be multiplied. There was a flash of heat under my collar with this notion, so supported by the popular press, that our political notions of Manifest Destiny had to repeat themselves in every individual man.

Grave Neena saved us, but only momentarily, when she asked why I preferred Mexico when she had read recently that Mexican savages had been known to kill American travelers, as our own Indians had many years before. I answered that the wildness of the terrain was a far greater danger than the people, and then told them of my friend Davis's fatal tumble from the cliff. We were in the middle of dessert and they fell morose at this story, and then Morgan with nervous pomposity said, "Surely, young man, you'll admit that these brown folks are far less civilized than ourselves and can present the gravest dangers to the unwary. The savages may not boil you in a cauldron for dinner as they do in Africa, but I've read they'll cut out your heart for lunch as did their neighbors, the Apaches."

At this moment I had become a welter of confusion and there was a peculiar quaking sensation beneath my breastbone as I ex-changed the longest look yet with Adelle, and Neena was amused as she watched this, and the mother pretended to overlook it. I found myself replying to Morgan just on the edge of impoliteness, "I'm half savage myself by birth so perhaps I sensed I had nothing to fear among my brethren. My mother was Oglala Sioux—Lakota they call themselves."

Morgan could not have been more startled had I fired a revolver into the ceiling. The table was aghast, and I cursed myself for admit-ting this which I normally kept to myself to avoid drawing attention, and being forced to answer so many stupid questions. At art school

Davis liked to introduce me to ladies as "John Indian" which oddly enough got my foot in the door with the more adventuresome.

"How wonderful!" Adelle said, breaking the leaden silence. Neena clapped her hands and Martha, the mother, smiled as if a joke had been played on her husband. Morgan pretended to be amused by his gaffe, but I could see I had immediately gone from being a possible suitor to a mere eccentric, albeit a rich one in his terms. Neena then asked me a curious question that had been asked by fellow students in Chicago, to the effect of why my language seemed a little *ancient*. I answered that I had been brought up rather remotely, quit school in the third grade, lasted but a month at Cornell, and my father always spoke as if he had just emerged from the Civil War, spending most of his ensuing time speaking with the Indians. Adelle piped in saying, "You're so peculiar," to which I replied, "I suppose I am." I bid them good night, and at the door Adelle whispered, "I'll see you early in the morning," after which I shuddered my brisk way back to the hotel.

I made my way slowly to the direct rear of the property then cut my way into the spring doubting my ability to do the whole circumference turning from the vivid past to the ordinary present. The sun was still warm enough at midday but it began to look a little ominous far to the northwest, the horizon glowering there with the energy of the front in a grayish smear. My legs were trembling, and my clothes damp with sweat as I lay on the sandbank of the creek, swigging rather too deeply from my canteen of whiskey. Seeing Adelle that clearly again in my mind made me wish to get drunk and die, which was merely repeating the pattern set after meeting her.

Adelle preferred the moon to the sun, and in the short time we were together, no more than a month of days in total, she seemed to come only totally alive after the late afternoon. The twilight and the night were her times, from which she drew a curious and manic strength. When she arrived at my hotel rooms soon after daylight she was melancholy and without energy compared to the way she fairly

glowed the evening before. At the time the hotel visit was considered daring and inappropriate for a young lady, but she carried a bag
of books and said at the desk that I was her cousin and tutor. I was
having coffee and still intent on making my Duluth train, and not at
all of the mind that she would actually appear as her whisper had
stated. She slumped in a chair and said nothing as I stood there in
my robe looking out the window but not actually seeing anything. I
finally sat down in an easy chair across from her, still unable to speak
a single thought. Then she abruptly got up and took a pull from a
whiskey bottle on the chest, coughed wildly and said in a broken voice
that she wished to become an "emancipated woman." Now it was my
turn to get up and take a deep drink. I managed to look at her fully
and at the moment thought that everything in my life was at stake.
There was still plenty of time to catch the train, an idea so idiotic
that I smiled. Why are you smiling, she asked? I was thinking of rush-
ing off to take the train, I said. She dropped her arms and made the
few steps toward me as if sleepwalking, but her eyes showing the life
of the night before.

She did not leave until Neena sent a bellhop up late in the afternoon to fetch her. I went down to the lobby with Adelle and there
was Neena with her school books thinking that Adelle should come
along home to avoid discovery. Neena had covered for her at school
and thought the whole thing "utterly thrilling," staring at me in particular with the awe thought to be deserved by kings. Then the two
sisters curtsied good-bye and off they went.

I took an evening train to Minneapolis, unable to reach Duluth
until the next morning, exhausted and puzzled by my day and more
than a bit embarrassed by my lips and neck covered by puffy love bites.
Adelle was born for the bed and in my young but not inconsiderable
experience I had never seen her like, or even close. I supposed it might
be the energy and grace of her dancer's body, and certainly her antic
brain, not to speak of what she had read that prepared her for the
day. I thought as I dozed on the train that if I were never to make
love again I had reached the pinnacle. In the dining car I ate two fair
beefsteaks to restore myself, and then was struck daft by the thought

"What next?" for I already missed her. The answer came after my first full day in Duluth with my friend from the Art Institute, the Swedish painter. It was Saturday morning and we were packing up for a trip up the north shore to Grand Marais to paint the drift ice when Adelle appeared at the door with a valise. My painter friend was well known and she had no problem finding the house. She had told her parents she was visiting a friend outside of Omaha but could only stay with me until Sunday afternoon, unless, of course, I wished her to go away, the last possible thought in my mind.

We went off to my bedroom and made love for a while, then the three of us gathered up a picnic and took a sketching walk along the Duluth harborfront. I told them about my stop here ten years before in the search for Willow, and Adelle wept at the sadness of the story, but then by late afternoon when we stopped at the same tavern of so long ago to drink and eat fish, she came almost too much alive and wanted to dance. The Swede took us off to a polka party at a Scandinavian hall and we had a fine, exhausting time, with Adelle stealing the show. I wasn't much of a dancer, but then few of the others in the crowded and drunken hall were much beyond simply jumping around to the music.

We were still in bed late Sunday morning when Frederick Morgan appeared at the door with two burly Pinkertons and a Duluth police lieutenant. "You're a bastard, Northridge," he said, simply enough. Adelle who had dressed quickly came forward saying, "I came here of my accord, Father. He didn't ask me." The Pinkertons and lieutenant struck me as disappointed at the civility of it all. In her morning mode Adelle went along meekly, down the steps, arm in arm with her red-eared father and with nary a backward glance. The Swede appeared behind me then, quite hungover, and said that I must be careful or she would kill me in one way or another. I said that was nonsense, but with little confidence.

Sprawled there by the creek and cautioning myself against my canteen whiskey I stared at the assortment of dead leaves that had gathered themselves in the spring, with some floating, a few suspended in the clear water, and the bottom of the spring pasted yellow and dull red with the others. I had once tried to paint this phenomenon, unsuccessfully in the minds of others because it is not the sort of thing one can see clearly. There was the odd thought, absent for years, that nearly everyone was ignorant of how they see, lost as they were in the attraction for the simplicity of photographs, which is not how anyone sees. We don't see all at once unless we work very hard at it. When I first saw Cézanne's work I was dumbstruck at his comprehension of true vision. I recalled how Adelle had an eye for the oddities, the peculiarities in the natural world. In the orchard the first apples coming past midsummer are the yellow transparents and she studied them closely, finding with delight that none were perfect, and that we shared imperfections with the dogs that followed us around, keeping at a discreet distance during our lovemaking.

Despite my caution I sipped again at the canteen and noted between the spaces of a group of ash trees that the storm had drawn closer. I felt overwhelmed by the sheer density of the reality around me, the water, the dogs, the impending storm, the still-warmish breeze pushing the floating leaves across the spring, the thicket perhaps fifty yards distant where I had found my mother, and lastly, this sandbank where Adelle loved to play as haphazardly as any mammal. We had camped here in a full moon on a warm August night when her ebullience came close to hysteria, and though I was young and half mad myself I justly feared for her sanity.

All of our idle, even enthralling thoughts of sexuality are the weakest possible shadows of the prolonged act from the very first meeting to whenever it may end. Our thoughts and our art reach so feebly toward the texture of our passion. Now I can smell her neck and the back of her knee with the sand stuck to her damp skin, the sand trickling into her footprints, her head emerging from the water, the rivulet of water between her breasts, her breath the odor of the green pears we had been eating, how she wished to make love like dogs do, with her back arched downward at her small waist, and how she ground her face into the damp sand, whipping her long wet hair from side to side. I saw her teeth in the moonlight when she said she wished to be called Neva after the Russian river for reasons only God could trace. She climbed trees in her underclothing and sang quite nicely. She rode fairly well in the English style but adapted immediately to my cow horses. She claimed to have swum the Missouri River late one night the summer before on a schoolgirl outing. I did not ask her how she got back. It was the sort of question one didn't ask her.

When I got home from Duluth after the Pinkerton incident there were two dozen letters from Adelle in the scant ten days I was gone. Her parents had aimed her at Pembroke College in the fall, part of the alma mater of her father, Brown, in Providence, Rhode Island. Instead of this she wished to marry me and we would live in either Paris or Mexico or both. She certainly knew I was "rich" enough to do this or her father wouldn't have brought me to their home for dinner in the first place. I was appalled by the idea that she thought me wealthy. Perhaps I was well off by inheritance in the terms of the society of that day but all of my nearly religious feelings about my art predicated a life of simplicity. To my friends at the Art Institute I was either "John Indian" or the "farmer" because of my agricultural background and my crude wardrobe. The examples of both the French and American artists I revered carried no room for the frivolities of society. The main problem she had to overcome, in this plan, of course, was that of her parents. She was sure she could change her mother's mind, but her father was adamant over the fact of my tainted blood. There were more than enough references to her father in all of her letters to make me think of their relationship as unhealthy, a popular euphemism at the time.

Meanwhile, she demanded that I come get her as she had tried to run away, been caught, and been confined in a private asylum for distraught and hysterical young ladies. She had been released on her promise not to run away again and when she objected to anything she was sedated. She was followed both to and from school and at her dancing classes by a disgusting Pinkerton.

There was also a letter from her father begging me to "act a gentleman" as his beloved daughter was of unsound mind, a condition I was exacerbating. He was confident she would be fine if I would only stay out of the way. He then reminded me that my financial "welfare" was also in his hands, which seemed a desperate measure on his part. I showed this to Walgren who became quite irate and telegrammed both the bank and Morgan's superiors in Chicago. I regretted this a little as it got him in some trouble and one of his colleagues was appointed my overseer. My regret came from my strategy's having energized Morgan's will to totally deny me any contact with his daughter.

I had no immediate idea what to do about Adelle so I hitched up a tank wagon and a double team of Belgians and spent a week watering trees against an especially dry May. I could neither draw, paint, or read, so troublesome were the daily letters. She filled my thoughts moment by moment and my indecision made me so sleepless I could only rest during the full light of midday. I kept reminding myself of my father's anger over my taking advantage of the obviously daft and mentally limited Norwegian girl, but then there seemed no similarity.

I then did an extremely stupid thing by writing a note to say that I was coming to get her, too distracted and thick to suppose her mail would be intercepted, but then my own will had been fueled by a letter from her sister, Neena, to the effect that she thought Adelle could not possibly survive the "brutality" of her father. By then I was unimaginably distorted by love and sleeplessness and spent an entire night deciding whether or not to take along my revolver. I left it behind which turned out to be a stroke of dumb luck.

I reached Omaha on a late May afternoon and went straight from the train to Morgan's house where I was attacked by two Pinkertons emerging from the bushes before I got to the door. I did fairly well with them before I was sapped across the forehead and lost consciousness, waking late at night in the hospital with a policemen dozing in a chair by the door. What saved me from a stiff jail sentence for "criminal trespass" and assaulting the Pinkertons was that one of the arresting officers was from my home country and alerted Walgren, who arrived the next afternoon accompanied by a youngish reporter from a socialist-labor newspaper. The word of this almost immediately reached Morgan who then attempted to detoxify the situation to avoid social damages. He was in my room within the half hour, beginning a prepared comment about his great love for his daughter. I shut him up quickly by saying he was fortunate I hadn't brought my pistol or I would have blown a hole in his miserable head instanter, and if he didn't bring Adelle to my room immediately it was he who would never see her again. He rushed off and Adelle was there with her mother for a short while, but then I had to be trepanned so great was the swelling behind my forehead that was split from side to side. I was in that accursed hospital for a full week before I left of my own accord. Adelle was my daily and nightly company, and it was her mother who worked out a not altogether satisfying compromise. She would bring Adelle to my farm for two weeks in July, but then Adelle must spend August catching up on the studies she'd missed with all of this "drama." She would then go off to college in Rhode Island but I would be allowed to see her over Christmas, and again in March during a vacation period. If we still wished to be married in June we could do so with her blessing. Adelle was disconsolate when I agreed, but then the meeting was during the day when the rhythms of her peculiar soul were at full ebb.

I went home then with my split forehead and a small hole at the hairline from my trepanation, stopping in Lincoln to order some new furniture, curtains, china, and suchlike. I aimed to present her mother with the living picture of a civilized savage. I brought in two painters from town to do the house inside and out, and hired a rather homely housekeeper to prevent temptation. I began to draw and paint again and the letters from Adelle were a bit more soothing with few references to her father, who had seemed a bit beaten in mind and spirit when I saw him the day I left.

The two weeks of her visit were perhaps the only time of my life I would dearly wish to repeat other than fragments of other days. The only drawback was a heat wave which was difficult for Adelle's mother who was slightly asthmatic. Other than a short walk in the early morning and evening she tended to keep to the den, kitchen, and parlor. She was the first I had ever met of that curious tribe of true Yankees to whom Boston was the capital and Providence an intellectual suburb. In the worst of the heat she spoke lovingly of her summers at a place called Wickford, where they would spend the warm weather sailing on Narragansett Bay. She assured me if things went well it would be a fine place for me to paint. I began to gather that she was the true force in the family rather than Morgan, both the source of their stability and money. It was inevitable that he'd prefer his daughter to marry an Eastern swell, or at least a Midwestern merchant, certainly not a half-Lakota artist. It seemed odd to me that Adelle's mother would be so fascinated with my father's collection of Indian artifacts which had not yet been moved to the subbasement, their intended hiding place, but then I assumed that it was because Easterners took a firm interest in ancestry. At her questioning, I told her what I knew which wasn't a great deal. She thought that it was melancholy that I missed half my "birthright" through my father's intention to have me fully adjusted to the modern world. It was years before I understood this and then only in the most private rituals where ceremonies of the blood tend to emerge.

The brief life, then, with Adelle took place out of doors with the tacit approval of our chaperone. We had our midsummer night's dream in field, barn, studio, at the spring and along the Niobrara where I taught her during one hot afternoon's swim to stalk waterbirds by keeping all but your eyes submerged, and then you could approach the bird with startling closeness. She tamed a Hereford calf so that it followed her on walks, and played the cowgirl helping myself and Fred, Walgren's cousin who had become my foreman, drive the cattle through the gated windbreaks to greener pastures. Fred was always red-faced in Adelle's presence, both because of her beauty and her frank language which she thought to be that of an emancipated woman. She was always eager to hear from me how the young women at the Art Institute acted, how "fast" they were in male company. It was obvious how much she loved her mother while she never mentioned her father except in oppressive terms, though never in her mother's presence.

Adelle had the strangest attitude toward mortality for one so young, and on our last moonlit walk together she spoke of a school girlfriend who had died of cancer the year before. It seemed out of character for one so vibrant to be flip about death, but other than for me, she didn't care if she died or not if her life was to become wrong for her spirit. She had spoken of suicide with her sister, Neena, who was without intentions toward the act for the simple reason that she would be cheated of her reading. Adelle on a moment-by-moment basis could not distance herself from a single emotion, however slight. I've often thought we are not fated to be quite that alive. I can't say that there was a premonition but on the morning that they left I was unable to imagine a future, whether for Adelle or myself. She passed me a lock of her hair through the train window and that was all, a not quite full smile and a lock of hair.

I can hear a roar of wind to the north and I'm quite suddenly fearful about being caught out here, though caught I will be in the center of our largest pasture on the south side of the property, fallow and un-grazed so that the grama grass catches at my ankles. I can see Naomi's house in the distance, far closer than my own, but I don't want to escape the storm there because I'm a little drunk which might cause alarm. I reach the far side of the interminable pasture and the wall of trees just as the storm hits me broadside with both a violent wind and a precipitous drop in temperature. I haven't been in this particular place for years but I recalled a pile of deer bones where a doe had caught or broken her neck jumping the fence. The bones were still there but the skull was gone, and I picked up a vertebra to study, then hastened along because it had begun to hail which stung my face. In the corner of the pasture where the shelterbelt was the densest, there was a thicket where Smith and I had built a lean-to and the remains of it were still there, offering a little shelter from the weather. I repiled the roof poles, pushing them together, and ducked under the front as a blast of hail rattled in the tree tops. Somewhere buried in the earth beneath me was an old tin box containing a photo of a half-

nude dancing girl that Smith and I had hidden there, a boyish trea-
sure that was a bow to a mystery. I could see the bare breasts in my
mind's eye, tilted upward and out a bit like Adelle's.

It was then my heart began to stutter wildly and I recalled I had
forgotten my pill for the day. I took two swallows of whiskey but that
sent me into a paroxysm of coughing with some of the whiskey going
down my windpipe. The heartbeat seemed even more irregular and I
curled on my side watching the ground whiten with hail, and then
stared upward at the rolling and turbulent clouds, shivering with my
drying sweat and unsure of how to proceed. It did not, for some reason, seem an unlikely place to die. My putative biography didn't
amount to much: he bought and sold horses, cattle and land, drew
and painted for a while, married a wife named Neena and was not a
good husband, raised two sons, and now somewhat looked after two
granddaughters. This became almost amusing despite a heart that
chattered like cold teeth. We are similar to beach stones that strike
us as unique but are pretty much uniform. My dreams were my own,
and early on the rare vision of art was mine, as were my loves. My
son Paul joked that in geologic terms we all share the same amount
of immortality. What we had supposed to be at least superficially real
faded in interest. In the protected hollow between two cedars ten feet
in front of me I could imagine Adelle until she took her specific shape,
but again the smile was not quite full and I began to helplessly weep,
and not the enraged weeping that came with John Wesley's death,
but that Adelle was there between the two cedars and I could not
gather her in my arms.

What I value is unknowable. What was the texture of her last
hours? And did she think me a coward that I had compromised with
her mother? Her letters in the two weeks after she left the farm didn't
say so. For Adelle the difference between all and nothing was very
close. What was gathered together from witnesses was this: on a hot
Thursday afternoon she threw her school books from the steamboat
pier, then managed to give the slip to the man hired to follow her in
the downtown crowd getting off from work. Just north of the city she
caught a wagon ride from two farmers, brothers headed north toward

their home after a full day at the market. She spoke with them rather slow but amiable and this slowness was determined to be from the nature of the drug, laudanum, that she took along with her and that had regularly been used to sedate her. The farmers said she got off short of De Soto but past Fort Calhoun and merely stood by the side of the road at twilight. She evidently made her way down a dirt road to the Missouri and there on a grassy bank her clothes were found, and the body discovered by fishermen well downriver the next afternoon.

Walgren brought the telegram and took the train with me to Omaha and I reached the Morgan home late in the evening. I embraced her mother, Martha, and Neena, who trembled wildly. They showed me into the parlor where Morgan stood beside the open casket with two of his business friends. I went to the casket and kissed her dead lips. I turned to go and Morgan followed me and I could not help but shake him like a rag doll in my fury. Martha and Neena stopped me, and kissed me good-bye. I did not attend the funeral.

2

JOHN WESLEY NORTHRIDGE II

November 1956

Smith came yesterday morning. Naturally it frightened me, but only for a moment. How would he know, or pretend to know, that this visit would signal the last year of my life? I lapse between petulance and awe over this man, my oldest friend when most of my friends, few though they were, have long since perished.

I was sitting in the den close after dawn having my coffee and staring out the window at a weak sunrise, when Lundquist came in announcing that there was an Injun standing at the foot of our long driveway. Lundquist reddened a bit after saying "Injun" knowing how much such terms irritate me. He added that the man had the dogs *buffaloed* and they were sitting before him and had paid no attention to Lundquist and his old dog Shirley when they had driven in. I had wondered why the dogs hadn't returned after their morning pee. All four of the Airedales were between middle and old age, and only Sonia pretended any vigor. She was a pain in the ass in most respects, but then so am I, though of late I have tried valiantly not to be so because of the enormous problems I will explain.

But first to Smith. He is the reason I began writing this again last evening. If you suppose you are to die within a year you may think there are a few more things worth mentioning.

Lundquist suggested he come along and that we take one of the shotguns, but I said no, it must be Smith, and Lundquist recalled that Smith was the Lakota I had been speaking with in the potato field in the rain four years ago after Tess had her last hunt. Lundquist then apologized for saying "Injun." It was the television's fault, he said, a passion of Frieda's that had nearly surpassed religion. He preferred going to the movies the once a week that they changed features in town as television made up things smaller than life, or so he said. I keep to the radio myself so that I may continue painting my own pictures of the world though, of course, only in my mind's eye.

I drove the '48 Studebaker pick-up down the long driveway reflecting that I had turned it into a junk heap but rather liked it that way. There was Smith inside the gate lecturing the Airedales as if he were a professor. As opposed to my cold reception in the potato field he smiled broadly as I got out of the truck. "That's a redskin truck. You hiding your money from the government?" he said. "No, I just don't give a shit. It works as well as I do." We shook hands and then he embraced me, and I couldn't but feel overcome. He pointed and said it was over by that dead tree that we pulled Sally and won a dollar. Sally was a huge and ornery Belgian brood mare weighing about twenty-five hundred. We had pulled directly against a neighbor's mostly Clydesdale gelding on a bet. Sally wouldn't quit and pulled the struggling gelding halfway across the ditch. The other kid tried to cut the rope to save his horse so Smith had leapt on Sally and pulled back her ears. We got them separated, and then Sally had tried to kick the hell out of the gelding and Smith grabbed her halter and she swung him in a circle shaking her huge neck. Even when we got her under control and were leading her away she kept turning her head and staring back malevolently at the gelding.

There is something weak about the light in November that makes things disappear at their outer edges. Even a footfall or a voice is flimsier in texture. Smith turned to release the dogs and they scurried over to greet me. "We'll likely be dead by this time next year," he said, with what must be described as a chuckle. "Suits me fine. I wore out long ago." I could not politely ask of his intentions so we let our memories unwind as we looked out over the fields. "Willow sends a greeting. She's up near Lodge Pole at Fort Belknap. You know, way up in Montana." This news brought an absurd heat to my old scalp. "Does she need some help?" I asked, lame for my own response. "Hell no. She's got a piece of land and a dozen cows. Bought the land with what your father left her. I spent mine in a week on a party and my head still hurts fifty years later." He again laughed then suddenly stopped. "I need something you have from the old days."

We drove up to the house then. I knew what he wanted and had actually gotten it up from the basement the day after I saw him in the potato field. It was an unadorned but very large grizzly claw that had once been owned by Kicking Bear who had been actually sentenced by a judge for various imagined crimes to two years of service in Buffalo Bill's "Wild West Show." My father had given it to Smith in the spring of 1906 when he was preparing to join a Wild West show headed for Europe. Smith didn't want to take it along because he might get drunk and lose or sell it, and plus, as he confided to me, the *old-time* stuff tended to frighten him. It lay in the safe in a small leather pouch of doe hide next to the photo and my sketches of Adelle.

We sat in the den and looked at the claw on the bare oak desk, then Smith put it back in the pouch, shaking his head. "Saw one in August when I visited some Wind River folks, and then I remembered this one was here. I heard they used to be way out this way years ago." I told him that the Spanish vaqueros used to fight grizzlies against longhorn bulls out in California way before we reached that state, and when it was still part of Mexico. There was the silent question who had won, and the equally silent answer, neither. My father had run into Custer and Ludlow on their early government expedition into the Black Hills. Ludlow and a group of his men, including One Stab, a Cheyenne guide, had run down a grizzly in a ten-mile chase, lassoed it, then released it after their resident scientist, George Bird Grinnell, had inspected the beast. Those weren't today's cowboys who spent all their evenings in town.

Smith went to the window. "I killed too many people back in the Great War. They took our horses away because they were useless against the Boche. I was a butcher, that's what I was. One of the finest things I saw was the Polish cavalry but they pretty much got wiped out to a man. I kept trying to get in World War II but they wouldn't let me. I was working horses up at Fort Robinson in the thirties." He paused until we could hear the last leaves skittering in the yard. "You didn't do too badly considering how we started out. The way I heard you were behaving you're lucky you didn't get shot."

I had had a number of pretty bad years, six or seven, between Adelle's death and the day I flippantly signed up for World War I on a bellyful of whiskey. Somewhat evasively I brought up the fact that our old lean-to and the dogs had saved me about a month after I had seen him in the potato field. I gave him the shortened story of my long walk and the memory of Adelle, ending up in the lean-to in the storm with a frantic heart but curled up closely with the four dogs for warmth. For his own peculiar reasons as a *wicasan wanka*, medicine man, he was animated by the story, saying "There's worse things than getting yourself killed by a ghost." He added that the dogs doubtless figured out what was going on so hung in there with me. I was immediately struck by these two different versions of what had happened, my own and Smith's, and perhaps the truth, however futile, was in between the two. If I consented to Smith's I might be insane, though that could not be thought of as a pressing problem.

We then, at his insistence, bundled back up and walked the mile or so out to the lean-to. Halfway there we stopped in our largest field and Smith studied the sky which was a dullish and solid gray, but a number of shades brighter than slate. Smith asked if I had noticed that the sky was an immense "pasture of light," and I said no I hadn't, but that was certainly a striking way of looking at it. "Well, that's what it is," he answered.

At the lean-to he pointed to Sonia and said she was likely the dog that had helped the most and he was right. I had put my coat half around her and she had lain close to my chest. Smith then began poking into the ground with a longish jackknife the French called a *mouche* for the silver fly on its helve. He paused in thought, then crawled to the back corner and began thrusting the knife as deeply as possible into the ground, smiling as he hit metal. He sliced the earth until it softened, then dug out the small tin box, opening it and revealing the photo of the dancing girl with the bare breasts. I attempted a jest but he shushed me, treating the photo as a holy object. He passed it to me and it seemed to have the same dense but almost plaintive eroticism it possessed for me as a boy. This is one area, I said to Smith, that I have stopped trying to figure out, and he nodded in agreement, then put the photo back in its tin box and reburied it, covering the site with twigs and leaves. I was struck by how light Smith was without making light of anything, or rendering those muffled opinions that are our habit.

On the way back toward the house Smith stopped to look at the sky in the same place he had before, saying that he used to love this spot. I reflected that it would be hard for anyone to detect it as it was a bit off center in the pasture and undifferentiated from its surroundings. He abruptly began to talk in fond terms of my father's Christianity which did not exclude the world of the Lakota or any other tribe. Part of Smith's point was that my father had made a beautiful place on the earth by using natural ingredients. Smith said my early aspirations to be an artist were the same thing. He gracefully didn't ask me why I had stopped after the war, but then I said that the war had evidently brought me too far down to earth. The grief and horror of war coarsens us and about the time I saw him in the potato field I had begun to understand life again without becoming enraged at least once a day.

Far off and between the trees I could see a man leaning against an old car near the foot of our driveway. "That's my grandson," Smith said, "the most pissed-off young man in God's creation." That unfortunately made me think of Duane who had disappeared two months before. Smith started to joke about the time we were about ten and decided one day we were tired of playing cowboys and wanted to become Indians. My father helped us out by gathering costumery from the then closed-off den, building us a fire in the barnyard, and dressing us like warriors. My mother painted our faces and we danced around the fire in the evening until we were exhausted with my parents showing us the steps. Quite suddenly my mother wept and ran into the house and that was the end of that game forever.

We were nearly to Smith's car when Dalva came galloping down the road on her gelding and Sonia broke away to greet her. Dalva was pregnant and certainly wasn't supposed to be riding but this sort of captiousness had to be dealt with by her mother not myself. Not giving lectures to anyone, including yourself, was quite a relief. Dalva unhorsed herself to greet Smith, saying, "I've heard a lot about you" with a smile, then glanced down the road with a start at the young man leaning against the car, thinking it might be Duane. She then got back on her horse, unable to talk, gave us a wave and thin smile, and was off.

"That young lady is having a hard time of it," Smith said, with a shadow on his face, and turning to me for explanation. I gave him a foreshortened and rather lame version of a young man who left town in September. He brought me up painfully by saying he knew the young man from Parmelee, also his mother, Rachel. He'd heard that the father was one of a group of three hunters she met over near Buffalo Gap just before the war. He peered at me closely then laughed at my stricken appearance, saying that we're just wonderful animals like the others. People, the earth with her mountains, rivers, prairies, animals weren't put here for our purposes but their own. I nodded in ready agreement, suddenly wishing for the first time that I hadn't given up my art. It was only what I did with my hands and heart. Nothing more. Why had I confused the entire heartbreaking issue when everything else in the world was well out of my control?

When I emerged slowly from my thoughts Smith was still looking at me, and then we headed to the car. Smith's grandson had muscles of stone in his face but was polite. He shivered in his thin denim jacket and I took off my thick sheepskin coat and said, "Let's trade." He glanced to his grandfather for approval and we made the swap. We checked pockets for possessions and he gave me back my red kerchief and a bruised McIntosh apple. I handed him a dollar bill crumpled to softness, a switchblade, and a popular brand of condoms. "I won't be needing these," I jested. "Yes you will. I smelled your girlfriend on your collar," the young man said. Smith sniffed and nodded, and I did too. Lena's lilac scent was there. "Maybe see you on the other side," Smith said, and they left. There was a slight odor of kerosene on the denim jacket and I had to let each of the dogs have a whiff.

* * *

In reverse of what might be expected I found it utterly liberating to think that I had but a year left in my life. I immediately drew a sparrow in the crabapple tree outside the window, then celebrated the clumsy attempt by making a piece of toast and putting on it the excellent crabapple jelly Frieda made every August. I drew eleven versions of the sparrow, the best with a smear of jelly near the branch. I felt less alone than in years. I began to tentatively forgive myself for being an angry and wild asshole much of my life, partly because forgiveness seemed to exhaust the alternatives. I put away the drawings with an abiding satisfaction and I didn't care whether it was temporary or not. The sparrow flew past the window and the length of that flying moment seemed to represent the length of my life, in addition to being a sparrow simply flying past the window. I took the photo of Adelle out of the safe and gazed at it on the desk, tilting it this way and that. I fell asleep with my cheek, I should say my wattles, pressed against it.

I was in the middle of a dream about a lost dog when Dalva set a cup of tea down on the desk. This cowdog with the unlikely name of Ed (Lundquist's idea) had been stuck in the well pit of an abandoned farmstead well to the rear of our property for at least a week when we found him. He was very pleased in his weakened condition to ride home draped over the swells behind the pommel of my saddle.

Dalva touched my shoulder to rouse me but I didn't want to rise and let her see the photo of Adelle so I said I needed a glass of water. She had told Naomi she might kill herself and she scarcely needed the encouragement of Adelle. I slipped the photo in the desk and she returned with the water, reminding me that Naomi was coming over with Ruth and her school friend Carol Johnson whom Naomi wanted to see my paintings. Naomi had shown me this young lady's sketches which were without particular merit but there was a little essay accompanying the drawings, "Why I Wish to Be an Artist," that was truly extraordinary for one so young. It reminded me of the level of skill of Willa Cather's high school valedictory address a friend from the University of Nebraska had shown me.

They arrived shortly thereafter and I recognized the girl as the thin-faced waif who washed dishes at Lena's Cafe where her mother was an employee. I assumed that she and Ruth were drawn together because of Ruth's obsession with the piano. While I showed the girl the paintings Naomi talked with Frieda in the kitchen, and Dalva was upstairs playing Bob Wills's music on the Victrola which made Ruth roll her eyes in embarrassment. I was distracted for other reasons as the music had the emotional texture of the music Davis and I had so loved on our trips to Mexico. And Carol standing shyly beside me was not so far away from myself standing before the French-woman talking about Courbet. These were but a moment's feelings but the continuum nagged at my mind. She paused a long time before a lesser painting of Stuart Davis's, then a Burchfield I had bought for three hundred dollars, which she found frightening for good reason. She blushed wildly at a Modigliani sketch and then regathered herself in front of a Gottardo Piazzoni and a Dixon. The fact that I had known the latter two, however slightly, amazed her. In the San Francisco of those days one had merely to stand a round of drinks, blaspheme common enemies and quarrel about technique to know another artist. Fame for everyone, such as it was, remained well in the future and was to be organized by others, mostly art dealers.

We were just sitting down to dinner when she asked me almost in a whisper if I cared for Picasso. I said there were seven Picassos and I liked at least five of them. Naomi felt the need to interpret this and I watched the girl pick at her food, her fingers reddened from her dishwashing chores. She hoped to go to the Art Institute in Chicago when she graduated from high school and wondered if I had liked it there. I said it was doubtless a good place but I hadn't liked it anywhere at the time. After dinner I gave her a sketching lesson at my desk in the den while Ruth played the piano. I showed her my eleven sparrows of that afternoon and what was wrong with each. I was so preoccupied it didn't quite register on me that Naomi and Dalva were close behind Carol and were watching intently. I had never acted the artist in front of them before and decided to let it pass as if they had caught me at something so simple as pouring a drink.

After they thanked me and drove off in the dark I remembered clearly the youthful feeling in the pit of my stomach, the hollow fear of my first days at the Art Institute. Davis had not arrived for the fall session yet and I was unable to make sense of a place so large as Chicago. A local attorney, who represented my father in the tree nursery business, had secured me rooms which I suspected were a bit nicer than they should be what with my romantic notions of the bohemian life I expected to unfold before me. I think it was 1903 and the noise of Chicago was quite maddening for one used to the silence of the prairie where you could hear the heart of your horse over its breathing, a far-off meadowlark, a cow lowing in the creekbed a mile away, even a delicate breeze approaching across the sea of grass. I spent my first few days in the silence of the museum which only served to intimidate me well past the fear of failure. One windy evening I walked north up the shore and the waves of Lake Michigan washed the air of other noises. Oddly, I spoke for a few pleasant minutes to a shopgirl from Kansas who was doing the same thing. Further up the beach I damned myself for not finding out her name or where she lived but the enormity of the city had made me so shy I could barely croak out an order for a meal. Finally, on my fourth day in the city, there was a reception for new students with everyone from Midwest states and further standing around stiffly in new clothes. One, an effete fellow named Simmons, from the city itself, took me in hand to an Italian restaurant where one received an enormous bowl of delicious spaghetti and a large glass of bad red wine very cheaply. It was a foreign place and the native babble of the working men made us feel quite artistic.

It occurred to me standing there and watching Naomi's car disappear that Carol Johnson would find Chicago, assuming that she made it there in a few years, no less strange than I had. I went back inside and for a moment I pitied this poor girl, not for her poverty but for her dreams that had made me so agitated. I looked at my not

very talented sparrows on the desk and had to laugh at my grand-
motherly sentimentality. Of course she must dream. Only our dreams
gave life any coherence. The common political fantasy was simply
to maintain America as a safe place to do business, which was short
rations indeed for a young girl scrubbing a meatloaf pan at a cafe.
When I had early on branded cattle, broke horses, dug irrigation
ditches, or simply hoed my mother's garden I could fashion myself as
one of Millet's peasants, or better yet, Turner watching the fog lift
on the boats along the Thames.

It had often come to me that I had let alcohol begin to destroy
my dreams after the death of Adelle. It was as if the dreams needed
to be sedated in this atmosphere of turbulent darkness, and then alcohol in such vast quantity had so diminished their clarity that by
the time I joined up for World War I, I was robotic, following the
structure of a hope rather than feeling hope herself. I certainly hadn't
the wit to understand that I was trying to die, though if I had had
any confidence in an afterlife in which I'd see Adelle I would have
put a bullet through my skull in a moment.

At first alcohol gave me an illusion of coherence because it kept
everything, including grief, in its specific place where it could be
relentlessly and inefficiently mulled over. At such times we drink so
as not to go mad, but then we have only found another sort of madness. I have also speculated that my Lakota half predisposed me to
this fatal and terrifying thirst with an emphasis on the fatalism. Of
course it is presumptuous to identify with another culture if it is unthinkable to live their life, but then Davis had upbraided me around
the campfire a few nights before he pitched off the cliff with the idea
that I "paint like an Indian." What he meant was that I was doing
what in modern terms would be near abstracts from the natural world
without a touch of the illustrator in them. There were no reassuring
forms in my prairies and skies and they were a bit reminiscent of the
contemporary work of Ad Reinhardt and Robert Motherwell that I
have seen in current art magazines. I have never viewed nature as a
homily to prod our tired asses toward heaven, or as a relief from groom-

ing the fleas off each other's skins, a balm for a life spent buying cheap or selling dear. My father's Bible was dead wrong. The earth was not made for our solace but for her own evolving magnificence of which we are a small part. I prate like Naomi who frequently wonders aloud why every acre of the West must be made comfortable for cows at the expense of all other creatures. My mother's people were sacrificed, in toto, for cows when they happily could have lived among them if the land had been shared rather than seized.

I was quite helpless a few days ago when Dalva spent the night and asked me why "nothing went together." She had lost the ability to make sense out of a moment, let alone an hour or a day. I did not interpret this as a slump caused by the biology of her pregnancy, re-membering how my own wife, Neena, had thrived on this condition, liberating her as it did to spend all of her hours reading rather than only half. At the time we could find no help she could abide more than a few days so I shipped in dozens of cookbooks and learned to fend for us in the kitchen. I told Dalva this which amused her, but then I added on, out of honesty, my own questioning. Your world fails to make sense, I said, because it doesn't for the present time. We have been taught for various religious, social, and economic reasons to keep our consciousness running on a track, somewhat in the manner of a train. This was clumsy indeed but I wanted it to be clear to her. It is convenient for us to agree to stay on this track, but then your lover runs off and you are fifteen and pregnant and all of the reality you consented to falls into shambles, mostly because it wasn't very real in the first place, just the most comfortable way to regard life. "Then what can I fall back on?" she asked, and I wished Smith had been there then rather than a few days later. Your "spirit," I said, rather than "nothing." It was still a lame response so I cast it in the light of how we can feel on first waking with the remnants of good dreams still with us, and how the world then is so lovely before our minds misconstrue its lack of intention for us. At this point I could feel Adelle in the pit of my stomach and rising slowly to my mind. I turned away then quite overcome. We were in the kitchen and I opened a cupboard and spied a jar of popcorn Naomi had grown. She read my desperation through the back of my head. "I'm not going to kill myself because it would disappoint everyone." I'd never heard a sentence in my life that so made me shudder.

We had an inescapably sodden Thanksgiving dinner at Naomi's with the roast turkey looking quite forlorn and barely touched. We could not rise above our collective sorrow as Naomi and Dalva will leave early in the morning on the long drive to Marquette, Michigan, where Naomi's cousin, a game biologist, and his wife will look after Dalva until her child is due in late April. The evening was nearly unbearable with no one able to speak with a full voice, and Ruth so overcome that she skittered off to the parlor where she practiced, unsuccessfully, Beethoven's Moonlight Sonata under a portrait of her father. Finally we gave up, embraced each other, and I left for home. We doubtless would have been far better off if we had wailed aloud as a family of Lakota would have felt free to do.

That thought jogged my mind and when I got home I looked in a journal for my recollection of what Rosenthal had said during our picnic years ago. It had been occasioned by my telling him a story about when I was seven years old, in fact the day before my birthday, and my mother had gotten word that her eldest brother had died up near Buffalo Gap. She lit a small fire out in the yard and sat there, covering herself with gray ashes, chanting and wailing all night long. I stood by my bedroom window and watched, quite frightened, my world delaminating from her grief and the eerie sounds she sang. My father came out and tried to wrap a shawl around her which she threw off. At dawn my father came for me and I sat next to her in my pajamas until the sun came up over the trees and she stopped abruptly. She then walked over to the full horse trough, doused herself, came back to us smiling and said it was time for breakfast. I was overjoyed as it seemed to mean that my birthday would not be overlooked.

Rosenthal was a bit melancholy at first with the anecdote and then spoke at length. My journal owns none of his fast-paced eloquence, but he said that I was fortunate to have seen something that has largely passed with modernity, an event that is now thought to be archaic since nearly all of us have distanced and sequestered ourselves from all of the highly evolved rituals and experiences surrounding birth, death, sexuality, animals, active religion, nature, even art and insanity. I felt I largely understood what he meant except in the realm of art, but he elaborated by saying that in primitive cultures everyone was an artist and storyteller, only some, quite obviously to all, were much better at it than others.

I could see the fair-sized waxing moon out the window and turned out the den lights to experience its peculiar warmth, remembering with amusement the alarmed reaction to my tales of moonlit walks at art school. Davis and I had made a sketching trip with his wild-eyed girlfriend, to the Upper Peninsula late one May, much further east than Ishpeming, staying in a seaside lumbering town called Grand Marais, quite unlike the Grand Marais in Minnesota, and far east of Ishpeming. It was there that I had a moonlit walk that was more alarming than any back on the farm.

At the time I was having great difficulty at school with an obligatory drawing class where we had spent day after wintry day sketching the marble busts of Greek and Roman heroes. It was progressive and you couldn't go on to the next bust until you got the current one correct, so I was stuck on Tacitus until my soul screamed while others had moved on well past Pliny and Virgil. The teacher was an Englishman of a militaristic nature who was particularly ruthless with me after I had asked aloud why we must draw from a work of art rather than life itself. For that impertinence I was made to spend a full week on a marble foot. Finally I walked out and flunked the course, which got me an audience with the director, William M. R. French, who was kind enough to move me on to the third or top form despite my incompetencies. This was my third slow year, but then I was a full paying student and was generally useful for my ability to write descriptions for brochures on the student shows, not a generally respected gift but then someone had to do it, and few were capable. In the top form I was finally liberated from the antique busts, fragments of sculpture, architectural ornaments, and moved on to painting and drawing from what was locally called "Life."

But it was spring, and my hand, which had finally been freed to do what it loved, froze itself into uncooperative meat. I had the briefest love affair with a supremely talented girl, who, along with Davis, was considered the most promising of the five hundred or so students. It was sad indeed to admit to myself that my resentment of her talent broke us apart. If it were not for the attention, however eccentric, of my friend Davis I would have chucked the whole thing, tucked tail and gone home for good.

When I proposed the week's trip north Davis was enthused but broke as was his girlfriend. That wasn't a problem as, again, my father was overgenerous with the allowance he sent. Later on I supposed that this was because he had little occasion to spend any of the money he was gathering from his tree nursery business and it was a way of spreading the general guilt over money. I did the same with my own sons.

By the time the three of us boarded the train that May afternoon I felt suffocated with people and was trembling with the sort of acute homesickness known best to nineteen-year-olds. If I couldn't have the grand void of the prairie I would at least have a week of the dense northern forests. I suspect the wild calls the loudest when it has largely disappeared from our lives and at that time I dearly ached for a peopleless landscape, averting my eyes and sipping from a jug of wine as the train passed by the fire-belching hell and smoke of the steel mills of Gary, Indiana, and headed north. Davis's girlfriend Sarah tried to tease me with peeks up her skirt but I was far too drawn and quartered to respond. I kept staring at my hand around the neck of the wine jug, wondering why it couldn't perform the feats of genius my mind envisioned. The hands of Gauguin and Cézanne doubtless did their minds' bidding, and were probably keyed to levels of perception of which the mind itself lacks consciousness. I was still a boy throwing a ball straight up in the air and catching it far less than half the time. For solace I had been attending symphony and chamber music concerts and had speculated that probably very few had been able to write down the melodies that the mind willfully concocted. There was nothing in the two volumes of William James that accounted for this phenomenon and I thought of writing a mock Emerson essay called "On the Disobedience of the Hand." I went so far as to speculate that my hand had broken too many horses, pitched too much hay, dug too many irrigation ditches and those chores had made it inept for this higher calling. Even the fistfights I was occasionally prone to couldn't have helped. A month earlier a very large butcher at a saloon near the school had swatted Davis unjustly, and I had hammered him prone with difficulty and my swollen fist had been unable to draw for a week.

We arrived in Grand Marais late the next afternoon, sleeping off the wine for most of the way except for the brisk train ferry trip across the Straits of Mackinac. We were advised to go up to see the locks on the St. Marys River in Sault Ste. Marie but I was impatient for the wilderness. It was disturbing to see between the Straits and the hundred and twenty miles to Grand Marais that most of the great white pines had been cut, though there were occasional patches that were a remembrance of former glory.

We found a simple hotel in the village, then ate an excellent dinner of lake trout. Davis and Sarah went to the rooms for their lovers' business, and I headed out east on foot, a fairly stiff breeze from Lake Superior keeping the clouds of mosquitoes at bay. Several miles from the village I paused in the twilight thinking I should return, but then I was alarmed by a great light through the forest which turned out to be a full moon rising. It was a reddish yellow from a forest fire far to the east that we had been told about on the train. I walked directly toward this spectacular moon and came upon the remains of a logging camp that was now inhabited by two old Chippewa men who were friendly and gave me a cup of their grotesque homemade wine. There was an old chestnut draft plug in their yard, a decrepit logging horse, and I offered them the generous sum of five dollars to take it for a ride. This vastly amused them but the older of the two somehow perceived my lineage and said "redskins" liked big moons.

At their instruction I crossed a wooden bridge, then turned south with the moon on my left, riding on a log trail along the bluffs of the Sucker River. The horse trotted just fast enough to keep ahead of the swarms of mosquitoes. She was broad enough to make riding bareback nearly comfortable, though she was incapable of the ease of a lope.

I'm unsure of what to call the state I entered but that scarcely matters. I was entranced by the moon and the forest, the huge stumps that were the ghosts of trees. The night and the moon shed me of my troubles, and I felt then deeply I must continue as an artist even though I might be doomed to failure, but that ponderous thought fell away in the glory of the night ride. There was a strong scent of perfume pushed by the slightest of breezes and I entered a vast clearing of several thousand acres full of flowering bushes which I later learned were mostly chokecherry, dogwood, and sugar plum. Their blossoms were as white as the moon straight above, and the vision transfixed me as if the strong perfume were opium. I rode through these overpowering bushes on a trail for perhaps another half hour until I came to a creek. I got off the horse to let her water, inhaling deeply from a handful of crushed flowers I had grabbed from a bush. Holy God, I thought aloud, where am I and do I care? I am simply at this creek at this moment, kneeling and drinking, rinsing my face in the moonlight, my senses as fully alive as any ancient animal's.

It was then I fell into a deep fit of laughter because the horse, after drinking deeply, had trotted off north on her long way back home. I tried to whistle as she disappeared back into the white-flowering bushes but couldn't because of my laughter. I lit a match and checked my pocket watch, finding it to be two in the morning. I drank again at the creek in anticipation of my long walk back, which I judged might be a dozen miles, setting off at a dog trot to outpace the clouds of mosquitoes. I felt pleased that I had maintained my legs and wind by hours of daily walking in Chicago, mostly a device of curiosity and to ease my muddy brain which had drawn the conclusion that I had been called to be an artist but not necessarily a very good one.

I walked fairly briskly until the first light came before five and the mosquitoes then subsided a bit with a freshet of cool wind off Lake

Superior. Far ahead, a hundred yards or so, I saw a dark movement on the logging trail and stopped, stock-still, with a jump in my heart, my eyes in distant focus on a very large bear sitting in the middle of the trail like an immense black Buddha. The wind was in my favor so she hadn't scented me. I eased off to the side and sat on a big stump to wait her out. There was a single cub frolicking around her and I knew it was unwise to proceed, to put it in its mildest terms. Now the cub began to nurse and the huge mother flopped on her back, sawing her legs playfully in the air. Several blue jays arrived and then a single raven. The raven saw me and then circled above my stump with a crisp fluff in its wing beats, and a sequence of raucous squawks, perhaps warning the bear of my presence. My eyes turned from the raven back to the bear and she was standing now, testing the air. She whuffed and sped off in the brush with her cub in tow. I waited for another fifteen minutes for safety's sake before proceeding. Quite suddenly my legs were nearly dead with fatigue, my mouth parched, and my head in a state of throbbing ache. The important thing was that my mind had settled itself and I had been witness to a consoling though utterly impersonal beauty. I had finally understood an idea that I still believe in that art is at the core of our most intimate being and a part of the nature of things as surely as is a tree, a lake, a cloud. When we ignore it, even as spectators, we deaden ourselves in this brief transit. The hand that swung by my side and earlier had plucked the flowers and reined the sorry horse would try its damnedest before falling still as all hands must. It was my nature.

When I reached the deserted lumber camp the Chippewas were asleep in the yard, doubtless having walked to town for a jug or two with my five dollars. The horse peered out from the shadows of a clump of trees and when I waved to her she retreated further into the shadows. On the stoop of the shack there was a half bottle of whiskey and I took a deep slug before continuing on toward the village.

Later, when I told the story to both Davis and Sarah, and my acquaintances among the art students back in Chicago, they were appalled at my lack of common sense, but it occurred to me it is largely a matter of birth and disposition. The prairie and the forest on a moonlit night are not threatening to me but Chicago and New York are, with Paris a little less so. In these cities, even among polite company, my skull tightens, and I sweat nervously from the degree of attention required to keep oneself out of a thousand varieties of trouble. My father often railed against "common sense" which he viewed as most often an essentially petty mixture of greed and self-interest, the inanity of the "Onward, Christian Soldiers" attitude that propelled millions of nitwits westward, utterly destroying much of the earth and all of the Native cultures. Of course he was a bit of a madman, but then he was knowledgeable of both the sound agricultural practices and the true Christian virtues that would have made the western movement other than the prolonged tragedy it became. On a much smaller and individual scale there is nothing quite so destructive as an artist acquiring common sense before he has utterly blown up the world of his perceptions and acquired the grace to put it back together again. I've read in *Harper's* that it's fashionable nowadays for universities to acquire living painters, poets, and novelists, to teach the young their craft, which will require of them a great deal of common sense while they drown in the deceitful morass of institutions. May the gods of art take pity on them. Art would have thrived better if they had become beggars or common criminals.

Hackleford has called to tell me we have two days of good weather in the offing. I've been waiting a number of days to get this Omaha trip over with, preferring to drive the seven hours or so with Lundquist, spend the evening and come back the next morning, but Frieda of late has so submerged herself in the world of television violence that she is too frightened to stay alone. If I am near her more than a split second she begins a tale of mayhem she has lately watched, whether of a fictional nature or on the news. Her preacher, a part-time furniture salesman from Tennessee, has also assured his parishioners that the blacks have fully armed themselves to strike back at their imagined oppressors. She is modestly outraged when I say, "One

can scarcely blame them," but I reassure her by pointing to the old
county map that there are very few, if any, blacks within two hundred miles and it is more reasonable to prepare for an attack from the
Lakota from the northwest.

Hackleford picks me up in his Stinson Voyager on the gravel
road in front of the farm, an extra-legal maneuver that we are both
happy to make. It would have been nice to take the ride in his
Stearman biplane but then we are both a year over seventy and an
open cockpit is chilly in December. It was Hackleford who took John
Wesley for his first plane ride but I can scarcely blame this fellow
geezer for my son's obsession.

We headed east, flying rather low along the Niobrara, and turning south over land when the river meets the Missouri. Once we
unwittingly followed the Missouri south to Omaha and north of the
city I was horrified to look down at the area where my Adelle had
drowned herself.

I suspect that flying causes reveries dangerous to a pilot. I've
always loved studying a river from the air and seeing the way a water-
course has shaped the land around it, the Niobrara braiding itself in
her delta, her cleaner waters merging with the darker Missouri. Neena
and I once camped on a high hill overlooking this confluence, one
of the happier evenings of our life and one of the few when she set a
book aside and looked closely at the world around her. To her credit
she could tell me the entire rather bleak history of the gorgeous area,
Indian and white, and the rest of the nation, and the world for that
matter. She taught the boys even more rigorously than my father
taught me.

Samuels, the senior partner of the law firm, picked me up at the
airport in his golf clothes, a sport he only took up after I had exhausted
both of us in my land dealings. The many years that I was so active
strike me as a bit pathetic as neither Dalva or Ruth show promise as
spenders. The government that dispatched my son had bought my
beef during World War II in vast quantity, an irony as sharp as a Japanese sword.

The unhappy business at hand was to decide the fate of Dalva's child. When Naomi had begun discussing the matter with me I favored keeping it, but was immediately disabused of this notion, bowing to her long experience as a mother and teacher. Some pregnant girls who are fifteen going on sixteen would be quite capable and disposed to raising a child, and some wouldn't. Dalva was in the latter category, and then there was my unshared knowledge of who Duane's father might be. Our aim must be to find a proper set of adoptive parents, and Samuels, my confidant in the matter, had come up with a junior member of the firm and his wife, a childless couple with whom we would have dinner.

I had Samuels detour for a melancholy drive past the Morgan home, now a big rooming house in a decaying neighborhood. No matter how irrational, it was difficult to accept that all of them were gone from earth. The parents were rather giddy when Neena and I returned from our impulsive elopement in the winter of 1917. For them I suspect, it somewhat healed the loss of Adelle, no matter that I kept my distance from Frederick. When we visited on occasion I walked the fashionable streets with a pair of coyotes I had tamed since they were pups and who were confident I was their parent. I joined the army three days after losing them up near Buffalo Gap on an April afternoon just before we entered the war. It was actually Neena's mother, Martha, who prodded me into a minor scandal when I walloped a United States senator. Martha and I were talking in a cloakroom after a big dinner when we heard a shriek and saw this senator bending his wife's arm and jerking her ear. She was a lovely and intelligent woman, though a bit flirtatious, and Martha said, "Do something" which I did.

At dinner at the Samuels' the young couple seemed perfectly suited as adoptive parents after I questioned them at length. They were a bit shy and frightened at first and I was reminded again how we can think of ourselves as fine fellows but appear to others as a bit on the raw side. The world has become quite modern and most men are somewhat less definite than they used to be. I was finally able to

set them at ease and the evening was over early when the young
woman became a little ill. The junior partner was from Minnesota, a
definite point in his favor, and lacked the slickness that had begun
to infect younger members of the legal profession. I was struck by how
deeply they craved to have a child, and felt confident that they would
be excellent at raising one. There was the disturbing thought that I
was doling out John Wesley's grandchild but I knew I had to let that
one rest.

Without reading my own thoughts the next morning I met Hackleford at the airport and asked him to fly straight up the Missouri despite Adelle, passing De Soto, then bearing left and over Winslow,
following the Elkhorn for nearly two hundred miles to its source
southeast of Bassett.

Samuels had felt relief over our successful dinner, and so did I.
Consequently we drank too much Calvados, a passion of Samuels's
who had always been one of those peculiar Francophiles one finds
among the prairie rich. I slept well until about 3:00 A.M. when I awoke
thinking that I heard Smith's voice telling me that nothing could be
avoided, that you couldn't change reality, past, present or future, to
suit yourself, thus I threw caution away and had Hackleford fly low
over the promontory on the Missouri where Adelle had drowned. The
noise in the Stinson was such that again I heard Smith's voice in my
mind, this time speaking with my mother in Lakota out near the horse
trough at dawn on the morning he left for good with my father giving him our very best horse and saddle and the small medicine bag of
Smith's grandfather's my father had from the old days after the warrior himself had died at Twin Buttes.

So I looked straight now into the great, swollen, brown river and
heard the muted laughter that came from Adelle in the late afternoon when her doldrums began to leave her. She was sitting on the
rock pile in the first large pasture behind the rows of trees in back of
the barn. It was still very warm and she wore only a white slip that
clung to the sweat on her body because she had been chasing her pet

calf around the pasture, and then it would chase her. The calf unnerved me a bit when we made love, standing so close we could feel
its milky breath on our necks and shoulders. I was trying to sketch
her on the rock pile with the calf off to the side, but she wouldn't
hold still because she was trying to catch some of the black snakes
that always sunned themselves on the rock pile. She couldn't catch
any of the larger ones before they slipped away but then she knelt in
the grass and caught several very small ones, cupping their writhing
bodies in her hands until they became quite still. She swiveled from
the waist, turning toward me with a rather mad smile, and raised her
cupped hands like a supplicant and placed the infant snakes on her
thick hair where they became alarmed with one wriggling down
her forehead until it fell in her lap, and the others down her shoulders and back. "I'm the Medusa," she laughed, and I could hear the
laughter and voice in the plane nearly fifty years later, now looking
down at the Elkhorn. She wanted to make love again so I drew her
away from the rock pile, not sharing her fondness for the black
snakes. Afterward, she began to talk, leaning over the back of the
calf, scratching its ears and stroking its flanks. *I want to be a boy or
man on alternate days. You're almost a woman while you're drawing. Your
face becomes softer and even when you talk you talk more softly. When I
say something your head turns slowly and you look up in the sky slowly.
Everything my father does is jerky and has sharp corners. Maybe paintings
should be round. My father thinks he is the engineer of the train of the whole
world. He sits in his easy chair after dinner farting because he's eaten too
much and reading financial magazines and talking to them in hopes he can
change what they are going to say next. I don't care for him anymore. He'd
be happier if he had a mistress but he's a little frightened of my mother whom
I don't think really cares for him anymore. Last summer we were sailing
in Rhode Island and he kept glancing at my cousin who is a very pretty girl
and he'd turn pink as a sunset. He thinks no one notices these things. Mother
says he has a small bully in his heart that on some days gets bigger. I just
think that he's one of those men who believes the world only exists inasmuch as it is connected to him. I'm sure you're not at all like that. I'm
sure that's one of the reasons I love you. Artists aren't like that at all, are*

*they? They paint the world so they can understand its beauty. I told my
father that John Keats was the greatest man in the history of the world and
he chuckled and chuckled and asked how I could overlook Teddy Roosevelt;
and then he said come back to me in ten years and you will have forgotten
John Keats. They all say come back to me in ten years to kiss the feet of
their wisdom. I'll have to take cooking lessons or will we be able to afford
someone to cook for us? On the boat to France we'll dance every evening
like we did in Duluth. When we come back to America we'll have a Buick
car and I'd like a black horse. On the boat you can't help but think how
deep the water is over the rail. Back at the spring this morning when we
were swimming how do you know how deep it is where that spring water
burbles so coldly around our feet?*

There was a brisk crosswind and we had a difficult landing on the
county road. Hackleford normally flew the perimeters of the ranch
so we could take a look but it was far too blustery at low altitude. He
brought the Stinson in half sideways and flopped her down with us
laughing all the way, not in relief that we were landing but in the
peril of doing so. Lundquist had heard us and was pulled to the foot
of the driveway in the pick-up. He nodded his head "no" when I
looked at him. It's been ten years since I cared about the mail but
ever since Duane left in September I've been hoping to hear from
him like a schoolgirl waiting for a catalog dress. Lundquist knows this
though it remains unspoken. I turn to watch Hackleford take off and
I almost said a prayer, an utterly unlikely thing in itself. Lundquist
said that Naomi had called from Duluth where she and Dalva are
stuck in a hotel waiting out a grand blizzard.

My heart has the jitters despite the medicine and I take a bowl
of potato soup, the surface of which I've made pink with Tabasco to
Frieda's dismay, into the den where I may listen to my wobbly heart
in privacy. Anyone who has examined and eaten as many deer hearts
as I have will suffer an equally vivid picture of this tough, meaty organ.
I am mortally tired out but then it occurs to me I have not led a tired
life. There is a great deal of uneasy melancholy in Wordsworth's

notion that the child is father of the man, and Smith's visit keeps drawing me back to the early, rather ordinary occurrences that seemed to have a later, momentous effect. At my age one can't help but wonder at how skewed and irrational life becomes in the living, how wondrously strange the accretion of effects that lead from one interesting patch of life to another. Something so absurd as a boyhood book momentarily captures the mind and never quite releases it. I'd often accompany my father on buggy trips to town for supplies, and spend an hour or so at the library during his errands. I knew he'd disapprove but I loved to read Buel's *The Century of Progress: A Story of Heroic Achievements* which was perfect fodder for a gullible boy with virtually hundreds of "true-to-life" illustrations of such things as the lamas torturing an Englishman, a flying African dragon, an orangutan tearing apart the mammoth jaws of a crocodile, seagulls fighting a giant octopus on the ocean's surface, the suicide of the bare-breasted consort of the rajah. The latter was my earliest pornography and it seemed a terrible waste of beauty. It first occurred to me to smell a rat in the illustrations when I asked my father if it were possible for an Indian to jump on the back of a moose and stab it to death with a knife. He only said, "Of course not." But then these images are not the less permanent for being so absurd.

It somewhat chills me to think that I have no real possessions excepting my memories and dreams. Money and property appear as too evanescent to be more than trifling. Once just a few years before they died I camped with my parents well up a creek near Long Pine and my father told me of the insanity and dysentery, perhaps cholera, that brought him so near to death the year after Wounded Knee when he was encamped with Lakota friends and my mother's relations in the Badlands. As he gradually recovered he realized again that he was a white man and despite his sympathies even his God could not make him a Lakota. We were eating some trout we caught except for my mother who did not care for fish, describing them as "Anishinabe" (Chippewa) food. My father said he had hung onto life by the merest thread for my own sake, and if he had died at that time, I would have doubtless been raised by my mother and her people as a Lakota. She merely smiled and nodded at this, so matter-of-fact was her attitude toward fate.

This has always been not much more than an idle speculation, but then it's impossible to avoid thumbing it over now and then. He wasn't saying that I was necessarily lucky that he had lived, only that it all could have easily gone otherwise. At the time, in the summer twilight, he quickly passed on to railing at the distant sound of an automobile. This was in 1908, I think, and I have since read that there were short of six hundred cars in Nebraska in 1905 and over two hundred thousand in 1920, an item that I still find astonishing. My father thought of the auto as anathema, a possible Antichrist and a tool of greed, and he jumbled the motor car together with Edison's work on the Victrola, and the silent pictures that had become so popular. He was a little less sure about electricity.

When I had jokingly told Rosenthal of my father's rant, "What will become of all the horses who will never be born?" he was less amused than thoughtful what with being so aware of the sweep of history. Rosenthal thought that the influence of such a parent, for better or for worse, had prevented me from fully entering the twentieth century. I am still less than confident in this matter a month away from 1958. All of our dire and often errant warnings about the world to our children tends to close the doors for them? I think that's what he meant. But then Paul and John Wesley showed little signs of timidity so I doubt I frightened them too much. Of course Rosenthal was speaking of my own father and his mental excesses, passing on the somewhat bitter notion that this place is my only possible refuge. Doubtless if I had continued in my art I might have sprung out of here more often as I did as a young man. I have to disbelieve that the landscape could be in my genetic makeup though it seems clear to me that it was in my mother's. It seems the problem must be more in the nature of my early years when my company was limited to my immediate family, horses, dogs and cattle, Smith and Willow. And then I've often thought if I had not lost both Adelle and Davis I may have continued in my art past World War I. Of course this kind of thinking is not the less absurd for being inevitable. I certainly can place no blame on my father whose selflessness in behalf of the Lakota drove him past the limits of mental stability inherent in him, and this after his experiences in the Civil War, beside which my own late in World War I are tame indeed.

It was a grim, cold Sunday morning with the air a whirl of snowflakes around the house, and in the fields, blowing lateral to the ground in rumply sheets. The dogs were restive early with even Jake, the oldest of the Airedales, coming in to nose at my pillow, a rare appearance, and then Sonia began to moan from the den and I pulled myself from a warm bed into a cold room and hurried to the den to find old Tess quite dead upon the leather couch, a small pool of blood beneath her muzzle. To be frank I wept like an orphaned baby with the dead, beloved dog across my lap, the heat already gone from her body. The other dogs, led by Sonia, joined in a chorus of mournful, wolf-like howls.

I dressed, had a cup of reheated coffee, and carried her to the south side of the barn where we have our dog graveyard near another clump of lilacs. I took a pick-ax from the shed to soften the partially frozen ground, then dug a fairly deep hole, wrapped her in a good woolen blanket she favored, and buried her except for her soul which had fled elsewhere. I reflected again how dog years leap ahead of us and we are left a little breathless by how much faster their nature speeds them along. If they have any complaints about this they are exchanged with us in gestures and glances that are informed by benign incomprehension. Their deaths more naturally embrace the eternity before and after their lives. Should they see God their surprise would be momentary and unreflective. It must be God, they'd say, then go about their business.

As I rearranged the cold sod I was puzzling over the Lakota name for dog, *shoohkah*, and horse, *shoonkawakon*. I remembered it meant either little dog and big dog, or little horse and big horse, but couldn't remember which. I looked at the weak sun that had peeked out enough to cast my shadow on the barn, and then the sun began to whirl and I sat down hard with an immense pain in my chest, my bowels loosening and vomit erupting. I was quickly soaked with sweat but oddly did not pass from consciousness. I remember glancing at my now shortened shadow on the barn and thinking that this was not a bad place to die. I dared not move nor did I feel able to do so. It did occur to me that Lundquist would find me in twenty-four hours frozen to the ground by my shitty pants. My nose began to itch and I had not the strength to scratch it but could only exchange looks with the row of four aging Airedales. I admit I became a foxhole Christian and prayed, for the first time since my youth, to survive this calamity, in order to help Dalva and Naomi through their troubles, and then I would die without a struggle.

I was a bit surprised by my lack of panic and wondered if all of my imaginings over this matter had somewhat diffused the actual event. My life didn't pass before my eyes nor did I have a death song to sing like my half brothers, the Lakota. Instead I felt calm though quizzical over the way time had pushed me before her, ran over me, and now was probably leaving me behind. There was another sharp pang in my chest, though far less severe than the first, and it struck me that my limbs were dead because my heart was digesting a lump. I was singularly ignorant of medicine but quite suddenly recalled the look of a particular cow's heart up on the reservation when I was a child and the government allotment was being butchered. I remembered touching this huge heart and playing tug of war with the intestines with a little boy with a burnt face until a dog raced in and won the contest.

It began to snow again but the wind had subsided and I could feel the flakes touch my face. A sense of life began to return to my limbs and I at last was able to scratch my itching nose. There was a consoling lack of drama in the whole affair except for the unattractive smell and it occurred to me I had nearly died in the manner of my beloved old dog I had buried perhaps a half hour before. I got up unsteadily, and shuffled to the house to the relief of the leaping dogs. I had a large whiskey with a hot bath, then slept a dozen hours until the present time, midnight, when I got up and fried myself an

ample piece of beefsteak, then sat down to make a short list of what
I hoped to accomplish before my death which apparently was drawing nearer.

I awoke later than usual and Frieda made me an enormous breakfast
thinking me a little pale. She fried some splendid pork sausage fresh
from the pig they had butchered on Saturday. I went immediately to
the den to avoid the chatter about television comedians, godless
Russians, Lundquist's grief over the pig he had dispatched, and the
subtleties of sauerkraut making.

Naomi called to say that she had gotten Dalva settled in Marquette
and was heading home. While we talked I looked over my list making
on the desk, warmly confident that I was losing my mind. The process had gone on until four in the morning and there was a litter of
sketches, snatches of sentences and paragraphs, and one larger sheet
of drawing paper I had finished the night with from an old tablet a
bit yellow at the edges. It was here that I'd made row upon row of
miniatures of sketches in the manner of the Chippewa hieroglyphics
discovered by Schoolcraft in his first exploratory voyage among these
people in the early 1800s. It would not have made the slightest sense
to anyone else but as I said good-bye to Naomi I recalled that I had
always liked the three-volume record of Schoolcraft's journey and had
wondered if the pages of hieroglyphic reproductions had made sense
to the entire sprawling tribe or if the signs, the ideograms, were more
individuated and localized or could they possibly be reductions of
larger works though I doubted this latter notion. I had been fascinated when Rosenthal had told me that the Chinese ideogram for
"writing" was actually a tiny group of animal tracks. I never found
out what it was for "painting" though I had meant to do so, and this
sort of vacant intention filled the spaces between the miniatures, the
interminable list of "I meant to do so," which now had become rather
more a puzzle than regret. I studied the large page, knowing what came
last with poignancy, but bearing down on each to try to discern what
I'd had in mind during my maddened night.

From left to right at the top were a series of a half dozen weathered fence posts, perhaps an eccentric idea to the nonrural but then fence posts seem to collect memories from their locations. Next was a rather fuzzy rendition of the spring bottom as if I were able to hover above it like a kingfisher. This was followed by a horse's nose, infinitely soft and quaky to the touch, quite mysterious when looked at closely while thinking of nothing else. There was a small morel picked near Trenary, Michigan, and a chanterelle from well up Mill Creek in Montana, both eaten years apart with intense satisfaction. The next was hard to figure out for a moment but then it acquired shape as my father's McClellan saddle stolen out of my pick-up near Chadron during the Depression. Naomi's profile had a bell clarity, but my long-held sneaking desire for her had only come clear to me last night, a matter of amusement rather than guilt. There was a minuscule warbler's nest blown loose from a dogwood which I had given to Dalva, and Lakota baby moccasins with intricate beadwork which I didn't want to part with but gave to Ruth because she wanted them so badly. There were then a group of small squares from paintings of Gauguin and Cézanne I had studied for a week in my twenties to my total distraction, thinking I might understand the secret of their genius piecemeal. I may have comprehended the technique in the haphazardly chosen squares but their randomness brought me to grief, leaving out the unsayable hearts of the two paintings. The attempt in itself was part critic, part a boy taking apart an alarm clock, a farm kid peering into his first engine cylinder. There were cattle from the air, and the stunningly intricate braiding of the Platte River, the gory wounds on the breast of an old Lakota warrior after the leather thongs broke loose during the Sun Dance. A simple blotch was my father's blood on the snow, and a stark, sitting body outline was my mother in her fatal thicket. There was a petroglyph of a wolf's outsized footprint from Utah, a girl's bottom from down near Sarlat in the Dordogne in France, certainly the bottom of all bottoms she showed me on my request when I was too ill and weak to lift a hand to touch it. Sylvie her name was, a nurse's assistant, who was confident I was death bound and saw no harm in this last wish. There were simple spokes of light from May 1918, when I saw from afar the German bombardment along the Chemin des Dames, some seven hundred thousand shells cast into the air landing upon the French and British troops. I was reminded again how the men who start wars invariably live through them to justify the behavior that has left millions maimed and dead. My eyes naturally flickered back to Sylvie's bottom, not as a symbol of life, but as a gorgeous bottom. A high and turbulent river during snowmelt had a dead deer draped over a log in the current, caught in a branch crotch, its limbs wobbling in the torrent in a parody of living motion. Peavine, milkweed, and hollyhocks were followed by the image of Paul's forearm and elbow which seized my sorry heart, his weight resting against them, looking up at me after I knocked him to the ground. My eyes blurred as they had the night before, making me incapable of anything beyond milkweed, penstemon and phlox, ineptly rendered.

Now I was troubled by my thoughts of Paul the day I saw Smith in the cold potato field, just barely over the lip of consciousness when seeing a Lakota child throwing a potato with a skewed intensity that reminded me of my older son. Perhaps, among other reasons, I am writing this to explain myself to him? I have never had a great urge to explain myself to myself, at least I don't think I do. In my teens I was early exhausted by James's notions of the consciousness of consciousness. Thinking of this overlong will send you to the barn to saddle a horse, at least it always did for me. Without the slightest question the striking of Paul to the ground was the most shameful moment of my life.

I impulsively called him in Arizona and his Mexican assistant with her peculiar, soft voice answered. I could hear dogs barking loudly in the background and when Paul came on the phone with his habitual "Hello, Father," I became unsure of what to say. He seemed to sense this and quickly mentioned that he had spoken to Naomi in Marquette. I broke in and dumbly stuttered out my apology and there was silence only broken by the sound of his dogs, and then he began by asking if I didn't remember that I had apologized on our hunting trip up to Buffalo Gap. I said I did but we had been drinking a great deal to which he laughed, "Sometimes that's what it takes." He asked about Rachel, Duane's mother, whom we had fatally met on that trip and I only said she didn't know where Duane was. There was the unspoken question of whether he had made love to Rachel, which I suspected he had, because I wanted him to be Duane's father rather than John Wesley whom she preferred. He didn't supply the answer and I knew he never would, what with his lifelong penchant for rejecting the obvious gesture. He asked if I had been "ill" and I said a little, but that I had been writing something for him he could read if he chose after my last gasp. I tried to repeat the apology but he would have none of it and introduced what I least wanted to hear, however true, his mother Neena's idea that war closes off part of a human, both the good and bad, and this portion of our minds is forever stolen by history. I would only admit that this was less true of me than others. I was unable to continue and we bid an amiable but clumsy good-bye after he said his dogs were waiting for their morning hike.

Absurd as this might sound to a contemporary, I had joined the army like many other artists and writers to preserve the glory of France, though the impulse came rather late in the fray compared to the hundreds who joined as ambulance drivers before the United States entered the war. All the talk in artistic circles, not the most historically conscious group, was that if the Boche were allowed to enter Paris they would pillage the Louvre, that sort of thing. Only the year before I had married Neena and fathered Paul, with Neena hoping for a girl which she intended to name Adelle. Neena never shrank for a moment from the horror of life, especially on paper, and I believe this led to her eventual decline. One must step back now and then.

Foolishly eager for battle, even if it couldn't be upon a horse, I was in France a scant week before I was struck down by a malaria attack which the army doctors accurately diagnosed having gained experience in the Spanish-American War. However, mine had been a Mexican mosquito, and the drugs didn't work as well, and my recovery was prolonged in a hospital in Tours. I was only out of the hospital a week when I caught a virulent form of dysentery, to which was added the flu I took on when I returned to the hospital. I had been sick nearly four months when it was determined I was well enough to be shipped toward the front to ferry the seriously wounded from field hospitals to a better facility near Paris. I was judged too weak to do any more than drive what was euphemistically called a gut wagon. It was, nevertheless, a great relief to be out of the hospital, beside which any Nebraska slaughterhouse could be thought charming. Those wounded by bullets or shrapnel, no matter how maimed, seemed fortunate beside the thousands of severely gassed with their howls and racked coughs, a condition from which there was no recovery. By great irony I volunteered in my own convalescence to write letters home for those who were shorn of their writing arms, just as my own father had done in the waning years of the Civil War. There is no more melancholy task than to help shape the thoughts of an armless farm boy from Missouri of nineteen years who will never guide a team of horses again. It seemed strange to hear no one curse God before they died. We are the eternal supplicants. It is a gift to have time to pray not to die.

It was in mid-May when I witnessed the great German bombardment which moved them only a dozen miles closer to Paris. Soon after that I had done a straight thirty-six-hour shift of driving the wounded when I was relieved, and drank two bottles of wine to put me to sleep. Within an hour I was roused, quite drunk, to drive again, and promptly badly smashed up the ambulance killing two of three severe gas victims who were my passengers. I was thereupon court-martialed for driving drunk with the extenuating circumstances that while they were sewing up my head after the accident the doctor, a wry Princetonian, discovered my trepanation scar behind by hairline that would have disqualified me from service had I admitted it.

I was saved by a rather pompous West Point colonel who hailed from Omaha and who successfully argued with the other officers that he had heard about me in Nebraska and my experience could be utilized by sending me south to help tend the fine French, British and American horses that had been removed far from the path of battle. It was by this odd turn of fate that I spent a comfortable time, except for another spate of dysentery when I witnessed the miraculous bottom, far from the butchery, an army horseman until Armistice. It could be difficult to imagine a less distinguished service career. John Wesley as a boy had always been quite disappointed in me when he demanded tales of the glories of war and I told him the not so simple truth. Of course Neena's contention was somewhat true. The exposed heart does not really recover from the smell of thousands of suppurating dead on an otherwise fine spring morning.

Lundquist saves me from these dour considerations by arriving with an article from a Minneapolis Sunday supplement and a request that I go with him to look at a very old Allis-Chalmers tractor for sale in a neighboring county. I feel a bit weak for an obvious reason but decide to go along with this lark. We have looked at this decrepit tractor a half dozen times in the past decade and the errand usually means that Lunquist has something he needs to talk about. First, however, I must read the article in what used to be called the "roto-gravure," and in this instance, a slightly silly piece about the "richest Swedes" in the upper Midwest with some of them very rich indeed in the areas of heavy industry, department-store chains, and the agra business. As we drive along in the cold but sunlit wind Lundquist wonders if his compatriots achieved their wealth by "fair means or foul." I suggest that foul is always a definite possibility, but then perhaps the wealth in some cases was achieved by hard work, intelligence and thrift. There was also the likelihood, as in my father's case, and to a lesser extent my own, that there had been no particular talent for spending, and in that way the money accumulates and multiplies on its own. He ponders this, muttering that one shouldn't "lay up treasures on earth where moths and rust doth corrupt" to which I am agreeable, still wondering what is bothering him. He errantly points out a crossroad, where I had had a nasty fistfight with a Norwegian farmer over a horse trade. I was in my forties at the time, the putative winner, but when I reached home Neena was so appalled at my battered appearance I had to promise on my actual knees that I'd never fight again. When they got home from school Paul was disgusted with me while John Wesley wanted a blow-by-blow. Lundquist mentions the time we had been attacked by young Italian men in Chicago when we were selling our prime beef to the Black Hawk, Chapin and Gore, and the Corona restaurants. It had been a wonderful business in the late twenties but quite naturally declined with the onset of the Depression. The young Italians in question were justified as Lundquist and I had walked out of a speakeasy with two women who were unfortunately married to two of our attackers. They were arrested because it was the policy of Chicago at the time to protect vaguely innocent visiting businessmen. I still had enough conscience at the time to send a bellhop to make their bail.

We never make it to see the Allis-Chalmers. Lunquist pulls off the gravel road and with a tremulous voice says that Frieda thought he was napping after dinner last evening and he overheard her gossiping to their minister about Dalva's problems. Lundquist clearly understands that this breach of confidence was grave, and despite the mixed fidelities involved, he feels he has to tell me. I reply, simply enough, that he must tell Frieda that she no longer works for me, adding that he should say I heard it in town and it could only have come from her. I then have to reassure him that this in no way affects the small farm I own that he lives on, and which I have given him in my will. He is forever trying to buy this farm with his savings, counting it his life's triumph that he has overcome primogeniture and saved enough to get his own place. I sympathize with his dream but have said his wife and daughter would likely need the savings if he passed on, to which he answers that he has already dreamed he will live to be ninety-three and that is that. The only way to get anywhere with this man is to change the subject.

It is somewhere in January and naturally I miss Frieda's vacuum cleaner. Lena comes out once a week with an odor of her cafe that perfume doesn't cover. She knits and talks about icy roads and her daughter, Dalva's friend Charlene, who is inevitably wayward in her terms, rather than being the delightful and rebellious young lady she actually is. The diseased strain of contentious Puritanism in America is never buried for long. Lundquist is sodden about his justifiably banished wife. The dogs are all cranky and semi-arthritic from the lack of their morning walk which the weather forbids but never really did before. That's why we have warm clothes, I keep reminding myself, though I'm quite frozen to my desk reading snatches of a dozen books at once. It takes a great deal of strength to keep January out of the soul and I've failed this year.

What wrings my heart and mind is that over Christmas we waited for an opening of good weather and Hackleford flew Naomi, Ruth and myself up to Marquette to spend the holidays with Dalva, but then she suddenly had become quite ill and was confined to the hospital. I hesitated to do so but I gave her a card and a necklace sent by Duane, the latter a simply set ordinary fieldstone attached to a leather thong, doubtless the only traditional "medicine" he had to offer. After I passed it to her I was happy I did as her connection to life seemed so tentative. I had a rather angry time with Naomi, a euphemism indeed, and convinced her that Dalva should be taken to Arizona to stay with Paul where there is the probability of sunlight rather than the Upper Peninsula of Michigan where a three-day blizzard was in the act of suffocating us. Naomi's cousin and I secured a logger's ancient Dodge power wagon, churned through the drifts and finally brought her home through the snow-clogged streets. The weather turned clear, the wind subsided off the dread Lake Superior and I managed to have a rather grandiose company plane from Chicago pick us up for the flight to Tucson. Paul was quite touched at the prospect of caring for her and on the flight home Naomi wasn't slow to admit that it now seemed a good idea. But all of that accomplished, I seemed to fall back into an unfamiliar darkness. When I kissed Dalva good-bye there was a strong sense of Adelle in her tearful distress.

Jesus H. Christ but these dreams are driving me mad! Several days ago it was God himself, or perhaps herself, and the voice was a billion deafening songbirds. I will tell you I hit the floor running on that one. I made coffee at three A.M. and woke up a grumpy Sonia, who is intolerant of moods, for company. At other times I might have been thrilled with the content of this dream but now I became querulous. Why hadn't I had this dream before? Why did it come so late in life? Would more like it be possible? Was Smith pulling some distant rigamarole on me? Of course I hadn't completely wakened from the dream yet and sat in the kitchen waiting for another billion-bird blast from the starless night.

At first light, and before Lundquist arrived, I went out to the barn and sat with the horses to give myself a firm grip on what I hoped was reality. I gave them all a good, vigorous brushing and I was delighted momentarily that I had made them happy.

Unfortunately for my sound sleep the following nights were chock full of Indian dreams, not just Lakota though they were in the majority, but Ponca dreams located at the confluence of the Niobrara and Missouri, Omaha Indians bringing Adelle back to life, Hopis dancing with snakes in their mouths, Chippewas in midwinter furs, the Tarahumara in their mountain fastness trying to put Davis back together. I took to drinking on an empty stomach which didn't help.

Today I wondered how the mind could make up dream people that the eyes hadn't seen. The whole experience was making me relentlessly irritable, if not more depressed. Sitting at my desk I finally had the wit to caution myself against becoming a goofy old bitch over the matter. I fetched Lundquist from the barn and insisted we go to town for a steak and a few whiskeys. He carried his old dog Shirley to the truck because she didn't care for walking in the snow. At the last moment we decided on the car and loaded all of the dogs in the back seat. After lunch we played pinochle with other geezers, then stopped at the butcher shop for dog treats. When I napped I had a fine Indian dream based on an experience back during World War II when some cousins of Willow and Smith showed up looking for a medicine bag their grandfather had given my father for safekeeping. I found the bag with some difficulty down in the sub-basement, fed them a big lunch, talked about old times, and sent them on their way with a gift of three steers because of their reminder joke about the winter of two thousand horses (1931) when the Pine Ridge Lakota had to eat that many of their own to avoid starvation. The government could be bounteous on paper with Natives but rarely forthcoming so that thousands over the years had starved to death, none of them congressmen it could be noted.

My heart lifted almost absurdly this afternoon when the rural mailman brought two letters from Dalva, one a postscript to the other. Paul had her taking long walks with his dogs every morning what with his "Mexican" notion that a strong body would make for an easier birth and recovery. She was studying hard to not fall behind in school though she admitted to having read *Wuthering Heights* again for the ninth time, having found a copy in Paul's library. Paul had also been teaching her the geology and natural history of the area, and would I prepare a special meal for Sonia, and give her two horses an extra handful of oats? The postscript was a bit stiff and was intended to remind me that if I heard anything from Duane I must call, and if I spoke to him I must tell him of her whereabouts should he wish to come and see her. I paused to damn the intensity of this kind of love that seemed to so deeply distort the rest of life, but then it was gone from my bones but not my memory. It was as inexplicable as much of the world and we could scarcely step off earth long enough for a clear view.

Lundquist tells me that it is mid-February and I have settled down to enjoy what I now truly believe to be the last year of my life. One part of my brain is no longer arguing with the other and I have made hundreds of sketches from memory. Yesterday was the beginning of a thaw and I sketched outside in the modest warmth when the sun was high and the shadows clean and crisp. I fetched my old elk-skin sketch case from a closet, overbundled myself, and went to the barn to saddle a horse, turning the rest out to frolic in the thaw, rolling, itching, rearing, with Dalva's mare running figure eights of its own accord. Finally it began to herd the other horses, showing its early cutting-horse training, but they would have none of it, racing to the pasture's four corners in unruly dismay at this attempt at discipline. I paused at my saddling to think of poor Lundquist who on that day was making the very long drive to Grand Island to take the "frazzled" Frieda to a "nerve doctor." She had flogged their ungainly daughter and Lundquist threatened to move with the young woman, and his dog Shirley, out to my bunkhouse.

The saddling went fine but when I put my left foot in the stirrup my leg hadn't the strength to lift me despite my hand pulling on the pommel. Jesus H. Christ, I thought, have I come to this. I tried again, and failed again. I felt and squeezed my leg for signs of a malady then cursed my two months of sedentary brooding that had atrophied my strength. The horse was getting restless with this nonsense so I went into the barn and got a milk stool for help, which meant I'd have to sketch from the saddle because I couldn't carry along the milk stool for remounting. I continued to swear under the mockery that there was something to blame other than myself. I got my first pony at age three and after sixty-eight years in the saddle I needed a goddamn milk stool.

I had meant to head for the lean-to but Sonia spotted a coyote track and roared off and the other Airedales followed. The horse, Rose by name, felt drawn to join the game and I fought her for a moment but decided my direction didn't matter. It was a brisk race indeed and my face burned despite the thaw but I was improbably enlivened, turning back to the house, a speck on the horizon, and wondering why I spent so much time within it. There are times when one is not only inept with other people but with oneself. The dreams and sketching were likely an unconscious prod in the butt to get me to live out my life.

I ended up well upriver and made several rather elaborate sketches of the foundation of Smith's parents' old cabin. Back in the twenties, after they had died, Lundquist said that Smith had come back while I was in Mexico and burned the cabin. I'm not sure what he had in mind but it seemed right at the time. Now there were a few charred timbers, a fieldstone foundation cracked by the fire's heat, dried stalks of nettle, milkweed, and burdock, and a root cellar full of snow. Out back were the remains of a privy and three apple trees with a few frozen apples near the top, out of the reach of the deer. I doubted then if one man could truly comprehend another's time, that the gaps were too large for our sensibilities. Smith's father had been so valuable at branding and round-up, fearsome and massively strong, and I remembered him pitching a good-sized steer to the ground by main strength, and not the kind of scrawny *corriente* used in rodeos. There should have been a Glackens or Bellows to paint this man in his prime. I recalled watching Glackens walk down Fourteenth Street in New York City as if he were eating the scenery. I followed him for several blocks but saw no point in introducing myself.

Back home I snoozed at the desk for a few minutes but was troubled by a thought and flipped through my notebooks until I found a passage from Kipling's "Notebooks" I had transcribed back in the twenties. "The Smithsonian, especially the ethnological side, was a pleasant place to browse in. Every nation, like every individual, walks in a vain show—else it could not live with itself—but I never got over the wonder of a people who, having extirpated the aboriginals of their continent more completely than any modern race has ever done, honestly believed that they were a godly little New England community, setting examples to brutal mankind. This wonder I used to explain to Theodore Roosevelt, who made the glass cases of Indian relics shake with his rebuttals."

The radio has announced this will be, sadly enough, the last day of the thaw. I head out for a walk with the dogs, still working out the kinks of my ride the day before yesterday. Naomi came over for an early breakfast on the way to her teaching duties. First she washed several days' of my dishes in a trice, and when I said, "I can wash my own dishes," she said, "But you don't." She now talks to Dalva daily on the phone, an indulgence of Paul's as country people usually keep long-distance calls under three minutes, but Dalva phones at length every afternoon when Naomi returns from school. We continue a modest quarrel of several years that started over, of all things, John

Keats. Two years ago in the summer Naomi had gone off to the university in Lincoln to take a short course in the English Romantics while Ruth was at piano camp and Dalva stayed with me. Naomi came home transfixed with Keats's notion that life, properly lived, is a "vale of soul-making." At the time I quipped, "Along with everything else and to what purpose?" This did not occasion a smile, and we were off on this bone of contention over my favorite boyhood poet, an enthusiasm that has stuck with me to the present. Naomi had a more ethereal view of Keats while I continue to think of him as like other men only more so, the volume and intensity of his sensibilities at sevenfold, urged on by his impending death. Adelle considered Keats too poignant to be bearable, but then she would have been an appropriate bride for him. I reminded Naomi that while she loved her Wordsworth I had noted that she also read Kenneth Roberts, Erle Stanley Gardner and Erskine Caldwell. But I'm not Keats, she insisted, to which I answered, Neither is he, but aside from his work he is an accumulation of our opinions about him. These discussions tended to become humorous. Last year when she passed on to me *By Love Possessed* by the current most critically acclaimed American author, James Gould Cozzens, I said that Cozzens reminded me of that farting old mare that used to pull the milk wagon around town.

Jake, the oldest of the Airedales, is a bit ill with his arthritis but not so ill that he doesn't growl when I force an aspirin upon him. I hold him on my lap despite his eighty pounds until he begins to snore and drool with the other dogs watching and questioning this privilege. There is an unknown car arriving in the yard and Jake roars off my lap, with one paw painfully using my nuts as a launching pad. I have become enough of a hermit to look out the window with irritation but it is Charlene, Dalva's friend and Lena's daughter. She is bringing a chicken casserole, the kind of dish I'm not fond of, but her mother, my occasional lover, has bet that I have prepared nothing for dinner which is true, and that I am drinking too much, which is not quite true. This said, Charlene stands inside the front door holding the casserole, without a coat, wearing her rather trim waitress uniform from which, with the rush of cool air, I can detect the slight fetor of her mother's cafe food. At first I say nothing and she is a bit unnerved, then stoops slightly putting the dish on the table. I adore this cheeky girl though I rarely see her. She is brash and intelligent and though I don't discount the gossip that she had made love to out-of-town pheasant hunters for money, it certainly means nothing to me, partly because I've been an out-of-town hunter myself with a weather eye out for a lady.

I offer her a glass of wine and she gracefully accepts. I open a fine bottle of Lynch-Bages and note a slight tremble in my hand as I pour. We go into the den and she sits on the soft leather couch and there is an unavoidable view of a fine thigh underside and she smiles. We talk about the weather, school, and Dalva and I'm grateful for her reassurances of Dalva's strength. Charlene is a year older and doubtless knows that I've made sure she's able to go to college. At least I suppose Lena has told her, though Charlene has straight A's and may get a scholarship of some sort. There's a bit of the Sapphist to this girl but that gives a wonderfully ambivalent edge to her sexuality. I notice this because it was always prominent in the painting community on my visits to San Francisco and New York where people who feel a bit odd seek others, the artists, who are naturally society's outcasts. I pour her a second glass of wine and we chat on, and then a third and we have finished the bottle. With her questioning I speak at length of Paris which she views as her "life's destination." Her dress has hiked up a bit and then she asks with an odd look, "Are you trying to seduce me?" I am so startled I do veritable back flips of denial, "Oh my God no, I could be your father, grandfather, great-grandfather." She laughs and repeats the popular vulgarity, "A stiff dick has no conscience," and then she comes to full consciousness with tears of embarrassment saying that she hasn't eaten much that day and the wine had hit her like a "ton of bricks." I am confused enough to say that I also haven't eaten and that she had doubtless read my pathetic thoughts. I put an arm around her to console her and she kindly says, "You're not pathetic." Now we are frozen in place for a full minute and then I mumble that I adore her but she had better go along. At the door she gives me a kiss full on the lips, and is off. I sit down at the kitchen table feeling absurd, a jelly-bean-sized tear running down my cheek. The experience possesses all the bittersweet melancholy of the milk stool and the horse. "I have a stiff dick with a conscience," I say to Sonia who shrugs her dog shrug of incomprehension.

It is now April 7, and I put this away for more than a month while I did hundreds of sketches of which I only saved a half dozen and burned the rest during yesterday's cool fog. It was a splendid deep orange fire and the dogs seemed to enjoy it except for Jake who was frightened.

My thoughts have put the dunce's cap on my grizzled head. Since death is such an apparent mystery I had hoped to describe it in the minutest detail, but only out by my orange fire did it occur to me I wouldn't be doing any writing during the last hour, or it would be most unlikely I would be doing so. Sad for you, Paul and Dalva, that you will not get this small peek at the void!

I laughed aloud and Jake crept out from behind the honeysuckle thicket near the grape arbor to check out the joke. These dogs have a sense of humor. Sonia will growl at a canyon boulder and when I check it out she'll run off yapping with delight. She did this only once with a pile of deer turds, perhaps understanding that it would only work for the first time. On occasion they'll run off to see Naomi in hopes that Dalva has returned. Naomi's not overfond of them but rewards their intentions with a bite to eat. The other day I said I was leaving a travel fund for her and the girls and if she did not use it each year the accumulated interest would go to the NRA in her name, scarcely her favorite organization. This brought on a pink-tinged "Why in God's name?" I said that there were plenty of good places for soul making on earth and she should at least take a look. She calmed down enough to ask me to make a list of places for her reference, then glanced off into the parlor where Ruth was laboring over Chopin and asked if I were thinking of dying soon, and I said not before October. We both laughed rather nervously over this selection of a month, both knowing the vast illusions over the control of our lives and final destiny when in the most naked reality we are but

trajectories. When my mind lends itself in this direction I always think
of Smith as a boy back when we were playing "Injun" and my father
had bought us recurve bows rather too strong for our age. We would
fire the arrows out over the big pasture to the south, then spend
hours looking for them. Once Smith found only two of his three
and strongly insisted the third had never landed. It was a magic
arrow and would only land when the time was appropriate.

I have tracked down Smith's location and am headed up to the
Rosebud at dawn to get some advice. The problem is that as Dalva's
time of birth draws nearer I grow more sodden with anxiety over
the matter, so much so that this nexus of worry has put a stop to my
sketching. I was this way over the births of both of my sons to the
point that it could be described as a torment. Neena was sympathetic and reassured me that countless millions of babies are born
every year. She then went back to her current book which I specifically remember was Stendhal's *The Red and the Black*. Neena was
quite the Francophile and I remember back in the thirties when I
came back in the house from branding and she was reading Proust
at the kitchen table. I was bruised, soiled and hungry and so were
the boys and she looked up as if we were aliens. We were suddenly
quite sure she had forgotten dinner but she nodded to the dining
room and then went back to her book. It was a hot day and there
was a turkey she had roasted and chilled, a potato salad, a green
salad, my bottle of whiskey, a bottle of white wine on ice, a pitcher
of lemonade for the boys, and a rhubarb pie. For some reason I hesi-
tate to write about my wife, either our joys or our horrors, as if this
marriage were a fundamental sacrament that might lose its worth
if babbled about.

Lundquist comes in from the barn after work, smelling of saddle
soap from keeping a room full of tack in fine fettle. He is a puddle of
despair over his wife's mental instability and we have a whiskey while
he questions me on the matter. I tell him that I have read that people
often become mentally ill over real, or imagined, but not quite ac-
knowledged guilt. I have already made the offer that Frieda may come

back to work if she apologizes for her indiscretion, but she has refused to accept this condition. She has opted for a world in which she has done nothing wrong, and that she need answer only to God. This is a not very rare version of God in America which is often viewed as a godless place, ergo, the most ordinary behavioral ethic may be ignored by Christians. It is a version of religion quite similar to Senator McCarthy's version of Americanism where all honor and civility can be righteously ignored.

Lundquist becomes more persistent about "mind doctors" and "nerve medicine" and I feel myself drift rather hopelessly toward the visual thought of the human trajectory, and how difficult it is to interrupt it in any positive sense. Frieda is being sedated and sits before the television like a big crock of lard. She doubtless misses vacuuming unoccupied rooms. My dear friend, her husband who is without guile, wants desperately, I perceive, for me to say she'll get better and I find myself saying, "She'll get better in the summer. I suggest you pull a tube or two on the television and maybe she'll turn back to gardening and religion." He's pleased with this garden-variety advice while I feel distressed at what little help I've been. I tell him I'm headed up to the Rosebud at dawn and he wants to drive me but I say best I go it alone. When he leaves I wonder again if my early obsession with art rendered me quite useless as a human being to my family and friends or if, indeed, everyone is quite useless to one another.

Before I went to bed I went down to the sub-basement to select a gift for Smith. I knew it was "de rigueur" to take tobacco but I thought something additional might be appropriate as it was likely our last visit. I made sure the railroad lantern had plenty of fuel and when I entered the earthen root cellar, past the wine cage, the black snakes became immobile in the lantern light except for a very large one that decided to challenge me. I pushed it aside with a stick kept by the descending stairs for that purpose and could not help but think of my beloved Adelle as Medusa in a damp slip. I rummaged through the big room with only the slightest of soul quavers when the edge of the lantern light caught the uniformed skeletons. The last straw, as it were, was when the cavalry officer, my father's nemesis, had thrown my rag doll into the fireplace. The rag doll had been Aase's, his tubercular wife, which had tripped my father's rage into the act of murder. I stood there overlong thinking first of the quality of Adelle's voice, and then the old Lakota warriors who had brought me back home on my ill-fated trip to rescue Willow. How odd that such men had totally vanished in my lifetime though there were likely a few left that kept themselves hidden from public scrutiny. In a specific way Smith was one of them and it was more a matter of will than lineage. When I had impulsively enlisted for World War I the sharp-eyed old recruiter down in Lincoln had asked me if I wished to enlist as a white or a Sioux. Can anyone actually be half of something, I wondered, and what part of me is my mother? This thought prickled my scalp and I hastily picked an ornamental bow made of Osage orange and wrapped tightly in two rattlesnake skins so that rattles hung from top and bottom. On the way out and up the stairs I shook the bow vigorously and the rattles frightened the black snakes in the root cellar. They disappeared into a hole behind a stack of potato crates. I decided I did not want to come down here again and I meant to call Samuels to add to my will that Dalva should deal with the collection when she became an adult. Back in the late thirties Paul had accepted a garishly painted buffalo skull he favored but John Wesley, in a rare show of superstition, wanted nothing to do with the room.

I left shortly after 4 A.M. and passed through Valentine at dawn, stopping for coffee and chatting for a few minutes with two very old stockmen I knew. On parting one asked if I was paying a visit to my "mother's people" and I nodded in assent and let it drop. Northwest of Valentine I hit the valley of the Little White River and gave a short ride to an old Lakota stumbling along the road and mildly drunk. It unnerved me when he said he remembered me from the only

Sun Dance I had attended, and that back in the early thirties when the ceremony was illegal, the U.S. Government having decided that the Indians that they were starving to death should not be allowed to puncture their breasts with thongs. Back then at the request of Willow's cousin I had brought up a bull that for reasons of its own had grown too fat to breed. The animal was admired through much of the ceremony during which he was fed heartily under a distant grove. I suspect he weighed just short of a ton and was devoured by the crowd with enthusiasm.

My hitchhiker knew Smith quite well and when I dropped him off at his one-room tar-paper shack he gave me more specific directions as Smith had concealed his dwelling. I tried to offer the gift of fifty dollars which he refused as he didn't want to drink again until it got cold in the fall. He furthermore refused my pocket watch as being too valuable and he also wasn't interested in what time it was. I said, "Neither am I" and we had a good laugh. He said then if I wished I could leave some money with Smith to buy his granddaughter and her children a milk cow as theirs had been stolen and doubtless eaten by marauding cousins from Pine Ridge.

I found Smith's shack with the door open, and the interior clean and nearly bare, with a spartan army-surplus cot and a small table with a patterned rose oilcloth. There was a Coleman lantern in the corner and a privy out back. I followed his trail down through a gully, crossing a creek that obviously emptied into the Little White, and then down the creek to a grassy bench surrounded by a dense thicket. I paused and whistled our boyhood signal and heard his in return, and thought this whistle was perhaps silly in seventy-year-olds, but perhaps not.

And there he sat before an old and worn but traditional tipi, smiling broadly. He adjusted a coffee pot on the coals of a fire, got up and bowed. I gave him a packet of Bugler tobacco and the ornate bow, the latter which he examined closely and then thanked me for. He ducked into the tipi and came out with a small leather bag which he handed to me. It contained a coyote skull with Smith's "medicine"

delicately painted on it in black ink. It was my turn to bow and we
sat down for coffee. He pointed off to a small sweat lodge in the bushes
and asked if I wanted to do a sweat. I said I had had a heart attack
and doubted if my system would take it. He had me describe the heart
attack and laughed with gusto when I said I had shit in my pants. He
said he had "let go a bit" when the longhorn bull charged down the
bank toward us. Now we laughed together and he said the last gift of
the government is when a hanged man shits his pants, then he asked
me why I had come so far to see him on a fine spring morning. I described in a rush my torment over my poor little Dalva giving birth
and he quickly corrected me saying she was neither poor or little but
a handsome girl of childbearing age, and since I couldn't give birth
for her I'd better calm my mind on the matter. He put some of the
Bugler tobacco and a few dried plants in the fire and said I should
pray for Dalva and not bother her spirit with my worries. That settled
that. I went on with my dreams about my mother and also Rachel,
Duane's mother, over in Buffalo Gap. He answered that I was dreaming about my mother because she was welcoming me to her world
late in the fall. She was only helping me get ready. With Rachel he
maintained her appearances in a dream several times meant she
wanted me to come over for a visit and possibly some loving. I said I
was getting pretty old for that and he said, "Bullshit." I then described
some of my animal and Indian dreams which he greatly enjoyed and
he said they were attributed to the landscape of my life since dreams
emerged from the ground. He was especially fascinated by how I escaped the German troops by becoming a huge bird and flying down
a river only to discover I was half bird and half bear. Smith said that
that dream was a real stroke of luck and I better work hard at my
life to make sure I was deserving of such a dream. I asked how I was
supposed to do that, and he answered if I didn't know by now I was
a cow flop. "Just do your art and be good to people," he added. "It's
that simple?" I asked. "That's really hard as you probably already
know." And that was that. He said a prayer for me in Lakota and I
didn't ask its specific meaning, then I felt drawn suddenly to wonder what exactly happened when we die. He said, "Got me by the

ass" and laughed, adding that it wouldn't do us any good to know and would certainly steal life's greatest surprise. He walked me back out to my car and said it would be good of me to go see Rachel so I headed west.

In retrospect it was the grandest of days. I stopped back through Valentine and had an early lunch with Quigley, a raffish lawyer whose people had come up from Texas in the 1880s. We had known each other so long in land dealings a midmorning drink seemed in order. I was feeling a tad drowsy but made it to near Gordon before I pulled off through a gate onto a rancher's two-track and took a nap with my back propped against a cottonwood. As I dozed off I thought of old Jules Sandoz, a friend of my father's I had met several times. Jules was an unappealing character in many respects but they got on quite well. His daughter Mari, who became a writer of note, was the fiercest young woman I had ever met and she eventually became friends with my wife, Neena, in Lincoln, and also New York City. I had also meant to ask Paul about Neena's diaries that she kept so relentlessly. I sup-posed he had them in his possession but had certainly never offered me a look.

When I woke from my nap I had slumped to the ground and was looking straight up at the pale green buds of the cottonwood just beginning to leaf. I turned sideways and stared off across the verdant pelt of grass where it seemed a great number of singing meadowlarks had collected, with each call trilling within my skull. Some were rather close to my prone carcass, perhaps thinking of me as a snoring log. I recalled that I had read somewhere that in the Middle Ages hell was envisioned as a place without birds. That thought increased their volume substantially as if they were giving assent to my think-ing. There was a trace of fear when their song merged with my dream of God's voice as that of a billion songbirds so I got up hastily and made my way to the car. I wanted to die at home.

I headed further west, turning north outside of Chadron, resist-ing an urge to go over to Fort Robinson for a look, thinking that it might decrease the sweetness of the day. I used to take the boys over for the polo weekends in the twenties and thirties when Fort Rob, as it was known, was a center of the game, and at one time the home base for our Olympic polo team. As the main remount station for the army there had been as many as five thousand horses at once. This was at a time when to be an army officer was considered a proper career for the young monied swells from the East with equestrian interests. The enormous emotional drawback of the locale was that it also was the site of the murder of Crazy Horse and on that day I wasn't up to a sidelong glance in the direction of his immense, doomed spirit.

My nap did not quite appease my drowsiness and I stopped at a country hardware store outside of Chadron, bought a thermos and filled it at the truckers' cafe next door with their wretched version of coffee. In this part of the country the closest place for a good cup of coffee, other than home, is Mexico. It occurred to me that my heart wasn't doing a good enough job to accommodate my before dawn wakening, a long drive, the emotionally fatiguing session with Smith, plus a couple of whiskeys and a T-bone for lunch. There was a corrective thought that my body was somewhat less than immortal, an idea that was getting repetitive.

I was troubled by the oddly crisp planes of light as the altitude grew after entering South Dakota, and the cooler landscape became more austere and less friendly. When I was young and arrogant I had tried mightily to paint this light which only puzzled the other students in Chicago, and later, my fellow artists, but then art and literature have always been rampant with xenophobia, and when in New York City I admitted I was from Nebraska I may as well have said I hailed from Ultima Thule. Showing one's art to others had always been similar to being limited to a bottle of bad wine when needing a drink. As far as they were concerned I may as well have been painting the moon. But then it is difficult to extrapolate the Sandhills from the Hudson River, or vice versa. We have always been regions rather than states or a country, and full of a tribal intolerance for anyplace else.

On a very hot August morning I had brought three of my paintings to Stieglitz's Photo-Secessionist Gallery in New York City. The great man, unfortunately, was in the country, a sane move during the heat wave, though the possibility of his being absent had not occurred to me. I knew the gallery had shown Marin and Hartley, both artists I admired. A polite assistant had a moment to say "How interesting," and then was off to lunch, adding at the door that I might come back in an hour. I came back but he didn't. I ensconced myself in a bar across the street, leaving fairly drunk in the late afternoon when he still hadn't returned. After a mostly sleepless night walking the city I tried to see Davies and Walt Kuhn the next morning. They were organizing the upcoming Armory Show to be held in February and in my wildest dream I hoped to successfully enter the competition to be shown there. The Kuhns turned out to be up on Cape Cod. I had a letter of introductions to George Bellows but he was also out of town. It struck me, and still does, that the only way to get your foot truly in the door was to live in this city or its environs. I had another introduction to a gallery near Washington Square that turned out to be closed for the month of August. I had enough vitality at the time to begin to think of the whole trip as quite comic. It was as if I had landed in Poland without knowing a soul or a word of the language. It was so hot I was without my ordinary interest in food and wine and I walked until my clothes soaked through with sweat. I will admit I was downcast a bit at the gallery that was closed for August and stopped at McSorley's for a half dozen schooners of ale, after which I walked out into the miserable slums of the Lower East Side where Glackens loved to paint. That was when I actually saw the man walking down the street which made me feel a great deal better, no matter the absurdity of the emotion. It was several hours after I left McSorley's that I finally noted that I was no longer carrying my portfolio of three paintings. I returned to the tavern without a trace of panic to discover that they were gone, thus escaping my post–World War I bonfire. I like to think of them in simple, middle-class drawing rooms where for years the generations of families have wondered idly over these peculiar landscapes.

By the time I reached my log hunting cabin near Buffalo Gap I was plumb worn out. Quite naturally Rachel "expected" me and had a pot of Mexican tripe stew called "menudo" that I favored simmering on her wood range. After bearing Duane she had left him with her mother in Parmelee and had gone off to Denver where she was a prostitute during the war years, in addition to being a severe alcoholic. She lived in the barrio and learned to cook a number of Mexican peasant dishes and both her phrases of affection and cursing tended to be a mixture of Spanish and Lakota. I had somehow caught myself a chill and was quite distracted by my thoughts which were still back in New York City in August of 1912. I called Lundquist so he wouldn't be alarmed by my absence but connected with Frieda who replied to my simple statement by saying, "Oh yes, sir. Thank you for calling, sir. God bless you, sir," an evident parody of some sophisticated fluff she had watched on television.

Rachel made me a peppery herbal tea and then I flopped on the sofa where she covered me with one of my father's buffalo robes I had given her. I quickly dozed but my unconscious mind would not let me leave New York. There in a dream was the immense sixty-story Woolworth Building they were finishing that summer. At the moment I set eyes on it I had doubts that there was any place for me in a locale where such a structure could be built, and though I was still in my twenties I was truly from another era. It was so hot that people came out of their stifling tenements to sleep on the banks and piers of the Hudson and East Rivers and in Central Park. In my night walks I heard singing in a dozen languages, and with my art left well behind, I became quite taken by this improbable music of the streets. I was a bit well dressed for some of the crowds and had been forced to pitch two attacking hooligans off a pier into the Hudson. I came awake when seeing the startled face of the second as he hit the river. I had left hastily and did not know if they had drowned.

Rachel was wiping my steaming face with a towel. She drew a bath as I had sweated through my clothes under the robe, but in the tub I still could not escape New York. On a dozen consequent trips I visited museums and the race tracks and did not pass by a gallery without a twinge of nausea. Mari Sandoz once told me that the briefest visit to her publisher's office would freeze her writing hand for a few days thereafter. If we move well forward to 1957 there appears to be a great deal of confusion with art and the art market, literature and the publishing business, in that the operative ethic of the country may be reduced to open and rabid greed.

We ate our menudo supper late and in the last light took a walk with Rachel's dog, a burly Labrador lost to a hunter which Rachel had adopted. This dog was not overly fond of me or of anyone except Rachel, keeping a weather eye out at me as if I were up to no good. We paused in the small log barn and Duane's buckskin came running toward us from the pasture, then the dog and the buckskin traded places, chasing each other in a game of tag. It was an especially fine horse if a bit headstrong like its owner. Rachel came in under my arm and I drew her close as if in the buckskin Duane was making a wordless visit.

That night heralded the first thunderstorm of the year and the frightened dog scratched wildly at the door. It normally slept in the barn with the buckskin but I got up and let it in whereupon it jumped on the sofa and quivered. I wrapped its large soaking body in the buffalo robe and then Rachel came out from the bedroom and out the west window we stared at the show of lightning against the distant Black Hills, a magnificent storm pushed in from the southwest so that when we opened a window the air was now warmer than it had been all day. We went back to bed with the dog following and crawling underneath, then growling when we inadvertently made love, so that we barely held our laughter until we finished. Despite Smith's admonition I could not have been more surprised on making love had I won the Olympic marathon. As I drifted into sleep the full impact of this golden day came upon me and I had the visual illusion of the surface of my life melting into the truer content beneath it. I was unsure if this meant anything but when I awoke frequently for moments during the night I could see all of the separate places on the farm back home that needed sketching.

* * *

I stayed three days at the cabin, and late on the evening of the third, Lundquist called to say that Naomi and the adoptive parents had flown off to Tucson because Dalva had entered labor, and then had given birth early this morning. Naomi would bring her home within a few days when she felt well enough to travel. When Rachel asked me if it was a boy or a girl I said I hadn't inquired. She was in tears so I called Lundquist back and he didn't know. I said to Rachel that perhaps we shouldn't know because by tomorrow this child would be gone from us forever. She wept bitterly, then became enraged over the idea that her son's child had been given away by the *wasichu*, the white people, when she could have raised it herself. What kind of people were we?

I left at dawn with Rachel sleepless and unappeased, alternately cursing me and pacing the room, though she did laugh a moment when the dog began to snarl and bark at me as if all of his suspicions had been confirmed. She did walk me to the car and kiss me good-bye in the gray light, though her eyes had become stones, her face impassive. I certainly could not admit that it had never occurred to me to think of her becoming the mother of the child.

On the long drive home Rachel's sadness left me, and I felt a little guilty that I could let it drift away by the time the sun rose above the horizon outside of Pine Ridge. I dismissed an urge to detour north for a last look at the Badlands where my father had holed up for nearly a year with the most recalcitrant Lakota after Wounded Knee, and where he nearly died of cholera. That was the slender thread between generations again, but then it was impossible to quite imagine that had he died I would have been raised as a Lakota in the most miserable period of their history. So much of my trip home was through virtually empty grasslands that once again it struck me as a horror that these people were not treated justly. Bartlett's Spade Ranch alone had been nearly a million prime acres and would have properly supported several thousand Lakota. One need not read very deeply in history, despite the otiose trappings of patriotism, to see how irrationally vicious we were with our Natives. We have rebuilt Germany in a scant dozen years and have utterly ignored our first citizens, and are confident in this sodden theocracy that the God of Moses and Jesus has been quite enthused over our every move.

I was not home ten minutes before I began sketching. Before that I got down on the den floor and wrestled with the dogs which I hadn't done for years, and then I was at my desk sketching Duane in the driveway, sitting in the road dust with his belongings in a burlap sack where Dalva had come upon him. He was an uncommonly strong lad but when he arrived his ribs were all visible beneath his skin while he washed at the horse trough. He was not so much embittered but taciturn, and Rachel later admitted she sent him along with the thought that I could curb the fighting tendencies that destined him for prison. It was at this time that on hearing from Duane that she was in a bad way that I had her move over to the cabin at Buffalo Gap. There was a childish wish on my part that Duane could be a replacement for John Wesley but he quickly disabused me of that. He seemed born a hard man whom life would doubtless make a great deal harder.

Naomi called to say that she and Dalva would be home in two days, and when she asked me what I was busy with I said I had months of sketching ahead of me. There were a few beats of silence before she said, "That's wonderful" and it occurred to me we had not spoken much except slightly in passing about my early life in art.

I impulsively went out to the barn and asked Lundquist to make me a one-sided stile to ease my getting on a horse. While he drew a plan on butcher paper I saddled up Peach and made it aboard without difficulty. Evidently my heart made me stronger on some days and weaker on others. Since I was no longer standing on pride I had Lundquist go ahead on the project.

Back in the house I did a number of sketches of Rachel, then of her dog, then of my own dogs which were better what with being drawn from life. My energies began to flag and I opened a bottle of wine to keep me going. It was nearly dark before I felt my hunger and was pleased to discover in the refrigerator that Frieda had sent over a pot roast. I dusted off our parlor Victrola and played a Bob Wills record during my dinner remembering dancing to the same music after a Fort Worth stock exhibition where Lundquist and I had lost track of each other for two days while in pursuit of separate nonsense. I had meant to continue sketching after dinner but fell asleep on the den sofa where Charlene had sat not very demurely.

It is a warm rainy Friday and last evening I went to dinner at Naomi's to see Dalva. They had arrived earlier that afternoon with Hackleford picking them up over in Denver in his Beech Twin. She was polite, friendly, but wan, and it seemed that everyone was near enough to tears to tread so lightly that nothing could be talked about. We said good night early and out on Naomi's porch Dalva said she'd pay me a visit the next day.

When I got home I reviewed my sketch pad but was so tired from my granddaughter's evident grief that I couldn't carry on, though at first light I was up with an aerial photo map Hackleford had made of our entire three thousand acres unrolled upon the desk. I marked at least three dozen spots I wanted to work with closely, and this has served to make me lose interest in writing my record which, after all, is not my "métier," but then my problem is that I don't really have a "métier," isn't it? I was quite spectacular in the cattle and land business but that doesn't quite "dollar up" as the auctioneers say.

I was saved from these dank thoughts when I heard the front door open and then Dalva was on the floor of the hall in her yellow rain slicker embracing the dogs who were twirling, jumping and howling. She let them out and I watched from the window rocker in the parlor as she ran around the yard with the dogs scooting through the burgeoning lilacs in the graveyard, down the wet ditch and around the tree that held the tire swing. They were fascinated when she was swinging, it being a game that was both incomprehensible and unavailable to them. She saw me through the window, waved, then came back in, shedding her slicker, cooing and chirruping at the dogs, getting them treats from the refrigerator. When she came back into the parlor she took Neena's old afghan from the love seat, approached me with a smile and asked, "May I?" I nodded and she nestled on my lap covering herself with the afghan and I rocked her as I had a thousand times since my son had died.

Oct. 9, 1958

I've become a bit daffy in the past five months which, on reflection, is not surprising. Anyone with any sense can feel the skull beneath their skin. I am not at my best but I'm having a very good time of it. Early this morning Lundquist drove me clear down to North Platte to pick up Dalva's birthday car I had arranged for on the phone. Naomi agreed on the idea of the car as Dalva has been driving an untrustworthy '47 Plymouth. Naomi had requested that I buy something "sensible," which irritated me, though when I reached the Ford dealership with Lundquist there was a definite feeling I may have gone too far. It was a brand-new aqua-colored convertible with a white top, spoke wheels, a big engine with four-barrel carburetors. Lundquist said, "Golly," and I quipped that I hadn't seen one in Nebraska before. When the dealer said, "Just the thing to recapture your youth," I didn't bother correcting him. While he and Lundquist went over the operator's manual I was remembering my sleek 1914 Buick Racer I had bought and made a mess of within a year on my extensive sketching and painting trips. I had driven it to San Francisco in the fall and had gone up the coast for a picnic with Piazzoni and Dixon, and fueled by a case of wine we had done a great deal of damage to the undercarriage backing over a stump.

I drove the convertible home, having brought along my somewhat tattered otter-skin coat for that purpose. The car had the feeling of a biplane and I was stopped for speeding outside of Thedford.
I was pleased to be let off though the young constable, whose father I
knew, asked, "Mr. Northridge, are you recapturing your youth?" and
I answered, "Not in the least. It's a birthday present." Come to think
of it, I have not the slightest interest in recapturing my youth. Once
is enough. Neena had a Blavatsky-type theosophist friend in Omaha
who was forever babbling abut reincarnation, to whom I asked, "How
do you know you're not coming back as a microbe buried out of sight
in a dog turd?" It was a pleasant after-dinner show stopper.

In any event, Dalva loved the car and Naomi and I watched from
the porch as Dalva, Ruth and Charlene sped off on a trial run to town
and Naomi said, "Think what a mess you would have made out of
two daughters." Feeling this might be too close to the bone she apologized, but my mind was already elsewhere, wishing I had painted her
portrait, and that I still owned my favorite vehicle, a 1925 Runabout
I had drunkenly driven into the Niobrara during spring flood. I was
occasionally quite the fellow in those days. Neena would pack herself and the boys off to Omaha, New York, or Rhode Island until I
cooled off.

I think I'm fairly close to the end. I'm frequently surprised and
thankful when I awake in the morning. My vision sometimes blurs
and often my heart flutters like an injured bird. I sketched, beginning at dawn, all summer long but by late July I could no longer sensibly ride a horse what with occasional dizzy spells. My last long ride
had been after Naomi had called to say Dalva had taken off for a walk
early in the morning and had been gone all day. She was worried she
might have been bitten by a rattler, that sort of thing. I said I knew
she had Sonia with her and I had never seen a snake without Sonia
seeing it first. That calmed her down somewhat, and then I added
that I'd go take a look. It was a lucky break that I had subdued my
pride and had Lundquist build the stile because I couldn't have
mounted my sorrel without it. I led another nag because Peach didn't
care to be led. I checked the thicket and pond spring first, then headed

north to the small canyon with the spring on the Niobrara where I found her. She seemed in good shape other than for a sunburn, and terribly pleased that I had arrived. I told her this was the place that at her age I had been thrown from a horse and busted my noggin.

In late June I had ordered oils from an art supplier in New York but had never opened the carton. A simple task like fetching a bottle of wine from the basement would be exhausting one day, easy the next. I had pretty much covered the places I had marked on the aerial map in late April, and by early September was resigned to an easy chair that Lundquist had hauled out to the south pasture with a pick-up. It was covered with a tarp against the rain, and I needed only to drive out, take off the tarp, sit down and begin sketching. We placed it in the approximate location that Smith had found so fascinating, to the puzzlement of Lundquist. A family of field mice quickly took up joint occupancy in the chair and I had to be careful when I sat down. Not being familiar with the power of humans they would scurry up and down the arms of the chair, across the sketch pad, and one morning a mouse perched on my shoulder as I sketched. The smallest of hawks, the kestrel, flying by would send them diving for cover. I took to carrying a coat pocketful of oats for them to feed on and they soon became smart enough to go for the pocket rather than waiting for a handout. I mostly sketched thickets from memory, also cloud formations, birds in flight, and some native grasses that surrounded the chair: bluejoint, buffalo grass, marsh muhly, side oats grama, sand bluestem. These reminded me of my father's botanical sketches, though not so finely rendered what with having a different intent. The thickets drawn from memory posed a bit of a mystery. I had not thought up to this point in my life that thickets were of such great interest. I drew riverine thickets near Durango, Mexico, where I had camped with Davis, a thicket a dozen miles from La Paz on Baja where the quail were thickly coveyed and hiding from raptors. There was a thicket near Sarlat in the Dordogne where a mare dropped her foal, and not far from the small hospital where I had seen the bottom that provided a miraculous cure, and dozens of thickets from Nebraska, especially from along the Loup, the Missouri, and the Niobrara. There was the idea that the farm itself appeared as a monster thicket from the county road, and that was where I had always retreated, lived and would doubtless die.

One cool rainy September day when I was somewhat angrily confined to my desk I timidly rechecked my notebook sketches from my teens and twenties to compare them to the work of the present. There was an interesting early drawing of a line of Negro infantry at Fort Niobrara outside of Valentine in 1902 when I was sixteen. I had been invited to lunch with these enlisted men and saw the odd phenomenon similar to Davis sketching the girls at the State Fair: all people have a peculiar fascination with artists as if they were some sort of lower-rent witch doctors. Many a young woman of high station and otherwise good sense will bed an artist before she will a stockbroker, perhaps out of curiosity. Davis thought this boon helped make up for an inevitable life of penury.

My work now seemed to stand fairly well with that of earlier years except that now the lines were a bit dreamier, more tentative, less likely to own a bold but inappropriate touch. But many of the journal entries were jejune and captious. At fifteen I had evidently discovered the word "hedonist" in the dictionary or *Britannica* and decided a hedonist was what I wished to be. That was a Modigliani, or hormonal phase, where a fanny and a Botticelli chalice are thought to be of equal value, with the judgment wavering to the former. Just the other day I had thought of having Charlene pose for me in the buff for a last look at the vision that has fueled so many nights and days. From May 1916, there was a not very intelligent observation leavened by humor: "If our actual lives are but parodies of our ideals, then when we hit periods where we lose our ideals we can become quite a mess. Written on a severe hangover, also recovering from a fist fight with a rather large and impudent cowboy outside the Bassett Tavern over a young lady who was trying to get in my car rather than his." Later in the month there was a sententious item, "Politics would convince one that life is a burbling cesspool, while organized religion sees it as a disciplinary system in which the administrators must be well paid. Only in the arts and literature, and natural history, are we led to that invisible altar where life may be sensed as the vast mystery that it is." Now, this is a noble sentiment but if it were a meal it would be thin gruel indeed. I somehow hear the droning voice of Eeyore, the donkey in *Winnie-the-Pooh,* a book I read to Dalva and Ruth so many times when they were little girls that the book became a fact of nature. All through life one hears nitwits bleating their versions of wisdom. I rather like Keats's notion of "negative capability" where one cherishes and nurtures the thousands of contradictory ideas in one's head, rather than trying to reduce them to functional piths and gists. What vanity! There is also the melancholy thought that you could study and write poetry from dawn to dark and not come off with a quatrain equal to what Keats may have written on the back of an envelope on Hampstead Heath and then discarded as inferior. Staring out at the downpour that enveloped the south pasture I had shuddered with the mad urge to eat and drink the ground, to swallow the sky with its rain, and then I slept and dreamt of Adelle, Neena, my mother and Rachel, standing out in the pasture in the rain, smiling quite fully and looking back at me behind the den window. I waved but they did not wave back. When I awoke I looked for them but it was getting dark outside.

I think I am quite close to my end, so much so that I have told Lundquist where to put the large manila envelope stuffed with this little story. He is quite frightened, perhaps sensibly, of our sub-basement and said, "I've never been down there alone." There are tears in his eyes and I cajole him saying that Lutherans are quite safe from goblins and suchlike. He admits that he's crying because he fears I will die soon to which I nod. I'm feverish from what I take to be bronchitis and the merciful onset of pneumonia, a disease said to be an old man's *friend.* Naturally he wants to fetch the doctor which is out of the question. There is an open bottle of whiskey on the desk for my violent coughing fits but he refuses, for the only time in memory, to accept a drink. I am so startled that I agree when he asks me to pray with him. We kneel and as he prays I stare through the ribs of my chair at the large folio art books on the bottom shelf of my library. I fix on Caravaggio who was said to be an unpleasant person, but then how does it finally matter who made the painting or book when the mystery is in the collective understanding, both unmeasured and immeasurable. Lundquist prods me, and I'm supposed to ask God to forgive me. I mutter that I'd rather ask forgiveness from those I offended but nearly all of them are dead. He asks again so to humor him I say, "God forgive me." He's so pleased that I can't help but think I've done the right thing. I grab the desk edge and pull myself to my feet. Now with his mission accomplished Lundquist is ready for a drink. We rehearsed for the last time our unique meeting down in Lincoln a few weeks after Armistice. Neena had met my train in from New York via Chicago but Paul, who was an infant, was only beginning to recover from the flu that killed hundreds of thousands in the U.S. that year. She wanted me to go ahead up-country knowing that I didn't care for her wealthy friends we were staying with, but then Paul who was only two seemed to enjoy my hospital visits. I took to driving out to the stockyards and the auction barn and the presence of cattle alleviated my homesickness. On the first day I had had perhaps too many sips from my whiskey flask and was critical at the way a feisty and muscular young Swede was sorting cattle. He marched right up to me and offered to kick my ass, at which he was chided by a superior because I was a rancher in an expensive suit. In the ensuing days I got to know this young man, Lundquist, from Minnesota and on the last day in Lincoln I drove out and offered him a job at double his present wage, plus the house I had bought from the Norwegians down the road who were desperate to leave the area. We were capable of going on endlessly with these memories, and there is a question of what else an old man has, when Dalva drove into the yard to see me and Lundquist left.

I looked out the window and could see Charlene sitting in the car with the sunlight gathering in her hair. Of course I should have asked her to pose. Dalva came in and hugged me and felt my forehead to check for fever. She said I was burning up and became tearful. She remains sure that she is the cause of my illness and I tell her I had this bronchitis well before her adventure. I also tell her the comic story of my first heart attack and she fails to see the humor. She begins to apologize again and I draw her up short by telling her to invite Charlene in and we'll have a short game of rummy. I tell her I have never been happier in my life which is utterly true.

What she did several days ago is jump in her car before dawn and race off to find Duane. Naomi came over at midmorning when she heard that Dalva had never arrived at school. I was sitting out in the pasture in my chair with a thermos of coffee laced with whiskey for my cough, enjoying a spate of late Indian summer and watching the dogs sleeping in the grass except for Sonia who was digging at the edge of the chair to get at the mice. Naomi came swerving through the gate and sped toward my chair, bouncing over the lumpish ground. On hearing the news I guessed that Dalva would have looked in Parmelee, and there she would have heard Duane was in Chadron in jail. I knew this because the week before on hearing from the sheriff of Dawes County I had asked Quigley to drive over from Valentine and bail Duane out and give him some money. Quigley did so and told me on the phone that Duane said he was headed for Oregon to be a logger. This sounded unlikely for a young cowboy but who knows? I said I would check with the sheriff in Chadron in case Dalva showed up at the jail, also with Rachel in Buffalo Gap in case Duane was there though the odds were against it. Naomi listened carefully then headed back to her country school, saying she'd return in the afternoon.

We were sitting in the parlor twiddling our thumbs when the sheriff called late in the afternoon to say Dalva had stopped a few minutes ago at the jail and he had her car keys in his possession. Naomi talked to Dalva and remained admirably calm. I arranged for her to stay with a family to whom I had sold a ranch at a fair price right after World War II, then I called Hackleford to arrange a ride. Naomi was so relieved she permitted herself a glass of wine and a tear or two. She teased, "If you are going to die in October you have less than a week," and I said, "I'll make it" and she became terribly upset. She was quarrelsome over having the doctor come out so I said I'd shoot him at the door. "What will we do without you?" she said. "You have Paul who is far wiser. He'll keep an eye on all of you." She repeated, as always, some of her confusions about money and I told her that what you do is spend some, or most, then save the rest.

Just after dawn it looked like it would be a fair day so I called Hackleford and requested his old Stearman biplane so we'd have an unencumbered look at the country. He thought it might be a bit cool but I insisted, a decision that damn near finished me off early in the trip. In fact we were flying low over the Carter ranch north of Springview when, despite being bundled up, I passed out from the cold a few minutes and never really got warm until we were on the ground a half hour in Chadron. The sheriff met our plane and I picked up Dalva's car and fetched her from the ranch up north of town. She seemed glad to see me and I was fearful enough of the onset of dizziness to ask her to drive. I thought, Jesus Christ, I don't want to die on the drive home so we headed the two hours up to the cabin at Buffalo Gap so I could rest up. For some reason I thought it would be appropriate that Dalva would meet Rachel and when we arrived I spoke with Rachel in my pidgin Lakota to keep her discreet on the subject of Duane. Dalva took off for a ride on Duane's buckskin and I told Rachel I was going to die pretty soon and she said, "I know it." I slept on the couch for five hours or so and then we left off for home. Before we departed and when I awoke I heard Dalva on the phone telling Naomi we should be home by midnight and I said an actual prayer to an unspecific god that I'd make it. My granddaughter had enough problems without me kicking the bucket, a phrase I'd always found amusing. He kicked the bucket. And spilled out, or somesuch.

We had a fine drive home, and though she protested I had Dalva put the top down. We stopped in Valentine and had a quick dinner with Quigley and talked about bird hunting. He was gracious enough not to express concern but I saw his alarmed look. My flask had run dry and we stopped for whiskey. The radio became beyond the range of a good station and I had Dalva sing to me, and I sang her some World War I songs that seemed to amuse her. "Here's to the Kaiser, he's on his last hitch/We're after his ass the damned son of a bitch." That sort of thing.

The twilight was radiant with the landscape suffused briefly in a yellow glow, and we heard hundreds of meadowlarks trilling good night. I awoke at home and Dalva tucked me in with my whiskey which, though I might wake with a hangover, now seemed to be keeping me alive. Before she left Dalva brought in Sonia to keep me company. Somewhere toward morning with a predictable headache I reached out toward this warm body thinking it might be Neena, and Sonia, who didn't like her sleep disturbed, growled. It's certainly not all in the mind but most of it is. This is as much as I can say.

It is five days later and I've had a few bad moments with this whole death experience, not exactly having prepared myself until this past year. What did I think would happen, how did I think it would end and where do I go next, if anywhere? Naomi came with the doctor this morning, and Paul is on his way up from Chiapas, down at the bottom of Mexico. I nearly told the doctor that I never actually made love to his wife but then he said my heart was "kaput," a rather homely expression, so I let it pass. I also have pneumonia and my general dreaminess can be accounted for by the fluid in my lungs. Thank God for big favors. When the doctor leaves in a concealed huff I tease Naomi with the fact that I know she sometimes refers to me as Lord Byron when out of my earshot. She reddens at this. I found this out from Lundquist who heard her and wondered what "Lord Byron" meant and I said he had been a fine gentleman who wanted to be buried with his dog, which sounded reasonable to Lundquist. The ex-governor who had tried to help the Rosenthals stopped by and we bid our adieus, and Rachel has come down from Buffalo Gap.

Rachel chants for me in Lakota as my mother had done for my father. I am charmed at this continuity though I have difficulty staying awake and my dreams are full of birds. I saw Mexican jungle birds, quetzals, that I hadn't remembered for a long time, also a sharp-tailed grouse flapping in a coyote's mouth up near Springview.

Paul is here and we talk about nothing until I am suddenly overcome and beg his forgiveness again for striking him to the ground. He kisses my forehead. Frieda Lundquist arrives and is kneeling outside my window, praying loudly. Paul helps me to the window and I give her a wave.

I've made it through another night and wake to find Rachel and Paul sitting beside my bed. I sleep again and hear those billions of birds again. Christ, what a grand noise. Dalva comes in and kisses me and Ruth says matter-of-factly, "I'm sorry you're dying." I ask my dear Lundquist to put away this journal. I want to sit on a hay bale against the barn as I did so often as a young man when the morning sun against the barn slats would warm your back though your belly would stay cool. Hail and farewell.

II

NELSE

Don't you hear your mother's call
In the north wind's frightful howl?
—Anna Akhmatova

June 1, 1986

I was pretty sure I felt the earth moving beneath my back. The sensation happened several times within an hour or so. The stars were wiggling a bit and intermittently blurred, my vision addled by fever: Virgo with Spica, Leo and Regulus, Boötes less defined except by overwhelming Arcturus.

Maybe I did and maybe it was an illusion. I can't say much for the difference which is a fine point we primates are always trying to transcend. It isn't a case study and neither am I. I was checking a kingfisher site on the remote banks of the Niobrara (seasonal employee, Migratory Bird Monitoring, U.S. Fish and Wildlife Service). I had stopped in Lincoln a couple of days before to file my field notes with my boss who had been promoted beyond actually having the time to study birds anymore except in his backyard. The irony of success—you are promoted from the outside into the inside. We discussed the spring fire a farmer had made of frozen sandhill cranes over near Fort Kearny. An error in phenology as some arrived too early and were caught by a blizzard. He said I was an enviable *nomad* as he popped three ibuprofen.

That chore done I called J.M. and we met at a bookstore. She warned me on the phone that she was just getting over the flu. I bought her an Octavio Paz as she must account strictly to her husband for the money she makes at a polite, harmless, ultra-clean strip club. She wishes to teach English and also has a minor in dance education. Her husband, a ponderous oaf from Sioux City of Norwegian heritage, has been working forever on his doctorate in anthropology. I remembered him slightly from when I was an unsuccessful undergraduate over eight years before. She told me he tries to talk with his pipe in his mouth. Inevitably some graduate students attempt to look like eccentric older scholars. They are prone to chuckle rather than laugh. Am I belittling this man because I'm fucking his wife? Probably.

We had a brief drink at the Zoo Bar and I looked at her closely. She was ever so slightly drawn from her bout of flu but I was heading for the Sandhills by dark and we didn't want to miss the chance. This was our third rendezvous after I had caught her show at the strip club in April where she had jumped into the air and landed in splits. I was a bit over-revved like a diesel engine, tossed her a hundred-dollar bill and left. The next afternoon by glorious luck and a minor search I saw her walking toward the campus with her gym bag. I drove a block ahead and let Ralph out to pee. He's now among the missing and writing his name clutches at my throat. I suspected he was part springer and part Labrador though there's no evidence, having found him as a pup in a field near a campground outside of Clayton, New Mexico.

She paused when she saw me, then smiled at Ralph who approached and gave her a good sniffing. She looked at my ten-year-old pick-up with camper shell, then critically at my clothing.

"I should give you your hundred bucks back but my husband knows I made it. I don't think you're actually a big spender." She stooped to pet Ralph and I caught the flex of her inner thighs before she tucked in her summer skirt. This flummoxed me and amused her.

"For God's sake you've already seen me almost naked. What do you do anyway?"

"I'm a nomad."

"I don't like to be teased. I guessed a construction worker. A few are dumb enough to throw a day's wage at me. Not often, but it's happened."

"I bet you're from up around Neligh. Maybe closer to Verdigre." She blushed a bit. Her voice was far too formal to come from a city and the speech patterns from up that way are traceable.

"Pretty close, smartass." She stumbled a bit on the "smartass."

Then we stood there a minute or two in silence with Ralph becoming a bit impatient. She reminded me of a snapdragon, one of my favorite domestic flowers, though I wasn't close enough to catch her scent.

"Would you like to take a ride? It's spring."

"I already said I was married. You wouldn't even tell me what you did and who you are."

I did a brief, safe sketch, while she looked off studying passing cars. She drew an imaginary X in the sidewalk and said I should be there in two hours and she would have made up her mind. When she walked off Ralph tried to follow her. She turned and said she had a sandwich in her gym bag and I called Ralph back.

And that was that. It was an ungodly long two hours and when I came back she was already there and got in my pick-up without a word. Within a few blocks she was nervously handling my botany and bird guidebooks, also Olaus Murie's *Animal Tracks*, flipping its pages.

"I won't go to a motel," she said.

"Neither will I. If you want a motel you'll have to go there by yourself."

She laughed at that briefly but her lower lip was trembling. She went back to *Animal Tracks* and asked if I could track her.

"Not on a sidewalk. Maybe out in the country." She turned and looked into the camper at Ralph who was irked that his seat had been displaced. This communicated, he went to sleep.

I drove thirty miles or so, out past Garland, to a woodlot where I had done a warbler count two years before. It was a warmish day in late April and her lip trembling stopped when we reached the full countryside. When I pulled into a two-track in the forty-acre woodlot and gave Ralph a biscuit for his patience she ran for it. She ran like a hurdler and I was impressed as she disappeared into the spring greenery. It had rained recently so the imprint of her feet weren't that hard to follow. I moved along at a good pace staring at the ground and then looked up in five minutes or so to find her sitting on a stump with her flower-print skirt held to her breast. There were mosquitoes in the air so I had her stand and I knelt and rubbed Cutter's bug lotion on her legs and bottom while kissing her sex. She made wonderful noises that seemed to belong in the woods. The first time she merely leaned over the stump. When we rested I identified plants, trees and wildflowers for her. Later, the only difficulty we had was scrubbing the dirt and grass stains out of her kneecaps.

Our second meeting a week later was problematical. She said she had *come to her senses* and this would be the last. There was a driving rain and she kicked a radio knob off the dashboard which embarrassed her. She would scream then blush. She was so firm from a mixture of dance, track, swimming, and work on her father's farm that I felt trapped within her. She put on some of my rain gear and we walked despite the prolonged squall. She had married her husband when she was nineteen, meeting him when he worked on an archeological dig up at the confluence of the Niobrara and the Missouri. He seemed wise and noble compared to the louts in the area and the fraternity boys she had met as a college freshman. That was three years before. She worked as a stripper as did several girls from the university dance classes because in a single evening you could triple what you could make as a waitress in an entire week. It also aroused her husband, a matter which seemed to puzzle her. "I must be an animal," she said and I said, "Of course," which pissed her off. It took a full hour to convince her that her admission was admirable. I let Ralph out and he killed a young woodchuck which didn't help matters. I had to crawl under the truck to get the woodchuck away from him and when I rolled out half in a puddle I looked up my raincoat at her naked bottom, an electrifying sight. I had been around a bit at age twenty-nine but there had been nothing quite like her. She looked down at me, laughed, and knelt on my nose and mouth with the cold puddle soaking my butt.

The third meeting was when I caught the flu before the trip to the Sandhill. After she warned me on the phone I said I didn't give a fuck if she had AIDS. This would pass for romanticism in my generation. But this rendezvous was made strange by my other preoccupations and her own. I had been in Santa Monica stalking my mother, stalking in the old sense, and my actual mother not my adoptive one, certainly out of curiosity rather than imagined affection for one I had never laid eyes on. On the way back to Nebraska to one of my *lairs* to think things over my pick-up was stolen at a truck stop outside of Tucson, Arizona. I had pumped myself a tank, got back in the truck, noted my water jug was low and hurried back into the station. When I returned the pick-up was gone. An attendant said he had seen a young Mexican "lurking" around. I had all my gear plus a full decade of my natural history journals in there, plus a small library, but by far the most important, my friend Ralph. I called and talked to the police, took a cab to a motel and waited there three days for news of which there was none, nor for some reason did I expect any.

J.M. was melancholy and used the phrase *come to our senses* again which seemed far off the mark for any problems we might be having. True sexual compatibility had been a rare item in my life and we certainly had that. She felt quite bad that I had lost Ralph but then picked on me for information about the new Chevy truck. I had already told her I lived on the six-hundred-dollars-a-month allowance left to me by a great-grandfather I had never met and knew nothing about. With this and what I could otherwise scrounge up I lived splendidly well below what she observed as the "poverty line." Since she came from a rather poor farm family she wasn't very sympathetic to the way I lived. I also didn't want to explain how I got the new truck. Despite the pleasant, sunny day we had made love only once in the first hour or so.

"Do you want me to run away with you and help you find your dog?"

"Of course," I said and she sat on my lap on the ground.

"I can't," she said. My answer, however, had pleased her when she sensed I meant it.

But I had to wonder what I was doing, or I had finally wondered what I was doing, just as she had already wondered what she was doing. We were mutual intruders and it was improbable for either of us to admit that anything that had started so accidentally could be

of lasting value. We made love again and she gave me to understand
that she wouldn't see me again. Having spent nearly a decade avoiding even the slightest of human traps I should have felt relieved but
I didn't. I had neglected the future for good reasons but I certainly
couldn't accept the fact I wouldn't see her again, a disappearance as
final as Ralph's.

On the way back to Lincoln we pulled off on a remote side road
and started to make love again and were waved at by a passing rural
postman. That ended that. I waved back but she slumped to the floor
in a clump of shame. The afternoon further degenerated when I asked
why a mailman seeing her tits mattered when she stripped three nights
a week? She took this as criticism of her job. It was the peculiar and
irrational situation where it suits a woman's purpose to misunderstand
you. She's trying to become angry so she won't see me again, I thought.
She wouldn't talk but when I dropped her off a few blocks from her
apartment she leaned over, kissed my cheek and tried to say good-
bye in a voice that was a mixture of a choke and a stutter. I stupidly
grabbed her arm, then released it. She walked away behind the truck
and I watched her above the OBJECTS IN THE MIRROR ARE CLOSER THAN
THEY APPEAR rubric.

What did I have in mind? I hadn't thought of consequences from
the moment I saw her. In the pick-up on the hot afternoon street I
felt like a shit-heel intruder. What did I know about her other than
a few poignant items: her 4-H Club Charolais heifer had taken third
place at the Antelope County Fair when she was twelve. She learned
Spanish from her mother who had spent most of her childhood in
Mexico where her father had been a mining engineer. Her mother
had studied one semester at University of Nebraska before she became pregnant by a farm-boy scholarship student ending up on a
mediocre one hundred eighty acres, enough for not very genteel poverty. Her mother viewed J.M. as being in essentially the same fix. Her
mother knew she stripped but her father didn't. J.M. had been impressed at a dean's reception for doctoral students and *the whole house
was carpeted*. She liked poetry in Spanish but not in English because
it was *mysterious*. Her parts were the most lovely I had ever seen.

Given the hyperbole of the age I should compare her perineum to the Sistine Chapel or somesuch. She said her parents hadn't been able to afford braces for her teeth and was demurely pleased when I said I didn't care for magazine teeth. This was about it except that she got all A's, her husband's favorite dish was sauerkraut and pork which she didn't care for. I judged her as far more intelligent than she assumed she was. In Nebraska only the strictly functional aspects of intelligence are much valued.

I only made it as far as Broken Bow that evening. I was so pre-occupied by J.M. that I forgot to eat until it was too late, curling up in my sleeping bag in an alfalfa field while there was still a trace of light in the west. I disturbed what had to be the second nesting of a meadowlark but she finally calmed down, approaching my head quite closely out of curiosity in the gathering dark.

At first light I was as hungry as I had ever been, plus soaked and shivering with dew, my protective tarp still in the truck. This stupidity made me feel generally raw and I was quite blind to the beauty of the morning, forgetting to inspect the windbreak for the owl I had heard throughout the night, doubtless a barn owl because of its wheezy cry.

A very large farmer stared at me from the window of a diner as I pulled up. When I entered he said I owed him a cup of coffee as rent for the square yard of his alfalfa I had slept upon. I nodded in agreement and sat with him for breakfast when he gestured me over. I told him I had been sleepy and if I had rolled the truck and it had caught fire I would have helped spread the noxious weed, leafy spurge, that I had seen in his ditch. He laughed at that, then we ate in silence as he listened to the dawn farm and stock report with the habitual melancholy of farmers listening to prices.

I reached my assigned location, a very large ranch up north of Bassett, by midmorning. I was shown into a den by a middle-aged woman whom I took to be the wife of a hired hand. The owner was an old gent in a wheelchair who immediately said I bore a resemblance to a long-dead friend of his. This made me a tad uncomfortable as I knew the girl who bore me had been raised within seventy miles of this ranch. I was startled to hear that the owner was ninety-one but then the Sandhills area is renowned for the longevity of its inhabitants. His voice was bell clear and he was amused and curious about the project. He resisted having government people on his property but something as benign as counting birds appealed to him. I thought of explaining that I wasn't actually an ornithologist, a profession as territorial as the species they study, but realized this would be a moot point to him. He said that one of his few regrets was that eighty years ago he had shot a golden eagle but that a half-breed Ponca cowboy had been joyous to accept the feathered carcass. He added that Poncas were more reliable cowboys than Sioux or Pawnee, but not nearly the horsemen that the Sioux were. It occurred to me that history was collapsing into the form of an old man who had been born a few years after Wounded Knee and had served in World War I. By contemporary standards he was wealthy with the ranch totaling close to a hundred thousand acres but there were few signs of it except an expensive telescope on the open front porch. He liked to look at the stars which had frightened him as a child for reasons he didn't explain. He offered the loan of a horse when I showed him the location I was aiming at on a topographical map. The closest two-track was a couple of miles away and the rangeland's underpinnings of sand were too fragile for my pick-up. I said I'd hoof it, not wanting to look after a horse. When we said good-bye he asked for a report on the numbers of the birds I was looking for on an eleven-mile stretch of the Niobrara, which were kingfishers, American bitterns and green-backed herons.

While I was gathering my gear a youngish cowboy you wouldn't want to jump in the ring with approached and tried to tease me about birds but then I said birds were real attractive compared to staring at a cow's ass all day. Any wimping out encourages the bully in such people so you have to draw a line. Rather than being pissed he agreed and marked out a spring on my topo and what he thought might be the best camping spot. He described his favorite bird, fluttering his arms to show the way it landed on a fence post. I figured it to be an upland plover, and then he asked how many kinds of birds there were on earth and when I told him he said, "Holy moley, don't that beat all hell."

On the fairly rough hike in I felt a little wobbly but still suspected nothing. My perceptions were slightly askew so when I came upon a yellow-headed blackbird it didn't look quite right and I paused to think it over beside a small slough. The bird was fine and maybe my mind wasn't. An otherwise dense early college roommate used to prate that "reality is mankind's greatest illusion," something he cribbed from a psych professor who got it from Erik Erikson. This bird looked newly minted in the dullish and cloudy afternoon light and there was the additional illusion that I could see it holographically, that all sides of the bird were simultaneously visible, a not infrequent experience earlier in my life due to a cognitive disorder (usual inane football injury).

I had also botched up the fairly short hike, about five miles or so, by being inattentive to my topo, scrambling up an escarpment when there was an easier way around. In the rumply West a compass is deceptive without a topo map and ignoring the latter often means you bust your ass when a lower route would be simple. I was also thinking of J.M. enough that I was a little inattentive, though just on the edge of my consciousness I knew I was in first-rate western diamondback habitat. A scant moment later I heard a staccato whir from a rock jumble and leapt sideways despite my heavy pack. It was a big sucker and without the leap my left leg would have been in range. I stood there admiring his irritability—some are relatively passive—then moved on.

I made camp about five and promptly fell asleep for several hours which told me I was becoming ill. I usually make a wide circle to study my location, noting its peculiarities, its geology and flora, the possible fauna, but this time I flopped on a bench formation on the hillside, stared down at the green and turbulent Niobrara for a few minutes and fell asleep with distorted dreams of a haggard J.M. and my adoptive mother making martinis from a gallon of discolored vodka.

It was nearly dark when I built a fire and fried myself a bacon and onion sandwich, adding a handful of peppery watercress I'd plucked from the cowboy's spring, but was only able to eat a few bites. I added a few green boughs for a smudge fire to discourage the overwhelming mosquitoes, cursing my ineptness for not camping well up the hill. Now, to be frank, I felt like fresh dogshit and the sight of thunderclouds in the west meant that I should set up my small tent when I much preferred sleeping in the wide open due to acute claustrophobia. More on that later, if ever; phobias are pathetically explicable but still hard to cure.

In the smoky firelight I almost regretted my impulse to see J.M., partly because my dick was so raw I couldn't sleep on my stomach, my accustomed position, and in part because I could feel my rising fever, my aching skin and joints. It was as good a place as any to have flu, the usual Nebraska euphemism. The sound of the river far below me became dizzying and my mind made colors of the surge of the water through riffles, the subsiding in eddies, the regathering of force as the river narrowed going into a bend.

Around midnight I checked my temperature which was just short of a hundred and three and the tent had become suffocating with sweat stinging my eyes. I crawled out and stood under a quarter moon with a whippoorwill's music coming from downstream. Not even Mozart could do that, the loon either. The last thundercloud was disappearing east and I was burning up and half enjoying it. Like my singular, youthful peyote trip it wasn't something you would bother futilely resisting. Then there were two coyotes and the whippoorwill again. They are intrigued and often respond to each other. Now my scalp ached more than my dick and I told the mosquitoes gathered on my skin to enjoy themselves. Only the soles of my feet felt good in the cool dew on the grass.

It was then that I lay down naked on the grass facing east. The cold grass was delicious on my hot back and I studied the constellations which were luridly brilliant this far from any ambient light. The stars were glossy, and the Milky Way was a milky broad belt across the sky. For the first time, no doubt due to my enfevered state, I felt palpably that I was moving rather than the stars, not the less startling for being true. Time closed down shop. It went away. I felt the earth moving ever so gently beneath my spine. There was a specific vertigo but I couldn't very well stop the earth from moving, could I?

The next day was negatively memorable. I couldn't keep water down for long, much less food. The breeze clocked down to the southwest and it became very warm and muggy. I was forced into my tent to get out of the sun but I left the flaps wide open to avoid any sense of confinement. Among my sparse collection of heroes is Loren Eiseley and he said, "At night one must sustain reality without help." This can also be true of noon, I thought. I kept recalling a minor spate of food poisoning I had while camped south of Deming, New Mexico. I'm rarely ever ill and Ralph had been extremely upset to the point that he had nosed into my sleeping bag in the middle of the night when I was cold and shivering from dehydration though well short, as now, of wanting the company of my mother.

In my fever I couldn't quite glue the several weeks together since Ralph's disappearance. Now I shed tears, conscious of delaying just as I had with my father five years before. He died at his desk from an aneurysm in Omaha and I dutifully came home for a couple of weeks from the east end of Canyon de Chelly in Arizona. I returned to my *lair*, as I call a number of places, and it was a full month after his death before its import struck me and I was able to roll around in the dirt and weep.

Ralph's absence began to overwhelm me there in the hot tent, partly because so often in the past I had set up the selfsame tent to shade him from the sun, his dark coat too absorbent of the heat. He was a marvelous coward and on hikes would bark, then scoot around behind me at any sign of danger, real or imagined. Several times on especially long hikes he'd balk and lay down and I'd have to carry his fifty-pound weight over my shoulder. I knew the odds were against it but if the truck thief had released him and he had been taken in by someone he could possibly be quite happy as long as he was fed by three in the afternoon. He wouldn't tolerate waiting past three for his grub. This loneliness for my dog welled up in my throat along with the half gallon of water I had just drunk. Tears and vomit. What could be added but blood? The memory of a lost dog was so clear and strong compared to a lost mother whom had been idly imagined dozens of times. Our dreams seem able to invent new people but it was no more than that.

I wandered clumsily down the steep hill to the river, sliding once on my ass a dozen feet, the fevered state making a joke of my coordination. I slipped into a coolish eddy grabbing a protruding tree root for security. It was sobering enough to let me notice a kingfisher flying downstream not all that far above my head. He landed on a branch and chattered at my intrusion. I pulled myself out of the river and crawled and scrambled back up to the tent. Before I slept it occurred to me I was at the end of a line, the nature of which I wasn't quite sure.

I awoke a bit after four A.M., an hour or so before first light, having slept nearly fifteen hours. I thought I heard Ralph bark but it was the yip of a coyote across the Niobrara. My stomach felt peeled but the nausea had passed and I wondered idly what I could have to eat that was harmless. There was a slight breeze from the west but enough to drive away the mosquitoes as I built a campfire. I glanced off at the setting moon and wished that J.M. were there with me, then tried to accept the fact that it was an unlikely idea. When the coals were right I cooked up rice and tea, thinking my gut wasn't quite ready for coffee, and dozed again. Now the coyotes across the river were in full chase and the yips had become a chorus, something I normally would have noted in my journal. I wondered when the disappointment would arrive over my missing journals but then doubted it would happen. I recalled that the last entry was campsite number 403 south of Ajo, Arizona, where I had somewhat shamefully followed my mother, then thought better of it when she turned back west on a two-track into the Cabeza Prieta. Up until that point I had convinced myself that I was simply overseeing her drive home from Santa Monica to Nebraska in her somewhat battered Subaru, an eccentric vehicle for someone who came from a moneyed background. It occurred to me well before I gave up the chase that her old car was a pleasant character point.

While drinking my tea and eating the rice I looked down the hill and saw a long-billed avocet wading on a reedy shallow flat in the first fuzzy light of dawn with mist curling around its spindly legs. I reached involuntarily for a missing journal and laughed for the first time in days. Our names are hoaxes! Agreed-upon sounds. That's it. Christian names, Muslim names, Buddhist names. I imagined my boxes of journals along a Sonoran roadside where they had been tossed having been thought worthless. No emotions arose. They represented an irrational human phenology: arrivals, departures, latitudes, longitudes, place names, fauna, flora, weather, an endless stream of thoughts wandering over the locations of nine years and questions about books being read, snippets of overheard conversations, descriptions of people met, the occasional woman bedded, infatuations, supposed wisdom, discarded ideas, word sketches of landscapes, clumsy geologies (never cared for the science), musings about my private and somewhat incoherent religion.

But it was my name itself that caused the sore belly laugh in the mental clarity of dehydration and an enforced two-day fast, a kind of *trip* in its own right. And after some snooping and research I found myself with two complete names which are worth exactly any slip of paper they might be written on. The long-dead patriarch of one family, dying, in fact, a few months or so after my birth, insists on giving me a legal name even though I, as a one-day-old infant, was passed on to an adoptive mother. My parents, properly enough, gave me their own invention, but this is neither here nor there within the absurdity of names.

Inside each journal cover in the upper left-hand corner is my name and my mother's phone number in Omaha. The whole idea of the journal came from my father one April when I finally and totally quit the university as a senior. There was a small item of violence, or so they called it. I tipped over a professor's desk, hopefully on him, but he pushed his chair back in the nick of time. A paperweight supposedly worth one thousand dollars was shattered and I spent the night in the Lincoln jail having modestly resisted the arresting officers. My father and a junior member of the Omaha law firm of which he was a senior partner came over in the morning. The young lawyer was a mouthy hotshot while my father only dealt with corporate law. For my senior paper in anthropology I had surveyed coyote stories among Nebraska natives, especially the Ponca, the Pawnee and the Omahas; several of the latter I had known since I had been drummed out of the Boy Scouts at age thirteen when I had brought a rather drunk Omaha to a troop meeting. My adviser, a melancholy young assistant professor who soon thereafter went back to his own father's auto dealership in Texas, had told me that I'd get in trouble for doing something so unscientific as talking to actual Natives when there was ample research material available written by qualified people. To make a dreary story short, a senior professor insisted that I do the paper over or he'd flunk it. He actually sneeringly called me a *romantic humanist*. I lamely said that I was a mixed-blood Lakota (really only about thirty percent which means next to nothing), a fact I had insisted on discovering at age eighteen to the dismay of my adoptive parents. The professor was one of those pathetic souls whose life was devoted to trying to establish anthropology as a true science, perhaps out of jealousy for the grant money available to archeologists, or the purer sciences. He said that my genes had nothing to do with it and neither was the obvious emotion I was betraying. Since I had had straight A's in anthropology and wished to go on to graduate school it was time I learned *scientific* discipline which hadn't been *sullied* by emotion. For some reason it was the *sullied* that lit the fire and I found myself tipping over the desk. He shrieked *you little fool* but I wasn't so little or I wouldn't have been able to tip over the ponderous desk with its stacks of books, papers and mementos. Naturally he pressed charges and said I also threatened to pitch him out the window which I may have said but didn't recall.

To be frank, it was quite a mess, but a suitable end to an academic career that had been already disintegrating. Only a week before the event a Ph.D. candidate had seen me reading Loren Eiseley in the front corner of the Zoo Bar and made a lame joke about my hero being a *romantic humanist*. It was evidently the curse of the season and I had also been too direct on that occasion. Probably the word had gotten around that I needed a comeuppance. It all seems pathetically comic in retrospect. The senior professor wasn't mentally ready for a sharp young Omaha lawyer at a private hearing before a judge. He was accused of racism, ethnic slurs, academic fascism and whatever. I got off by paying for the antique paperweight.

But not with my father who was terribly embarrassed both by my behavior and that of the young lawyer. On the way out of the courthouse he apologized to the professor who had gone from the apoplectic to the merely flustered and sad. I watched them out of earshot and my father's decorum angered me because I still felt I was the wronged party. The young lawyer was nervous because he thought he might have gone too far in his zeal to win for the son of one of his bosses. And he certainly had, according to my father.

At lunch, to which the young lawyer wasn't invited, I tried to sink in the hard chair in shit-heel shame when he reminded me that when I had been filled in on my ethnic background a bit at age twelve, more fully at age eighteen and without the names of course, it was to be the final discussion of the matter, and certainly not to be used as a weapon against a "smug old fool but a learned man." Tipping over a desk was more disgusting than anything the professor had done to me, or so my father thought. I countered with the question of whether when someone is unfairly breaking your balls should you just go ahead and let them? We didn't make it through the impasse and maybe we never did. The lunch ended with "Now what are you going to do with your life?" He had liked the idea of graduate school as it ran soothingly counter to the various scrapes I had been involved in. I said I didn't know but would try to find out. He asked if I'd come home so we could talk it over at length and I said no. This hurt his feelings but I sensed waves of claustrophobia coming at me from every direction in the restaurant, actually a club for Lincoln's high and mighty, and I needed to get out of there. Of course I understood his disappointment with my blowing the whole thing up when I was ninety-five percent done with the work toward my degree. I stood up abruptly, we shook hands and I was out the door with no protest from him because he could see I was on the verge of a phobic attack. I didn't see him until seven months later at Christmas. I hit the road, free, pretty much white and twenty-one.

Nine years later what had seemed like a heart thumper, with me drenched with sweat running to my apartment, clumsily packing the truck and heading northwest, now has become quite comic. And I doubt I'll see a green-backed heron this far west, more than a little out of their range. That's the immediate problem, though a mere overlay to Ralph and the fact that I'm about seventy miles from my actual mother whom I saw walking past while I sat on a park bench on Ocean Park Boulevard in Santa Monica. She was attractive though she wore the loose bulky clothes that many attractive women wear to hide their attractiveness.

What my father was referring to about my *ethnic* background came about in an odd way. Back in the late sixties I was riding my bicycle around a slummish area of Omaha against parental wishes. I didn't mean to be contrary but it apparently was part of my nature. A warning against anything made that *thing* an interesting probability. I was helpless before my impulses at the time. Even J.M. said the other day that my so-called inner and outer child were the same. I said to cut that psychobabble shit out and she got teary. That's what I mean, she said, you only like nouns. Life can't just be nouns. Dog, earth, truck, birds, pussy. Am I just a pussy? I'd never thought about it quite this way before and it stopped me cold. That's what I meant about J.M. being more intelligent in an original way than she thinks she is. I can imagine her husband loathes many of her perceptions.

Anyway, I was riding my bicycle through this semi-slum and I stopped for a Popsicle at a small store and two Native Americans, probably Omahas, were standing out in front laughing at a fire hydrant. I was curious and went over to see what was so funny about this particular fire hydrant. They were ragged and smelled of sweat and my mother's sherry. One turned to me and said, "Go back to the rez, you little dickhead." That evening I asked my father what "rez" meant and he said "Indian reservation," and that possibly meant that one of the men laughing at the fire hydrant thought I was one of them or somehow connected. I should add that this wasn't a big deal at the time. Two of my classmate friends were also adopted and didn't make much of it. I was quite dark complected and my two sisters were tow-headed. My parents thought they were sterile when they adopted me but a couple of years later my mother had two daughters in two years which evidently happens sometimes when the parents relax.

The ethnic question came up comically while we were having our habitual Sunday dinner at the Happy Hollow Country Club (actual name!). Rather than our usual table we had to wait for a table right in front of a window because of another of my problems. A few months before while at a Boy Scout spring camp an older boy had given me a painful kick in the ass for not obeying orders and I had thumped on him. Boys are sensitive to age and a seventh grader is not supposed to beat up a ninth grader. A group of older boys got together and captured me after a chase through the woods. My punishment was a faux-Indian custom where they buried me with a supposedly hollow reed in my mouth. The reed wasn't hollow enough and by the time they dug me up I was bluish and went into convulsions. An ambulance came and I spent three days in the hospital. There was no permanent damage other than claustrophobia, a minor infirmity, and rather boringly one on one with the cause.

So my parents had to greatly enlarge the windows which looked out into our backyard, I had to sit near the door in the classroom, near the window at the country club, and the movies now were out except for a drive-in at the edge of the city which was splendidly tacky. But the Sunday dinner mudbath came about while my parents were gabbing with table-hopping friends and I told my sisters the fire hydrant story as if it were a scary mystery. Lucy, the youngest, shrieked, "That's why you get a better tan," and Marianne whispered, "This is just some more of your bullshit." Lucy prodded my parents who were startled and I had repeat the hydrant story. My parents were quite nervous and I was willing to drop the matter but that wasn't the inclination of my sisters who, no matter how often they were shushed, were experts at getting in digs. Lucy laughed too loudly, patted her mouth and went *woo-woo-woo* like a cartoon Indian. My mother reddened and grabbed Lucy's wrist, then my father spoke very softly which he always did when he wanted our total attention. Yes there was a *bit* of Indian in my background, maybe a quarter, but that was neither here nor there and he forbade us to talk about it again. Marianne who was a dog lover (she now has seven) said to me, patting my arm, "The very best dogs are mongrels." My mother ordered a second Bloody Mary in defiance of my father who thought one drink a day was quite enough.

Perhaps I was a blockhead or simply not very sensitive but I didn't think about it much again until my eighteenth birthday when my father took me for a ride for an hour or so up the Missouri. That's when he told me about the six hundred a month "the other people" had left for me, oddly worth about half as much now as it was twelve years ago. The money was a sore point to him as if it implied he wasn't a capable wage earner, or perhaps that there was a string tugging on the legality of his fatherhood, or maybe that his control which was anyway diminishing would disappear. He continued by saying that I had another name if I wished to know it and I think I consoled him a bit by answering that the name I already had was quite enough and since I'd grown up with it I couldn't imagine ever changing it. My first name, Nelse, was his own father's name, a man I had cared for deeply, a former game warden and unsuccessful farmer up in Minnesota who had died when I was fourteen.

He parked and we walked down a hill to a small park known as Adelle's Point after a girl from a prominent Omaha family who had drowned herself there over love back before World War I. (The name meant nothing to me then but certainly did after I did some research last winter.) It was humid and sprinkling and the mosquitoes along the Missouri swarmed in great blurry clouds. Along the banks there was the litter fishermen leave, worm containers and beer bottles, tangled birds' nests of monofilament, chunks of broken Styrofoam coolers. He said that while he knew I despised our fancy neighborhood, a vast understatement, he hoped that wouldn't keep me from coming home for a visit. I was too self-sunken at the moment to understand what he was saying: when I was graduating in a month I was leaving forever, first to Absarokee, Montana, for a summer job at the ranch of one of my mother's cousins, then in the fall to college. The son is leaving and can't wait to do so. The father understands this rationally but his emotions are a jumble. No more fishing trips, Saturday hikes, no more football or baseball games though the latter two had been out for quite a while. No more helping out with youthful legal blemishes that could be overcome due to political influence in Nebraska: a drunk-driving charge, marijuana possession, assault and battery (I was actually attacked by two servicemen from the Strategic Air Command base but the patriotic judge figured a conviction was less injurious to my record than theirs. All they were trying to do was to drag a doped-up girl I knew into a car outside a disco for a little fun).

We stood by the Missouri swatting at the mosquitoes and talking idly about the fact that mosquitoes never seemed to bother Grandpa who could manage a canoe standing up with a long paddle. Once while we were fishing up in the Quetico Superior area along the Canadian border he told us over the campfire about a Chippewa friend who was a flier. This was from his early game-warden days in the thirties. I was about ten during this fishing trip and was quite disturbed when it occurred to me that the Chippewa *flier* didn't use planes but simply flew his body around this wilderness, according to my grandpa who swigged at his pint of Guckenheimer. My father was amused by my discomfort but said "Nonsense" to reassure me that this was a fib. I wasn't sure while I stood by the Missouri, which in the seventies we had only begun to determine the weight of its filth. Grandpa was filtering off into the haze above the river and we had turned back toward the car when my father said that since I had turned eighteen I had the right to know more about my background. I said,

"No thank you" because one set of parents was quite enough at the time and the memory of my grandfather's marginal life was at that moment quite appealing.

I was wondering if this kind of truth about my life is no longer very interesting because it's not really the truth, or is the truth of a very limited sort. A girlfriend of mine in college called this *monkey brain*. She was appealing in an ethereal way and was raised by two bachelor uncles in Minneapolis who were not very appealing. They were preciously ascetic and wouldn't let me smoke in their house, worked as computer programmers during the day and were mostly involved in Buddhist activities after work. The uncles were bony faced and I suspected she would eventually become so. She took me to the local Zendo and I rather enjoyed sitting on a cushion (they call it a zafu) for nearly an hour in silence. She was pleased over this but I ruined it by saying that as an amateur naturalist I often sat still out in the boondocks a great deal longer. It's not the same thing, she said, and it probably isn't though I'm not sure what the difference is. In the natural world you don't think about anything while you're sitting there as it prevents you from being attentive to what's happening. She wouldn't make love at home but at a cheapish motel near the airport she hooted with an uncanny likeness to a barred owl though she didn't care for this comparison. We broke up because she wanted me to take a summer group trip with her and other Zen students to Japan, a country poorly suited for a claustrophobic. But then according to her I maintained this phobia because it suited my purposes, which probably it did and still does. I said you don't cure someone's fear of snakes by dropping them into a snake pit. She took this as an implication that Japan was a snake pit. She was just coming out of the shower when she said we were all through, giving me a gander at what I'd be missing. But then I rather like the monkey-brain notion to the effect that one part of our brain can't reliably observe another part. It's a nice idea except that *reliable* strikes me as an economic term, something like *stand on your own two feet*. Who wants to be reliable in this shitstorm? She left behind a pair of blue underpants as a memento, or out of forgetfulness, a perfect dinner napkin. I must add that a permanent memory of our affair came about in an odd way. The bald master of the Zendo in Minneapolis told us during his brief sermon not to try to change reality to suit the self. What a monstrous notion. It still comes up at least once a day along with the vision of her bare bottom when she stood on a chair to fix the venetian blinds in the motel.

Incomprehension can be pretty interesting. Once something can be seen from all sides, figured out, resolved, whether location or idea, it seems to lose its juice for me. Of course I frequently discover I've been shortsighted and have to go back for another examination. For instance I had some difficulty in the northern forests of Minnesota with my grandpa after being buried in the scouts (I can still smell that earth packed in my nose). I began to dread the closeness of the forest while I followed him and my father to our brook-trout creeks and beaver ponds. But the creeks and ponds themselves broke up the density of the woods and I would breathe more deeply and my nervous sweat would dry. This was only a tentative solution and I stayed away from northern Minnesota, Wisconsin and Michigan for a full decade until I had an absurd dream that I should walk the edges of the forests and either natural clearings or plains or abandoned farm areas. So I did, being without other instructions from the gods, like, get a good job.

Ralph's collar has a brass tag with my mother's Omaha phone number. Why has no one called? Does this mean he's been carted off to Sonora, destroyed by a dog catcher, is with a family with no phone or conscience, is with a family who loves him, or is plain dead in a weedy ditch? Ralph's name is less a hoax than our own because there's no real attachment. You could teach him his name was Bob in a day or so with proper treats. His favorites are beef jerky, fried fish skin and, for inscrutable reasons, marshmallows for which he will spin in a circle.

* * *

It's evening on the Niobrara and I've caught a rainbow trout to go with my rice and beans. I saw two kingfishers today on a mile hike and will be ready for a full day's outing at dawn. You can get quite a mental jolt from the recovery of even a short illness. I missed discovering the location of the kingfisher's nest in a hole in a claybank because of two questions J.M. had asked during a rest in the Garland woodlot. Did I still feel lucky that I met her during a nervous breakdown, hence available? Yes I did, but then I looked at her closely. Was I so obtuse that I didn't realize she was having a nervous breakdown?

The second question which quickly followed the first was whether I ever got tired of being so peculiar. I wanted to reply, "No, Mom," but sensed she was coming from a different slant than my mother so I said that I had spent a lot of time being reasonably invisible, or not sticking out like a sore thumb, a mediocre idiom, so that not that many people noticed that I was peculiar. I bet I'm not your first affair so someone sure as hell noticed, she said. I pondered this and said that she lived in an academic community which is obsessive about scrutiny. Why don't you write down a hundred of your peculiarities and I'll decide for myself from a simple farm girl's perspective, she said. A farm girl who was thrilled when I bought her the collected Octavio Paz, I said. She tweaked my balls for vengeance, then said that when she was a girl both pig nuts and bull nuts struck her as the silliest things in creation. Later on, she said, I added men's nuts though you're only my third set. It was neither here nor there if I believed her but I had to defend nuts though they are visually pathetic. A cunt is not exactly the *Mona Lisa*, I quipped lamely. But it is if you think about it, she replied so seriously that my brain spun. She stood up then, a child's-eye view of a naked aunt or mother, not bad at all. She shook a finger at me like a schoolmarm and demanded five peculiarities, if not a hundred, which she admitted might be giving too much of my heart to a virtual stranger.

I looked in my mind for something harmless with her sitting down on my lap facing me, and pretended that I was revealing dire secrets. Since I was nine, I said, and an erstwhile member of Junior

Audubon I've worn greenish clothes in summer, brown and dark yellow in the fall, black and white in the winter, pale green and light brown in spring. She whistled at this one and I explained that our leader, Miss Fetzer, was my first love, albeit rather homely, totally ordinary at nineteen but owning a luscious body. I would not dream of obeying my parents at the time but Miss Fetzer said these colors would help us blend into the natural settings. I told my mother this and since she loved to shop it was quickly accomplished. I still stick to the same regimen depending, of course, on where I am in North America (or Central).

"What happened to Miss Fetzer?" J.M. rearranged herself on my lap, feeling my arousal.

"Who knows?" I said, in that I didn't want to admit that I had tracked Miss Fetzer down to Wyoming where she was married to a game biologist for the Park Service. I was twenty-four at the time and cracking up, though that's an inadequate excuse but an adequate explanation. She was happily married and had eight-year-old twin boys. It took a week to seduce her after which she sucker-punched me in the nose, then left the motel room in Jackson Hole to get ice to help stop the bleeding. I still think of this as one of the more shameful items in my life because it plainly is.

"I tend to count the birds I see during a day and jot down the meaningless number before I sleep."

"That's no big deal. You're getting away with an easy one."

"I walked thirty hours in a row including a bright, cold moonlit night near Canyon de Chelly when I fully comprehended my father was dead and I wouldn't see him again. It was a long walk."

She felt my legs as if to check if this were possible, noting that the mention of death had an immediate wilting effect on my dick. We looked down at this peculiar organ and I rushed on.

"When I was twelve, that was in 1970 I think, I was leafing through my mother's *Vogue* for the underwear ads, which had a great effect on my pecker, and after I relieved myself I read an article by a writer named Bruce Chatwin on nomads. Parents are always so worried about the effect of pornography on their children that they forget the other stuff. Well, I read this article a dozen times with the help of the dictionary and *Britannica*. Much of it was fairly easy like, The best thing is to walk, or Drugs are vehicles for people who have forgotten how to walk. I didn't always obey the last one but it was a good reminder.

"What's peculiar about reading an article?"

I was irked enough that I began to wilt again. My heart actually beat faster as I explained that after reading the article I had discovered my mission in life which, simply enough, was to be a nomad. Chatwin even referred to children which struck home to me and I was able to quote a whole paragraph, not that hard when you've read something dozens of times when young. Think of the feeble-minded "be good" poems we had to memorize, the prayers, the banal songs, even the Pledge of Allegiance. "Children need paths to explore, to take bearings on the earth in which they live, as a navigator takes bearings on familiar landmarks. If we excavate the memories of childhood, we remember the paths first, things and people second—paths down the garden, the way to school, the way round the house, corridors through the bracken or long grass. Tracking the paths of animals was the first and most important element in the education of early man."

She became opaque as if carried away by the quote into a location invisible to me. She sighed and leaned back so far that we became disconnected but she seemed not to notice, and then she spoke. "I know what he means. The path around the back of the barn to where cow bones were. The path to the apple trees. The path to the vegetable garden. The path in the woodlot to the secret place I had with the neighbor girl. My dad who is pretty much a dipshit told me when I was a kid that if I was lost just follow a path. Well I got lost at a family reunion on a farm up near the river getting away from my boy cousins who were wagging their dinks at me and a girl cousin who just laughed. I ran for it and followed a path like my dad said but the path just led to the river. I was pissed off at both the river and my dad."

After hearing this I wondered at my ability to ignore the dimensions of other humans. It was only the barest beginning that she was an attractive female, that I saw her flexed butt in splits and my skull popped. Now what did I have here beside me? I picked a mosquito off her breast leaving a tiny blood smear. I resisted the pointless urge to locate us anthropologically drifting backward in time to mating primates. Licking faces and rumps. A shaft of sunlight grazing her shoulder. Her full lips open and the consensual sounds of language through teeth good at both bones and vegetables. A Cooper's hawk shot by a hundred yards behind her left shoulder.

"Is that four or five? I could use one more before we go," she said, glancing at her watch, her only adornment.

"Twice a year I stop at a big urban library and read the Sunday edition of the *New York Times* to see what the world thinks is happening to itself."

"Oh bullshit. You know very well that's not enough."

"It probably is. Didn't you do *current events* in school? It was repetitious."

"I don't want you to end with something that lame." Her fanny made a circular grinding movement and the whole business of talk had become a little abstract. I reached for her and she pushed back. "One more. But nothing dirty. I want something to think about tonight while I'm dancing. There's a convention of grain-elevator owners in town and I want to ignore their big, beaming faces."

"After my sophomore year I took a summer course in wetlands botany which turned out to be six weeks in a vast swamp helping a Ph.D. candidate collect plant specimens. It was at the Seney Wildlife Refuge on the Upper Peninsula of Michigan. Before we left I imagined the locale to be rolling hills with both hardwoods and pines broken by idyllic tamarack marshes. Instead, it was bug hell with about seventy of the hundred thousand acres mostly covered with water and mosquitoes and black flies blurring the air. We heard a wolf one night and our leader said it wasn't supposed to be there according to his information. We also saw a moose and he said the same thing. He was strictly a plant guy and rarely looked up from the ground. The local rangers of the refuge didn't care for him which pretty much cut us off from contact with others. There were eight of us counting the teacher and we were his Linnaean slaves. It had none of the grace of an archeological dig which, according to my major, was where I belonged but then the only one available to me was in Arkansas and I didn't want to go south in the summer. The following year I was on the Norden dig on the Niobrara, an archeological survey because the government was thinking of building a dam and it was totally wonderful. Anyway, the bugs were obnoxious and sometimes I'd just lay down in the water to avoid them, and the leader would say, 'Get serious or you'll flunk.' I made a call to my sister and had her mail a couple of Niobrara plants that I slipped in with my specimens to fuck up this creep. He sat there under a Coleman lamp in a state of confusion, glancing at me suspiciously. Of the seven students only two were girls, lumpish botany majors who seemed fond of each other. However these junior lesbians were wittier and more fun than the others and we formed our own little group. They both advised against my plan when I showed them my material, a dozen peyote buttons, small dried hallucinogenic cacti a friend from Albuquerque had wangled for me. As was my habit I slept outside a good hundred yards from the others who quartered in a nasty Quonset hut. The stars are the most soothing objects for the claustrophobe. Anyway, an hour before dawn I restarted my small campfire and gobbled up the peyote buttons, all of them which was a foolhardy dose, also nauseating. At daylight my voyage into the nonrational began and I still had the wit to put a few miles between myself and the others. I was actually eleven miles away when they found me just before dark."

I stopped then and watched J.M. draw on her undies and glance at her watch.

"Hurry up. What happened anyway? I never tripped so how would I know?" Something had made her irritable.

"Nothing much happened. I wandered around all day, in and out of the water. I ate some water weeds and vomited. I became a turtle for several hours at least. I got fairly close to a group of otters that were driving suckers into a reed bed and gobbling them down with choking sounds. I chewed on a piece of sucker left behind and three of them stared at me questioningly. Later I talked to a big fat bear out on a slender peninsula of a deeper lake. He was probably just trying to get back past me but I gurgled and babbled so that after he walked by he paused and listened carefully for a minute. I saw all animals and birds holographically, I mean all sides of them at once even from the top. I had had the experience before but never this intensely. It started after I had two concussions playing football in my sophomore year in high school. When a ranger found me I was just coming down from being a sandhill crane."

"Jesus H. Christ, that's peculiar." She French-kissed me and quickly finished dressing.

"Why were you pissed a minute ago?"

"I was jealous that you had enough money to go wandering around the country while I'm stuck in marriage and showing my butt to morons."

"Seven grand a year isn't much money. I bet you pay that much for your apartment in a year."

"Oh fuck you," she said, then blushed. "I can tell there's money somewhere in there. It's in your speech, your manners. Your hiking boots."

"I haven't taken any money from my family for nine years. I sleep outside and mostly cook for myself. If it's raining I sleep in the back of the truck. Why fault me for my birth? I was a foundling, a bastard who was adopted because two teenagers fucked. Why blame anyone for their parents? I've got two whole names and so do you. You want to get married?" That left me sucking wind as I had never said such a thing before.

"I don't want to get married. I'm already married. I'm just being a pissed-off kid. Why did I get married at nineteen? Maybe I'm a dumb shit and I have to accept that."

Dawn. A yellow day. I'm off as soon as I can see to walk. I forgot to tell J.M. about the marsh marigolds and swamp irises when I was weaving and floundering on peyote seeing the backside of the moon behind me in the first hour so that I was frightened and had to douse myself. When I came up from under the water a loon cried. Hard to tell her if she won't see me again. Who wants their life blown up? Not her. Keeps me from a seventy-mile trip to see the woman who conceived me, evidently at fifteen or so my mother said this spring.

I saw the kingfisher enter the hole below a sod overhang with protruding roots. An hour later she emerged during which time I entered my dreaded fugal state and a few tears fell. It was only the second time that year, the first while camped under a full moon down on the Seri coast of the Sea of Cortez near Desemboque. Sat up on a mountainside on a crunching shell midden and stared at the moonlight glimmering off the windy and rumpled water of the strait, and off the mountainous island of Tiburon itself. Eiseley came up again, saying, "At night one must sustain reality without help." But now my brain was welcome to wheel as convulsively as it wished because I wasn't leaving the thicket from which I could see the kingfisher emerge, if ever. This life is perhaps coming to an end. My brain began to clock the prospectors I'd met in the outback of the West in my search for a niche, the perfect lair, a peerless thicket, an ultimate hideout, so childish as I had lived my life so no one would look, trying to make up the soul's habitat as I go.

I glanced backward and saw a rare daylight badger well upwind and then he, she, hit my track and vamoosed down a gully in a blur. It sometimes is discouraging to be the eternal enemy. Speeding up with marsh wren's song from the sloughs off the flat of cattails. In a blowout on the hill across the river I glass reddish penstemon. My mother in the backyard kept saying, "What kind of bird is that?" but she couldn't remember a single one save the robin. "I guess that's my bird," she said. My sisters fled upstairs when she came home crying from the shrink. Willa who worked for us, a Latvian woman with thin chest and a huge butt, went into the pantry and closed the door. Why are you crying, I asked, curious rather than sympathetic. I think I was eleven and was eating a jar of strawberry jam. She said my doctor said I must quit drinking forever. Her mind doctor. I patted her sobbing back, jam on my Peterson opened to wrens. I kept a Polaroid photo of a naked girl on the brown thrasher page. The night before, sleeping as always in the backyard even before my suffocation, the stars sucked me up into the sky. Dad put his foot down when he woke me for school one morning and there was snow on my sleeping bag. So angry in his tight, white-pursed-lip way. She kept crying and I went into the pantry, where Willa just stood there, and poured a glass of vodka. I gave it to Mother and said, "Tell him to mind his own goddamned business." She really sobbed then and poured the vodka in the sink with me beside her, fumes rising into my nose. Whew. Isn't drinking better than crying, I asked. But I do both, she said.

The avocet again. Jesus I've become lousy at this and sometimes I cheat a little. I should quit. I asked my boss if I could do Northridge's and he said that quadrant is out for years to come. I said please make the inquiry for me anyway because I'm curious and he said okay but it's on your dime. I did an aerial reconnaissance with an osteopath named Hackshaw, of all odd names, who lives in Grand Island. I knew him in college and he thinks I'm enviously worthless. The owner's name is Naomi. She's my grandmother but won't know it. She teaches at a country school.

What I meant about prospectors is that they have the disease of secrets and I'm too much like that, or becoming so. They're alone so much as the nonromantic heroes of minerals they lose their peripheries and become self-babblers. I remember clearly having a beer with one in Fallon, Nevada, in a tavern where there were *fados* on the jukebox because the owner was second-generation Portuguese. To the somewhat wrenching love-and-death music I listened to a geezer named Mike talk about his *secret* mines that were going to *pay off big.* I ruined it a tad by asking him what he was going to do with all of the money. He said he was going to buy a big ship and pilot it through the Panama Canal where he had been stationed in the army from 1947 to 1949. Then he resumed his jawing about his hidden gold, sluices, screens, and the fact that they don't make shovels like the hundred-year-old Ames shovel he used to own. The bar owner sat down with us and teased Mike about his odor which resembled oily rags, then I bought Mike lunch which moistened his eyes and made me embarrassed. He implied that life was all in the digging. The owner played a truly remarkable Portuguese song called a *saudade* and the

voice of the singer, Cesara Ivora, was that of a vibrant ghost. At my
insistence we listened to the song three times so I could commit the
music to memory. *Saudade* means homesickness for a place, a woman,
an experience that can't be returned to. Perhaps more.

The kingfisher emerged. Victory in our time. Christmas on earth
(some poet said). I hiked on upstream making a slight jump for a bull
snake which has the coloration of a crotalid but is not poisonous. I've
heard that like king snakes bull snakes kill rattlers but am not sure. I
walk and walk, a round-trip of eleven hours, fording the river in
order to come back on the other side. Three kingfishers and nary a
green-backed heron though a single black-crowned night heron and
a bittern in which you see the remote connection between bird and
snake, almost as much as the profligate-shaped anhinga in the South,
certainly a winged reptile. Jesus, almost back to camp, and there's a
sora, plus a rare ferruginous hawk. In the last hour or so before dark
a few rain clouds and a light sprinkle enliven snipe, a dickcissel, a
redstart. Sitting still I see more but that's a compromise to checking
out varied habitat. Sardines and rice are penance. I'm getting the fuck
out of here though it's gorgeous. I'll call J.M. and tell her she owes
me five peculiarities and that I'll keep a weather eye out for passing
mailmen. Call mother and see if there's word about Ralph. My sisters don't call often to avoid instructions but she has forever dropped
that with me. I'll say to J.M., let's run away and ruin your life as my
own is impervious to any definition of ruin. You can't hit a moving
target and no one is aiming. I began packing up in the dark for early
departure, hoping that the stars wouldn't draw me upward, as they
often did for an involuntary flying expedition. My occasional sanity
problems are harmless but that wasn't always so. I dream too vividly
of the Omaha Indians well north of the city. I don't even like to tell
a piece of paper about them.

I hiked out double-time starting at dawn, glad to be back within my
body unlike on the trip in. Near a small alkaline lake I saw a huge
flock of crows and made a brief detour to determine the nature of their

gathering. No clue. Near a playa south of Wilcox, Arizona, there were thousands feeding on emerging salt-tolerant worms. Give me the Corvidae: ravens, crows, magpies, jays, opportunistic scavengers, whom I feel akin to as a mongrel. Look it all over and take what it gives you assuming you maintain the wit to recognize a gift.

I made the ranch in a couple of hours and the old gent had his help cook me breakfast. Steak and eggs and potatoes and a cold beer. He sat in his wheelchair with an afghan around him despite the warm morning. We chatted about his ranch, the birds, the Niobrara. He mentioned again that I reminded him of an old friend who died in the late fifties that he used to bird hunt with, then wondered if I'd like a few months' work come fall, the upshot being that he had trouble with poachers and trespassers. His regular hands were busy then with fall round-up. It wasn't so much that the outsiders shot up the game but that they had cut fences a few times and tore up some fragile pasture with their ORVs.

"You look tough enough," he said with a twinkle.

"Maybe at one time but I retired from it." I went ahead and told him about it when he raised his eyes questioningly. I had been camped over near Devils Tower in northeast Wyoming two years ago and returning to my site after a hike I discovered three natty rock climbers drinking up all my water supply. Two of them were embarrassed but the largest one merely said, "Tough shit." I was getting the best of him when one of the others hit me over the head with his walking stick and the big one booted me in the groin when I was down. That was enough for me. I didn't tell the old rancher that the head whack had more than rattled my composure and that between swollen nuts and jumbled lobes it took a while to recover.

"You just let it go? I doubt that," he prodded.

I looked at him closely, then figured he was a safe bet. "The next evening someone, possibly a Native American, built a campfire under the gas tank of their Volvo station wagon while they were singing folk songs with some ladies at another camp."

"Sounds fair to me," he said, trembling with laughter. By then I was looking at a curious landscape on the wall, an oil of bluish gray sky and prairie, half and half. It was rather eerie in its simplicity. He said he didn't care for art in general but the locale was a place he used to bird hunt with the friend who had done the painting. Then he said he needed a nap and I was free to use his phone and please stop by whenever I wished. He began to wheel off, then swiveled and asked if I needed money. I said, "No, sir. Thank you." He tipped his imaginary Stetson and left.

I had an immediate head-snapper while dialing the wall phone. I could see through the partially open door of the den and there above a littered roll-top desk was a photo of the ranch owner and "J. W. Northridge" with their English setters beside a Model A Ford raising whiskey pints and a brace of sharp-tailed grouse. Relative indeed. He didn't look so kindly, this man who helped raise the sixteen-year-old who released me into this life. Nowadays it wouldn't have happened at all, I thought, dialing my Omaha mother who sounded sprightly, a morning phenomenon. It was a bit much added to the photo but there was a note with a Green Valley return address saying that they had found the dog I had "abandoned" and had given him a nice home a month ago. Ralph's name was now "Sweetie" and he was accompanying them to their summer home near Port Townsend, Washington, until November. It had lately occurred to them that maybe the dog hadn't been abandoned because some people down the street in Green Valley, a retirement colony, were also from Omaha and told them the address on Ralph's collar was "well heeled." My mother thought this term antique and funny. She also said that the note's handwriting was "squiggly" as if written by a palsied old hand. I told her I'd get the address later as I had had some minor difficulties in the state of Washington and couldn't very well roam the Port Townsend area. Attentive cops notice roamers. Ralph a.k.a. *Sweetie* would have to wait for November though I was delighted he was alive. Last year I had taken up with a pleasant though neurotic woman in Seattle for a few days. She had a bunch of fine paintings in an otherwise modest apartment and I was simpleminded enough to drop one off outside of Bozeman, Montana, for her at one of those immense, absurd log cabins they're building in the West these days.

When she was arrested and made bail she was polite enough to write a warning note that they had been tracking her for months and I could possibly be implicated for the delivery of stolen goods. She was a desperately paranoid pot smoker and I wasn't, but however unlikely the possibility of arrest I certainly wasn't going to tempt it.

I then called J.M.'s number in Lincoln but got her ogre of a husband.

"This is Vernon Schultz. Regional Director of the 4-H. You know, Head, Heart, Hands and Health."

"We're having lunch," he said after a pause.

"I trust it's Nebraska beef. Could you put on the little woman? We used to call her Miss Blue Ribbon."

It was a minute before J.M. came on the phone and I felt a touch of hyperventilation. She was quick when she caught my voice, saying, "Sorry I can't see you and the gang, Vernon. I've got to work the next two nights."

"Do you want to see me?"

"I don't think so. I don't know. I got finals next week. Maybe. Maybe not." She whispered, then he bellowed in the background, "Lunch!" She had told me he's an awful cook but thinks of himself as inventive and beyond cookbooks.

"I love you," I said.

"Don't say that!" She hung up the phone.

On the long drive toward the southeast I had another spate of mind whirls, and there was the not infrequent temptation to give a week's time to the study of the human brain. Since one professor told me years back that I was a *Pleistocene holdover* maybe I should begin with primates. My aversion came from my mother's addiction to various therapies which she passed on to my sisters. My father was appalled at their frequent *overhauls*, as he called them, the cost equaling what would support a normal family and it seemed to come to nothing. She clearly thought of herself as too special for something simple like Alcoholics Anonymous about which I'm unsure.

I swerved for a gopher but heard the mortal thunk. And regret. There's the usual quarrel among ornithologists but it's commonly agreed that at least a hundred million birds die hitting windows every year. The evolutionary curve has been too slow to make windows comprehensible to them, somewhat like deer and car headlights. This wasn't the habitual needle in the eye and I wondered what I was still interested in with the poignancy of my feelings for J.M. My father told me in my early teens that I was saved from the problems of my mother and sisters by my "healthy interests," avoiding on his part any genetic assumptions since they are clearly impossible to deal with. Nature and nurture versus each other is a can of inextricable worms that raises all sorts of suppurating ethical and political questions. The simple fact back then was that I was obsessed with the world we haven't made: birds, mammals, botany, and I began getting a subscription to the *Journal of Plains Anthropology* when I was fifteen. Absurdly enough, I very early could chant out the whole expanded Linnaean hierarchy which I memorized while listening to the Rolling Stones: *kingdom phylum subphylum superclass class subclass infraclass cohort superorder order suborder infraorder superfamily family subfamily tribe subtribe genus subgenus species subspecies.*

So what? I can't see the virtue in studying the natural world, just that everybody should do it. It's the only world you're going to get as far as we know. You read up a bit then look at it closely. Why are people adverse to it? I'm not sure but suspect it's because it's not immediately functional in the economy. Of course my obsessions are mostly my obsessions. My parents' trump card of admonition used to be, "What if everyone were like you?" I wanted to say, "But they're not" or "What if everyone were like you?" but I never did. My dad's implicit politeness seeped into me and still is there in a slightly crazy form.

I stopped to watch a prairie falcon trying to stir up a meadowlark for lunch east of Brewster, still nagged at what I'm still interested in and whether this infatuation with J.M. would be a short phase. I've thought inanely that I'm impervious but ventilated, like a first-class raincoat. Also, that periods of doubt have kept me from going off deeper ends, such as becoming a guerrilla in any of a number of locations in the world. The fact that going off a deep end appears to be a requisite to doing anything of consequence in this life has not escaped me. My anthropology tells me in a pukey little whisper that I'm feeling a late mating urge, that my nine years of wandering around and looking things over were a ritual I had devised to frame reality, that the search for *secret places* was basically a primitive religious impulse. My mother's analyst who ran a tight ship would tell me briefly (I only stayed fifteen minutes) that my penchant for sleeping outdoors was totally caused by my phobia though I told him I did it a great deal before my near suffocation. My point was that I'd rather look at the moon and stars than a neutral ceiling.

My primary fuel for this wandering seemed to be simple curiosity. During my boyhood all late fall and winter my father would take me to the public library on Saturday mornings and at least once a month to a bookstore, both breeding a unilateral curiosity which isn't always a "blessing" (one of my mother's favorite words). Frankly, it was a grace note a few years back when I figured out I was quite ordinary, especially compared to all the creeps and flotsam I run into on the road, or to the all too normal folks whose lives are utterly blinded by the green of money and whose singular motive seems to be simple greed. As a formerly devout student of anthropology I can't say that I detect any connection between my modus operandi and blood or genes. Historically and in the present we've always had lots of wanderers in America. There's a sweet, vaguely scary feeling in disappearance.

I headed for the freeway south of Grand Island, something I usually avoid. Most of my driving is done by a dashboard-mounted compass as the freeways and the speed required to not be a pain in the ass to other drivers kills your attentiveness to the landscape. There was a memory jolt when I passed a sign for the Stuhr Pioneer Museum and Village, a fascinating place in that the way our grandparents lived has pretty much vanished. The jolt came when I thought of S.C., a girl who lived down the street from us. She was thin and if anything her parents were thinner. I only mention this because it's a rarity in Nebraska (I checked it out and Wisconsin and Missouri are also porcine states). S.C.'s mother had supposedly been a ballerina in Chicago but I had my doubts as my own mother's *art life* had only been of a year's total in New York and Paris. Anyway, S.C. had a flair for acting spooky and was precociously interested in witchcraft. On a field trip to the Stuhr in Grand Island for we so-called bright students when we were sophomores I sat next to S.C. because no one else ever would and I was quite sunken in my dad's sense of politeness, though I already had reservations about our first sex talk, "Treat every girl like your sisters." Despite my kindness S.C. liked to poke fun and mimic my formal speech which came from my reading in natural history and from my father who was a third-generation Swede. My mother occasionally mimicked him when she was drinking, one of the few things that pissed him off. S.C. liked to think of herself as quite naughty and had given me Henry Miller's *Tropic of Cancer* and *Tropic of Capricorn* which my sisters had swiped and turned over to my irate mother who threw them in the fireplace, saying "Don't make a beautiful thing dirty." Of course I bought fresh copies and was urged on to read them promptly, thinking, This guy is sure alive. In return I gave S.C. a copy of Clyde Kluckhohn's scholarly *Navaho Witchcraft*, a key book in my burgeoning interest in anthropology.

I had some distance from the material and S.C. didn't and the book put her over the edge for a period. Her haughty father stopped me on the street and told me not to give any more creepy books to his daughter. He was walking their Tibetan dog and wearing his sport coat over his shoulders with his arms not in the sleeves and a robin's-egg-blue ascot. I was irked and thought about crushing the skinny shitsucker. That night, a warm breezy September evening, S.C. snuck over through the backyards and I actually smelled her coming by the scent of the patchouli incense she used in her witchcraft rites. Now she was crying with rage because she'd been told her father gave me a tongue lashing. I consoled her by saying I didn't give a shit. She slipped into my sleeping bag without asking. She was the end of the line for any girl who made me feel turned on and she was distracting me from a meteor shower. I was, however, startled to discover that

her butt that looked too thin in clothes was what we called "nifty."
She said she had read a book about Oriental sex and I must say we
had quite a time, the first full-fledged *all the way* for both of us. After
quite a spell she whispered she had been able to seduce me by stealing one of my footprints, a technique she had read in *Navaho Witchcraft*. At the time I didn't doubt it because she was scarcely what my
friends called "boner material." We performed these essential services
for each other about once a month until we went off to college, she
to Bennington and me to a humbler place predicated by my bad
behavior. I had heard she was now married to a guru of some sort and
living in New Hampshire.

I began to feel a specific despair the closer I got to J.M. and Lincoln.
It was difficult to interpret her phone voice as encouraging no matter how confined the circumstances with hubby braying for his liver
or whatever. I was a half hour from town and it was still several hours
before she was due at the club so I pulled off an exit to a spot near
the West Fork of the Big Blue to perhaps watch birds and take a
snooze. There was a sudden impulse to head for Manitoba but I had
made quite the study of the insubstantiality of moods, the way they
float in and out of us from a thousand origins. My Zen girlfriend used
to say that we paint our own lives to which I replied that there are
lot of hands on the brush. This irked her and made her resemble more
closely her clenched-assed uncles, one of whom had lived in California and was quite relentless in his psychologisms and other silliness, so that once when I entered their house he said, "We are what
we eat and I smell a poisonous hamburger," to which I replied, stupidly of course, "We aren't what we shit, and if we didn't we'd weigh
thousands of pounds." In that company it was one of my best lead
balloons. After we broke up and just before she went to Japan I ran
into her at an environmental protest and she had shaved her head.
She teased me that her appearance made her look nonsexy which it,
in a curious way, didn't but rather more feminine. I was feeling sentimental and admitted I was the main hand on the brush as far as

painting my life, but then her new boyfriend emerged from the crowd and I was nonplussed to see that he looked like her uncles though he seemed very good humored.

Off the exit I slowed to a stop beside a sandy-haired young man in his twenties working on a decrepit Dodge with the hood up and grease to his elbows. He appeared to be dismantling the carburetor while his wife walked and dandled a plump baby in diapers and a girl about five was chasing dragonflies in the ditch. I asked if he needed help and he shouted a kind of liturgy. "No help! You can't help! I don't need help! No help!" It was harshly loony but I noted both the wife and daughter ignored his shouting as if accustomed to it. When he finished his chant he buried his face in his dirty hands and wouldn't peek out. There was a rose tattooed on his bicep rather than the usual snake, panther, bleeding dagger. I drove slowly past his wife who wore jeans and a soiled Coors T-shirt. She looked off at a cornfield but the baby smiled at me. The man had resembled so many you see holding cardboard signs saying, "Will work for food," but then they usually didn't have visible families, or were well past that juncture where the family is abandoned with relatives, if any. It struck me for the thousandth time that when you were on the move you noted the bottom third, at least a third it seemed had become social mutants and were scratching along as minimum-wage menial laborers and without any reliable way to get anyplace else for a fresh look; those in Washington who could help simply had never noticed these people, that there was something about the xenophobic power trance in politics that made them unable to extrapolate any other reality than the effort toward reelection. They were making a mighty effort to rigidify the society to protect the top, and the bottom third were being openly sacrificed.

I thought without humor that consciousness of others is a very big hand on the paintbrush besides your own unless you hide out in a toilet. I admit I was trying to focus on the family with the broken-down car to try to get rid of them. My father who instigated my journal writing in the first place so I wouldn't simply "drift" didn't much care for my social commentary when he read the first few years' worth.

The passages admittedly weren't very astute and came under *xeno-phobic highlights*, basically an anthro-oriented rundown of human behavior in a locale. He said I was too full of cynical "nay-saying" and I shouldn't write about people as if I were Jane Goodall writing about chimps.

I made my way into a thicket along the creek not quite fully prepared for memories of the other times I had sat in this thicket but not really giving a shit. The little girl chasing dragonflies while her father wailed tended to minimalize my interior quibbling. We are all trapped but some a great deal more than others, I thought, applying my mosquito dope and getting some painfully in my left eye. Jesus, pay attention. How limited am I and what limits me? I felt a rather startling wave of fear over the idea that J.M. would never again have anything to do with me. The fear was as palpable as when I was fish-ing the Bechler River in the southwest corner of Yellowstone, a breeze across the water covering my scent, and a grizzly had strolled by. My bowels trembled but he decided to ignore me and ambled on, the breeze rumpling the fur along his hump, the fur not really conceal-ing the vastness of his musculature. J.M. fading in the gathering twi-light may as well have been a grizzly. Would she be physically involved again in my personal phenology, my wanderings that were directed by bird migrations, available sunlight, the births and deaths of wild-flowers, the activities and movements and hibernations of mammals, or the slightest urge of curiosity while studying maps by flashlight, or at dawn, or while listening to the rain rattling off my pick-up camper, crawling toward my huge now missing map folder. J.M. hadn't so much rattled my cage (we are truly zoo inhabitants) but had tipped it over and she, along with Ralph, the flu, and my long-delayed in-tention of looking up my original mother, had derailed nearly nine years of habit. I had experienced three clinical depressions, one in high school and two in my nomadic life, and they all seemed to have their inception in a sense that I had worn out a way of being. Natu-rally I didn't seek *professional help* as the modern-living pages of news-papers call it. The main thing I noted at depression's core, which rather than red hot is more an ice sculpture, was that the brain grows

very tired of the accouterments of its zoo cage. High school and college students are obviously susceptible to depression (buzz term!)
because of lively hormones and the utterly repetitive strictures of their
existence which also pisses in the whiskey of them learning anything
durable. Some adapt, and some are strikingly less evolved and can't
quite wear the armor. They tend to be neither more nor less intelligent than the successful ones.

But later, on the road, seeking out those empty areas cartogra-
phers call *sleeping beauties*, during two enormous pratfalls, I had to
learn and relearn that my self-appointed nomad state wasn't enough.
You also had to be a mental nomad, and your curiosity had to stay as
lively as your movement. Ethnology can become as banal as sporting
events. The creatures you study lose their inherent dimensions. The
mind minimizes and codifies, and the journals become slack and
dreary. Before that point I try to anticipate and take a job however
menial, once as extreme as washing pots and pans in a Laramie,
Wyoming, restaurant which was soothing for a scant week. Hard
physical work was generally the best, whether bucking hay bales,
digging cement forms, or as a shovel man for contract archeologists
which was more in line with my training. You usually worked in
advance of the building of a highway or a gas line (the best as they
frequently traveled through uninhabited areas) to make sure that
nothing of archeological value was going to be destroyed, but the site
had to be awfully good to slow down commerce. Hard labor fatigues
the entire body except the mind which is allowed to rest from the
frittering endgames which precede depression. Of course there are
comic aspects. My mother once told me during her pre-dinner martini session that she hoped I wouldn't become an artist because life
was treacherous and artists were "sensitive plants." I was on the sofa
a few feet from her marking time before dinner by leafing through a
large pictorial botanical guide which she couldn't have noticed other
than subliminally. My sisters didn't look up from the carpet where
they were cheating each other at Scrabble. My father peeked at me
with a frown from behind his *New York Times*—he was a news junkie
and Omaha newspapers weren't enough. I had the clear choice of

baiting my mother about "sensitive plants" about which I was the family authority or deferring to my father whose frown meant he was anxious for the pot roast.

I was trapped in the thicket for longer than I wished for fear of driving back past the woebegone family. I looked in my wallet and found eighty bucks and last month's check. If they were still there I intended to pitch the cash out the window toward the woman and keep driving. I looked at a patch of burdock and milkweed, not very sensitive plants which I'd like to identify with: ubiquitous, homely in their plenitude. It's not very unique to set out to find out what you want to do with your life but then only find out clearly what you don't want to do. My fragility irked the shit out of me. One of the big problems about the so-called open road is that you don't get to wear a horse's blinders. The bird through the binoculars doesn't exclude what you saw on the way to the swamp, the crippled kid stacking firewood near the shabbiest of mobile homes. We waved at each other. Who knows if he's interested in my sentimentality? How much melancholy did I get from my father who got it from his diabetic mother who saw woe buried in the bluest of skies. Dad again. Not to speak of mother. When your mind races you see the speed at which your parents aged, somewhat less accurately in yourself, and you wonder why bother doing anything you don't want to. Not very pure and not very simple.

Lucky for me I was saved by an image of J.M's butt under my rain slicker and I recalled the sound of the rain on its oilcloth. Feet, ankles, knees, thighs. The image was more real than my sodden thicket, and the warbler right behind me whose voice I couldn't quite identify would vamoose the moment I moved. Had one land on my head in Canada and couldn't see that one either. Wish I could say a physical prayer to that bottom. I stood up abruptly to the disappeared warbler and my lower legs had gone to sleep so that I stumbled the first few steps out of the thicket.

* * *

My true father was a real piece of work, or so they say. This information kept rising to the surface no matter how hard I struggled to ignore it which, of course, encouraged its presence. Samuels, the retired
senior partner, told me that and a great deal more not long after my
father's death four years ago. Who would care to think about such a
thing? Samuels's knowledge, though, ended at my birth in Tucson
where I'd lost Ralph, of all places.

    I know a great deal but not very much. My chest swelled but I
couldn't get enough breath. When I reached my truck I thought I
might simply drown in personal bilge. Mixing creatures and plants
I could name thousands but there was an urge to take a ball bat to
my new truck parked there in the weeds. I had so much to get rid of
before I could function again without mixed bullshit. Breathe deeply.
Hike with a clear head. Chase the mysteries of the natural world with
my old intense curiosity and a light heart. If I had a journal I would
have been witless enough to write them down. I was going to see J.M.,
and then my mother in Omaha to ask her some questions. Then I
would go west and see my actual mother, and then in the fall I'd go
further west and find Ralph. This sort of planning was alien to my
nature but I could see no way out of it save falling into a petrifying
slump, something I was already verging on. One thing I'd noted over
and over about men my age in my lost journals was the sense of their
free-floating *pissed offness* which was still of indeterminate source to
me. And I was unlikely to find out by chanting my vocal tranquilizer
of hundreds of names of birds, flowers and other plants. My immediate solace as I neared the freeway was that my tormented family wasn't
there and I hoped to hell I wouldn't see them down the road.

She wasn't there. This had not occurred to me as a possibility. I stood
there like a feeb while the bouncer, a pleasant monster, repeated it
three times, then said, "You need a drink," and got me a whiskey.
The words "she's not here" were not quite comprehensible. I waited
for Lolly, J.M.'s friend, to finish her routine and her name gave me a
boot backward into prehistory. Lolly. Jesus, not something you could

repeat ten times. The loner pops in out of the dark into darker. Lolly hurried over only to say that J.M. had abruptly decided to go home for a few days because her father was quite ill, giving me the slightest of winks to indicate the information was bogus in case the manager two tables away might overhear. Lolly made childish burbles with her straw and cola belying her outfit which nearly didn't exist, the tits that became pink eyes in my air-conditioned brain. I left so quickly she chased me to the door with J.M.'s farm phone number and two college boys yelled "Lucky dog" at me as I pushed through the door. Lucky ape looking for the hoped-for mate. What in fuck is love that hollows the chest thusly, and makes the brain stutter?

I found a motel on the east side of town and simply didn't give a shit about my claustrophobia as I sat down by the phone and mis-dialed twice, getting her mother, Doris (not her real name), on the third. It was late, she said, eleven o'clock, but there was a tease in her voice as she called J.M. to the phone. Her voice was too small and the laugh was quite shallow when she said that someone had told her husband about seeing her in my truck. He had thought it over for days, then this morning confronted her in the kitchen and she had said, "I was with my lover." He knocked her to the floor and now she had a black eye. Her mother wanted her to press charges but J.M. had said no. I found myself speaking in the monotone my father spoke in when he was angry. I said, "I'll take care of it." She said, "No, you fool, this is my door out. Don't go near him or you'll ruin it." She wouldn't see me the next day because she felt trembly but the day after would be fine. She gave instructions which I couldn't listen to carefully because my brain was humming, and then she said, "I'm just glad you called," and hung up.

I waited awhile to hang up as if pretending to further the con-versation. A professor once said that reality is when you peek through a keyhole and someone sneaks up behind you and kicks you in the balls. The room began to get smaller as I knew it would. Sometimes I slept out in a woodlot near the Lincoln dump when the wind was right. Nearby was a large skeet range where I won money in college. My father quit pheasant hunting after a partner kicked a bird dog so hard it had to be put down. I was pleased not to be there as I doubt if I could have been constrained. A jungle gym had been installed in the backyard to rid me of excess energy and though I was only fifteen at the time I'm sure I would have pounded on the jerk. Anyway the wind through the window was from the southwest which made the dump woodlot out of the question and the ambient city light made the stars hard to watch.

Quite suddenly I was interested in how small the room would get. The sweat had begun to pop from my skull. J.M. could have certainly helped me get through it but then she was a hundred and fifty miles away. When I thought of her butt the room began to resume its shape. I had been mildly vertiginous but had cured myself over a few days of cliff standing near Moab, Utah. There were ants near my feet and the deer in the valley straight below me looked like ants. My Zen girl's uncle told me there was a sect in northern Japan that stood on cliff edges to keep *attentive,* the only interesting thing this bald dickhead ever said. Jesus, being irked shrunk the room radically and made breathing difficult. I felt like a not very smart mammal that had fallen through the ice, survived, but spent a life being terrified of lakes. I tried the television for thirty seconds but that made it worse. I'm worthless at television and movies and have to avoid them because there's too much movement. It jangles me.

If you watch television near a window you note that life doesn't move all that much outside unless you're near a highway or crowded city street. You keep making subliminal primate adjustments to all that fast action on television and end up with a scrambled mind that takes a while to regather itself. Your accomplishment is that you've quite literally killed time. Movies are a bit different. About twice a year when I get the urge to see one I call my sisters for a consensus. They are sophisticates who follow the work of certain directors. However, the movies replayed on television are too small and you can't get all the way into the screen where you belong.

Bed. Front windows looking out onto an overlighted parking lot. Toilet and shower room. Sink area. Desk. Luggage rack. Closet with folding door. A print of freaky-deaky ibises by someone who has never looked at one closely. It's squeezing closer to a locked shed. The air is burned spaghetti from the restaurant vent next door. Bible by Gideon in the bedstand drawer. Since the room is physically obtuse and can't move a micrometer I'm going to deal with it. I'm not covered by dirt in a ludicrous ritual. I sit down at the desk and try to draw a picture of J.M. but it looks more like the head of a bluestem pricklepoppy, a flower I've sketched in my journal. Why bother as I can shut my eyes and see her? She is beside the truck, fully clothed, showing me how high she can jump.

Out of fear I wrote down the names of two women, one seventeen and one thirty, that had brought me closest to this condition before. How had I messed up my other approaches to love that had at least a portion of this energy? Everything is not my fault. I've been told that this attitude is as hopelessly self-sunken as to think you're right on every occasion.

All I really seem to have is consciousness. This ordinary possession will have to be enough to win out over a bullshit phobia, though indeed I've used it to my advantage. My ears and sinuses begin to clear and my head stops humming. The mild hyperventilation stops. This is a start. L.G.'s hands were always chapped. She was the daughter of my hero, my mentor, my high school biology teacher who had been a POW in Korea. She was the middle of five children. Her parents were from Chicago and thought to be politically radical, members of the Dorothy Day's Catholic Workers Party though the mother was Jewish. My mentor was also versed in history and literature, rare for a science teacher. He was so brilliant and his students did so well when they moved on to college that his politics were overlooked by the community. He was treated by the powers that be as a harmless and beneficial oddity like a cranky beloved poet on a college campus tolerated because, though he was somewhat beyond their ken, there was a suspicion that his unorthodoxy held something of value.

L.G. was so intense it unnerved all other young men though she was thought to be attractive. She dressed more poorly on purpose than her parents were. I loved her in my senior year of high school though she didn't love me, not a unique story. She thought my mother's sta-

tion wagon vulgar and certainly wouldn't have gotten in my father's
Lincoln Town Car (a partner's cousin was a dealer and the firm got
discounts). I had wrecked my old Jeep for the third time on a weekend trip to the Sandhills to see the aftermath of a blizzard, saddened
that it had missed Omaha. L.G. once had gotten arrested for demonstrating against nuclear arms outside the fence at SAC headquarters.
She was alone and twelve at the time. I admired her guts with fervor
but she didn't love me. At her house we ladled out goulash from a
pot on the stove, moving sprawled books on the kitchen table for a
place to eat. Everyone talked at once. She only tolerated my company for a couple of months. I asked her to the prom and she laughed
directly in my face so I didn't go either. I got drunk, took speed and
smoked pot with some other malcontents the night of the prom and
slept in L.G.'s yard. It got down to the mid-thirties that night
and her dad retrieved me at dawn when he let out the dog. The dog
peed on me which became a family joke. Even I thought it was funny.
She said she loved my bird and botanical mind though she thought
anthropology had warped me. She read Virgil to me in Latin and
St. John Perse in French. She was at all times a captious pain in the
ass. She told me her secret love was our black football star and he
liked her but didn't want to mess up his life with a white girl. She
was bitter about this but accepted it with understanding. I don't mean
she was harder on others than on herself. She was hard on everything,
right down to slamming doors, and scrubbing the linoleum in their
kitchen. I made love to her once—I can't say she made love to me—
and that was when I returned from Absarokee, Montana, just before
we both went off to college. She was a National Merit scholar and
had a full ride to Northwestern near Chicago, her father's alma mater.
We ate a pizza and went to a pathetic movie. I felt squirrelly in the
theatre and left halfway through, walking down to the Missouri on a
hot late-summer evening. The Jeep had been repaired but I was to
get my graduation pick-up the next day. When I returned she was
looking at one of my bird guides with a flashlight. She glanced up
from the book and said she was ready to make love. I had long since
given up the idea in despair and was dumbfounded. We drove north

a half hour until we reached a suitable two-track in a cornfield near the river. I was so jittery I almost failed, not that she was much help. It's impossible in a Jeep so I spread out a not very clean blanket which she decided unworthy so we leaned against a fender. She tugged at me too firmly and I told her to ease up, then I couldn't get it in. She even said, "We're going to get it in if it's the last thing we do." It was apparent to me that she didn't want to go off to college in a virginal state. I tried to go down on her, something I had read about but hadn't done, but she screeched, "Nothing doing." She didn't have any lotion in her purse but settled on Chap Stick, working on my dick as if she held a crayon, with strokes which were a bit harsh. This made me come off all over the place but I stayed firm enough, and we settled down on the blanket for a while until she actually cried out "Uncle." We both laughed hard at this so the evening ended without melancholy for her though I was a mud puddle of yearning. In the Jeep she checked herself out for anything that might be noticed by her brothers and sisters or parents. It was very erotic under the beam of the flashlight as she wiped her thighs with tissue. I wanted to continue but she said, "Are you kidding?" so we drove home.

I slept an hour in my clothes having decided the plug-ugly room wasn't going to crush me, but then awoke with a sweaty jerk after a dream about a Ponca from whom I'd gathered a few coyote stories, an *informant* they call them. I still felt bad about the whole experience though not for the professor's reasons. I was an arrogant young pissant collecting wonderful stories in exchange for two bottles of Boone's Farm wine. We met three times on successive days, though on the third he mostly gave me the Ponca names for a couple of dozen birds I'd seen at the Bazil wetlands nearby. He had warmed up when he learned that rather than using the local motel I had merely flopped on a hill in a sleeping bag. He asked me twice in a teasing way if I had a little *skin* in me which I denied (you'd scarcely admit to a Ponca your smidgen of Sioux if you wanted information). He'd tweak the hairs sprouting from a wen on his chin and try to pass off a story on how Coyote learned to play hockey on the frozen Missouri. It was as if I was gathering stories from an absolute alien in our culture when it was we who were aliens. I took him to a small cafe in the town of Niobrara where he ate three orders of deep-fried chicken gizzards admitting he hadn't had much to eat in a couple of days. I was nervous when a large smirking cowboy approached but he only offered twenty bucks if my informant would trap the raccoons that were bothering his wife's garden.

Of course the point is that he shouldn't have told me shit but then he was first of all a friendly human being with a breathtaking sense of humor. I think at last count in my absent journals I had encountered at least a single member of thirty-seven different tribes. I never wrote much about them, probably out of the modesty my dad passed on to me. The bookstores are chock full of serious treatises on human behavior, including that of Natives. I'm discounting self-help trash. After quite a bit of exposure to Natives, though, the scholarly texts I had read as a student and the quasi-serious books I had read afterward didn't seem to jibe accurately with my experiences. I clumsily accounted for this by thinking that though the books may have represented a lot of field work they were written elsewhere, say in a college town or in Washington, D.C., where people, no matter how fresh to the job, are only in touch with themselves.

Power and money rule the level of discourse and no other considerations are seriously considered. But I could read K. Basso on Apaches and confirm it in my own wanderings because he still hung out in the area. How can anyone else, including me, present definitive conclusions without being fluent in the primary language on which the Native sense of reality is based? This all began to be quite funny in the shit-sucking beige motel room with its moving walls and ceiling. It isn't always better to run for it, I chided myself. What's the point in pretending you know more than you do? I couldn't seem to bear down on this life I was living but was lost in the arena of vague intentions. There was no question that losing Ralph had something to do with this not-very-free-floating anxiety about making some solid moves. I even began to miss the flea markets, fairs, rodeos, the diners I regularly visited until about a year ago, or the evening I stopped without irony at a Nazarene church to check out an event billed as

Puppets for Jesus. It is fascinating how people will grasp at figments that assure eternal life. On a seven-day solo hike you occasionally have to remind yourself you're part of the human species no matter how many of the avian and mammalian species you've seen that could very well have reminded you.

It's after three A.M. and I'm feeling stupid. Oh, J.M., why don't you wake up and give me a call? It's no fun feeling dumb when the most consistent reassurance of your life is that you're intelligent. I note that this feeling lowered the ceiling a foot and consequently sweat emerged on my forehead. It was a full hour before I would hear the first birds. Carla, not her real name, always reminded me of a canyon wren, no doubt the musicality of her voice which contrasted oddly with her straight-razor wit. I saw her twice at a Mexican restaurant in Espanola, N.M., with her three-year-old son who was remarkable as the piggiest young eater in creation. She looked Chicano with a few other things mixed in, slender, quite attractive but not overwhelmingly so. She was much more sedately dressed than others of her background and the waitresses deferred to her, picking up her son's mess with smiles. It piqued my interest that she was reading a psychology text, a subject I could fairly describe as my bête noire. The next time I saw her in the restaurant I was at an adjoining table and her son threw a piece of tamale which landed near my plate. I smiled and said "thank you" and he screeched, reaching to have it back, his eyes glittering with anger. I brought it over and he quickly threw it again while I stood there, leaving a splotch of red chili sauce in the middle of my shirt. Carla dabbed a napkin in a glass of water and tried to wipe it off. She said that I had a nice hard tummy and I said thank you, then she tried to offer five bucks to get my shirt cleaned which I refused. She grabbed her son's arm as he prepared another toss. He howled and I quacked like a duck which pleased him. She checked her watch and left in a hurry. Two days later while I was still camped near Bandelier—I like the irony that a gorgeous old ruin was so close to the atomic arms factory at Los Alamos—I drove over to the Puye Cliff Dwellings and there she was sitting in the shade of a boulder reading the same text. She acted pleased to see me and

the boy was thrilled with Ralph who, unlike many dogs, adored children. She wore the kind of loose-hemmed shorts so that when she
was sitting you could look down into a fine stretch of underthigh.
My ears seemed to buzz. It's not all that odd that under a blast of lust,
the furze, the stubble of culture, utterly disappears except as a convenience to get you where you're trying to go. Could I invent chatter
that would make her fuck me?

No, it was evidently for other reasons. She asked enough questions so that it was an interview, or a real-life supplement to the psychology text. How we will grovel before a fine butt and thighs, getting
our brains slammed and bruised like young antelope with their first
surge of desire. It is so nakedly silly but still somehow poignant to see
our feet turn into hooves. I answered all the personal-history questions and she looked into the back of my pick-up camper. The little
boy joined Ralph in some dog kibble. Carla regarded my neatly
stacked camping gear, my food chest, my small library, my sea chest
of clothing with a cold eye. Meanwhile, I hastily leafed through her
textbook which dealt with abnormal psychology, a true barrel of symp-
tomatic worms. She said in her musical voice that I obviously verged
on being a sociopath, also an anal-compulsive loner, blah, blah, blah.
I said, "Oh, fuck you," which she accepted as a possible suggestion.
She then looked off at the grandeur of the scenery and said that it
was God's country. I said she was another xenophobic twit and that
I had been to at least a hundred places in the United States that the
misty-eyed locals described as God's country. She said with manic
anger, "Don't call me a twat," and I said, "Twit is not twat." I crawled
into the camper where her son now was sleeping using Ralph as a
pillow and got my dictionary. She was not totally pleased with *twit*
but gave me a hug. My hands slipped down a bit and she pushed me
away giving my crotch a deft tickle. She then gave me a woeful tale
that her son was actually fathered by her uncle! I was stunned. Her
brothers were dope criminals and would beat up anyone who cared
for her. She was escorted three days a week down to the university in
Albuquerque by an obnoxious bodyguard. If I wished to spend time
with her I'd have to be sneaky.

She had me follow her a few miles toward her house, stopping well down the road. I used my binoculars as she pointed out her mother's house at the bottom of a hill, a reasonably nice place with a few horses and a chicken pen, and then her own reddish brown adobe well up the hill. I couldn't come in the front way but there was a two-track off a county road behind the hill that would bring me within a few hundred yards of the house. I was to arrive just after dark and if the back-porch light was on the coast was clear. She gave me a peck good-bye and I drove around to the other side of the hill, found the two-track and did a hasty scouting foray on foot. It seemed simple enough so I drove back to my campsite and gave myself a good scrubbing in a creek, singing a little song to Ralph about how I was going to get laid and he wasn't. Ralph is particularly drawn to very large female dogs and is often punished when he tries to be flirtatious.

Anyway, the first night went splendidly and so did the second and third. I was in love and it was obvious that I had to rescue her from her evil family. She was frankly quite savage in her lovemaking and I began to wonder when I was going to get a rest. The house seemed peculiarly cultured for a narcotics family and a locked door led to her criminal brother's den, or so she said. My suspicions arose when she asked me to fetch her a tequila and soda with lime, and I hobbled out of bed to the kitchen. I found everything except the soda and opened a closet door, taking a bottle from a case there. I also noticed a stack of framed photos behind the broom, mop and dust mop. They were sideways and I tilted my head to see the top one, a gringo in a hard hat being handed an award from a man in a suit. I heard her bare feet padding up the hall toward the kitchen and quickly closed the door.

It was just after dawn and flies were already buzzing in the room and at the back-door screen when I got up to take a pee. It occurred to me that the house wasn't very secure for a drug lord. There was a simple hook for the screen door and the inside door had a loose knob and no dead bolt. Mixed in with the rooster's call from down the hill I also heard a canyon wren, an impeccable piece of music. It was very lucky that I had undressed in the living room because the sound of a pick-up roaring up the hill overwhelmed both rooster and wren. Carla screamed from the bedroom, "Run. He'll kill you,"and I did.

I stopped a hundred yards down the hill in a grove of scraggly juniper and hurriedly dressed. I had lost a sock and both feet were painfully bone bruised. I reached the truck and didn't stop until I made Albuquerque a couple of hours later, and by then had begun to wonder about the photo of the man in the hard hat in the kitchen closet. What else was in that stack of framed photos and what was really behind the locked den door her son had tugged at, screeching his lungs out? I still loved her but as a major league fibber myself I was beginning to think she hadn't been honest with me any more than I had been honest with her about my background. Since I had made extra money working for a contract archeology group up in Utah I checked out the Yellow Pages at a service station and stopped at a private detective who had a crisp little office in a shopping mall. I made up an elaborate story about an extortion attempt at which he yawned and asked for two hundred bucks in advance. I walked across the mall parking lot for breakfast and when I returned in an hour he gave me what he called the "goods." Real banal stuff: she wasn't enrolled locally but had graduated from the Las Cruces branch of New Mexico State University. She worked part-time as a legal secretary and her father was a respected loan officer at a local bank. She was married to a graduate of Texas A&M who was an oil geologist who spent a lot of time on the road. She had no brothers and neither she, her husband, or anyone in her family had any criminal record.

I sat there for a minute like a mound of ground beef with the detective concealing his amusement by arranging papers. He was trying to let me retain some pride. There was no charge beyond the original two-hundred-buck retainer. On the wall there was a reprint of the old White Rock beer calendar of a girl kneeling beside a spring with long hair and lovely breasts. I glanced at it overlong as if to stem the rush of blood in my face, the prickly embarrassment. I said thanks and rushed out, heading south for the Bosque del Apache where I watched birds from a camp stool for several days, the soles of my feet too bruised for hiking. Every time I put my feet down for a few steps

Carla arrived in my mind not all that pleasantly. It's probably been several hundred thousand years since we could run barefooted over rocky terrain.

At first light with sparrows walking in the bushes outside the window I took a shower and had a momentary touch of fear that J.M. might also be involved with disguises. I hoped I had accumulated enough knowledge about women to avoid a major pratfall. My dad always made a large item of learning from the valuable lessons that life taught us, but then he appeared to have a much less than total comprehension of my mother. Human beings make for confused lessons. At Carla's adobe there had been long shelves of mystery novels, the reading of which seems to make people's lives more interesting. I knew from watching the Corvidae, especially ravens, that boredom tended to create random behavior. When nothing is happening, make something happen.

What the fuck did I know, anyway, outside the natural world where my antennae are truly operative? This was getting quite tiresome and when I stopped at a diner for breakfast it hit me quite directly. I had some time to waste in that it was six A.M. and my mother was never functional before nine A.M. In the diner a group of codgers was listening to a replay of a presidential news conference about Irangate, as they called it. Over pale eggs and pathetic sausage I listened to the words falling on the air as if it were sprinkling dogshit. What I couldn't specifically figure out because of my failures of perception outside the natural world was why the language of both the president and the questioning reporters struck me as babble compared to Bartram, Thoreau, Beston or even *The Wind Birds* by the contemporary Matthiessen. I knew there had to be an obvious answer but I lacked any of the specifics. I strained to recall what a young English professor had said about Foucault, a Frenchman, and levels of discourse but I couldn't remember the main points other than power controls discourse. At the time it only meant to me that the environmental movement was screwed because they were forced to do their dealings in the language of the enemy camp, the government and developers. There was the idea while I concentrated on the edible fried potatoes that I might sit still for a few months and simply read which is hard to do on the road because of fatigued eyes. J.M. seemed to read widely and she could probably give me a hand in literature. When I reached a camping destination I stuck to reading up on the natural peculiarities of the area. I knew that when I was reading clumsy texts in any area I could see my skull at work, laboring over the words, but then with good stuff the skull disappeared and you read with your whole being.

Back in the truck there was a slightly desperate urge to lighten up, a possibility in the company of my mother if you weren't raised by her. When my sisters were around the three of them laughed a great deal but then I was described as the thorn in her flesh, a peculiar idiom from Saint Paul. After my younger sister learned I was only a stepbrother she became aggressively fond of me, including climbing into my bed naked. This was unnerving to the point that I installed an inside lock on my bedroom door. My parents noticed the way she mooned around me—she was thirteen and I was sixteen at the time—and took me aside for a discussion on the matter. My mother's mind doctor had described this as a *phase*, an expensive way to find out nothing. Anyway, my parents hoped I would treat the situation with adult good sense. We were driving north of town for our talk and while they were droning on I was pleased to see a rough-legged hawk, comparatively rare in the area, and I said that I had enough girls to fool around with without tampering with my obnoxious sister so don't worry. My dad fairly screeched off the road onto the shoulder and they turned to me with red, angry faces. I was thinking you can't win, and speedily assured them I didn't go *all the way* with my girlfriends and they seemed relieved.

I had never asked my mother why I had seen her necking with the assistant golf pro on the eleventh green early one morning. I was bird-watching in a nearby thicket with a friend who thought the whole thing very funny but then he was cynical because his parents were divorced. I told him not to tell anyone or I'd pound the living shit out of him. The selfsame assistant pro was later released for being a seducer, or so went the gossip. I don't think I was especially troubled at the time, age ten, but instead filed it under *incomprehensible* in my very young brain. Later, when she was trying to bully me, I was tempted to bring up the subject but my father had taught me politeness too strongly and I held back. At the moment I was inclined to think everyone on any given day is vulnerable to anything at all.

When I reached Omaha I pulled up at a dealership with a huge lot of new and used pick-ups. I spent a half hour wandering around, waving aside two different salesmen who approached. I didn't care for my own new truck, a gift from my mother after the other was stolen. The new one was insufficiently modest. It was garish and smelled of prosperity, plus I was only six hundred bucks ahead in the world and my tentative plans didn't leave time for earning any more. In a back row I found a green '82 Ford with a small yellow lightning stroke painted on each of the doors and was drawn to the daffiness of it. I beckoned a salesman who was tracking me and asked how much I could get for my new Chevy. I was treated like a nut case in the office when we talked it over with his boss. My papers looked clean to them and I could see greed beginning to seep in. They doubted my general reliability so I gave them the name and number of my father's law office partner, also my mother's home to let me know when it was all clear. I was losing a bunch but would have five grand to try to get J.M. to run off with me. We'd go find Ralph and whatever. Stop and see my actual mother. Go see the ocean. Camp in my favorite spot near the Seri Indians on the Sea of Cortez in Mexico. Climb trees. Go to Veracruz for the immense hawk migration. I had a fair amount left in my sister's care from a life insurance policy my dad left each of the three of us but it never seemed appropriate to touch it. My mother had a bunch before she married my father, including the home that came from her own mother. I suppose her family was technically rich. I have nothing against money except that it mitigates against leading an interesting life in my terms. I know my terms are limited but I've never known a rich person, including all of those I grew up with, who leads a life I could bear.

* * *

When I reached home the house looked a little smaller with the shrubbery larger as it always does when I return, usually once or twice a year. My mother's new housekeeper at first wouldn't let me in but I told her to check the photos in the den, which she did, then reappeared, squinting at me until I flashed my driver's license under her nose. She was a fine mixture of the servile and snarky and said that my mother was out for a morning walk with her boyfriend who I figured must be her art dealer pal, Derek. I had met him the year before and liked his gentle nastiness about the world. My mother had gone to New York City a number of times with him and the trips drew her out of the fairly long depressions she had experienced after my dad's sudden death.

I went up to my room, putting a sign on the door saying that I had been driving all night and to wake me at noon. Yet another fib, but then someone had to do something about reality. I opened the whole row of French windows that faced the garden, took off all my clothes and slumped to my bed, my mind buzzing like a june bug against a screen. Above me the ceiling was covered with my old astronomy charts and the walls were papered with bird, mammal and plant photos and posters. The only thing changed in my nine years of absence was a missing photo of Jane Birkin's bare bottom I had cut out of a magazine but that had been gone for several years, a victim of either my mother or a religious housekeeper. I never inquired though I missed what I thought of as the finest butt in creation.

I had to get up to open the closet door which was closed and I have to have it open, for what reason I'm not sure. Other than ancient suits and sport coats there was a rack holding fishing rods and several shotguns, both my own and my father's. The shotguns were Parkers he had bought in the early sixties before they got expensive. I went into the adjoining bathroom and took two aspirins, avoiding a glance in the mirror as counterproductive. I got back in bed almost praying for sleep. Just an hour, dear whomever. I stared at the jukebox in the far right-hand corner, not a big one but a jukebox nevertheless, and thought of playing a Charlie Parker tune, one of my dad's favorite musicians from back during law school, or so he said. The jukebox had an odd origin. By mid-year in the sixth grade my studies had fallen apart and my parents promised me a grand present if I got all A's which I did, and then I demanded a jukebox. They tried to hedge but came up with one, unsure of the reasons as even then I couldn't bear the radio or TV. I like live music if I'm way in the back or well off to the side for obvious reasons. I was drawn to the jukebox because you could stand there and watch the intricate way it worked. There was also a happy memory associated with a fishing trip up near Leech Lake, Minnesota, with my dad and grandpa. We were camping but it rained hard for two days so we moved into a tourist cabin near a tavern on a lake. We went to the tavern for dinner and ate hamburgers and delicious fried fish. It was a warm, muggy evening with great bolts of lightning above the lake and the whine of mosquitoes through the screen door. While we ate the tavern filled up with local people rather than tourists and everyone drank a lot including my dad and grandpa. My dad escorted me back to the tourist cabin then returned to the tavern. I waited a reasonable amount of time and then snuck back and watched through a side window along with several other kids, including a big plump girl who smelled of molasses and who kept hugging me. Now the jukebox was very loud and a lot of people were dancing and I was startled to see my father dancing with a blond woman with jiggly breasts. The molasses girl told me they were dancing the "schottische." I had never seen my father look so happy either before that evening or after. Even my grandpa danced, both alone and with a barmaid. In my nine-year-old mind I connected this happiness with the jukebox that had an orange and purple glow so that when my father's blond dance partner bent over it to select another tune it made her look very beautiful or so I thought at the time. Consequently I felt it was worth studying hard to bring a jukebox into the family.

I slept and dreamt consciously in my old bed, if that's possible, though I'd never researched the phenomenon. It had become almost a habit while camping out in some pretty odd places where the prospect of danger was quite real, thus my ceiling covered with man-made stars phased into actual stars including far too many comets and I thought the world was ending before I had a chance to see J.M. again. Even the clock on the wall whirled and I heard J.M. talking, guessing again that she had had a slight speech impediment as a child. What was she doing talking to my sisters Marianne and Lucy when she didn't know them and they were telling J.M. what was wrong with me using Spanish words I was unfamiliar with. I asked what the words meant and they said, "We're inventing these words so you won't know."

Of course with that I was wide awake blinking at my paper stars, and then my mother knocked, coming in with coffee. For a radical change I felt quite happy to see her. How in hell do we become something else, I thought, as she sat down nervously. She looked better than usual with a tinge of color in her face and her hands less shaky. She still spoke, though, in a dithery rush about news from my sisters, Lucy and Marianne, and why for God's sake did Marianne have seven dogs in the Kansas countryside. "Why not?" I answered and she moved on, looking away when she said an inquiry had come from someone representing my "biological mother" and that as a gentleman I should look the woman up out of common courtesy, a favorite phrase. "Biological mother" is a simplistic term if you think about all of the strings involved, including the umbilical. A man called from the auto dealership and why was I selling the truck she bought me a month or so ago? Too fancy, I said, it makes me a target for thieves. I didn't admit the lack of money which was the sorest of points, what with her wish to push it upon me as it had been pushed upon her without questioning the effects. Somehow she caught that I was fibbing again, perhaps because it was also a habit of her own. She still tells people I went to Macalester rather than University of Nebraska, but then both she and my dad went there as did her parents and this fragile continuity means something to her.

"How in God's name could you possibly think taking a little money would matter now?" she asked, looking up at my stars. "You're more set in your ways than the oldest person I know."

"I don't live on applesauce and cottage cheese. I prefer sardines."
She rolled her eyes at this because one year when I was in Costa Rica
and didn't make it home for Christmas she asked what I wanted over
the phone and I had said a case of sardines. It took me three months
to see a jaguar up near the Nicaraguan border.

"We used to pray every night you'd settle down."

"No you didn't." This prayer stuff was new. "But if you did now
and then it was an intrusion. Maybe I pray that I have the balls to
keep looking things over."

I could see she was on the verge of deciding to be offended by
"balls" and I regretted baiting her with it. What was the point anymore? Evidently I had reached a phase where some of my behavior
was becoming tiresome.

"I was thinking of getting eighty acres and eighty books I need
to read. And some cows. I'd build a three-sided cabin with an open
front."

"Why cows? You always said cows were destructive." She was
hesitant, not wanting to be tricked into believing me. She was referring to years ago when I was a little involved with an environmental
group in trying to get cattle off public land.

"I'm trying to be honest. I can't give up beef. After ten thousand cans I can't deal with sardines anymore." She actually believed
that at one point I had attended Michigan State to study cattle when
I'd actually only spent a month working in their research cattle barn
cleaning pens and stalls.

She unclenched a hand and stared at a piece of paper, recalling
what it was for, then said a nice-sounding young woman had called
me about an hour before. I fairly leapt from the bed in my skivvies
which made her titter as she left.

I don't recall a more difficult conversation in my life. It was by turns
endearing, angry, hesitant. She and her parents doubted if it was wise
if I came up the next day. In addition to an ugly black eye, an X-ray
had revealed a slight crack in the upper part of the cheekbone. Her

husband had called several times in apology and her father had
grabbed the phone and said if he called again he was driving to Lincoln with a shotgun to blow his fucking head off. Her mother was
worried over the idea that they couldn't afford a decent lawyer. I lied
then and said a close friend was the best divorce lawyer in Omaha
and would handle the matter free. This lightened her up and she asked
several times if it was so. Then her mother came on the phone and
expressed crisply her doubts about my visit. We compromised by my
agreeing to just stop by for an hour, and she said maybe two hours as
it was a long drive. J.M. came back on and I told her I loved her and
she didn't tell me to shut up. There was a long pause and a breathing
sigh and that was that.

I called my dad's friend and retired senior partner, Samuels, and
he told me to stop by and we'd discuss it, and that I was lucky I caught
him because he was going back to France in two days. It was utterly
against my nature to ask favors but then I'd never been against the
wall in quite this way before. Samuels was as close as I had to a godfather and had been involved in one of my "scrapes," my father's term,
when Lucy's doped-up musician boyfriend had beaten her up and my
father had been too overwrought to deal with it. I had called home
from Browning, Montana, near the Blackfoot Reservation, to get my
check sent only to have my sobbing mother tell me about the incident. I drove straight through to Omaha in thirty hours, found the
creep and demolished his guitar collection against his body. His
friends tried to interfere with one of them nicking me on the hip-
bone with a kitchen knife. A neighbor had called the cops and I resisted somewhat. Samuels got me exonerated as I had what the judge
called a justifiable cause in my sister's beating, plus had been knifed.
The fact that Lucy began seeing the guy again a few months later is
one of life's mysteries. Now she is apparently happily married to a
young State Department guy and lives in Maryland.

I walked the few blocks over to Samuels's home with the unpleasant sensation that the sidewalk was thin ice, but then sidewalks
are an infrequent experience for me. I was plainly wavering in the
face of a larger picture than I was accustomed to. You can convince

yourself that you're brilliant when you're by yourself, but then a few blocks in the old neighborhood bring on the same vertigo as a Utah cliff. The only tonic was in the humor implicit in the houses themselves. Big houses for people with real big principles, enacted to their satisfaction on the job, at the brokerage, church, country club, part of the current Republican trance that required of the poor only that they behave and keep out of the way of the money-making possibilities. The whole country had apparently become comfortable with the greed frenzy of its top one percent.

Samuels was not what I expected him to be. I had known him closely since childhood and always thought of him as my father's best friend. The year before, when I stopped to see him he had been strong and jaunty though he was in his mid-seventies, but now he was querulous and distant. Yes, he would arrange a divorce lawyer for J.M. but why had I fallen for a married woman? I was so disappointed in his response that I almost ran for it. He stared at me long and hard with his rheumy eyes, then quite suddenly admitted that his second wife, twenty years younger, was quite ill at a hospital in Lyons, France. He had only one more day to tidy up his affairs in Omaha and was getting out for good. This struck me as so improbable that I was unable to say anything. He had retired shortly after his first wife's death which took place the same year as my father's. She, like Samuels, had been a Francophile and was a close friend of the Frenchwoman he had married. His disappointment was so palpable in the air that I felt drawn to console him but was helpless to say anything. He shook his head to break his reverie, then abruptly told me that now that I was older I more closely resembled my relatives, which further put me off balance. I said that I was sorry he was having such a hard time of it, at which he finally smiled and said he doubted if anyone accurately foresaw what it was like to become old. He then asked about J.M's "character" and background and I talked about her a few minutes. He was suddenly afraid he'd forget my favor and called the law office, during which I scanned a few shelves of his library which had impressed me mightily when I was young. He poured two small glasses of brandy and smiled again saying I probably avoided liquor because of my mother but, properly used, it wasn't bad stuff. We drank and I was overwhelmed by his age and the way time had passed for both of us. Always a dapper man he looked critically at my clothes, then asked when I was going to stop acting like a poor boy, if ever. I said I didn't want anything to ever interfere with what I had hoped to do which had been basically an effort to understand the world, especially the natural world as I seemed to draw up short on human beings. He pondered this and poured us another brandy and I recalled I hadn't eaten yet and the first drink had already made my skin prickle. We clicked glasses and he said this was good-bye, and to go ahead and hang out with my goddamned peopleless nature as there were quite enough folks messing up the world. I nodded and then he searched for words coming up with the idea that if I married J.M. I should listen to her carefully as everyone was nearly deaf to each other but men tended to be deafer than women. I was amazed at this and got up to go. He stood and we shook hands and then he gave me a hug. I was overcome though it occurred to me again that wealth and power didn't mean shit except on a temporary basis. The question of why we had to grow old and die is an evident one to an amateur of natural history. Because everything does, including Aldebaran.

Back home I ate an unsightly mess of fried beef and scrambled eggs under the watchful eye of my mother who was amused at my booziness which she hadn't seen since I was a teenager. She mentioned the time my dad had been away in Kansas City on business and she had been called to the police station to pick me up whereupon I vomited in her new station wagon. This memory stopped me halfway through my lunch, though I remembered Samuels's admonition to listen carefully. She then said that she wondered why her children thought they were so special that they couldn't even give her a grandchild. I said I didn't know, went up to bed and slept for five hours, the solidest sleep I had had in the house since my teens. I reckoned that though I still might loathe the neighborhood it had somehow become disarmed and that over a decade later I was finally safe from its debilitating influence.

* * *

I awoke in a dank sludge from the brandy and lunch and entertained and rejected the notion of a city hike. Because of a toad dream I looked through my haphazard college journals until I found the record of a field trip I had taken for a term paper for an ornithology course taught by the famed Paul Johnsgard. Naturally I had to travel the furthest, a critical failing in my dad's view. Drink the most. Fight the hardest. Smoke the grandest joints. Bring a drunk Native to Boy Scouts. Chase the prettiest girls. Hit the most violently in football so that my brain became perhaps permanently rattled, all of which bores the piss out of me now. This can be filed under fatigue rather than wisdom.

Anyway, I was fascinated by goshawks and drove some twenty hours to a location in Michigan's Upper Peninsula, about thirty miles north of my ill-fated peyote summer session near Seney. There was a record of a local birder, Brody Block, having located a goshawk nest near a fairly dense riverine system that, however, abutted an open area of several thousand acres. My obsession had begun with an old article, found for me by a high school teacher, by Frank and John Craighead called "The Ecology of Raptor Predation." I only had had two scant and fleeting sightings of the goshawk, one near McLeod, Montana, and the other near Bear Butte, north of Sturgis in South Dakota. I bypassed a clot of dreary notes vis-à-vis latitude and longitude, local flora, weather, the nearby river severely ravaged when used to transport logs nearly a century before.

May 23, 1977. Maybe the best day ever? Started early after a miserably wet, cool night with a stiff wind NW off Lake Superior. Misdirected myself by forgetting the nature of the horseshoe bends of rivers so that I was nearly a mile off the next mark on my topo map. I was scrambling through an alder thicket into a small clearing when I was startled by the hind end of a large black bear (Ursus americanus) thrashing into another alder thicket just ahead. I had surprised him at toilet and there was a large steaming scat between two young aspens with the scat showing signs of fawn predation (white spotted chunk of brown fur). My eye was then caught by a movement a few feet away.

A largish garter snake (Thamnophis sirtalis) was swallowing a very large toad (Bufo americanus) with the toad's head and forelegs still protruding from the snake's mouth. I curled up with my eyes only a few inches away with the toad and I blinking at each other but the snake's eyes steadfast. I judged it a mortal predator attempt as the snake's jaws were cracked and bleeding profusely. A raccoon or coyote would certainly have a feast. Two hours of meandering later I came upon a red-tailed hawk (Buteo jamaicensis) carcass splayed on its back with the breast missing plumb in the center of a logging trail. The carcass had no sharp odor so was reasonably fresh. I guessed myself to be within a few hundred yards of the goshawk (Accipter gentilis) nest and clapped my hands to irritate it to the point it would make itself visible. It did so, a female, within seconds and I felt it necessary to drop to my hands and knees to save my scalp. I dodged into the shelter of a sugar plum bush and she made several passes at me with a loud *kek-kek-kek*. It was easy to see why this creature is the bane of grouse, rabbits or any other bird in its path.

Not included in the journal was a manic evening in a bar, driving my pick-up in a ditch, a short romance, running out of gas which entitled me to a ten-mile round-trip walk, sleeping with a protruding bare foot and waking to find it swollen with blackfly stings, eating damp bread and cold spaghetti out of a can. I knew even then that a real naturalist tended to be prudent, ruminative, disciplined and my own manic energies were better suited to anthropology though I proved to be a flop at that also. With the passing of years, and arriving at the not very ripe age of twenty-nine, it certainly occurred to me that the weight of mental idiosyncrasies will prevent me from having what the culture refers to as a profession. Until I met J.M. I wasn't upset at the prospect of carrying on my modus operandi until I dropped dead.

Derek (not his real name) cooked us an elaborate dinner, the likes of which I do not recall having had since I accompanied my mother to France for two weeks during my junior year of high school. The bribe was the Jeep I got for my sixteenth birthday as a trip to France with my mother would have been the end of their marriage, or so my father said. She was in her late forties at the time, a menopausal stage that included her heaviest drinking and a free-floating goofiness that tended to chase the whole family to their separate rooms which did not prevent her from knocking.

I had met Derek only once before and thought he was English and gay, though he turned out to be from New Hampshire and straight. So much for thinking you can discern the mystery of another's personality after a brief meeting while you were loading your truck with a case each of refried beans and sardines. This time I sat in the kitchen while he floated around preparing dinner and chatting with the irritating presumption that we were quite alike. He had spent the sixties in London so I wasn't really wrong on the accent. He meant that we were alike in that he had left his family for a decade because all of their presumptions about reality ran contrary to his own. This piqued my interest somewhat as I had made close observations while still in high school on how my parents, Lucy and Marianne each lived within quite different perceptions of reality. Derek had hoped to become a painter like Francis Bacon but ended up as an Omaha art dealer. He regarded this as quite a plunge in his aspirations but had accepted the limits of his artistic talent which he viewed as nonexistent after working hard in London for ten years. The only painting that survived in his care was a seascape done in a hurry on the ferry from England to St.-Malo in Brittany. His mother had stored a number of others in an attic in New Hampshire in the family home now lived in by his sister but he had no curiosity about them in that he could remember every square inch of each of the paintings and found the memory "flatulent."

We talked from seven until midnight, certainly a record for me since college. At first I felt a little simpleminded but we examined the feeling together. The core of his thinking was art and the art world while mine tended to be nature and the study and observation of the natural world, thus our discourse was structured by the character of what we knew. People are limited by their central obsessions, from which the nature of their language emerges, whether it is sports, raising cattle, the stock market, anthropology, art history or whatever. I added location, thinking of the xenophobia notes from the four hundred or so locales in my journals. It certainly wasn't a matter of states or their governments but fairly intact regions. Derek had assumed that television had leveled the differences but I insisted this was true only in the minds of television people. My mother was bored with this conversation so I rushed through a litany of distinct regional differences with some states such as Texas and California having at least a half dozen apiece. Derek wanted to hang onto the train of thought as he had limited himself to a specific class of art buyers in Omaha, memories of New Hampshire, New York City and Europe. My mother interrupted by asking of what practical use was my knowledge of four hundred locations and I said, "None whatsoever." Derek disagreed and said the main effort in life was to keep yourself from being braindead and visual images did the job as well as other considerations including natural history. This put me in a reflective trance and it occurred to me he was right and I said so. Everything was based at the start of experience by the senses all primates shared. Conclusions could come later. I gave the approximate latitude and longitude of Caborca in Sonora, meaningless data, and said Navajo know where they are by bowing to the six directions every dawn. I visually described the landscape, the flora and fauna, on an imaginary line from Caborca southwest to the Seri area south of El Desemboque on the Sea of Cortez. I even described visually some of the hundreds of plants used by the Seri in their enthnobotany. It was oddly hard work to think in strictly visual terms but for the first time I could imagine a shred of what it might be like to be an artist. My mother shyly said that she made visual squares or rectangles of everything interesting she saw and Derek leaned over and kissed her forehead.

The kiss was oddly uncomfortable for me. A man not my father kissing my mother! A lump formed in my throat as my mind saw J.M.'s bruised eye. I was now thirteen hours away from seeing her. I was further kicked off my feet when it turned out that Derek had known

Bruce Chatwin in England, the man who had written the nomad article that had helped fuel so much of my behavior. Derek also quoted William Blake, saying, "Still water breeds pestilence." I was pleased that I knew a Blake quote given me by a goofy ornithologist in Mississippi, "How do we know that every bird that cuts the airy way is an immense world of delight closed to our senses five." At least that's how I remembered it. Derek wanted me to go *deeper* about what I saw southwest of Caborca so I described the underbellies of dead scorpions, also a rattler run over on a gravel road, the lateral scaly lines and the one eye that still moved. I also described the three stomachs of a *corriente* cow I'd helped an old Mexican couple butcher, the cow so starved and scrawny that the tripe for menudo would be the best thing her death could offer. We rubbed the strips of tough meat with salt and crushed chiles and hung them up to dry in the sun and I got the idea that the old couple was mostly Papago (T'ohono Odom).

It was getting late and I didn't want to drink more wine so I led them out in the backyard and tried to teach them how to tell specific time by the star clock beneath the North Star, and near the pointer stars that lead to the Little Dipper. This twenty-four-hour clock, of course, runs counterclockwise. There was too much ambient light in Omaha for me to do a good job and I wondered what the fuck I was doing in a place you couldn't clearly see the stars and then I remembered. They both liked the idea of a clock running counterclockwise and the act of subtracting four minutes a day, but that was the limit of their interest other than that the star clock has only two days when it doesn't need this adjustment, September 2nd and March 4th.

It was a pretty good evening partly because it helped pass some of the time until I could see J.M. Near the end my mother reached for the brandy bottle and Derek said, "Ta-ta-ta" and took it from her. She only smiled and shrugged, a pleasant reaction. Derek said I probably talked about Mexico because he had served shrimp ceviche as a first course, and that our minds are limited to one thing leading to another unless we can mentally jump around like true intellectuals. The roasted striped bass with fennel should have reminded me of Italy but I had never been there. He was appalled at this but my one Euro-

pean trip had been the mostly cantankerous trip around France by
train with my mother to see what she called her "old haunts." I had
climbed Mont Ste.-Victoire near Aix-en-Provence while she spent
a hungover day in bed. At dinner she lectured me on Cézanne's painting of this mountain and I pissed her off by saying it was a successful
mountain far before Cézanne painted it.

I found myself hoping that Derek wouldn't stay overnight. Perhaps he sensed this and didn't. Of course, it would have been less
grievous than her kissing a golf pro. Before he left he delivered a ti-
rade I wish I could have taped though it verged on the incoherent. It
started with my mother telling a fib in her slurred, late-night Judy
Garland voice. She said my own sense of the injustice of life, which
she felt deeply for unknown reasons, had come about while I was in
the Peace Corps in Central America. I had spent time there but hadn't
made it past the first "psychological" interview for the Peace Corps
in Washington, D.C., when in a mood of irritation in an especially
small, dirty, green office I admitted an inclination for chasing pussy,
taking various forms of drugs, and the lost art of fist-fighting. It was
the close quarters that made me do it and the slightest mention of
the organization over the phone made me a member in my mother's
addled brain, which had at least showed a few signs of clearing up
during the evening.

Anyway, Derek chided my mother, saying justice had always
been an accident of birth and that democracy was no more than a
hoax for the bottom half of our population. The rich and the upper
middle class were now seething with resentment over protecting their
position and were demanding an enforceable mono-ethic which was
gradually turning the country into a fascist Disneyland. My mother
was still upset over this when Derek left so I gave her a warm hug
which she insisted was the first she could remember.

In the morning I tried to leave without calling my sisters which my
mother viewed as a duty every time I stopped by home. Lucy was easy.
I caught her at her Washington, D.C., office where she worked on

some sort of antipoverty program, a decided improvement over her music groupie period. I ineptly suggested that she have a baby at which I got an ear-burning lecture, including the fact that I as a hopeless *sociopath* should avoid giving advice. I unluckily got Marianne who lived near Lawrence, Kansas, with what I suspected was an honest-to-God girlfriend though my mother didn't have an inkling of this. I was on a roll so suggested a baby to Marianne which only drew forth a long silence, not counting barking dogs in the background. Finally she said, "Oh fuck you" and suggested if I finally was in the mood to help the family I could try to retrieve the two hundred grand that mother had lent to her art dealer buddy, adding details. This took my breath away and I lamely asked how? She said since I'd always been good at violence I could "threaten to drown the cocksucker." I said I didn't have time today but would think the project over.

After I picked up my green truck with the lightning strokes that didn't look as good as they had the morning before, I drove past Derek's gallery in an old, restored part of the city. I parked and sat there trying to think of where to store the five grand cash I'd gotten on my idiot truck deal, also what to do about Derek. I went into the gallery which was being watched over by a homely young woman with an excellent build that easily dispelled the homeliness. I fanned the five grand under her nose and said I'd buy a painting for my sister if she made me a cup of coffee. She went into the back and I stepped through the opening of an office cubicle on the side and made off with a big Rolodex that was perched on Derek's grand mahogany desk. The whole matter nauseated me but I thought the amount Marianne had mentioned was a high payment for companionship and that I might somehow correct the matter.

Ground zero. I'm early and take a stroll along the Elkhorn, avoiding a dense swale that looked tempting but then I wanted to appear presentable. A farmer sees me and slows his pick-up. Probably his land so I raise my binoculars to a distant raptor and the farmer picks up speed. Fat cows graze and I keep a wary eye on a holstein bull. For some reason dairy bulls tend to be more hostile than those from beef herds. I think of the farmer regarding my harmless pursuit of birds and how nature obsessives in hard-headed America are often referred to as *tree huggers*, or better yet, *prairie fairies*. One thinks in despair of the deeply imbedded theocratic notion that God gave us the land to scalp and destroy after the nasty business of exterminating the Natives, thus nature lovers are thought to be kooks.

My heart was eating my stomach this close to J.M. I can think of myself as generally a fine person but there have been too many big fuckups and I desperately didn't want this one to be included. Given the specifics of my background it was hard to present myself to parents as a golden opportunity for their daughter, though by some definitions I was one. All of my radical theories about money and my proven contempt for it were loosening under what anthro nitwits call the mating drive. As I circled back toward the truck there was also the discomfort and confusion of my twenty-four hours at the homeplace. I tried to dispel this by gazing at the lovely farm I was trespassing on. The tilled fields were set back far enough from the Elkhorn to allow a sizable riparian thicket. The pastures were judiciously grazed so there had been no invasion of weedy species like spotted knapweed. There was a pang from my early youth when for a few years my dad would haul me off to Sunday school at the Lutheran church. We little boys were taught by a gawky young railroad worker to pray for our heart's desires and I had prayed mightily that our family would move to a farm by a river in the country. Here it is, I thought, though I'd prefer to be further west.

When I got in my truck the farmer returned and pulled up alongside me, a real ham-armed grain-belt monster. I hurriedly fibbed that I thought I had seen a goshawk and, before he could say anything, I asked directions to J.M.'s parents' farm at which he smiled and pointed up the road. "Three miles," he said, waved and proceeded on.

If I had known what a gut-churner I was in for I would have delayed my visit but I never do. My premonitions have generally been inaccurate enough to totally ignore them and making my way slowly up their long drive I was experiencing what mammal students call displacement. Under threatening circumstances you yawn and pretend to be interested in something elsewhere.

J.M.'s ancestors had chosen a site on the wrong side of the road if indeed there had been a road then. Rather than the lush, fertile flatland along the Elkhorn they were on the other side in a rumpled landscape of hills and gullies, with rather makeshift patches of corn, oats and barley, a smallish dairy herd in a pasture adjoining the barn. There were two older Farmal tractors near a gray shed, a corn-picker in reasonably good shape, a thresher rusting in a lush patch of burdock.

The driveway curved around a tall grove of lilacs, a row of half-dead Lombardy poplars, and there they were sitting on the porch, the three of them, a small, terribly unhappy family. I parked next to a gray pick-up older than my own, a decrepit Subaru, and J.M.'s Mazda. From a hundred feet I could see J.M.'s plum-colored face, her father glaring straight ahead, her attractive mother staring down at her own lap.

I never made it past the porch. The lump in my throat grew as I approached them, and tears welled at J.M.'s appearance as she seemed to be looking just over my head and then her father reached out and put his hand on her arm as if to restrain her but maybe to comfort her. Her mother spoke in a low even voice, nailing my head to the air where I stood.

"You said you had a friend who was a lawyer. Well, he's not your friend. He works for this big firm in Omaha. I know about it. He says there's no charge. I want to know how and why you're paying for this. How is this any of your business?"

"I love your daughter," I croaked, not the voice I hoped for.

"You don't have a job. How do you aim to get by?" her father asked, leaning forward, drilling me with his eyes. "She had one asshole. She sure doesn't need another."

"I can get plenty of good jobs," I insisted though I'm sure it sounded lame.

"We want her to finish her education and that's that." Her mother got up and passed through the screen door, followed by her father who first glanced out and saw the yellow lightning bolts on my truck, shaking his head.

J.M. came down off the porch and walked out to my truck without looking at me. In addition to the purple and yellow hematoma she looked nearly haggard. I followed and when we reached the truck she allowed me to take her hand but turned away from a kiss.

"I want to kill him," I said.

"That's a goddamn stupid start if you want to see me again. Why did you lie about having a lawyer friend? It was embarrassing. Dad said you're just trying to get me to be your whore."

"Let's go get married now," I barely whispered.

"I'm already married. Fuck marriage for the time being. My husband came over this morning with his parents who drove all the way from Sioux City and Dad wouldn't let them out of the car."

A wet mongrel came up the driveway approaching J.M. apologetically. She stopped and began picking burrs off his coat.

"How are you paying for that lawyer?" She was insistent.

"It's just a guy from my dad's old office. It's only a favor."

"Am I supposed to think about spending my life riding around in a pick-up truck? I want to teach school."

"I've been thinking about settling down." I got down on my knees to help with the burrs but the dog turned and growled at me.

"Oh bullshit. When and where?" She was at least smiling now. "Did you think I'd run off with you today even if I wanted to? Maybe I want to but I'm not doing that to my parents. Give me some time to think things over. Write me letters, then come back and see me in a month. Do you write letters?"

I was stopped by that and tried to invent a fib which she read through and laughed. We looked up to see her mother coming toward us with a glass of lemonade which she handed to me.

"We're not rude people. This had been a hard time," she said, looking at her daughter for a clue of what may have transpired. J.M. dropped my hand and took her mother's which was clue enough and her mother had a trace of a smile.

"I'm sure it's been hard. It happened to my youngest sister." I left it at that, of course, not wanting to talk about my reaction in that incident.

She nodded and I gulped the lemonade. J.M. took the glass and said, "Keep in touch" and they walked back toward the house, pausing out of my earshot to talk about a flower bed. The dog stayed for a few moments as if to make sure I was leaving. When I got in the pick-up I gave my head a good crack forgetting the door jamb was lower than the new one I had traded in.

A scant hour down the road I'd rehearsed the scene a hundred times, a process so confusing I had headed in the wrong direction and had to double back to get Route 14 up through Verdigre to Niobrara, a small town near the confluence of the Niobrara River and the Missouri. I was slightly fearful because my head seemed a bit scrambled by the thunk it had taken and I couldn't quite isolate the pain at the base of my neck from the pain of seeing J.M. in that general condition. I became too confused to drive well and turned off on a small gravel road for a mile or two, parked, and walked off across a pasture to what looked like a consoling thicket.

Actually I sat down against a tree and wept. Why lie to myself? You're not obligated to be manly when you're alone. For a change I didn't even identify the tree I was leaning against. I was close enough that I thought I'd look up my old Ponca informant of ten years back who was only a half hour away. He wouldn't be as comforting as another Native friend, an Omaha who lived over near Bancroft, but then I didn't want to be comforted as much as I simply wanted to talk to someone not drowning in their own mental septic tank. My Ponca informant used to piss me off by asking me to identify a bird, tree or plant at which he'd yell, "Bullshit, that's not what it calls itself." But then I know he had talked to anthropologists a number of times before and delighted in confusing white people. Was everything food for words? What did I really have if I said "maple tree"?

My weeping stopped and I tried to rebuild my time with J.M. moment by moment from the periphery inward. By ordinary standards the house needed painting. Her father's forearms were scarred. Her mother's black hair was striking. The screen door had a tuft of cotton to keep away flies. The yard smelled of mint and ragweed, also milkweed. The lilac bushes were covered by dead brown blossoms. J.M.'s jeans had a hole in the left knee I wanted to kiss. She smelled like coffee. I didn't get to embrace her. Now I heard an oriole, a sweet sound for so small a feathered throat. How can I write letters when I never have except to Grandpa way back when. "May I come up there and live with you? I don't like it here. Everywhere you go are just houses. Your grandson, Nelse." That was when I was thirteen and had spent a summer with him after a friend and I tried to grow some marijuana plants. My sister told on us. All summer we dug a new foundation under their old cabin, raising it with hydraulic jacks, and laid new courses of cement blocks, then lowered the cabin. We fished for brook trout in streams, or for bass and pike in a lake every evening and sometimes early in the morning. My grandmother was sick and sat in a rocking chair in the yard and watched us. I also weeded her garden. She died the week before Thanksgiving and it was a cold white world when we all drove up to Minnesota for the funeral.

I picked up a couple of bottle of cheap, sweet wine in Verdigre and the clerk asked me if I was okay. I was honest and said probably not, that I had bashed my head on the door jamb of my pick-up. I was getting a few of those blank moments when the world stops and I don't quite recognize anything. That's what happened after the football injuries when I was *Nail* instead of Nelse.

Of course I had thought J.M. might sail off with me. I've noted that I have no control of the world beyond my skin. Here I am standing on the sidewalk in Verdigre on a hot afternoon struggling to focus reality. There's a pay phone fifty feet away and I remember I should call Derek and make my threat. I don't suppose my mother is actually rich though the cut-off there is uncertain. Maybe it's when you don't have to work to live well or what they think is well. My dad used to say, "Life is work." In my terms I can't say it did him much good. One trip through J.M.'s yard served to remind me that I don't know shit about money. A full tank of gas and a few hundred bucks and I was flush. I was bored with prosperity because that's how I grew up and it ran counter with anything I was interested in. So what? Others must be more bored with the struggle of poverty. I've watched it on the road a thousand times and it's not the same because they have no shield at all save religion. The prosperous have so many layers of shields that they're blind as human bats. Even their language excludes all other considerations except their own. I don't want to talk the language of the enemies of my heart.

I called Derek's gallery and got my coffee-making lady. Derek was very upset, she said, and I said tell him to give my mother back her money or I'd write everyone in his Rolodex and tell them he's a crook. She said, "That's awful," and I hung up.

I ended up visiting the grave of my Ponca informant. I know his sister remembered me but chose not to acknowledge it. She said she was a Christian and didn't want the wine so I left it at his grave which overlooked the Missouri where he told me the Poncas had devised the game of hockey. I stood there so long the afternoon sun moved a few inches, after which I headed west where I intended to talk to my true mother, the only thing left on my vaunted itinerary, other than buying some stationery.

Dear J.M.,

Encamped here at the confluence of the Keya Paha and Niobrara Rivers. Longitude 99 degrees, latitude 43 degrees, you're no doubt burning up to know. This isn't a great region for stationery but I bought a buck's worth from a motel lady, the paper older than either of us. Bide-a-Wee is a homespun place and if only you were along we would have stayed there rather than camped. Don't have a fire as I'm trespassing as usual and am not sure where the closest ranch house is. But I have moonlight, starlight and a flashlight, not to speak of the whine of mosquitoes, my true friends as they follow me everywhere in the USA. Tomorrow I hope to look up my birth mother or whatever she should be called, or at least her mother named Naomi on whose ranch I have permission to do a bird count. I am nervous about this whole thing but as you suggested I better get it out of the way. Naturally I hoped you'd run off with me and I'm trying to understand why you didn't. Maybe I can as I have proved that pressure is what I like the least. You said or thought I couldn't settle down but I'm sure I could for you in the right place.

Love, Nelse

I didn't say I was fine because I wasn't and could see she had small tolerance for my white lies, fibs and just plain lies. It was two A.M. by my star clock and I could only sleep in ten-minute increments before coming back to sweaty consciousness because of an orange light in my brain, deep red around the edges. It had been years since I had seen the orange light, the last time in Utah crawling under an overhanging boulder where there were signs of an ancient basket-weaver encampment. I stood up too fast catching my head on an overhang and then fell to my knees for a while. After I recovered enough to walk I made my way further down the canyon and through a crevice so narrow I had to take my pack off, as per the instructions of a free-floating grizzly bear lunatic I had met up in Montana who had also drawn a map for me of Seri country. Anyway I found the petroglyph under another vast, sheer overhang, and there it was, large wolf prints plus dancing creatures, half human and half crane, also snake squiggles, and a lone humpbacked flute player, Kokopele. I had a modest seizure and stayed there staring at the petroglyph until nearly twilight, too unstable to crawl back to the crevice to drink from my canteen. I was lucky enough to have a big moon for the long, perhaps two-hour, walk back to the truck over the smooth, lunar caprock.

A trace of orange now stayed with me when my eyes were open, a frame for the immense star clock above me. I thought hard about my old favorite anthropological writers, Mary Douglas and Loren Eiseley. If ritual is the framing of reality what am I doing now with bats fluttering between my body and the stars? Jesus. In Sarlat down in the Dordogne, my favorite place in France, I tried to go in the narrow caves to see the rock paintings but couldn't for the usual reasons, so settled for the museum while my mother was back in the hotel sleeping off her wine. At dinner she had been careful to only drink a single bottle out of which I had asked for a rare glass to irritate her, but that night from my adjoining room I heard a room-service waiter bring another. At the museum a very bright visiting Parisian told me I was in the area of the birthplace of the Occident. I was as impressed as a junior in high school could be, that is, I was knocked off my pins but didn't show it.

Jesus, again. I had a good twenty-minute doze with a dream of J.M. draped over my face laughing, then awoke to what I thought was an orange sob and it was actual lightning from a storm coming up fast from the west where the sky was a starless black lit by intermittent yellow light. Bullbats croaking. A poor-will upriver. Saved by nouns which J.M. teased me about, and the western sky split by lightning, closer now. This time I have my cocoon-shaped tarp with only my face clear to get wet.

The first drops of rain help questions fade, like will I resent slowing down, or better yet, if I don't believe in the reality of others what do I do when my own disappears? The answer comes when the rain beats down so hard I have to turn my face to the east. One Christmas afternoon before the aneurysm sent him into the void my dad said in anger during a snowy walk that if I wasn't careful I would disappear up my own asshole. Maybe so but nouns will be my savior. Or so I hope with lightning a vast strobe on a mile of river, the glow so strong tree and bush shadows are still crisply lighted despite the blur of rain.

Dawn. My nose near pokeweed (*Phytolacca americana!*) but I'm not sure it's supposed to be here. I saw a coral snake in pokeweed in Arkansas. Clouds still roiling low as if I were sleeping at altitude. I thought it was the day to see my brand-new grandmother but a brief look in the truck's outside mirror was homely indeed with an ugly lump partly emerging from hairline and eyes as red as a tertiary drunk's. A kingfisher. A heron. Common mergansers. Pied-billed grebe. A wild turkey up the hill a half mile away.

I made coffee with a gizmo machine powered by the cigarette lighter. Another gift from my mother, ordered from one of the three hundred and thirty three catalogs the mail brings her. I could ask, Where am I to go and what am I to do but then my effort has been to be at home anywhere, most of all a riverbank on a June dawn with nary a squeak from humankind in the air. Just birds and clouds.

I burned my tongue and spilled some hot coffee on my dick which betrayed cloud intelligence. My dad gave up on me well before he died. Not that he didn't love me but that he knew I wouldn't *pan out* as the gold-miner idiom goes. I could see the realization in his face one late evening around Christmastime when the overspiked eggnog had put my mother and sisters to bed early. He was reading my journals and, other than being mildly disturbed by what he figured out was the sexual code, he was fascinated by the southwest entries, an area he had never seen. What pissed in the whiskey that evening was a journal quote from my revered Mary Douglas, "The more that society is vested with power, the more it despises the organic processes on which it rests." Like any boy who came to full consciousness in the Great Depression my father was a devout believer in progress, but he still loved the memories of a simple, utterly basic life. Did Douglas mean that everything we deem natural was going to disappear under societal pressure? Of course, I said, probably too flippantly, adding that it certainly had in this house where the bathrooms are carpeted in white and the merest mention of sex is taboo. He said the old life is still everywhere, though he admitted mostly among the poor. Or in Mexico I added, but whatever is left is passing with your generation as a boy. You had a huge garden, chickens, three pigs and a steer for fall butchering. A lot of people who eat them now have never had any actual contact with a cow, chicken or pig. They're supermarket abstractions. Even when I was small you had a vegetable garden and now it's only flowers a black man comes in once a week to tend. I became too busy, he said, and I said, Maybe ignoring is equal in a way to despising. No it isn't, he said, I goddamn hate the way you despise the way we live. I don't really despise it so much as I simply don't want to live this way myself, I said, then added, You don't seem that happy yourself working seventy hours a week when I think mother already has some money. This struck home but was probably impolite. He said, I pay the bills around here and besides it's natural to want to be successful. I disagreed, at least for myself, and he implied that the exception proves the rule, a notion I find absurd. We were at an impasse where neither of us wanted to be. I wished that we were back when he asked me why there were three different kinds of quail in New Mexico while there was only one kind in Georgia. He abruptly poured a rare drink for us and asked why I didn't become a game warden like Grandpa had become in his thirties when he became tired of farming. This calmed us down for a short while and we laughed about how Grandpa had been reprimanded for punching out a man who had shot two bearcubs. I said I couldn't be a game warden because I probably would have gone further. This brought him up quite short and he gave me the briefest look as if it were occurring to him that I wasn't a blood relative after all.

We rushed to another subject and he asked with a smile if I'd think it was ludicrous if he started going back to the Lutheran church again which he had done rarely since I was a young boy. I said not at all. One thing I did learn in anthropology, I said, was that religion at the very least frames reality for we poor lost souls, not mentioning again the dread name of Mary Douglas. I also said our civilization is its own religion and that's why we're such a total mess. But we're not a mess, he said, it's the fact that you think it's a mess that makes your life so problematical.

I called Derek from Springview. He gave me a little lecture, doubtless rehearsed, about the dangers of blackmail, especially a lengthy jail term for a claustrophobe like myself. "I'm pleased you know my history but they'll never take me alive," I joked. He wanted me to say more but it's long since been a habit to let the other commit first.

Finally he allowed that he understood my motive in wanting to protect my mother but the loan had been freely offered. "By a pleasant
nitwit," I said, "no doubt under the influence." There was a longish
pause and then he offered to return half the loan assuming I FedExed
the Rolodex. I liked all the X's and said I might do so after a secretary in a real estate office finished xeroxing it so that I had a copy to
protect myself. He said that the other half was already invested in
paintings for resale and for me to call my mother who was outraged
at my behavior. "She always has been," I said, suddenly feeling that
if I did win the victory would be Pyrrhic. This caused a dose of despair and I suggested that I'd settle if he'd return three-quarters of
the money and from now on he could deal with my charming sister
Marianne. He had met her several times and said, "I'd rather not,"
and I answered, "I don't blame you" and hung up. I was sick of the
whole matter and a grocer helped me pack up the Rolodex for the
UPS pick-up even though it didn't entail an X. I imagined that
Marianne's main worry was that Mother was loaning money that
would otherwise eventually end up in her own pocket and I certainly
didn't give a shit about that. How much is enough?

I set up camp near the Niobrara south of Norden resolved to regain
my good appearance for my next day's meeting with my new grandma.
I even stretched out some clothes on a line to smooth the wrinkles.
The area was the scene of my greatest temporary happiness during
college and I felt a bit of heat in my ears over the fact that I had been
excommunicated from the project for causing "morale" problems. The
university had been engaged to do an exhaustive archeological survey of the area prefatory to the Army Corps of Engineers overseeing
the building of a large dam for the usual phony reasons of flood control, irrigation, recreation. Moving water offends the developer in
certain souls while lakes thrill them. It was the spring of my freshman year and I thought I was chosen for the crew because I had
straight A's, and was sturdy enough for hard outdoor work. I didn't

know at the time that I was the youngest member of the group because my father had interceded with the university president. This justifiably pissed off some of the professors and graduate students in charge. I think my dad only wanted to avoid the pratfall of the summer before when I had worked on the ranch of my mother's cousin and had sucker-punched the foreman for clubbing a horse. He was a big guy and I had to get the drop on him. I left in a hurry and roamed Montana for a month in my Jeep, neglecting to get in touch with my parents, and coming to a halt when I got in a tiff with a Yellowstone Park ranger for camping in an illegal place (I didn't realize to my later embarrassment that I was in an area of troublesome grizzlies).

But up at the Norden site I was still, a year later, an overly hormonal stripling, a bit quick to anger. I was relegated to the lowest job, a pure shovel man, though I knew quite a bit about the simple artifacts, including a number of buffalo-hide scrapers I improperly pocketed, thinking these might have been owned by some of my ancestors. The knowledgeable graduate students would walk up the river valley in front of me and stick in transact flags at likely sites. I would then dig until they decided if the site was worth further looking into. The digging was quite wonderful as I got to burn off the irritations a young man is heir to.

Unfortunately it rained hard for two days in a row and I was discovered having a love bout with the girlfriend of one the graduate students and this caused an argument. I was accused of smoking wild hemp I had gathered, also taking acid which wasn't true as my goofiness came from some quaaludes I had brought along. I drove over to Valentine with a couple of girls who were crew members, got drunk, and wrecked the vehicle. Luckily we weren't hurt other than some bruises but I was arrested for drunk driving. A local lawyer friend of my father's named Quigley got me out of jail and shipped me back to Omaha in a rancher's Piper Cub. I spent the rest of the summer on foot in Omaha working on a landscape crew, still behind a shovel but not happily as I had been up on the Niobrara. I felt a general navy blue shame but couldn't think of an adequate penance in my parents'

terms. My dad's probing question was how could I be at the same time
so dumb and so smart, while my mother made a project out of finding me an appropriate shrink. Of the three we tried the only one I
could deal with was a Jewish fellow from New York who was just starting out. He was hyperintelligent and seemed daffier than I was. We
only talked for three sessions but at the time he made me feel less
freakish though it was a disappointment when he said that he thought
my talents were more metaphorical than taxonomical, thus I was a
poor prospect for the sciences. Though I liked him I refused to go to
him any longer after he became too intrusive by asking what I seemed
to think was so virtuous about being an "outsider."

Fortunately they never built the dam at the Norden site. It wouldn't
have been a crime on the order of Glen Canyon but would have
constituted, nevertheless, a criminal act worthy of explosives. There
I go again, while sitting out the midday heat and planning an evening
hike. I've been glassing a buckskin across the river who fades in and
out of a willow thicket. He or she, I haven't determined yet if it's a
mare or gelding, wears a halter and I suspect it's a runaway as the
immediate area is fenceless. For the past hour there's been a miniature ice cube in my brain that says that rather than having gone too
far I haven't gone far enough. It's been months since my brain has
extended itself into one of those prolonged voyages into the bodies
of a mammal, a bird, the stars, a creek or river, even a wild field where
I could imagine everything that was happening upon myself. It's probably fear holding me back. But then I'd read enough on the subject,
perhaps too much, especially back in my anthropology days, to know
it's foolhardy in the sense that you are supposed to have a teacher,
and my own self-taught methods plus books are not quite enough.
Once while camped near Grassy Butte in western North Dakota I
spent the whole of a cool, blustery May afternoon being a goshawk
and had difficulty finding my actual body and reentering it. I slowed
down on these practices for a while after that because it is an all-or-

nothing proposition and I shied away from the final threshold. It's not wishy-washy spiritualism but a specifically physical process. Say you see a goshawk quartering into a stiff spring wind and the bird draws upon you. You sit still for an hour or so and empty out all your mental contents and then let your imagination enter the bird. It does so completely and you easily leave where you already were. For obvious reasons it's much more vertiginous than becoming a badger, a mammal I've always admired for its capacity to bury itself in minutes. Also, you can't get anywhere unless you truly know the nature of what you are entering. For instance, I've flunked on white-tailed deer, mountain lions and Cooper's hawks, because I don't know them as well as mule deer, bobcats or prairie falcons which have been notable successes.

Dear J.M.,

I'm sitting on a grassy bank on the south side of the Niobrara near Norden where I was a pain in the ass as a worker on an archeological site. My parents never thought I was very good at self-judgment but I've had some regrets. For instance, yesterday morning I didn't get to see your mare Vinnie you've talked about. I've also wanted to own a horse or two but have never stayed in one place long enough. Right now there's a loose buckskin across the river staring out of a dark thicket at me. I don't stare back because I don't want to make it feel uncomfortable.

Frankly my heart is way up in my throat and I seem to be feeding on it over what I'm going to do tomorrow morning. It's not so much the primitive but normal emotional stuff like, "Why was I given away?" Maybe it's a bit of that, but more so it's the idea that my view of the world and my life will alter. That can't help but happen. It's like one of those terrifyingly emotional Spanish poems you are fond of. I've somewhat avoided that sort of thing in favor of the natural world though it often has occurred to me that that's part of the natural world too. I remember in ninth grade English I was reprimanded after a teacher read a Keats poem for saying, "If that guy really means it we're in a whole lot of trouble." I only meant that if Keats's world is the real one then we're not living in it.

I miss you a lot and keep thinking of your gorgeous bare knee poking through your jeans. I could have used a whole lot more. Love, Nelse.

P.S. If we get hitched up I promise you horses, dogs, cats, and I will learn to endure your musical taste.

Before my late-afternoon hike I checked the truck mirror again and other than seeing I was improving I wondered at the actual connection of what we look like and what we are. I mean beyond my parents' usual insistence that the durable impression we make on others depends on our grooming and tailoring. My sisters kept watching the *Planet of the Apes* series with amazed delight though my mother would prattle at them that evolution wasn't a proven theory as if changing species care about our conclusions. In the same sense I couldn't draw any conclusions from the mirror or lift myself up off the ground to determine my mammalian density. Lift your dick slightly to avoid peeing on your pant leg. Human limitations were suddenly consoling. Perhaps I'm ten percent too fucking dumb to save my hide. I do know that one hour ago I ate the last mixture of sardines and rice in this life. The easiest eating move becomes sufficient. I'm dumping the contents of the remainder of the sardine case on a likely raccoon path by the river. It will be their first taste of a saltwater species.

I was a scant hundred yards into my hike when tears formed from an unlikely direction. I had come back from the Sandhills to visit my sister Marianne who was in a hospital clinic that treated bulimia and anorexia. I brought a fading mixed bouquet of wildflowers including violet wood sorrel, show peavine and spreading pasque flower. She was a senior in high school at the time, about five foot eight and down to less than ninety pounds. She refused to let my mother enter the room and only tolerated my father and Lucy for the briefest visits. I sat with her for a full three days and made a great effort to teach her how to tell the entire world to kiss her ass. This included refusing to go to Macalester, my mother's alma mater, and instead going to Stephens in Missouri where she could take her horses. Dogs and cats were taboo in our house because of my mother's nonimaginary allergies. By the third day I went out and got cheeseburgers and spaghetti which made her vomit but improved her morale. Her recovery was longish but she began to live a great deal more on her own terms. I didn't get blamed for her new rebelliousness because my parents preferred a live daughter and she had been going in the other direction.

I had supposed the tears came because it was the singular successful act in someone else's behalf in my life, certainly not counting beating up Lucy's boyfriend, or doling out my limited funds to other wanderers down on their luck. Instead, as I made my way down a deer path along the river, the tears increased and surrounded the idea that J.M. might finally say no to me. No to my existence in her life. I finally had to sit down and try to compose myself with the idea that she hadn't yet said no. Something underneath was arising and it was the somewhat blurred features of my real mother walking down the sidewalk of the Pacific side of Ocean Boulevard in Santa Monica. I couldn't quite accurately reconstruct her features. I didn't feel I could endure the sort of weeping collapse that had happened over my father's death when I was well up Canyon de Chelly flopping around under a crabapple tree.

At this sodden point I was lucky to hear far-off crows and stalked my way downriver toward the growing cacophony, moving up into the high-bank brush to conceal my approach. Crows are difficult to stalk unless they're quarreling, though less so than their Corvidae relatives the ravens. I was startled by what appeared to be a rattler but turned out to be a hognose which flopped over in a parody of death, their main defense other than their rattler appearance. I glassed down a rock and scrub-strewn bank to see the crows feeding between a closer patch of rice cut-grass and the river bulrush tight to the Niobrara. The prey looked to be a smallish mule deer that perhaps had stumbled on the steep slope while being chased by a coyote pack.

In any event the carcass had to be torn open by coyotes first in order for the crows to feed as they are unable to penetrate a deer's tough hide by themselves.

There were enough glances up the hill in my direction for me to know they knew I was here, doubtless alerted by the scout crow in a tall pine across the river. I pulled myself into a seated position and watched them bully each other noisily to be in the prime feeding place. It wasn't as quarrelsome as it could be because there was plenty to eat. For some reason Ralph hadn't liked crows and when they flew over he'd run in circles, his head craned straight up, barking, and frequently running into something.

I used to be a little nervous about this Sioux country. I'd made a foray northwest of here on a day off back during my archeological dig mudbath, driving from Wewela over to Keyapaha, up toward Mission, then on Route 18 west past Parmelee all the way to Pine Ridge. I had left at dawn in a mood of great enthusiasm, returning by nightfall with my brain clubbed to jelly by what I'd seen. I had read a great deal and should have known better but then I almost never do. The question in mind was, How could I think my less than a third blood had any meaningful connection to the people of the Rosebud and Pine Ridge? The poverty formed the main energy in this lesson of humiliation. How could this have been allowed in the United States? Easy, evidently, I was to learn as my road life progressed well off the main traveled routes and their deceptive prosperity.

Of course I was nineteen at the time, an age of intense vulnerability when the heart is usually either soaring or plummeting, or mine was anyway. You think you're meant to understand everything and when you don't you stew dankly in your own juices. But now, after a dozen or so trips into the area, I tend to think of genes as a scientific artificiality and my only connection to the original culture might be my nomad's life and my attention to the natural world. Growing up the way I did I probably had a solider relationship with photos of Marilyn Monroe. I was pleased after my father's death to find a nude photo of her in a locked desk drawer in the den. The enjoyment of this was leavened by an envelope bearing my name with a recent date.

I'm not sure, of course, if it was a premonition or an act of a doubting conscience. "Dear Nelse, Why not live the way you want to? What do any of us really know about how our children should live, short of trying to prevent them from ending up in prison. Keep an eye on your mother whom we both know doesn't have both oars in the water. Love, Dad."

I sat on the bank until it was nearly dark and the crows had long since disappeared weighted by full bellies with the soft flap of their wings fading in the twilight air. Among other things, I'd rehearsed my arrival at the Northridge place. I recalled that in the letter I'd asked my boss to write, tomorrow was the actual day so I'd been inadvertently right. I'd be strong and silent and let this Naomi do the talking. We'd spend two days on the bird survey and my new grandmother would doubtless introduce me to my mother and neither of them would have any idea of who I was. Whether I divulged this would be up to me and it would obviously depend on the emotional content of the meeting. Were they vaguely compatible? Were they intelligent? That sort of thing. Samuels had told me in his usual guarded, lawyerly way that they had some money and this was a strike against them to me, though he had added that they had never been "spenders." At the time he said this I thought I might look at these people as an anthropologist would a freshly discovered culture which I now realized was a fundamentally creepy attempt to build some armor around myself.

I made my way back carefully in the near dark to my campsite, my stomach fluttering with butterflies as if it were the eve of being shipped off to war. I'd thought about the insubstantiality of moods numberless times but there was no denying the real weight of this one. I mean especially the triggers of moods as thoughts and images arise in your brain: first mother, second one, Ralph, J.M. looming in the gathering night, before or after lunch when the brain is duller, shit-stained politics, overgrazed land, the first naked girl you saw other than your sisters, pointed out by her brother as you hid in the shrub-

bery and peeked in the window where she lay pinkly bare the hair
thatch twisting as she turned over on the bed, three days of cloud
cover interrupted by a flash of sunlight that primally lifts the spirit, a
new birdcall a blessed question mark in your ears. For instance, I look
up at the stars which are normally a friendly sight, but tonight they
look cold, remote, almost brutal, utterly inexplicable, and it will be
gentler to look at my pocket watch than to tell time by these alien
lights. I lie there talking to myself, adding mental words to each side
of the scale, trying to balance what I'm going to do in the morning.
If only I could nudge Ralph during his dog snores or calm him when
a noise would make him scramble to get into my sleeping bag but then
that wouldn't help tonight. J.M. alone could soothe my brain until
at least dawn but then neither of them are here except in spirit. And
maybe this mood of relentless talking to myself is schizophrenic. Who
am I talking to? I am my own cattle prod. The brilliant black graduate assistant liked to quote an Englishman named Laing who said,
"The mind of which we are unaware is aware of us." I remember this
because after ten years it still puzzles me, as much so as the fact of
stars. In Sonora while gazing at the clearest stars ever I put an old
palo verde log on my fire and black scorpions scooted out of the holes.
Oh to be for a while a scrawny bear in June feeding on beach peas
and wild strawberries, nosing the flowery air near the beach. Time is
a slug or snail tonight. Let's have a hearty smile from the stars so I
can note the time without a flashlight. What is J.M. wearing in bed?
Tricksters trick themselves. Coyote burned off his balls chasing a
Ponca girl, or so the dead man said. Will I screech when I die? When
we flew over the Northridge place coming way up from Grand Island
I saw a good, mixed square mile for phenology, the dated arrivals and
departures of all flora and fauna, mammal mating and whelping, flowering of plants, leafing of trees, time without artifice, time without
the vulgarity of clocks. Two merging creeks, a pond and slough, the
creek emptying into the Niobrara. As a junior anthro I was always
ready to reduce the dimensions of people in order to see the pattern
but that is also done with birds. That temporary shrink way back when

said our predominant emotion is dislocation. Yes or no? I don't know. God might be a he or she but is definitely not human if I can trust my own authority which I can't. Julian Jaynes said that when early man talked to the gods they were certain he could hear their words. I suppose that in this century since we no longer believe in evil as a force we can't believe God listens. A whippoorwill! Just what I was waiting for. Even the implacable stars warm up a bit, soften.

I left an hour before dawn, having given up on the idea of more sleep. I was clutching at my sleeping bag as if it were my anchor on earth and maybe it is, the anchor worn to a big lumpy rag like a child's favorite blanket. Just get in your truck and drive, you dickhead, I thought, before your stomach creeps up past the heart already in your throat. I even turned on the despised radio for the livestock and weather report followed by lachrymose country songs, including an old one by Merle Haggard with an improbably fatal line, "I turned twenty-one in prison doing life without parole." Here was a call for empathy I couldn't begin to muster.

I arrived too early with just a tinge of light in the northeastern sky, so I drove down a dwindling gravel road north toward the Niobrara for a few miles, passing the driveway to the old homestead, the location recalled from my aerial reconnaissance. The gravel road dead-ended at the river where curling, diaphanous mist moved over the water and a heron decided to ignore me near an eddy bordered by cattails. I made coffee in my cigarette-lighter gizmo and had momentary praise for modernity.

After making my guts raw with coffee I doubled back and on a sudden impulse headed up the drive toward the homestead, passing through a rather grand acre or so of lilac bushes that must have been overwhelming in bloom. The shelterbelt trees that had lined the gravel road continued to confuse me on my way up the driveway and into the yard though I knew there had been many European introductions in the late nineteenth century, sold as rootstock by nurseries in Illinois and Iowa. I noted deciduous caragana, wild plum, Russian olive, and the larger green ash, black walnut, European larch, and a great deal more. How eccentric.

My stomach was thumping as I made a quick turn around the oval drive noting my mother's battered Subaru, and an old aqua-colored Ford convertible without a top. The house was largish and resembled a Connecticut farmhouse, again from the nineteenth century, with a broad porch, and the paint faded to the point you couldn't quite determine the color though it was probably white. Despite this everything was in crisp repair with multiple flower beds, and a tire swing hanging from an elm branch. When was there last a child here, I wondered. It certainly wasn't me. I sped up as a pen of geese started honking wildly. Further back there was a corral of four glaring horses against the big barn, several outbuildings, including a bunkhouse with curtains. My skin prickled and my heart fluttered at my sense of trespass so I stepped on the gas and the gravel in the drive rattled under my fenders. My mother might be a late sleeper like the other one and these pinging stones wouldn't help.

Back on the country road I was still hyperventilating and slowed to watch a group of red-winged blackbirds, one of my favorites. Above their chatter there was the melodious trill of meadowlarks announcing day. The air was coolish but I was beginning to sweat. Onward and presumably upward, goddammit!

Naomi, my grandmother, was sitting on a porch swing drinking coffee when I came up the drive. The house looked nearly a replica of the other but vaguely newer, with a largish vegetable garden off to the side and the trees not so large. The outbuildings were in trim shape but looked as if they had been unused for a long time.

I pulled up behind a ten-year-old Plymouth sedan, the typical schoolteacher's car, and nearly stumbled as I got out. There was a single noisy crow above me in an ash tree and I paused to look at it and regather what was left of myself. As I came up the porch steps the crow glided close to my back and I nearly stumbled again.

"I raised him," she said, smiling and standing up, offering her hand, but looking at me rather closely.

"Nelse Carlson," I said, "and you're Naomi. I hope I'm not bothering you. It shouldn't take over two days at the most and then I'm off."

We spoke briefly about the Breeding Bird Survey and I was more than a little unnerved by her sidelong glances which, though restrained, seemed to hold more than ordinary curiosity. There was a suppressed urge to babble out the whole business but I was sure this wasn't the right move and besides, how did I know I'd be welcome? I mean if your fifteen-year-old daughter got pregnant by whomever you might wish to keep the memory forever in a well-locked closet. I glanced down at an open bird book on the porch swing where she had been having coffee and the sight of a green jay on the open page helped lessen the prickling on my scalp. It turned out we had both seen the bird in the vicinity of Harlingen, Texas, where she had once been to observe migrating warblers, though only briefly as the spring vacation at the country school where she had taught was a short one.

She insisted on making breakfast and inside the house there was the problem of tunnel vision. I couldn't make myself look around the parlor but followed her to the dining room where she had laid out maps of the farm, including aerial photos, and a few monographs by ornithologists dealing with the immediate area. One was quite recent which betrayed the fraud of my invented project but she didn't mention it when she returned silently from the kitchen with coffee and orange juice and caught me flipping the pages. One end of the dining room was solid books including a library ladder to reach the highest shelves. I got up and looked them over, feeling melancholy over the collection in my stolen truck when I saw so many of my old favorites, including William Bartram, Audubon, Thomas Nuttall, John Muir, Bent, Beston, and Matthiessen. A nitwit high school English teacher had said the prose in my essay assignments was "old-timey" and wondered why. I said I thought it was because I had spent so much time with this kind of book but he wasn't familiar with many of the names which was an eye-opener. I wondered at the time and still do why they allow people to teach who don't read.

She called out to ask whether I wanted my eggs *over* or *up* and when I turned I saw three portraits of three men at the far end of the room, obviously three consecutive generations and I couldn't tell at this distance if they were photographs or painted. None of them looked particularly friendly but then that was probably my mood which resembled that during my visits to the Haida up on the Queen Charlotte Islands, and to the Hopi. These were people who taught me that this is truly not one world. Their legacies were ancient, their customs particularly their own, and without our intervention they would have remained *virgo intacta* in their unique traditions. They had no need for the slightest incursion from the rest of us. I only became a bit agreeable to them by keeping my mouth shut and loving the landscape in which they lived, and by knowing the animals to which they were drawn.

I was still twisted in my chair and staring at the portraits when Naomi put my breakfast before me. She politely broke my trance by going over to the portraits and telling me who was who as a mock schoolmarm might. The first John Wesley Northridge started the farm in 1891, the second spent his life here, and the third, her husband, had died as a pilot in the Korean War. Of course I was the prodigal by no fault of my own but my eyes had turned to a photo of two young women on a fireplace mantel. They were sitting on the porch swing raising wine glasses, and Naomi said, "These are my daughters, Ruth and Dalva."

Now I'm alone at twilight, camped near the pond and creek I had noted from the air in the heart of the property. Naomi said it had never been touched to any degree by cattle but was from the beginning the family camping spot, two hundred acres or so bordered by thickets and shelterbelts, and composed mostly of marsh with a few hummocks of higher ground that held trees, a pond on the south side, and a slow creek moving north toward the Niobrara.

I don't recall spending a less focused day. I refused dinner saying I had to collect my notes and she had freely offered the camping spot when we had lunch on the sandbank of the pond. Now in the evening I admit to the sudden weight of resentment when it occurs to me that this marvelous habitat could have been my own to grow up in. This thought is really pissing in the wind but is, nevertheless, there to tug at heart and mind.

I was so inept today that I'm sure this woman thinks I'm clumsy as hell as a birder. Warblers were never my strong point but I wouldn't have normally fucked up the yellow warbler, yellow-rumped warbler and yellow-throated warbler. All of her corrections came in the form of a polite question. "Mightn't that be a spotted sandpiper rather than a western sandpiper?" Why yes, of course, and I'll try to get my head out of my ass before I run head-on into a cottonwood. She was amused when I told her a story from my college ornithology course about how the girls in the class had T-shirts made in honor of the female spotted sandpiper which is energetically promiscuous for a bird. The young men in the class were irritated. When she teasingly asked me if I had been irritated I said I was only an exception because there were hundreds of things that irritated me more than the ordinary squabbles between the sexes. For instance, outside the classroom building which was nearly all glass I found dozens of songbirds that had bashed themselves to death against the windows. She had heard estimates as high as over a hundred million a year of birds that had died thusly, adding as threats broadcasting towers, power lines, pollution, cars. We dwelt on the evolutionary curve and wondered jointly if birds would ever learn about windows. We doubted it as we with our very large brains had never learned about war. She said that way back in the Middle Ages in Europe hell was envisioned as a place without birds. To lighten up she told me an entertaining story from two weeks back about how a visiting historian from Stanford had gotten very lost in this area and had to be rescued by a makeshift posse of locals.

Dear J.M.,

I'm sitting here at twilight by a pond eating a very large pot roast sandwich with mustard and raw onion, possibly the best sandwich of my life. It was made for me by my new grandmother,

Naomi, who is an interesting woman. I have grave doubts about
how I'm handling this like I'm acting with too much backspin.
This has caused me to have doubts while I'm sitting here about
having to stay away from you for a whole month. As an old song
goes, my heart cries for you, sighs for you, etc., that kind of romantic malarkey. But it does. It's the solstice and my thoughts are not
on planetary specifics but you. Today I was strictly Daffy Duck, my
boyhood comic favorite who was arrogant, inept, pretentious, in
short I was a fuckup. I tried to cover some avian misidentifications
by being more theoretical, blabbing about bark glean, commensal
eating, possible migratory strategies, and lekking species. That sort
of thing. I suspect she thinks I'm peculiar. Aren't we all? But then
that's a cop-out. She's a Scandinavian of some sort and her
husband, my grandfather, died way back when in the Korean War.
I saw a nice photo of my mother and her sister at your age. I think
she's suspicious, but pleasantly so, as this kind of nesting survey
should have been done several weeks ago. My mother is a couple
of miles away on the ranch at a house Naomi calls the *old place*. I
drove in the yard for a quick look at dawn. Countless thousands of
trees were planted around the turn of the century because the
ancestor was from New England and wanted his pastures and tilled
fields protected from the wind and also as a source of wood for
heat and lumber. Naomi's house itself spooked me for a number of
reasons I can't locate. The furnishings and decorations appear to
be from back around World War II or older. It reminded me of the
furnishings of our neighbor Samuels who was always sort of my
godfather. Did I tell you she's been a schoolteacher for forty years
at a country school? Perhaps I can see why you want to be a
teacher. For instance, I pretend to hate anthropology but it should
be taught in high schools so young people know who the hell they
are other than money-grubbing Nebraskans. Anyway, I'm going to
call you because I can't stand not to. Why should we be limited by
a bunch of perimeters? It's your business if you won't talk to me. I
love you. Nelse.

* * *

I must say I slept like an actual log, not so much from the long day's walk but that I had begun to resolve the core of my life. A big item! At dawn I had barely stirred the coals in my fire while watching a blue heron spear frogs, and was thinking of a cryptic statement of my Zen girlfriend's to the effect that ashes don't return to wood, when Naomi showed up with a thermos of coffee and a fried sausage sandwich. While I ate the sandwich she modestly identified the dozen or so birds we could hear while we sat there with the sun rising through a thicket fifty feet away so that we were speckled with pieces of gold light. We were quiet for ten minutes as this golden light also burnished a section of the pond, diffusing itself as it rose through the canopy of thicket until the top looked like it was burning with sun and rising ground mist. Three mallards came in for a clumsy landing when they saw us and tried to reverse course, bawling us out with their nasal quacks and hisses. We talked about preferences in birds, which one can't help having, and hers were for the ordinary local residents, meadowlarks, bobolinks and longspurs. My own, goshawks and northern shrikes, seemed pointlessly masculine, except for the canyon wren of the Southwest.

   We finished the checklist by early afternoon when we were at the edge of a mile-long pasture near the old place. She wanted me to meet her daughter and her houseguest which put my heart back in my throat. I hoped she hadn't sensed this but I entered a stream of fibs to the effect that I wished to pay her for her time, and that I had to drive way up to Minneapolis to file a report. This was barely out of my mouth when I realized she'd know that the survey was headquartered in Lincoln. I tried to cover up two fibs with yet another by saying that if she was interested there might be more work in a week or so.

   She stopped me in the middle of the pasture and asked if something was wrong with me. I blurted out that I was terribly afraid that the girl I loved didn't love me as much. She nodded, paused, then continued walking without saying anything.

   Luckily no one was home but a large ungainly housekeeper woman named Frieda who was picking lettuce and peas. She was a cranky sort but gave us a ride back to Naomi's in an overpowered

Dodge pick-up which she drove straight-armed like a race-car driver, her big right arm deftly speed shifting. I was afflicted with pounding temples and couldn't say a thing when Frieda nearly spun out, swerving to miss a hen pheasant. Naomi gripped my arm, then gave my hand a squeeze, whispering in my ear that she was sure my girlfriend would come to her senses. The delayed reaction was poignant to me as it seemed meaningful.

I went immediately to retrieve my gear back at the pond, running most of the way in a mixture of anxiety and rage at myself. All of my rehearsals for this visit which had begun when I saw Dalva walking in Santa Monica, and in other forms before that, had come down to a self-administered mudbath. What the hell did I have in mind. All I wanted to do now was cut and run back to the safety of the cab of my pick-up.

I quickly packed up my gear with my lungs struggling for breath, then sat myself down unintentionally hard on the sandy bank of the pond somewhat, I thought, like a child will injure itself during a tantrum. Holy shit, what a fool. I stripped to my skin and dove into the pond. How did I think reality would match my intentions for it? And with me in control as if I was godlike at the steering wheel, as absurd as Frieda squealing the tires from gravel to blacktop. I had all of the rapacity of the culture I assumed I loathed. I'll see if they're worthy of me, indeed.

I swam underwater along the bottom of the pond, noting in the sand the indentations of small springs, until I reached the area that had been burnished by the rising sun, then came up at the last possible moment when my eyes had begun to darken. The question was why didn't I during those lovely moments at dawn merely say, "I am your grandson." The worst she could have said was, "Go away," and I would have been better off, or so I supposed with the usual all-or-nothing absurdity.

When I reached the house Naomi was back on her porch swing with classical music coming through the screen door, drinking lemonade. She offered me some and I refused, now itching to call J.M. and certainly not from here. I thanked her and said I hoped we could work together again. She smiled, then had a disturbingly quizzical look that said without words, "Why don't you tell me what you're thinking." But I didn't. I left.

I called J.M.'s home from a pay phone outside a tavern in a county seat a couple dozen miles down the road, waiting first for two teenage girls who were shrieking into the phone to boyfriends. They wagged their asses at me as they left. Ample asses, at that. After five rings which reverberated nastily on my brainpan, J.M.'s mother answered and said that J.M. was out haying with her father. Naturally I had expected J.M. to be sitting there politely by the phone. Then her mother asked, "Did you get to meet your people?" and I answered "Just the grandmother but I didn't admit who I was because I couldn't." There was a long pause and then she said, "Oh for Christ's sake, it's not my business but you should clear this up. I trust my daughter and from what I hear you're a good man. Maybe a little peculiar but that's up to her." There was another pause and then I said I had to see J.M. soon if it was possible. This brought on full laughter and she said that I had twenty-eight days to go but that tomorrow was Sunday and relatives were coming though Monday would be fine. My ears still rung with the *twenty-eight days* for a few moments before it occurred to me that she was saying I could see her daughter in a day and a half. I said, "Thank you" and then her voice came on cool, almost harsh, saying that if I wished to prevent J.M. from finishing her last year of college she would do all she could to make my life unpleasant. I promised I wouldn't and her voice softened again saying she looked forward to seeing me on Monday.

I'm not much of a drinker for obvious reasons but I headed into the saloon after looking up and down the heat-shimmering main street, noting all the bustle of ranchers and farmers and their families in town on Saturday afternoon shopping and visiting. It might seem quaint to some but it wasn't.

The tavern was quite crowded with burly types in whose hands beer bottles looked small. Out of habit I listened to the collection of

voices to trace accents, coming up with mostly Czech and Scandinavian and one brash metallic voice with a trace of a whine from a
red-nosed man in his late thirties with a very old farmer who, despite
the heat, wore his denim jacket buttoned to his Adam's apple. The
younger man was being teased a bit by others and it occurred to me
he was the Northridge houseguest, the Stanford historian, who had
been quite lost in the not very challenging landscape. He drank beer
straight from the bottle, tipping the bottle up and chugging as if he
had been weaned too early. He was an extreme form of my favorite
kind of college teacher, one who broke through all polite academic
restraints by the force of his obsession with his field of study. In common parlance they were fools but give me a fool anytime, like the
poor young ornithology graduate student who rode a bicycle thousands of miles around America for three years toting up his species
count. This scholar and houseguest, Michael by name, told me, as
we played a game of pool, that some of the soil in the area was still
likely moist with Native blood, and that other than southern New
Mexico with its remnant Apache and Comanche conflicts at the end
of the century, this was the last area in America where the full collision of cultures had taken place.

I'm not exactly an amateur in this area of study but it wasn't the
kind of thing I wanted to talk about in that I was still savoring the
prospect of J.M. come Monday. I moved over to a corner with a fresh
beer and watched the old man in the denim jacket bounce around
playing a miniature violin and singing. This must have been a common occurrence as others joined in. Through the window I could see
women and children sitting on a long bench chatting animatedly,
doubtless waiting for their beer-drinking husbands and fathers. I left
when two behemoths started bellowing about shipping fever and
cattle, then began wrestling and knocking over tables. I crossed the
street to Lena's Cafe which, just short of five o'clock, was already full
of senior citizens eating their dinners with the slow relish of the older.
I sat at the counter where I was waited on by a young Viking woman
whose pink name badge spelled Karen. She had taken in her waitress dress so that it was tight across her fanny and I missed my mouth

with a forkful of mashed potatoes looking at it. She bent over twice
to fetch coffee cups directly in front of me. Even antelopes would leap
and fight over this butt. Dear J.M., I'm only looking. When I left she
gave me the pouty look favored by females in skin magazines that
dweebs look at to pulverize their weenies.

I headed toward the southeast, lacking the energy for driving fast
which would have been for no good reason. Suddenly I felt immensely
burned out but then the day had started long ago at the pond with
Naomi's soft footfalls coming up behind me. She scarcely fit my pre-
conception of *grandma* and I guessed her to be in her mid-sixties
though her appearance was well short of that. She was quite the
walker and she said she generally walked before and after school, in
the morning to compose her mind and in the afternoon to let her
mind settle back down after a day of teaching. A few summers back
she had taken a Lindblad voyage up the Amazon but the lack of
walking possibilities had made her irritable, and besides it would have
taken a lifetime to learn the area like she had her "homeground." I
felt slightly addled about this notion as I had just been somewhat
bragging up my hundreds of varied camping spots. She was curious
about my favorites and I rattled them off and she was pleased they
included this part of Nebraska. She was also curious about Ekalaka
in the area of the Powder River in southeast Montana, the state highway coming in from the south still gravel. I had to describe the place
for her in detail which made me wish I hadn't lost my journals. Reading a few sections might impress her and then she would say, "I wish
you were my grandson" and I'd say, "I am."

This was goofy enough that I blushed and drove off the road east
of Brewster for a doze, recalling our discussion of birds as miniature
flying dinosaurs, a current ornithological quarrel. Naomi also didn't
care for airplanes, partly because her husband died flying one, and in
part because she wanted the bird's-eye view to remain in her imagination. I admitted then that I had had to limit myself and wear blinders as the world I loved tended to exist in only small pieces here and

there. National parks were far too crowded and one dared not fall in love with any beautiful national forest land as on returning it would likely have been clear-cut. Washington and Oregon might look good from the ground but from an airliner window you could see they had cheated and much of the land was a savage mess. This had made her somber but then she teased me that as a nomad I certainly had enough hideouts to last a lifetime.

I had fallen asleep deeply enough to pitch my head forward and thunk it against the steering wheel. The small orange fire that erupted was a bonfire my grandfather started for me in a blizzard up in Minnesota on a family trip to see my grandmother after she became ill. I liked the idea of grandparents and regretted the idea that my mother's parents had died rather early, from too much booze my father later told me. Anyway, my mother was hysterical that she was trapped by a blizzard in a log cabin. My father and I failed to soothe her and my sisters were luckily always able to ignore her by playing double solitaire. My grandfather took me outside and we roasted bratwurst over a fire in the driving snow. He had a shed full of dry cedar kindling which smelled wonderful.

I sat there yawning and made a cup of coffee in my lighter gizmo. With my binoculars I could see across the Loup River to where I'd camped for a few days back in college when I was writing a paper on native grasses. A rather progressive young rancher had let me camp on his property and suggested a ten-acre niche near the Loup which had been fenced off from cattle for a family camping spot for generations. It certainly hadn't been as splendid as the Northridge holy ground but I had found a number of my favorite grasses: sawbeak sedge and slender flatsedge, reed canary grass, porcupine grass, redtop, prairie dropseed. The grasses diminished and the view through the binoculars faded with the image of J.M. squirming out of her jeans in the warbler woodlot near Garland. I could be as angry as I wished over not being raised by the family I belonged to but then I would inevitably be swept away by the fragilities of time and location and how minutely it is broken down to the series of accidents and coincidences known as life. It was ironical to forgive those who gave me up because otherwise I wouldn't have met J.M. I wondered what side of this interior argument was irrational, or were both? The fact of our existence is so inalterably raw that you cringe when you look at it too closely. An infant is given away and at that moment its familial predestination is radically changed. And no doubt the mother, however young, keeps mapping the child's possibilities in her imagination.

Another hour down the road and it occurred to me I didn't know where I was headed. This addled me in the twilight and I stopped to check the map as if to confirm my existence. For some reason a truck cab didn't seem as safe since I'd met Naomi and it had already diminished a lot after my second meeting with J.M. when I perceived I was a goner.

Just before dark I reached Dannebrog and figured I'd camp along the Loup (splendid name) on the property of a professor I liked way back when. He was a huge burly fellow, an expert on the Omaha Indians and also a folklorist in an age wherein actual folks were disappearing at a startling rate unless you knew how to look for them. There were no recent tire marks on his two-track so I concealed the pick-up in the bushes and made my way to an ancient log cabin he had moved there and reconstructed. There was a proper fire ring and I spread my sleeping bag beside it and made a minimal campfire. I expected insomnia because I had been hit hard by an obvious question: Why had I been such a chickenshit and not simply sat in that yard until my mother returned? The grandmother wasn't the point. I felt like the goddamned coward I must be when it came to my deeper emotions which now were crawling around on the surface of my skin. I lay there drifting for hours, pleased that the foliage above was thick enough to keep me from tracking my star clock. I'd trotted to this thicket like a wounded lapdog and I don't know enough about her to speculate an ounce other than where she lives now and her photo on the mantel from when she was younger than me. Maybe she's like her mother which would be fine. Give it up. See J.M., then go back you goddamned fool. *Back to that inland sea, Lake Superior, so fresh it smelled like flowers rising up with faraway ducks bobbing in this estaurine wave lap. You don't have to lift the binoculars every time, with clouds, mare's tails they call them, highly scudding, then stretched until they can no longer elongate without disappearing. Dad and Samuels took me fishing in the ocean way down in Islamorada but all the birds were near shore in the mangrove islets intersected by aqua and greenish tidal channels. They just brought up fish that were clubbed and died. A single sailfish, amberjack, one wahoo. The old book calls it mare tenebrosum, the sea of darkness when you look over the side straight down, but I like the in-betweens of everything where life is, the edges between field and forest, the edges of green clots of mangrove and low-tide nearby sandspits where birds feed. On the night of the third day eating weird new fish I asked if I could see birds and Samuels went to the desk of the lodge. Maybe I was eleven years old. Next dawn a lady made of leather showed me all day long thousands of birds. The sun made her into leather though she wasn't Indian. The roseate spoonbills popped my young skull. She peed over the side of the boat, then said fish are like underwater birds so I leaned over the skiff deck and watched the passing creatures in the tidal thrust. J.M. has never seen the ocean. Will you take me there, big shot, the first time anyone called me that. Are you upset all those men have seen my butt? Testing me I guess. No, I'm the only one in the cosmos who really understands your butt, dear. I added dear which pissed her off. That's for when we're over fifty. Every shred and ounce of nature equals mortality. We must not stand up to this but absorb it. I dread J.M.'s records though perhaps I could use some music. Lucy was good at the flute which wasn't bad from the next room. I shined a flashlight up at my ceiling constellations in the worst depths of winter when I couldn't sleep outside. Dad sent off for the best sleeping bag, good enough for Tibet, and I'd awake to the early Omaha traffic in the distance with snow covering my sleeping bag where I was warm as a womb baby. Who are we in the dark anyhow.*

Sunday morning and spiffy people coming home from church. I approach Mother's house so slow the truck lugs in low gear. A dapper man squints at my lightning strokes, sees my face and waves. That man was always trying to give boys a squeeze which we thought was funny but it's somehow serious now. There's a new BMW which you don't see in Nebraska outside of Omaha. Money is a terrifying problem. People with a lot are always trying to get more and when you ask them they're not sure why. When they run out of things to spend on they even insist their kids look rich. But then the country isn't at all what it largely thinks it is. The money is too thin and unevenly spread. People crave to be what they see they're supposed to be on television and few of them can. Of course in other cultures this money could be green stones rather than greenbacks, or cows or horses, camels, ivory, grain, goats, whatever. There was the sudden errant thought that my six hundred dollars a month wouldn't take us very far if J.M. married me. The concern was jumping the gun a bit but still there. That amount was food and gas money with not much left over. There was some insurance money left by my dad in a bank account but my sister Marianne looked after that sort of thing. She's a business whiz and along with her girlfriend they've bought and redone a number of houses, and lately an apartment house, down in Lawrence, Kansas, which is also the location of the Corvus Society. Of course Marianne has told me that I'm the "biggest fucking neurotic in the world" about money. Maybe so. It's always been an unpleasant abstraction to me, a tool of control. Is the house where I'm parking my truck worth ten years of a well-paid person's salary? Ten years of time which has a tendency not to replace itself.

I won't say my Omaha mother was glad to see me. Without so much as a hello she demanded why I, along with Marianne, had bullied Derek away from her. He went to New York this morning without inviting her. Yes, he paid back three-quarters of the money but wasn't that her business? That was her own money and had nothing to do with what my father had made. She had always offered me money and I had always refused. Why had I become such a lazy, greedy bastard that I would interfere with a loan to her boyfriend? I knew it was serious as I couldn't recall her ever using the word "bastard." I tried to slide it off by saying the greed aspect belonged to Marianne and that I was only following my dad's request to keep an eye on her. She fairly screamed that she didn't want my eye kept on her. I attempted to pass through the house and out the back door to a thicket

I'd planted myself: Japanese bamboo (northern), dogwood, Russian olive, for maximum concealment when I was ten. It surrounded a lean-to I'd sleep in when it rained. However, she caught me before the back door and called me a miserable, insensitive bastard. I aimed low and agreed that technically I was a bastard, regretting the quip on the spot. Her face blanched, contorted, then she ran upstairs as she always did when truly pressed. On the way out to my thicket I reflected with amazement on how fast she had covered the stairs. Must be her aerobics class.

I sat out there at least an hour, pleased that there was a mating pair of orioles in the yard. In my thicket it was hard to believe you were in Omaha, the density of the greenery baffling all but a trace of the ambient sound, say the shriek of a golfer a few hundred yards away. I dug up a metal container of arrowheads and marbles, rattling them together with fondness. A childhood buddy had swiped our mutual collection of dirty photos including the most powerful nut-buzzer, the butt of a French actress named Jane Birkin. We agreed that she would likely never appear in Omaha. Later I found another photo of her for my bedroom wall.

Three alarmed English sparrows fled and then there was a tinkle of glass and footsteps. She arrived with two wine glasses and a bottle of red. If it took alcohol to resolve this I was willing. "I should be shot for saying that," she said, plunking herself down, despite an expensive dress, in the dirt beside me. I took the bottle from her trembling hands, also the corkscrew. We toasted and the wine tasted better than usual. Her eyes brimmed with tears and she repeated that she deserved to be shot for calling me a bastard. I was kind enough to disagree, and then she said, "Just because you're older and your husband has died doesn't mean you can do without a boyfriend. I'm only sixty-one." I knew she was sixty-three but to try to smooth things over I offered to go to lunch with her at the club which used to be a Sunday family ritual. She pondered this for a few moments and I could see the contents of the cartoon light bulb above her head and then she smiled. "I never know what to say when my friends ask what you do." When she said this I wondered at the nature of her recent inventions about what I was doing. Back before my father died during my last trip to the club I'd told table-hoppers that I was an explorer, and when they'd ask, "Where?" I'd say, "The good old United States." Many had had enough problems with their own grown children not to pry any deeper. There's also a slight interior yelp for freedom among the involved strictures of prosperity so that the idea of going someplace without an elaborate itinerary has at least a minimal appeal. I could see them thinking, Nelse is an explorer of America, with their forks poised above their Sunday chicken hash or lobster Newburg.

We settled for corn soup that she'd frozen last Christmas after my one-day holiday visit (fleeing Marianne's butch girlfriend who fashioned herself a societal interrogator, also Lucy's Washington husband who insisted he could *wangle* me a conservation *watchdog* job). Corn soup was another household joke that had begun back in my pre-suffocation Boy Scout days. Scouts were traditionally taught a polite amount of *Indian lore*, but not enough to do any damage to their potential citizenry. I went a bit further and before I was a teen I'd already read Densmore on the Chippewas, somewhat romanticized versions of the frontier in Washington Irving, Walter Edmonds, Kenneth Roberts, Hervey Allen, the last four from my dad's thin library, which were oddly incendiary books if you were expected to finally enter the greed rampage of the late seventies and early eighties. Anyway, I came down with a not very severe case of pneumonia and demanded corn soup with marrow like the wounded Jim Bridger ate, or warriors ate before and after an arduous war. My father no longer hunted but got venison from friends and my mother boiled up chunks, adding a package of frozen corn. I would eat nothing else for weeks. What a pain in the ass I must have been. Boys who are no longer quite boys lying around tweaking their engorged weenies, dreaming of valor in the wilderness, wrestling bears and pioneer girls in thin flour-sack dresses, or mating an Indian girl in a hidden place behind a waterfall, then regaining their health only to face again the torpor of the schoolroom.

We spent a pleasant enough afternoon and evening backing well away from our bastard blowout which, while scarcely a psychodrama, was a pretty big deal in this household. We sat for hours in her "art room" with her leafing through dozens of coffee-table-type books to show me her favorites which were invariably nineteenth-century French. I'd bought her an Edward Hopper book once for Christmas but she had found him depressing. We also spoke at length about our trip to France though her rendition made me think we must have been visiting separate planets. Her Omaha travel agent had concocted an itinerary that properly would have required amphetamines and blood transfusions to enact the whole thing. We stuck to the game plan for a week before we figured out that my mother's pidgin French could get us by. My regret afterward was that I couldn't get her to spend more time in two areas I'd warmed up to, the Morvan and the Massif Central. Despite the fact of their population density most of their cultivated areas looked less fucked-up than our own partly, I suppose, because they had to be more judicious while we still felt we had infinite freedom to sprawl. She preferred Paris and the Louvre, and wandering not all that far between the Café Select and Café Flore for her timidly ordered glasses of wine. I did, however, see a hoopoe, in Burgundy, a marvelous bird that looks a little like a roadrunner with a heraldic crest.

I'm a wine amateur or I would have kept my mouth shut. It sneaks up on you in thick velveteen shoes. I had begun to wonder at midevening why I had so strenuously avoided this guileless woman when I errantly dropped the fact that I had spent two wonderful days looking for birds with my grandmother. Other than rebuking me for not sticking around to meet my "birth mother" she asked me reasonably lucid questions about the landscape, and pointed questions about the interior of my grandmother's house. I noted that her eyes had begun to fill with wine tears and there was the specific idea that I should run for my truck. "I suppose you found yourself wishing you had grown up there," she blurted out. I had enough wine myself not to shut up and let it pass. Instead I agreed that it had been exactly the kind of area where I'd like to have grown up, that Rock, Brown, and Cherry Counties together were bigger than Massachusetts and collectively had less than twelve thousand inhabitants. Why the hell wouldn't I have preferred growing up there given my obsessions? The absolute stupidity of the whole thing was mutual between us, as if there were a parallel universe where actual alternatives to our lives could take place. We had suddenly dropped into a hole and while I was struggling to get us out of it she was buried there by the weight of tears, wine and the kind of thinking that had never lent itself to rationality. She fairly shrieked about my birth mother's grandfather, starting at the beginning with a dinner with Samuels to arrange the adoption. My father had been angry because Northridge had been a bully and she said his face looked like a crude *brown* boxer's face (a racial slip), and he wore a pretentious antique English suit drinking water glasses of whiskey and gulping down wine. "He even insisted we name you after him. How arrogant! And then he gave you that allowance that ruined your life." I said how for Christ's sake can six hundred bucks a month ruin someone's life? You have thousands of times that much money in the bank, did it ruin your life? Probably. "Don't you dare attack your mother," she said, then continued on with the "fact" that this man was known as one of the biggest bullies in Nebraska, that he had swindled ranches away from people in the Depression, then sold them all after World War II. She had met the two sons when she was young and their mother came from a fine family but the father was a monster using money as a club.

　"But I didn't grow up there," I said. "I grew up here. You forget they gave me to you. It's happened a lot with babies for one reason or another. I grew up here in the same way Dad died. You can't change a goddamned thing starting a split second ago."

　"I'm alone," she howled and I went up to bed, coming back down in the middle of the night to cover her with a blanket where she still lay on the couch in embarrassing disarray.

　Jesus Christ, I thought, improvement can be splotchy. Now it's nearly four A.M. and I doubt I'll have any more sleep after seeing her in that corpse-like condition. I almost checked her breathing. Squabbling primates, and one couldn't neglect the way comedy pitched in with what had never been, and could never have been. I wished I had a few powwow cassette tapes that were in the stolen truck. I surely

didn't know what the hell was going on in the music but it drew me
the furthest away from an emotional sump which is where I am now.
I had been to about a dozen powwows over the years, keeping a discreet distance from the activities, so much so that I didn't even record
the visits in my journal. This was odd enough that I've wondered if
there were secrets you even try to keep from yourself. I saw Frank
Fool's Crow at two different Sun Dances, so old his face looked like
a shucked walnut. Men with leather thongs attached to their bleeding breasts. Why not? I studied the steps to the Grass Dance closely
and once when I was in a distant place near the Escalante in Utah I
stuck in the tape and danced until I sweated through my clothes. That
was just once. Afterward I felt exhilarated but eventually bogus. It
was evening when I started and I danced right into the dark under a
big moon with a chorus of coyotes near the end. I danced until I scared
the hell out of myself with the sensation I was seeing the moon for
the first time, and all sides of it at once. I admit it was only last year.
Ralph curled up under the truck and watched attentively as if he knew
it was serious stuff.

It was a struggle to stay in bed until daylight. During a brief doze there
was a disgustingly obvious dream about living in a dollhouse with J.M.
with the exit door so small you had to crawl out like a ground squir-
rel. Will I have to give up Veracruz up near Jalapa where I had been
twice, once in April and once in November, to watch a million raptors migrating north and south? Am I such a bad bet for permanence
that I shouldn't offer myself? Nomadic cultures are extraordinarily
civil until you try to confine them to one place.

    I snuck out of the house at daylight and made it a whole block
before I was stopped by a patrol car. Doubtless my lightning-stroke
truck looked unpromising in the neighborhood. I sat there tingling
with adrenaline until the approaching cop yelled, "Nelse" and he
turned out to be a high school acquaintance, much swollen now by
bodybuilding which cops do to look overwhelming. We shook hands
with him glancing down at my lightning bolts and shaking his head.

He smiled and said, "I heard you were a hippie. You getting much?" a slang reference to pussy. "Quite a bit," I said because it was easier. We chatted a few minutes about the old days for which he had more enthusiasm than I did.

I reached J.M.'s by midmorning but no one was there. She had said her mother worked and then I remembered she was helping her dad hay. I found them in a field down the road with J.M. driving the tractor pulling a wagon, her dad throwing on bales and a kid too slender for the job struggling to do the stacking. J.M. waved and her father nodded, vaulting on the wagon to help the kid, so I began pitching the bales. I had bucked bales a fair amount to pick up change and it was a pleasant way to get rid of the horrors of the night before.

We finished by noon and back at the house her dad heated up a pot of chili while J.M. took a shower. Her facial bruise had subsided somewhat but her eye still showed redness. While I drank a couple of glasses of water at the kitchen sink I again pointlessly rehearsed murdering her shithead husband. You jerk up his sternum and tear out his heart, that sort of thing.

Her dad still hadn't said much and was staring into the heating chili. He glanced at me as if sizing me up physically, and then said that the other asshole had never lifted a hand around the place. He then offered his hand and we shook awkwardly. I tried to pass it off by saying I had proved myself better at manual than mental labor which he smiled at.

J.M. came out of the bathroom in a short yellow sundress that made my ears buzz. Her dad teased, "You're assuming you're done for the day?" She merely pointed at me and said, "He can pick up the slack," then served the chili. They were a little disappointed that I wasn't upset by the pepperiness which J.M.'s mother, having grown up in northern Mexico, added to the dish. I explained that I had spent a lot of time in the Southwest. Then her father, Bill by name, asked what it was I actually did. The best I could come up with was that I was looking things over before I settled down. This was quite lame but J.M. interrupted with the suggestion that we take a ride. Bill stood politely when we got up but shook hands with me as if testing my grip. "Thanks for the help," he said, sitting back down and beginning to roll a cigarette. I had the briefest flash of what he was like at my age before, like my dad, his liveliness began to disappear. Was it necessary, I wondered, following J.M. out the back door. What was it beyond the obvious factors of success and failure, and notwithstanding them, that diminished men so relentlessly as life gradually passed. For a change I wanted to reject previous thoughts to the effect that we've been around the last million years and only in the last one one-thousandth of that time, or less, have we been very civilized and simply squatted in one place. To me the advances were questionable and tended to ignore our true nature.

J.M. wanted to drive my truck so I simply sat there, a rare thing in my solo career. I developed a lump in my throat just looking at her legs and the way her hem hiked further up when she worked the clutch. There was no indication that this ache was mutual but my mind was certainly foggy as we drove along. I agreed readily to anything she said in her chatting such as that we had to live together a full year before we mentioned the word "marriage," and then she repeated she was finishing her BA which would take up the coming year in Lincoln. My pecker was swollen enough that no iron curtain dropped at the word "Lincoln." I don't mind any city if it's a quick in and out which wasn't what she implied in her next suggestion. Why didn't I finish my degree since I was so close? The lump in my throat began to take on a different nature and I tried mightily to observe the landscape. Finally I said that all I had to do was totally rewrite my senior paper but I was unwilling to do that. I added that my dead Ponca informant would rise from the dead and strangle me if I left him out by changing the paper to jerk-off academic specifications. They could shove the mortar boards up their asses sideways before I'd do that.

She reddened, stiffened and slammed on the brakes. "It must be nice," she said, "to throw away something that the rest of us work so hard for." I was appalled at the strength of her reaction, but then she went on to say that her dad had a real prosperous cousin, an older man who had been to their house on Sunday. This man had saved their neck when they got behind on the mortgage. It turned out he had known my own father and Samuels. Why had I lied about being a rich person? This man said he'd heard I was a "layabout" which upset her own father. And since I was a rich person why was I interested in her? People who say that America is a classless society are full of shit, I thought, jumping out of the truck and bellowing, "I am not a goddamned rich person! I'm a goddamned adopted half-breed! My parents are not my goddamned fault! If you can't understand this simple fact get the fuck out of my goddamned life!"

She drove off so fast down the gravel road that I had to turn around quickly to shield my face from flying stones. Naturally I didn't feel very intelligent standing there so I crossed the ditch and sat under a tree. It was quite hot and my throat was raw from shouting, an act I couldn't recall committing since college. There seemed to be a clear question of how much of my arms and legs I'd have to cut off to fit in the world she was imagining for me. I could say to myself she was only twenty-one but that didn't encompass the problem. It didn't strike me as appropriate that love would immediately demand the most shit-eating compromise possible in my scheme of things. Within my own coda or private religion leaving school over a principle such as I had was inalterable. To suggest otherwise was to put my nuts in a vise, or so I thought sitting under a larch tree beside a hot dusty road. A long-billed curlew flew over heading west where it belonged. What the hell was it doing here? Not to speak of myself, an alien leaning against a tree on a hot summer afternoon in eastern Nebraska with my hands stinging from nettles from when I had walked blindly through the ditch.

It was a full hour before she returned, at first coasting by without seeing me and then I shouted and she backed up. She slid over to the passenger side and tossed her pale blue panties to me with a blank face as I approached, then held up a pint of blackberry brandy, of all things. I took a glug before I got in the truck and we made love right there on the front seat, with her kicking off a radio dial with a sandal. We slid partway out of the cab, and I stumbled backward when I finished, then fell, imbedding some gravel in my bare ass. She man-

aged to hold onto the steering wheel then frantically helped with my
trousers because we could hear a car coming and I was still part coma-
tose. It was the rural mailman and rather than being mortified as she
had a number of weeks before she waved and smiled. He waved then
politely looked off in the other direction, the dust his car left behind
settling on our sweating skin in a dry brown cloud.

We headed north, turning left in Verdigre, then eventually
north again to reach her favorite swimming hole on the Niobrara. I
mentioned idly, and it turned out to be a stupid move, that we were
about one hundred fifty miles east, but on the same river where I had
tried to visit my mother. What do you mean by *tried*, she asked? Why
was I so evasive? Did I tell my new grandmother who I was? Hadn't
it occurred to me that she'd perceive who I was? Her own mother
felt I acted stupidly after my phone call. I was irked and said that rather
than teaching literature and dance she might do well as a private
detective. We had just pulled up to the river and she hissed, "Oh fuck
you," jumped out and headed west on a path. I followed but her track
experience came into play and it was a while before I caught up. Her
tracks on a sandbank ended near bushes with her yellow sundress and
sandals on the ground. I glanced at a river eddy and she emerged from
the water and threw a handful of mud and sand at me. She intoned,
"The course of true love never runs smooth," as if addressing the
United Nations. I undressed while she stood in waist-deep water singing mock versions of "the course of true love never runs smooth,"
explaining that that's what her 4-H sewing instructor had told her
and a group of other little girls when they reached their teens. They
thought it was quite funny as they already were dealing with horny
farm boys by then. We bravely made love on a sandbar in broad daylight then stared at our imprints in the damp sand wondering if a good
tracker could figure out what had happened there.

I only stayed one night and half of the next day before we had worn
each other out with permutations of the quarrels we had already had.
It was as if the strength of our affection peeled our nerves other than

when we were making love. There was the notion that I had never had so much at stake and didn't know how to handle it. I even began to think if the bruise on her face hadn't been so relatively recent she would have been easier to deal with, one of the stupider thoughts of my life. For a brief hour on a hike in the hills behind the farm we seemed to see the mess we were in quite clearly, she more than I. Her idea was that she had begun with her severe depression over her marriage in the spring, then met with me several times which had utterly rattled her brain, and then her husband had clubbed her to the floor. She went home and I quickly showed up and arranged a lawyer. Now I was back again without even a week passing rather than the month we both agreed was appropriate. My "evasiveness" hadn't helped, a word I bridled at because my parents had used it a fair amount to describe my shortcomings. I had always wondered, and said so, why you had to tell everyone everything right from the starting gate, and she said you don't but if you think you love someone you should. I had made a start with my list of the peculiarities I had admitted to, but I had left out a lot. I knew she meant the money thing so I suggested we get in my truck and go visit my mother which would give her a big dose of reality. That made her angry and she asked how the hell she could meet my mother with a big fucking purple and yellow bruise on her face? She began to cry and I felt like my stomach was going to drop out over what an insensitive asshole I was showing myself to be. I held her and we began to try to make love but her dog wouldn't allow it. In fact I came close to being bitten and got a pant leg torn. On the way back down a series of diminishing hills to the farmhouse I had to walk at least ten feet behind her with the dog turning and growling if I came closer. She thought this was very funny and I did too though it made me miss Ralph.

The only long truce period was during dinner and the evening when her father expertly grilled some local chicken halves which her mother served with a blistering red chile sauce, and then the four of us played an involved card game called pinochle which I caught onto reasonably fast. It was pleasant to have all my bleak nervous energy absorbed in a card game so that for three hours, other than the exchange of wistful glances, J.M. and I could slam down trump cards as wholeheartedly as her parents. It was a little disappointing when her parents went to bed and we were left behind with difficult and separate selves. I offered to sleep out in the yard but she gave my pecker a tweak and said she was sure her dog wouldn't allow it. He even growled at me through the screen door and J.M. gave me a piece of beef from the fridge to try to make friends. He accepted the meat on the front porch but growled while he ate it. The consolation was a big moon and J.M. had me recite some constellation details which I could tell from her comments she wasn't listening to carefully but I didn't give a shit.

I was a little worried about her room but it was big enough with plenty of windows, not at all frilly but stacked with books and 4-H mementos, including some small trophies and photos with J.M. and prize calves and heifers. Her husband had so far refused to ship her main collection of books and the mention of it made her flare with anger. I wondered how long this sort of thing would last. Her voice slackened a bit with fatigue and when she exacted a promise from me to see my birth mother her heart wasn't in it and she began to sleep. I stared closely at her hoping to develop a subtle language that wouldn't pinch her sore spots. I turned off the night-table light and looked out the western window and tried to imagine if this mother was really looking for me and why. I supposed that I wasn't capable as a male of fully understanding giving away a baby you had made with someone you loved. Samuels had told me her grandfather and mother couldn't keep her away from this half-breed Sioux hired hand who lived out in their bunkhouse. It must have been the one with curtains out near the geese and horse corral, I thought, then fell into the deepest sleep possible.

I awoke to a red-tinged dawn, tried to make love but she pushed me away and slept peacefully on. I heard noises downstairs and decided to help her father with any chores in the offing. While playing pinochle he had referred to J.M.'s husband as a "mouthy marshmallow" and I didn't care to be categorized like that. His auger attachment for his tractor was hopelessly broken so that he had to do postholes by hand, a talent at which I was expert I'd told him over cards.

He was surprised to see me and put extra bacon on. We talked about pheasant hunting and he said J.M.'s obnoxious mongrel was pretty good though you had to run for a downed bird or the dog would make off and eat it. We then talked about grazing and I told him about a new theory and practice I'd read about where you partition your grazing land in seven pieces and move the cattle every ten days or so. That way your weight gain went up at a surprising rate with all the fresh grass. He countered with the simple fact that that was a lot of fence to build and I said I was up for it. He asked why, and I said I was taken by his daughter, but it all seemed too antique and idealistic for him. Maybe so, but I'd be glad to do it. I could see he'd had his ass in a sling over the farm often enough to have adopted a proper cynicism. The farm had worked well for the previous three generations but now all the crop moves he made, not to speak of the cattle, were "a dollar short and a day late." This morbid talk began to sink us both but then the mother, Doris, appeared for a cup of coffee and a bowl of cereal on her way to her office job in Neligh. She seemed happy enough and looked handsome in a blue terry-cloth robe. Then the phone rang and she answered as J.M. came into the kitchen as if she didn't quite recognize it, still half asleep. Both father and daughter were concerned about a phone call this early so I went out on the porch. She could be a real puzzle, I thought, remembering that during the hillside growling fiesta she had said, "No greater dog hath man than his love." I said you got dog and love backward, and she said, "No I don't." Bill came out on the porch looking pissed off and distracted and I asked if I could scythe the burdock around the barn, and he said, "Go ahead, I got permanent tennis elbow but not from tennis."

I found the scythe in the barn where I'd seen it the other afternoon, also a metal file on a workbench in the corner. I put the scythe in the vise and sharpened it, then headed outside for the burdock. My grandpa had taught me how to scythe and I remembered you had to swivel your hips or your shoulder would wear out. I cut a few swaths while worrying about what was happening in the house and also about a period the year before when my mother had gone through some New Age spiritualist bullshit which, according to Marianne, had cost her a bunch of money. Though they quarreled incessantly Mother kept badgering Marianne to move back to Omaha so they could keep each other company.

I had just about finished scything when J.M. appeared and said my so-called friend, the lawyer, had called to ask if they would come down this afternoon because he had a hot chance to go fishing in Wyoming and wouldn't be able to keep an appointment later in the week. Her father was pissed because it was his night for nickel poker with his friends though he wouldn't admit that was the reason. Her mother couldn't miss work. Naturally I offered to take her but that was out of the question because she was only twenty-one and her parents didn't think she was capable of handling it without one of them. There was a flash when I wondered whether when you married someone you also married the parents. I mean I liked them fine but it was an illusion I'd noted long ago when we think of parents as anything but an older version of ourselves.

Her mother waved at us as she drove away and J.M. asked plaintively if I'd keep on writing her. This meant I was dismissed but for a change I could understand why. The family didn't want me to share their private mudbath. I embraced her and she said I could use her shower. Then her father came out looking quite affable and I recalled how often my own father had acted pleasant and gentle to my sisters when he was eating out his guts over their problems. He put his hand on J.M.'s shoulder and asked if we were up to the final couple of hundred bales of hay as the radio said it might rain before they got back from Omaha. I was relieved at the chance for something menial and it only took us a couple of hours. While I showered J.M. made me a Spam sandwich to travel with, a specific delight as my mother had never allowed the stuff in the house. The same with catsup and bologna, which drew me strongly to all three. J.M. kissed me so ardently good-bye that my heart and mind purred like a cat. She said, "Don't forget what you're going to do and give me a couple of weeks this time."

Rather than doing what I was supposed to do I headed north instead of west for the simple reason that within a mile down the gravel road it had struck me with dreadful finality that if I was going to join up with J.M. my career as a nomad would be over. This overshadowed the question of my Sandhills mother and I kept stopping along the road as if the lack of movement would make a decision. There was the usual yes, no, yes, no, yes, no. If it was yes was I truly capable of it? My sister Lucy liked to joke that I'd make an excellent traveling salesman covering the entire country except the eastern seaboard. I said yes if I could sell rain, or moonbeams, or leftover wind. But then what the fuck were decisions of this sort when J.M. had said we'd have to live together for quite a while in order to figure out if we could manage the long haul? How flowingly realistic compared to my geometric-decision bullshit.

I made my way north, passing up the idea of visiting a friend in Morris, Minnesota, whom I'd met in the Yucatán. He spent half his year in Morris as a civil engineer, then went native on the Yucatán coast for the fall and winter, but I doubted I'd be good company. He probably would advise me to see if J.M. would settle for a half-year marriage. For a number of miles I very much missed the advice my father might have given me despite our essential quarrels.

About an hour before nightfall I reached my grandpa's land, about fifty miles east of Moorhead and fairly close to the White Earth Reservation. I set up camp on a hillock covered with sumac for concealment. From what I wondered? I was only about a hundred feet from the Buffalo River thinking the sound of moving water might soothe me. It must have rained the day before because I could smell the charred damp odor of my grandfather's cabin not far away, carried by the slightest of western breezes. The cabin burned the summer after he died and the local sheriff had suggested it was probably lightning which my father accepted cynically. There had been a local storm that evening but not very severe and it was my father's opinion that it was likely arson committed by one of the many poachers my grandpa had arrested as game warden. That was in my early teens and I remember thinking I had lost a possible home.

Lying there and watching my beloved stars gather in the growing dark didn't prevent a modest tailspin about J.M. Life unwinds in the living and on this particular night my brain's machinations were not worth a badger fart. My dad had said when irritated that my life was not unlike a hobo's during the Great Depression but for less reason. Hoboes had begun by moving on to look for work but after a while they just moved on for the sake of moving on. Mother said one night in the backyard, her voice a little slurred, that the universe above us was God's brain. I had agreed for a change which delighted her. But I know looking up at the stars that we don't have even the sorriest clue to what is ultimately going on. The French writer Camus said we were supposed to be brave about this simple fact. I tended to like Camus in college because his name spelled backward was "sumac" which might betray me as an idiot. Once in Montana a girl in the middle of the night asked if I didn't think it was wonderful that God created the Big Dipper. I smugly said that the stars were there before dippers so I doubted He had that in mind, which made her withdraw her affections. I had to start being careful because at that moment I felt I'd rather die than ruin J.M.'s life.

At dawn it began to rain fairly hard and I began to brood in earnest. Brooding leads to more brooding as if you were going to achieve some sort of clarity by continuing to stir the mud puddle. When it's raining hard and you're confined to a small mountain tent you're bound to come up short in terms of self-judgment. Maybe a single life doesn't amount to much but perhaps it should at least drift toward the common good.

I stayed there for three days and never got dried out. I wrote one ink-smeared letter to J.M. but mostly walked the perimeter of Grandpa's forty acres over and over like a well-programmed bird dog. The excessive moisture caused blisters on my feet and I swathed them with a tape with the attractive name of "moleskin." I got very bored talking to myself and talked to the hordes of mosquitoes and flies. I prayed for sunlight as a child might on a Saturday morning but it made me feel weird as hell. Even while walking I stewed in my own rank juices as if the overmemorized landscape from my youth was incapable of drawing me out.

On the morning of the third day I drove over to Naytahwaush on the White Earth Reservation (Anishinabe) to look up an old friend I hadn't seen since my early teens when he'd occasionally fish with my grandpa and me. His mother still lived in a tar-paper shack and out back there was a remnant of long bluestem, an original prairie grass from when buffalo still roamed the area. I never feel more embarrassed as an American citizen than when I visit an Indian reservation. Nothing so much emphasizes our moral fraudulence than the way we treated these people from the time we hit shore to the last fifteen minutes. God must squint, turn his face and puke, when he's not busy elsewhere.

The mother was there and smiled broadly when she saw me. She was as tall as I was, six feet, and her arms proved she had split the immense pile of firewood outside the shack. It turned out her son was in prison in Missouri. I asked when he was due out and she said, "Never." Her two daughters were fine, though, and both had jobs and husbands in Minneapolis. She served me coffee and I tried to give her fifty bucks to send to her son but she wouldn't take it because he had "free room and board." I left the money on the table for her and she gave me a ten-pound bag of wild rice. Then she said that I should visit my grandpa's old girlfriend down the road. I was utterly startled that my grandpa had had a girlfriend, also mildly delighted as my grandmother had a big share of bully in her, perhaps a reason my father had always been oversubdued.

I was allowed a piece of starlight only a few minutes long that night and at dawn I packed and left in a steady downpour. For some reason the rain had purged my sentimentality and I was only interested in the business at hand. I stopped for gas in Sioux Falls and called my bird boss in Lincoln, and tried to wangle a few days of work for Naomi and myself. He said stop by in the afternoon, but then laughed at the idea of paying Naomi in that her father-in-law used to be one of the largest landholders in the state. I didn't say anything more though I doubted the truth of what he said, or else Naomi made a fetish of living simply.

I reached Lincoln in the early afternoon and since it was also raining there I checked into my claustrophobic motel. I was given a room with a print of a sad-eyed donkey wearing a garland of flowers which barely beat the more usual purple twilight in snowcapped mountains. I didn't want to but I called my mother in Omaha out of duty and she announced gaily that Derek was coming for dinner. I said, "Wonderful" and then she knocked my wind out by saying that Dalva Northridge, my "birth mother," the term she insisted on using, had met her for a drink and a chat at the club yesterday. For want of anything else I said, "Thank you," and then she continued on rather shrilly that I was obligated to look for this pleasant woman who was looking for me. My mother had had enough art not to mention to Dalva my visit to Naomi. I didn't listen carefully and hung up, forgetting to say good-bye. I was back in my truck and driving downtown before it occurred to me that I was certainly entitled to go see her if she was already looking for me. Despite the clouds and rain the ceiling lifted quite a bit, a great deal, in fact.

I parked near the office which was adjacent to the university, standing in the parking lot in the rain with a case of admitted tremors over the phone call. I remembered thinking on Ocean Park Boulevard in Santa Monica that I could simply walk up to her and say, "Pardon me but I'm your son," but then I imagined that she might say, "Oh for Christ's sake I live way out here to get away from my family and past." But now all of those doubts were slipping away and

I spent a half hour in the nearby Nebraska Historical Association to check out something among the vast collection of old photos. I had been there a number of times in the past few years to compare the photos of the grasslands in the western part of the state, including the Sandhills, in the 1880s and 1890s with what they looked like now. Since I am habitually sunken in the justifiable pessimism of my generation I was startled to discover that the rangeland looked marvelous now compared to the supposed good old days (except for the Natives) when the area was miserably overgrazed and overpopulated with cattle. Of course this is all private ranching and not within the apparent misery of Bureau of Land Management control visible throughout the "great" West.

The curator of photographs, a burly crank of great knowledge and curiosity, dug up a number of photos of old Northridge, the man who had doled me out to my Omaha parents. There was a pic of him standing next to the governor and John J. Pershing at the groundbreaking of the new State Capitol building in 1924, another at the State Fair holding the reins of a team of champion draft horses, another in 1920 standing outside of a mansion in Omaha, dressed in a homburg and a topcoat with a fur collar, holding leashes with two obvious coyotes. This was a bit puzzling in that he looked more feral than the coyotes, as if he wished to bite the world in the neck and shake it, a mood similar to that in the portrait in Naomi's dining room. His head looked too large but then so were his shoulders.

There was a niftily dressed young hotshot talking to my bird boss when I entered the office. He represented a private environmental group, I think it was the Nature Conservancy, but my heart was elsewhere and I wasn't listening carefully. My bird boss offered me a few days of work checking out fledgling Swainson's hawks in nests in the Sandhills, also a possible rare breeder, a ferruginous hawk in Sheridan County, if I would make a list of areas, from my hundreds of camping spots, I felt needed preservation. We ended up talking a couple of hours and it seemed odd that I might know something of value to these professionals, but then it is easy to forget that few could

equal the way I had covered the map. Obsessions don't seem extraordinary if it's just the way you are. I ignored my slight sense of invasion of privacy as I rattled off a dozen or more of my favorite locales,
feeling a growing irritation that a man younger than myself had an
actual job that J.M. would find acceptable, though he was also probably suffocating in paperwork.

I was back in my motel, still very agitated, and trying to write
a letter to J.M., when it occurred to me that the room wasn't
making me feel claustrophobic. I had read enough on the subject
to know that phobias can become intermittent. The college roommate who had conned me into reading Henry Miller was frightened
by heights. Three steps up a ladder and he was lost, or anything
higher than the third floor of a building and he felt he might be
sucked out the windows, doubtless a genetic remnant of our primate
brain. In exchange for my reading his main enthusiasm, Henry
Miller, I insisted he had to read volumes by Mary Douglas and Loren
Eiseley, also Edward Abbey's *Desert Solitaire,* and Aldo Leopold's
Sand County Almanac. Oddly, after the initial discomfort of having our brains expanded, possibly the real value of college, we felt
it had been a good deal though Miller had sent me off on a sexual
rampage.

> Dear J.M.,
>
> Good news for a change. Dalva was in Omaha looking for
> me! She talked to my mother. As you have noted I've been timid
> about this. I never thought of myself as fragile but I guess we all
> are somewhat. I hope that your trip to the lawyer wasn't too bad. I
> have a terrible urge to call you but think it might not be a good
> idea for a few more days. I don't want to suffocate you. I mean I
> probably want to but you have that divorce problem. There
> doesn't seem to be much good advice floating around on the
> subject of falling in love with someone but I don't want my
> obvious shortcomings to scare you away. Perhaps you could let
> your father know I'd actually enjoy putting up that fence on your
> place. Love, Nelse.

It was now ten in the evening and I had forgotten to call Naomi. There's always a touch of the moron in this kind of mental agitation. Luckily she was awake and reading and, after a long pause that made me nervous, she said she was up for a raptor trip but would have to be back in three days for a family picnic. Then her voice dropped in volume and she said that I might enjoy meeting her family. There was a stroke of suspicion here that she might be onto my deceit but I dismissed the idea as unlikely.

As I tried to sleep a few tears formed from Ralph's direction but they quickly absorbed themselves when I thought of his adoptive parents which was ludicrously coincidental as many things are. If I hadn't been at the campground in New Mexico I never would have found him whimpering under some balls of tumbleweed near the back fence. If I hadn't gone to that particular truck stop on the outskirts of Tucson near the air force base my truck wouldn't have been stolen and, with it, Ralph and my journals, a life's work but only for my life and eyes and heart. If a rancher's fifteen-year-old daughter and a mixed-breed Lakota hadn't made love I wouldn't exist. The bottom line was manifestly simple like the billions of galaxies which, no matter how inconceivably vast, had an existence with origins as mysterious as our own. If it all was based so resolutely on chance it seemed by far the best course to seize what chances were offered. Come to think of it, I hadn't been in a strip club for several years until the night I saw J.M.

I left the motel at four A.M. and reached Naomi's a little after eight. She was on her porch swing waiting and received me like an old friend. I sat on a stool in the kitchen while she made breakfast and I babbled on about the beauty of the morning and the birds I'd noted after I got past Broken Bow and could see more clearly in the diffuse light that occurs after a long rain lets up. I spread out my topographical maps and pinpointed the Swainson's hawk sites, also the supposed ferruginous site over between Gordon and Walgren Lake. She didn't seem to be looking at the topos carefully but instead gazed directly at me. I looked down at my nearly empty breakfast plate, then back at my topos, and then out the kitchen window at her semi-pet crow looking back in the window at me.

"Don't you have something to say to me?" she asked.

"I don't know," I said, standing up so abruptly that I tipped over my chair. I rolled up my topos and carried her bag out to the truck, standing there sweating in the coolish morning air as she came down the steps of the front porch and walked toward me. "How did you know?" I asked.

She laughed and stood there shaking her head. "How could I not know? I knew from the instant you got out of your truck the first time. You simply look like the product of my daughter and her godforsaken boyfriend." She got in the truck and I stood on my side looking in on her and wondering if there was something further to say. My temples and heart were drumming to my own foolishness, but then my stupidity no longer seemed to matter so I simply got in the truck and started it. She patted my shoulder and rubbed my neck, then laughed again. "I don't know who you look like more but you act like both of them at once. Maybe that seems unlikely but it's true. Of course you're truly the son of those who raised you. I understand that but I'm very happy you showed up. No one is more welcome."

I couldn't think of a single thing to say for the first half hour down the road. My dreary self-consciousness was choking me, and I felt like a dog who has been caught at a terrible deed and is convulsed with embarrassment. Finally I slowed the truck to a stop and asked if we shouldn't turn around and go see her but Naomi said she thought Dalva was off near Buffalo Gap in South Dakota for a few days, and then she stopped me cold.

"What do you want from her?" she asked, staring straight ahead.

"I don't need any money." I didn't quite know what she meant.

"I don't mean that. I know she's been looking for you but I told her that I suspected that was wrong. If there was any looking to be done it was up to you. I didn't want you to expect too much, or her to expect something impossible if she found you."

"I want to know what her life has been like and who exactly my father was and what he was like," I finally said, stuttering.

"She'll have to tell you that. She'd want to. I'm just relieved. I prayed for this moment because it's only fair. She made herself a very hard life just like her father and grandfather." She smiled and added, "She even told me she wished she had taken after me."

I started driving again to cover the anguish of what I had to ask, "Why did you folks give me away?" I glanced at her and her eyes had teared up and she looked away. It was miles before she answered and I kept wondering if I had had the right to ask that question. I felt I did despite her evident sorrow. The answer came in a jumble as she said she was mostly overcome because her younger daughter, Ruth, had behaved so horribly when she didn't get to see me, the baby, who had been born in Tucson. The grandfather had wanted to keep me but Naomi said he was the most difficult man she had ever known though he certainly hadn't seen himself that way. In her long career as a teacher a number of her students had gotten pregnant and a number of them had kept their babies, but Dalva hadn't shown the barest thread of the maternal. Naomi had disliked my father but years later realized that Dalva was equally at fault, probably more so. There wasn't a remote prospect of immediate marriage because of the nature of the two and this was a difficult area to bring up an illegitimate child. The grandfather had died the year I was born and she felt ashamed to be relieved that the quarrels had ended. Countless times she had wondered if she shouldn't have raised me and perhaps it was selfish but after her husband's death in the Korean War her sanity had depended on her teaching at the country school down the road.

"I'm not blaming anyone anymore," I said, and that was that for the time being.

We did fairly well at our Swainson's hawk chore mostly because of Naomi who had an antique sense of responsibility. By the afternoon of our first day out it had become hot and humid and I was having a relapse in my interest in birds. My curiosity about my original family was incessant, and maybe a little clinical in the anthropological sense, but then I felt I had a right to know. Naomi refused to talk about my mother and father, saying that it would be improper, and that since I had hesitated this long two more days wouldn't matter. She mostly spoke, at my insistence, of the background of the family which was eccentric enough for me to tirelessly want more.

On the second morning we were over at the Fort Niobrara refuge near Valentine and found two nests before noon and also saw three fine plump western diamondbacks. I came intentionally close enough to the third for it to coil up in anger. "Why bother it?" said Naomi, and I said in defense, "You could at least tell me his name."

"Duane Stone Horse," she said. "He was half Lakota the same as Dalva's grandfather. I met his mother who was a fine woman."

I didn't dare go further beyond our implicit agreement, but she then asked if anyone had mentioned my own small share of Native blood, and I said mostly when I was younger. Children are quick to recognize differences, however slight. Later on it seemed to depend on how much time I spent in the sun, often a lot, or in college when my hair was very long. Once after an anthro class a Wahpeton Chippewa, who was a leader in the Native activist group, asked me why I was *playing lily white* and I said I was playing nothing. To show him I attended a meeting but my own privileged background made me feel like a hoax. Naomi listened to this carefully and we walked another hundred yards before she stopped abruptly and took my arm.

"Sometimes it must be terribly hard work to be a loner," she said.

This was rather close to home and I wasn't able to say anything. She sensed my discomfort and told me a wonderfully bawdy and sad story about their houseguest Michael, the historian, who had gotten himself involved with an underage local waitress. There were photos and angry parents, the father slugged him, and now his jaw was wired. He was staying at Naomi's where he worked all night and slept most of the day. She was amused that I could identify the girl as the obvious knockout at Lena's Cafe in town. She then asked me how my girlfriend was and on and off all afternoon I talked about J.M. and what I should do. We were eating dinner at the Peppermill in Valentine, where I was intent on proving to the owner that I could actually eat the two-pound porterhouse I had insisted on, when Naomi looked at me blankly and said, "God knows why she'd marry you at this point. She doesn't want to be your anchor. That's an improper job for a woman because she'll soon be resented."

This was a little disappointing but I wasn't able to respond because an old rancher and his wife stopped by to say hello to Naomi. I was introduced as her grandson which gave me a tingle. This woman said, "Why yes, Ruth's son," and Naomi said, "No, Dalva's son," which blanched the woman somewhat though she seemed pleased to the point of beaming at me. When they left Naomi said that this wasn't an area where anyone could hide unlike a city. You were welcome to have all the privacy you wished but people knew your family history from day one. She suddenly looked as tired as I was but said she hoped she hadn't sounded cruel about J.M. Marriage was impossible enough without going into it with an unclear mind. I wasn't sure I agreed but I had asked for advice not a quarrel.

Back at our motel we were saying good night and about to enter our separate rooms when she added that if I truly loved this woman I better give it all my energy because for both Dalva and herself it had only happened once. This was a cold thought that made my room seem very small indeed. In fact the ceiling was descending until I called J.M. who deftly reassured me. How could I think anything was wrong? Let's stick to the plan. We'll see each other every day if we wish. Surely with my apparent brains I could find a livable area where she could eventually teach. This all reminded me of my sisters who, when they hit the bottoms of their private hells, could still see a continuity in life that escaped me during all but my best equilibrium.

There was the vacant thought of how totally ordinary my "problem" was. A young man looks for the mother he's never met other than within the confines of her womb, blood-warm and wet, discovering life in absolute but comforting darkness. She doubtless rode a horse while she was pregnant so I felt that! Newspapers, television, magazines and books have covered the situation. My Omaha mother was always sliding them my way, thinking it was my main torment rather than the daily view that the natural world was disintegrating. The comic aspect was that the distance between mother and son in the common mind could go away because the reports had been sequentially digested. That was that. Except for those who lived it every day. Like everyone else we were only supposed to behave and follow the national, interior manifest destiny of profit that was evidently the reason for the country and its inhabitants existing. The millions of rules were rather localized, my first poignant lesson being the dogs I saw in restaurants in France, and later, the countless miserably poor in ghettos, barrios and Native reservations, not to speak of my beloved nature which was everywhere scalped and diminished so that the lords of progress could make more bucks. Why would I wish to fit in this schema? All I had to do was find a more stationary niche because I loved J.M.

We left by dawn driving all the way over past Gordon to Walgren Lake only to discover our ferruginous hawk was a fiction. Birdwatchers can be both wistful and hopeful and send in inventive reports. My bird boss had a relentless informant who kept insisting he'd seen any number of gyrfalcons near Hastings, a notion much more remote than world peace.

Naomi started laughing over the matter while I was quite pissed off. We'd only seen two harriers and by midmorning it was almost ninety degrees during our long walk back to the truck. She laughed until there were tears in her eyes and finally it was infective enough for me to join in. We left our valuables and binoculars on shore and walked into a reedy lake up to our necks which was even more funny. We sat in the shade of the truck for an hour half-dozing and chatting, then decided to bag it and head home.

This was a bit of a fuss when we reached Naomi's at midafternoon. Frieda, the housekeeper at the old place, was testing the strength of Naomi's porch swing with her big body and swollen face. She gestured at a screened window from which Michael's snores emerged, and said that at his insistence they had drunk a full quart of butterscotch schnapps, the mere idea of which made my belly tremble. I had regretted not seeing him the other morning after Naomi had told me the nature of his work dealing with land conquest and Sioux extermination. She had said there was no point in trying to talk to a man with wired jaws.

I had already asked Naomi if I could camp back at the pond and she had joked that the idea was appropriate as she thought I was probably conceived there because Dalva and her "boyfriend" had used it as a hideout. She then blushed and threw up her hands, believing it an indiscretion. She made me a large ham sandwich and I was off until picnic morning, though not before Frieda told me that it was beyond her why any "asshole" would want to sleep outdoors, adding that she had done so dozens of times in the army in Nevada where she had met a Basque rapist that kept her captive. I stood there boggled by the information until she waved me away saying, "Go to it, kiddo."

I sat plumb still for several hours the better to absorb the landscape, or better yet, become absorbed by the landscape. You don't really become it but it becomes you. I felt as much an earthling as the red-winged blackbird that landed on a cattail a few feet away only to flee with a squawk when I batted an eyelash. True stillness always seemed to be a hard to accept gift. A great blue heron landed in the shallows of the far side of the pond where the creek began to form. Beyond that was an ultimate thicket, dense looking as a deep ocean. Not that it mattered but if Naomi's quip was true this was a good place to be conceived. As time filtered away into the landscape the birds set up their good-night chorus like excited children. Here I am whoever wants to know. Their names didn't matter and if you knew their nature well enough you'd know what they call themselves, so said my Ponca friend. Maybe the names we give them mean no more than the names we give ourselves, a fragile hedge against mortality.

At twilight I lit a small fire and ate the ham sandwich, dead smoked pig and damned good at that. Ralph would have gone swimming a dozen times by now for no reason other than he liked to do so. Rather than toting dog food when backpacking we shared our meals. It was fair exchange for my using his vastly superior scenting abilities. As the fire burned down to coals I curled close to it adding a little grass as a mosquito smudge. My head was as light as my beloved birds.

Naomi appeared about seven A.M. with a thermos of coffee and some cheese biscuits. She said she couldn't stay long because Dalva's uncle Paul and her sister Ruth were being picked up in Denver by a neighbor's small plane and she wanted to get to the grass strip right after they buzzed the house. I said I'd walk over the back way whenever she wished, and she said late morning was soon enough. She looked at me quizzically and then said, "Are you sure you're going to show up?" For want of anything to say I gave her a hug and watched her walk away, raising her binoculars for a moment at a larkspur I'd heard singing.

I sat back down for another three hours like the evening before, thinking it might be good training for my mind in addition to being a fine thing to do. My lost master map would have appalled any sedentary souls. For a change one part of my mind didn't have much to say to another except when it started talking about food. My guts were fluttering when I stood up and I had to remind myself I wasn't going to my execution. And when I started the hour-long walk I had to put my feet down hard in order to feel the ground. It was so disconcerting I changed courses and walked back up the mile-long slope to Naomi's to get my pick-up. In my remnant of snake brain there was the thought that I didn't want to be there without a means of escape.

No one was at Naomi's so I guessed I better head for the picnic. I couldn't feel the gas or clutch pedal any better than the ground. I was relieved that after I went up the long drive and into the yard Naomi came out of the house to greet me. She introduced me to

Dalva's uncle Paul, a tall, slender man in his sixties, and then to his ward, a young Mexican boy who wanted to ride a horse. The old hired hand Lundquist was carrying a saddle out of the barn and I took it from him and put it on the horse, who was nervous. I took the reins and calmed the horse, whispering nonsense and letting it smell my breath. Lundquist adjusted the stirrups and then Naomi tapped me on the shoulder. I turned and there was my actual mother looking quite frightened.

"Dalva, this is your son," Naomi said.

"I know it," she said, and we walked slowly out toward the driveway and down it for a quarter of a mile until she stopped and looked at the ground. "This is where I first met your father."

"Looks like a better place than most," I said, staring off at the immense pasture to the south. She seemed a little wobbly so I took her arm.

"Why didn't you say something before?" she said looking away. It was startling to perceive that some of her features resembled my own.

"You've just been home a month, and I wasn't sure you wanted to know me. Naomi figured it out a week or so ago when we were working. I tracked you down this spring. A few days ago I called my mother, the other one, and she said you two had met. So I figured it was okay." I hadn't breathed during this little speech and felt dizzy. We hugged each other stiffly and I added, "Naomi said my father was quite the young man but not necessarily the kind you wanted in your living room."

"She was trying to look out for me but I guess it didn't work," she said. Now we were both smiling and we walked slowly back to the house and up the back stairs to her room which had a fireplace. On the mantel there was a photo of my father on a buckskin, darker than myself but the resemblance was so clear my breath was short. She said that she hadn't seen him again after she became pregnant until the day he died when he'd insisted that she come to Florida and marry him so she could get his armed service benefits. She said he shot himself but he was as much as already dead from war wounds

and the battering of Vietnam. I was unstable on my feet and she ran
downstairs, returning with a bottle of brandy. We toasted each other
several times straight from the bottle. I said she didn't look old enough
to be my mother and she said, "Oh my God I was only a kid when I
had you." I hugged her while she cried for a minute, and then we heard
music and went to the window. It was old Lundquist and his not very
expert miniature violin wandering around gravestones in the lilac
grove. Naomi looked up at us and we waved and she covered her face.
What was left of her whole family was down there around the picnic
table. I couldn't say it was my family but it was a start when we went
down to join them.

III

NAOMI

Oct., 1986

I suppose that the most intimidating thing about teaching at a remote country school is that you are actually teaching those of ages
five through twelve how to look at and understand the world. After
1953 the young people of high school age traveled the forty miles
to the county seat with some of them boarding in town, but were
only nominally out of my reach because they often visited. On cold
clear winter mornings when it was still dark we'd assemble in the
school yard to look at the stars through my birding binoculars, a
fine pair of Bausch & Lombs John Wesley brought me home from
World War II. The average number of students during nearly forty
years was fifteen and we'd stand there in the snow-crusted yard
passing the binoculars and looking at the constellations while a half
dozen horses tethered at the rail would steam from their rides to
school and we'd hear the steady munch of hay and distant crow calls
in the winter dawn. I remember that a rather limited farm boy
named Rex would bellow out, "Jesus H. Christ, what's going on up
there?" and quickly pass the binoculars. I didn't chide him for swearing because he was so shy over his lack of intelligence that he'd
rarely say anything. After passing the binoculars and vigorously
shaking his head Rex would go over to his tethered horse, Dolly,
lean against her for comfort, and stare at us until his world regained
its shape. His nickname was "Badger" because he was a student of
the ground, always looking downward and trying to catch things,
including rattlesnakes. The nickname came from when he was still
very young and tried to dig up a badger he'd seen disappear into its
hole, losing his small dog when it tried to protect him from the

cornered beast. Now thirty years of age his livelihood is putting up
fences, hand digging the postholes in difficult terrain, the kind of
work all others wish to avoid.

Of course by the mid-sixties nearly everyone had a television
and for better or worse some of my duties were lightened, but from
1945 until that date I was the student's main access to the world, along
with the parents, whose solitary concern appeared to be discipline.
For instance, everyone cuffed Rex, his schoolmates, his parents, his
sister the most ardent punisher as if to differentiate herself in the eyes
of others from her slow-witted brother. Now he stops by once a month
on a Saturday for a short visit but won't come into the house. He
brings me samples of grasses, weeds, wildflowers, and descriptions of
birds but he rarely remembers their true names. His visits delight me
even though in winter I have to bundle up on the cold porch. I've
never stopped wondering about the particulars of the world he thinks
he lives in. Rex is confident that the sun sets on Edson Gale's ranch
some seventy miles west of here, and the westward perimeter of his
world. Typically, it is only Lundquist who speaks to him with enthusiasm. All others are put off by his shaggy wind-burned appearance,
his old dirty clothes and bad teeth, his speech which is barely more
than a mutter and inept at consonants.

Which brings me to the sudden appearance of my grandson,
Nelse, this summer. The mind is a curious thing indeed and since
they were the same age I had always imagined my unseen, unknown
grandson in conjunction with the very real Rex. Any relation between the two is, of course, a mere incident of brain chemistry. For
instance I first read Rachel Carson's *The Sea Around Us* out in the
yard near my bed of dianthus when they were flowering, thus this
noble woman is fixed in my brain with the flower. But Nelse had
pulled on me for thirty years, and five years after his birth, and adoption by the couple in Omaha, I would look at the two boys who were
my kindergartners that year and wonder how Dalva's son was doing
in his distant kindergarten. Of the two little boys I was teaching one
was a bright, towheaded Norwegian and the other was Rex who
mostly offered the problem of peeing on the cloakroom floor. Know-

ing that Duane was the father of my grandson I certainly had to discount the well-mannered miniature Norwegian and settle on Rex as
a focus point.

How many thousands of times have I thought I should have
raised Dalva's son and then halfheartedly blamed my father-in-law
who'd insisted it was out of the question. My dead husband was the
only one on earth who could remotely stand up to this man who acted
the gentleman but whose eccentricities were always bursting through
the seams, often not pleasantly. But then my husband had his own
obsessions, perhaps as strong as his father's, and always acted rather
than reacted, a tendency passed on to Dalva.

Which brings me back to Nelse, who seems to be cut from the
same cloth, as we used to often say before people stopped making their
own clothes. When he appeared that early summer morning in a
peculiar green pick-up with lightning bolts on the door panels I had,
of course, no idea who it would be other than a seasonal employee of
the Department of the Interior and that seemed odd as we had done
a bird survey only a few years ago. He had barely taken a step out of
the pick-up before I recognized him to be the son of Dalva and her
misbegotten lover. What else could a mother think when her fifteen-
year-old becomes pregnant? His immediate mannerisms were almost
too male. There is such a thing, God knows. When he came toward
me from the truck I actually prayed I'd like him as the opposite was
possible. Shyness and arrogance can both be close to narcissism and
he seemed to possess both, though I very soon recognized that like a
few of my students over the years Nelse, rather than being arrogant,
had simply made up his mind about too many things when he was
too young. His speech was abrupt as if he had held onto what he was
going to say moments too long, paused to reconsider his surroundings, then let go. When we first sat on the porch there were the briefest
of sidelong glances while he was evidently deciding that I didn't know
who he was. I had trouble keeping my composure because after a few
minutes I could tell I would like him in part because of his resemblance to my daughter, and in part because of his immediately obvious interest in the natural world.

While I cooked him breakfast I enjoyed his discomfort sitting
out there in the dining room trying to understand all of the resonances
of where he was. Why didn't he simply introduce himself as he was?
But then I quickly decided there might be some modesty involved in
the idea that given the circumstances of the past he might not be
welcome, and if not quite that, perhaps I myself was on probation.
There was also the eerie sense that when Duane had appeared so long
ago he already looked familiar which was impossible at the time but
which I later discovered had a basis in truth. I really didn't want Duane
around because given Dalva's volatile nature he was simply the sort
of young man she would succumb to, as perhaps I would have so many
years before that.

When I served him breakfast I teased Nelse with the identity of
the three portraits at the end of the dining room, wishing I could add
that he would make a not awkward fourth to the male part of the
family line. It was then he made mention of his decade of camping
out and that offered a crack in the linoleum revealing the dark pitchy
nature of what was beneath the pleasant surface. First of all, why in
God's name would anyone put themselves through that optimum
level of discomfort? Of course he didn't see it that way, but then my
student Rex had no idea how strange he was either. What could such
a number mean? Four hundred and three camping spots? I said, "Four
hundred and three?" and he nodded, then we both allowed ourselves
a smile at the tentative silliness of numbers. "I prefer stars to ceil-
ings," he said.

I studied him unobtrusively while he ate, my eyes flickering down
at some topographical maps I had laid out, when he glanced my way.
He had Duane's eyes but his mother's cheekbones and chin, Duane's
thickish dark hair but Dalva's rather delicate mouth. His forearms
were striated with muscle in a way that belied his upbringing. I certainly couldn't pry as it would have been improper and would imply
that I knew his background.

So we had a fine day and the following morning together. He
was only fair to middling at birds but that appeared to be an indication of his turmoil. At one point he walked directly into a small cot-

tonwood down by the spring but seemed not to notice the collision. He had little gift for small talk and admitted he wasn't partial to the radio, television or newspapers. Collectively they didn't reveal the world he wished to understand. His deepest injury seemed to be his loss by theft of this pick-up in Arizona which contained his journals, small library and, most important, his dog.

When he left I felt tremulous, fearful that he wouldn't come back. I did my best to conceal this from Dalva who had returned and was likely preoccupied with settling in and the almost daily problems of her houseguest, Michael, who was thoroughly obnoxious but somehow still charming. Way back when she was at the University of Minnesota she had brought home an equally brilliant oaf. I suppose there are women who find intelligence erotic. Not many certainly, but some. That was one of the qualities that Ruth found appealing in Ted, his homosexuality notwithstanding. I liked him enormously but the whole thing was quite damaging to my daughter Ruth, also to my other grandson, Bradley, who, it seems, has permanently withdrawn from all of us except Paul who finds him interesting but unpleasant. Bradley is involved in the new world of computers in Connecticut. Paul loaned him some ungodly sum to start a company despite the fact that Bradley's father, Ted, has done very well in the entertainment business. Ruth told me that this hurt Ted's feelings but then Paul explained by letter that he had already forgiven the debt in favor of Bradley giving up any eventual claim on the property here. I asked Paul why he would do such a thing as his visits here are rare. He said it was only his bachelor sentimentality about where he grew up and if anyone ever ruined the property it would be that "money-grubbing little bastard Bradley." This statement is very unlike Paul who is grave and kind while his brother, my husband, was impulsive and temperamental like their father. I liked their mother though all she really did was drink too much and read. She moved back to Omaha when the boys were in their teens and I never had the chance to know her well.

What did I ever wish but that my family, torn apart in various ways, would come back together in this place. Of course they did for our summer picnic and I now feel that Dalva might stay. There is no larger event in my life than the birth of my daughters except when Dalva finally met her son that hot afternoon. Ruth's love of music makes this a poorer place now. How could two daughters be so unlike each other, as unlike as Paul and my husband, as unlike as I and my brother who though quite the success as a wheat farmer was seemingly born a brute and a bully. The head can spin thinking of this. If I look at the class pictures of all my years of teaching at the country school I can recall the nature of the voice of each student. None of them were actually alike. Not their voices and not their characters. Maybe that's why we are startled by good mimics? Of course their behavior was less unique. Boys with tough and laconic fathers tended to act tough and laconic, aping their father's gestures and speech mannerisms. Certain of the very tight-lipped girls were either the first to eventually become pregnant and marry before finishing school or to leave, if possible, at sixteen when they were entitled to quit school for Denver, Rapid City, Grand Island, Omaha or Lincoln . Of course the tight and embittered faces revealed an unhappy home life, parents in disarray, or perhaps featuring an uncle or hired hand who didn't wish to keep his hands to himself. I wish the latter weren't so frequent as it is, or that it at least was less frequent in church-goers. There aren't apparently so many clues to the way men are except the way men are. Explanations for truly bad behavior are always inept, pathetic. One little girl, barely ten, confided in me and after I told the parents a hired hand was beaten just short of death. I'm unsure of the ethics here. I do know that when our houseguest historian, Michael, seduced (or vice versa) a senior in high school and a waitress at Lena's, he didn't deserve the beating he got from the father, but then I have known both father and daughter from their infancy and the outcomes in this case were predictable. When Karen was only in the sixth grade she got a group of five boys in the thicket behind the school to take off their clothes by lifting her own skirt. She had them turn around, then grabbed their clothes, ran to the front of the school and threw the clothes in the horse trough. It wasn't the sort of event that I would threaten to share with the parents, furthering the boys' shame as they sat in wet clothes all afternoon. She was notoriously devious and by the time she was thirteen caused many fights among the athletic boys at the county seat, and among young cowboys at rodeo time. But then perhaps she is better fit for the world we live in than most. She has gone to California by way of Michael's contacting Ted and it will take a shrewd man in that state to take any kind of advantage of her.

After all of these years of keeping track of my thoughts I've begun to doubt my ability to stand outside my life and give it a fair look. Some parts of the experience are similar to a tongue probing a sore tooth. You momentarily add to the pain, then back away, depending on your "mood" which in itself is suspicious. Say you are on a long Sunday walk early on a May morning and you see an uncommon bird in a thicket, then move up and over the knoll that overlooks the marsh and creek. You, of course, remember camping there with your husband, now dead, and you first pitched your tent near the creek but the mosquitoes were thick so you moved the tent up to the knoll. It is a wonderful memory in this habitat despite his death soon after. You made love at sunset and sunrise, a perfect balance. But such a memory can be unbearable on a Saturday morning in January when the electricity is off because of a blizzard, and you start the woodstove and the light is so dim at midmorning you start two kerosene lamps for cheer that doesn't arrive. Out the kitchen window the bird feeder is empty of birds, and the millions of individual flakes of snow are but particles of the dark and brutal ghost of the past. Your husband's chair is empty as it has been for over thirty years, but emptier yet than it has ever been. Your throat fills with tears. Your mood makes you remember quarrels rather than splendors, a scorched pot roast rather than a well-cooked feast, the vivid tremors you felt when he called from Bassett to say he'd wrecked the plane in an alfalfa field in a thunderstorm, admitting he shouldn't have been flying. You didn't weep because your little daughters were having breakfast. Or more closely, what does it mean when you remember in a good mood Dalva at five helping her father pluck pheasants and sharp-tailed grouse out by the barn and when you brought him a cold bottle of beer she seemed so preoccupied, then suddenly bit down on the plucked breast of a bird and solemnly stared at her teeth prints? You laughed at the time and often in memory, but at other more melancholy moments her act seemed a little appalling. She simply had to try everything in life and biting the raw bird was only the smallest of omens. Though it was a male country song she seemed to personify the lyrics of, "Don't Fence Me In."

Last winter a rather new, re-occurring mood stuck during another weekend blizzard. All the first night the house was buffeted and creaked. In the morning the windows of the ground floor were covered because the snow had started as wet before the wind turned to the northwest and became much colder. There was the unpleasant sensation of living within a spacious cocoon. After having coffee and reading the Bible (King James Version) I bundled up to go out to the garage to feed my crow whom I call merely Crow because I rather like the name, just as my first childhood cowdog was named Dog. Outside I noted the birds huddled in the thicket of barberry, honeysuckle and Russian olive I have planted for that purpose. The wind drove the snow so it was what we call a "whiteout" and the garage, only a hundred feet from the back door of the pumpshed, was barely visible. Back home on such a day we'd unravel a ball of binder twine when we fed the stock, having heard dire stories of frozen unfortunates, mythical or not.

In the garage Crow wasn't in his winter quarters Lundquist had made of potato crates with a perch and one crate wrapped in my old terry-cloth robe so Crow could retreat into darkness. The door of the cage was always open so he could go and come as he liked, and was positioned on a slick metal pole so no stray cat could reach him. I was somewhat snow-blind and put my handful of pork tidbits into the cage expecting him to gently pick at them. He wasn't there and I squinted up at the rafters but then he snapped a windshield wiper on my car, which he liked to do, squawked, fluttered and hopped to my shoulder where he preened against my hair and tugged at my stocking cap, a sixty-year-old stocking cap my mother had knitted. I asked him, as always during bad weather, if he wished to come into the house. He said no, and my eyes had adjusted enough to see why. He had somehow managed to catch a mouse and had tucked it against the windshield wiper and there was a small smear of blood on the window. He crowed mightily as if proud, a bit hard on my contiguous ear. Then we turned to the open garage door and stared outside at what was nothing more than a white sheet of snow stretched across the door. The mood was a delicious and particular sense of nothing as if my thinking mind had closed down. I focused on the perfect whiteness out the door feeling the animal warmth within my clothes, the crow against my ear, the wind moving the garage ever so slightly, and I shuddered from this wonderful nothing.

I was in this mood early the morning Nelse arrived again, after calling the night before about another likely invented assignment to check nesting raptors. I stood there after serving him breakfast, watching him study a sheaf of topographical maps, and thinking he'd never make a spy or businessman as he was no more deceptive than a rooster. Way back in the second grade one of my classmates, a diminutive Lakota girl, did so accurate a rooster imitation that even the dumbest boys were embarrassed. Nelse was so enthused over his breakfast and topo maps that he had momentarily forgotten his mission whatever he might think it was.

But a little while before when I still was sitting out on the porch swing waiting for him to arrive I was struck again by the splendid mood of nothing. Of course I was delighted that he was returning, to the point that my body felt hollow, but then I let my anticipation and worries go. I could hear both meadowlarks and the gentler-sounding longspurs. Crows' wings were open for a morning sunbath, perched nobly on a fence post. Far off I could hear my neighbor Athell Dodson cultivating corn with one of his antique collection of tractors he kept in repair with simpleminded intensity. I stared up at the sky until mental pictures of my life disappeared and there was nothing left but sky. I did not talk to my departed husband as I often do in the morning except to say, "Your grandson is coming again." I seem to have disappeared for a while before I heard Nelse's truck coming from the wrong direction, from what we call the "old place" where Dalva now lives. She belongs there and I never quite did, mostly because of the personality of my father-in-law. It was not simply because he was a somewhat awesome and generally furious man but because I couldn't bridge the gap that any of a dozen paintings in the house were worth more than what my own hard-pressed father could make in a dozen years. Old J.W. saw the world only from his own locus. I admit I was a little surprised to see how the death of his namesake, my husband John Wesley, so utterly crushed him. I was quite nervous about the way he so readily adapted to being a second father for Dalva, much less so for Ruth, but the influence struck me as measured and positive. I've taught enough young girls without fathers to know that it can present a long sequence of problems. It was odd indeed when in his last year he returned to his early obsession of art and became a gentle, if daffy, old man with no trace left of the overbearing scoundrel. The joke in town was that he used to act as if he owned all the women in Nebraska, and anything over the state line couldn't be vouched for. Paul, with typical wisdom, said that the danger of art when the calling is obsessive and becomes ingrained is that there is no way to turn your back on it.

Nelse was nearly finished with his breakfast when I asked, "Don't you have something to say to me?" and he stood up so abruptly that he tipped his chair over. When he glanced at me after righting his chair he looked just over my head, mute and stricken, grabbed his topos and my satchel and rushed from the house. I quickly rinsed the breakfast dishes and joined him, getting in his truck as if nothing out of the ordinary had taken place. He then peered in the driver's-side window and said, "How did you know?" My answer was along the line of "How could I not know?"

Why didn't I marry my husband's brother, Paul? It didn't seem the right thing to do though I certainly know it was almost obligatory in certain Native tribes. This question is always the most poignant in September and October when so many species of birds group up and fly south. How I miss them. But when I mentioned this to Paul a scant year after John Wesley's death in Korea he said that was why he favored his retreat near the Mexican border of Arizona. I suppose I very nearly loved him but not quite enough. I warned Nelse this summer over his beloved J.M. that such passion for most of us occurs only once in this life and seems quite unlikely if there is a next. Neither Dalva nor Ruth know of the dozen or so meetings with Paul over the years. Both had cajoled me in their late teens toward my getting remarried but I only said the talent pool in this part of Nebraska was rather shallow.

It was a full half hour down the road before Nelse could gather himself enough to ask questions but I refused most of them saying that it was proper to take them up with his actual mother. The hardest, of course, was, "Why did you give me away" which I had to address as it certainly wasn't Dalva who gave her son away. I fibbed a bit. Perhaps "lied" is a better word. My father-in-law tore my mind to pieces over this and I did the same to him. We took both sides of the question and never met in any middle, reversing our previous positions on alternate days. After the decision to give the infant away we did not so much as glimpse each other for a couple of months despite our proximity. We all seem to have a touching conviction that for every problem there is a solution. There wasn't and isn't. Our two choices were both clearly wrong.

It was not until the next morning over near Valentine that I began to wonder about genetics, and then for only an hour until I abruptly gave up. There is so much in educational doctrine that says a child is in most respects a "tabula rasa" but then, after thought, I doubt if anyone believes it. Despite the surface good manners of the way he was raised there seemed to be a large quantity of his birth parents within Nelse, an "all-or-nothing" attitude toward life that I doubted came from his adoptive parents. I certainly had suspicions that such a quality could be transferred genetically but he nearly convinced me otherwise. I filed this mentally under things we are not meant to know or understand though in the future they might devise some means to accurately penetrate such a biological idea. Nelse seemed to have a good share of the acuity of Paul's and Dalva's intelligence but tempered by his father's feral impulsiveness. Up near the Ainsworth Canal which is adjacent to the McKelvie National Forest, Nelse vaulted a fence rather than climbing it or crawling under. I know that Duane always did so, landing once rather too close to a rattler. The rattlesnake is beside the point but the vaulting is an almost violent gesture. He admitted that he had a nagging head injury left over from high school football which he recently re-injured on the door jamb of his truck. I told him that all the fauna he so admires have a measure of caution for survival. He nodded gravely in agreement but later in the McKelvie he climbed a pine tree for the view, a branch broke and he slid a dozen feet downward tearing his shirt and bruising his midriff. Of course his physical appearance could have been deceiving me, and I could not help falling back on breeds of dogs, horses and cattle. For instance, as you grow older you tend to slowly recognize that you are less unique than you thought you were earlier in life. Perhaps my mind and heart, as full of thanks as they were for his arrival, were trying to make Nelse into truly our own. And if he were so that would relieve me of the last portion of guilt over giving him up as a baby.

I will reach sixty-five in December. There are somewhat comic realizations in the aging process that you thought you understood previously but it was very much a surface understanding. Primary among these is that it all happens just once. Back at our pond I watch the cottonwood leaves begin to descend after the first frost, and within a month the trees are shorn, and on the bottom of the pond when the light is correct you can see the huge aureole of yellow leaves pasted to the muddy bottom from the shoreline to the depths. I see the features of my daughters change in ways that I do not notice in my own because the daily view of my own, pleasant enough, involves changes too gradual to notice. But often my daughters would only visit once or twice a year making the maturation process immediately apparent. You could always immediately read Dalva's face but Ruth's was so restrained it took study. Dalva never withheld herself from men she was interested in while Ruth spent months pondering the issue before opening her heart a bit. She even did so in high school and college well before her unfortunate marriage.

Reading your own face is, of course, a different matter. It often becomes so tiresome you don't really see it. The idea that you are passing this way only once is well beyond mirrors to tell a significant part of the story. A long time ago when Dalva was at the University of Minnesota she sent me a pair of snowshoes at the onset of what appeared would be a hard winter. I set out alone on these contraptions which take some getting used to but after a while enjoyed the freedom of entering swamps and thickets that are barred to you in the winter if you are using cross-country skis. I had turned for home at midday on a long Saturday walk, crossing the snow-covered frozen pond which is fed by a dozen springs and from which the creek that runs north toward the Niobrara emerges. Anyway, I slowly and helplessly broke through the ice and floundered there quite wildly. I kept thinking of a girlhood experience when I watched a young deer struggling desperately, caught at its midriff by the high fence my father had built to protect a stack of hay. The snowshoes pressed down large sheets of thin ice so I sank quite slowly as I listened to the shrieks and chirrups I was making, my heart pumping spasmodically with fear. A crow flew over with only the briefest downward glance. I had verged on accepting my fate when the water was breast high and my snowshoes touched bottom. I fairly shimmered there despite the cold blustery air that was driving the snow around me like ground mist. I realized quite quickly that I was on the deepest edge of a sandbar familiar from swimming and wallowed toward the near shore, half scrambling, then crawling where the ice was considerably thicker near the bank. It had been barely more than ten degrees when I left the house so that my wet clothing froze and crunched as I walked and gave me some relief from the wind.

My clearest memory of it after I reached the house was that the experience had been beyond prayer. Naturally I was thankful on the long walk back, a mile or so, but during the event itself I was simply another desperate animal facing very possible death. The

deer stretched over my father's haystack fence had also twisted itself
free, not helped at all by my girlish tears. When I shed my clothes
before the stove I spoke to my absent husband, mostly saying, "Your
widow nearly joined you," and he answered, "You only have to do
that once." I agreed and said no more though his words hit me deeply
because they covered both the bad and good of the idea of "only once."
This strikes me the hardest at the times of the solstices, by which I
mark my years. In the winter I'm pleased when the days get lighter
but in spring and summer I often dread the passage of moments with
the clearly banal thought that this summer will not re-occur except
in intermittent memories.

When I think, as I often do, how my life before my marriage was so
totally swept away by my marriage I now also think of Nelse. One
early September dawn while we were birding I asked him if he had
any regrets about showing up and meeting us all, and how that so
utterly changed the routine of his life. He looked back in the direction of my house a couple of miles away, and then in the direction of
the old place where Dalva lived, as if to truly locate himself, then he
said he couldn't have done otherwise. There was a specific rawness
to the way he looked and spoke. J.M. had left for Lincoln the morning before and I had heard them quarreling in the distance when they
walked down the country road just before dark. It was apparent that
evening how unnerved he was by the radical change in his life and
how upset he had been when Dalva had completely sided with J.M.
over how much time he would spend in Lincoln. He was bargaining
for three days a week in Lincoln and four up here and J.M. insisted
on the reverse. He had stood up from the supper table waving a
chicken drumstick and said, "Goddammit" very loudly. This somehow shocked and amused me. I had only taken "the Lord's name in
vain," as we called it, once in my life when I had driven over to Bassett
to pick up John Wesley after he had wrecked his plane. It was early
evening and he was standing there leaning against a fence with several farmers passing a bottle of whiskey. I fairly howled, "Goddammit"

and the men turned from me and looked at the crumpled plane. Men like to give foolhardy things a patina of rationality. John Wesley simply loved airplanes though he didn't care for airports, thinking they somehow diminished the glory of what he called his "sport." Of course on our road, his landing strip, there were many days no cars passed at all except the mailman. I am mindful of the fact that Dalva yelled out when she was twelve that if it were up to me nothing would have been invented. In defense I said I approved of books and binoculars and antibiotics but then began to run out of steam.

Nelse's "goddammit" resounded with the ache of a male trapped by females. The dinner table was a cage we had built for him God knows why. We even tried to make him eat too much. Dalva brought over some nice wine from the old place, where Nelse insisted on staying in the bunkhouse like his father. He admits to being an occasional claustrophobe and he and Lundquist tore out a big section, making a screen out of a wall. Presumably glass will be installed later, I thought, but they built swinging doors like a barn door for when he is gone. Almost idiotically he said that on cold nights he likes the cold, and on warm nights he likes the warmth. Dalva thinks that part of his unrest came about last weekend when she showed him the Native artifacts in her sub-basement and asked him to help redistribute them to their proper place. He said there was no longer a truly proper place but he'd think it over, then he stayed down there an entire night which upset her. I think she should make the house her own and that shouldn't include caring for the family ghosts.

My own family place was over southeast of Gordon, not all that far in Nebraska terms from where Mari Sandoz of *Old Jules* fame was raised. No white person ever looked more clearly at our extirpation of the Natives, particularly the Sioux. Pine Ridge and its infamous site of Wounded Knee was but a hundred miles north so that Sandoz wasn't some distant scholar. She was very much my hero by the time I reached my teens and the very thought that a local young woman could become an admired citizen of the world thrilled me. Perhaps my heart is weaker now because I no longer can bear to look at some of her books, especially *Crazy Horse* and *Cheyenne Autumn*. The cruelty of what happened to our first citizens is too great in dimension. But it's not just the books, it's because I was born and raised with stories of Native tribulations that had become the darkest part of our own family history. My father had told me that his own father had left Sweden to escape government oppression, including the draft, only to arrive in northwest Nebraska well before the Wounded Knee Massacre. Such aspects of local history were more thought about than talked about but we were no more ignorant of them than German civilians during World War II were ignorant of the death camps in their vicinity. The answers to childhood questions were the harshest because the children have so few buffers to their feelings. My father was a mediocre farmer but had a good mind and was an amateur student of our history. Oddly to most, his own social trauma was that he had married a Norwegian girl to the disapproval of both families. This seems garishly stupid now but the young couple was as much as forced to move from their mutual roots in Loup County to Sheridan near Antelope Creek.

Nelse knows so much of Native history though I'm pleased his contact with our historian, Michael, was limited by Michael's inability to speak and by the time his injured jaw was unwired he was quite ready to leave. Nelse's temperament is such that I knew he'd admire Michael but the influence wouldn't be positive at this time. (I just sent Michael a check as a "loan" for the benefit, supposedly, of his lovely daughter but I have my doubts.) Michael could shape all history into a continual reign of terror. I have never met a man less in touch with the "dailiness of life," so relentlessly blind to his immediate surroundings. Nonetheless, it was easy to be carried away by his wit and learning. Even austere Paul indulged him for the few days Paul was around when Michael could resume his talking. There is certainly a wicked streak to most tertiary alcoholics I have known. They are so utterly self-referential that the world only exists inasmuch as it relates to them. Paul and Nelse are both a bit remote with alcohol, Paul certainly because of his father, and Nelse from what he had told me of his adoptive mother, though this wasn't apparent when he brought her up for a short visit in September. When I mentioned this Nelse said she doubtless had some booze in her suitcase. He speaks of her as his biggest problem though he treats her with courtly affection. Besides, his obvious biggest problem is the idea of whether or not he wishes to settle down and marry J.M.. He has begun his year-long phenology of an approximate rough-edged section of land containing the marsh and pond, and following the creek to the Niobrara. He has also started the planning with Lundquist for some sort of agricultural experiment the nature of which he hasn't completely announced though it involved fencing seventy acres into seven different portions. He even asked the county agent out for advice and I was teased in the county seat while shopping that this had to be the first time in an even century that a Northridge has asked anyone for advice. They are rather jolly about not holding me accountable for my husband's family. There is also the idea that a country school teacher is a passive heroine and though she may have a secret life that would make the God-fearing upchuck, she is beamed at wherever she goes.

Dalva's problems seem to be half drowning her. If it weren't for Nelse and her horses and puppy I'd be fearful. Her man friend, Sam, has a sullen edge about money that he can't quite control. I didn't tell her that better she know this now, as I doubt the problem can be overcome. J.M. has a bit of this too, but is convinced somehow it isn't Nelse's fault. Even more problematic and wearing is Dalva's job which failed to get adequate government funding after the original announcement of an appropriation. The Department of Agriculture prefers glowing items, and the rising amount of farm bankruptcies in the southern area of the county is a dominant item only to the press and the suffering families. One fourth-generation farmer hanged himself in the barn he no longer owned right after the auction that dispersed his cattle and equipment. Dalva spent several days with the wife and adult children and a number of relatives right before a program conference in Lincoln where, she admitted, she shot off her mouth enough to be called a "communist sympathizer" by a state congressman which she didn't accept gracefully. I certainly have doubts about her career as a civil servant. I suppose an effective psychiatric social worker must learn to blunt perceptions and feelings to survive. She has also been harried by a number of museum curators, no doubt because of Michael's big mouth, about the propriety of keeping such valuable paintings in "an old wooden farmhouse." She has refused any attempts by the curators to visit.

I have often wondered why her fascination with natural history is so slight as if my own skipped a generation and landed on Nelse, but then she has never been one for details. The happiest I have seen her recently was last weekend when she was helping Nelse and Lundquist put up fence. The fence master Rex had also been hired at my suggestion and Lundquist's agreement. Dalva drove the tractor with the power auger and Lundquist mostly supervised. He's in his eighties but not really weak as he is most frequently carrying his dog over his shoulder. I brought over a picnic on Saturday but Rex wouldn't share the food. He lives in a shed on his mother's small place and each morning she gives him a modest piece of meat from the freezer. In his ragged denim coat he carries a small iron frying pan and by lunch the meat is thawed enough and Rex builds a fire. This is clearly a delight for him and he is not averse to carving up the good remaining parts of road kills, from deer to woodchuck to the occasional rattler which he skins to sell as hatbands. He rides an old balloon-tire bike with a basket, plus saddlebags for his fencing tools. Nelse has offered to pick him up and take him home but this is out of the question, though it is a matter of seventeen miles each way. "I like to ride my bike" is all he'll say. There is much grumbling among ranchers who employ him because each summer Rex's mother takes a charter bus with several dozen other women out of Scottsbluff bound for Las Vegas and there is the offensive idea that the money Rex makes is poured into slot machines. The whole notion of an evil mother is hard on men's sensibilities. Way back in third grade Rex was in obvious pain one morning but wouldn't tell me anything so I asked his sister who smugly explained that their mother caught Rex "playing with himself" and beat his genitals with a coat hanger. We had no social worker at the time so I called the sheriff and there were no more beatings. The sheriff let me know that he told the woman if anything happened again he'd skin her like a deer. This is scarcely good law enforcement but it worked.

I've been having a long-distance quarrel with Paul. The only grace note is that we're conducting it by letter, mostly because Paul thinks a multitude of problems are caused by trying to conduct serious matters over a telephone. His contention is that who among us can speak aloud their mind precisely enough, while the process of writing it down requires hard thinking. It began when he offended me in August one evening on the porch when he said it was hopeless for me to try to shelter Nelse. He said that it's as if I'm trying to prevent Nelse from running screaming off into the sunset. Paul is obsessively taxonomical in all matters and prefers the human world without shadows though he knows otherwise. He has in his possession an old manuscript of his father's which he calls a "false memoir" because as a son he saw it all quite differently. Paul views the memoir as "engaging" and thinks Nelse should be allowed to read it since in a blinding week he already read the notebooks of the first J. W. Northridge. I refused to read the manuscript myself but, of course, Dalva loved it since he was in so many respects her father and could do no wrong. She thinks my objections on the matter of incest are absurd because the meeting of her and Duane was unintentional. The fact that my own husband was possibly the father of both of them grieved me terribly when I discovered it. I suppose it was the overriding issue in why we finally decided to give Nelse up for adoption. It wasn't my husband's infidelity that hurt me the most but the final result of it, a horribly biblical event where the illegitimate son, now nearly an adult, comes out of the hills and unwittingly mates his half sister. This was sheer accident. But why should their own son know? Isn't it enough that he was given away? Dalva, untypically, has said that it's up to me. She is quite tired of talking it over and is ever so vaguely suspicious of my motives. I can't convince her that it's not my husband's infidelity that bothers me. If a man goes off on a hunting trip of two weeks' duration he is an easy mark for temptation. Despite a lifetime of church-going I can't see that the human animal has evolved beyond being circumscribed by ordinary lust that is imme-

diate and spontaneous. And a hunting camp would have few barriers. Certainly not the presence of a brother and a father, the latter
being a renowned reprobate himself. So it's not sexual squeamish-
ness on my part. Paul further irritated me the other day in a letter
by suggesting that I never had a son to mother and since they are
rather more slow to learn than daughters I am taking advantage of
the situation. I wasn't sure what to make of this as there was a nagging feeling beneath my breastbone and I couldn't quite locate the
cause.

Dalva came over for Sunday morning breakfast and we made potato
pancakes like we did long ago. She said Nelse and Rex were working
on the fence despite Lundquist's lecture against working on Sunday.
It was very warm for October and after breakfast we sat on the porch
swing drinking too much coffee while she had a laughing fit over the
possibility of losing her job after only two months. The state congressman she insulted is demanding she be fired and has managed to
get ahold of some unfortunate comments from her work record in
Santa Monica. Her superior in Lincoln has called to suggest that the
best she can do at the moment is to offer a written apology and Dalva
said that that would be like apologizing to a cow flop for the unfortunate experience of stepping on it. Evidently she had been asked
pointedly by the state congressman why she thought the government should step in and help save a farm when the farmer couldn't
save it himself? She admits she was being a little flippant when she
replied that all sections of the economy tend "to feed from the public trough," including the congressman's business in oil and gas leases.
The expression was a very old one she got from her grandfather who
was neither left nor right politically but merely crushed all forms of
opposition to his land interests.

We went for a walk back to the pond and when we stopped to
look at a patch of wild, dried-up globemallow Dalva quite suddenly
said that Paul was correct, that I feared that if Nelse knew everything
he might run for it. She thought that unlikely and besides his natu-

ral curiosity would finally pin down the truth. The little pang beneath my breastbone began to jiggle and I sat down to draw my breath remembering when my own father had left us though only for a scant month. My mother could become quite depressed but aggressively so, and usually she'd become quarrelsome. My oldest brother, Gus, about fourteen at the time was enough of a bully to ignore this, but Erik who was twelve would go out and sleep in the barn. I was ten or so and I remember clearly my father yelling out in the hall that if she wouldn't make love to him he would go to North Dakota. And he did for a month. I think we were partly frightened because it was mid-March and by late April my father would have to begin getting the fields ready or there would be no crops and we'd lose the farm. Of course he returned in plenty of time but this mental vision of a man running away stuck with me and was further driven home when I was eighteen and Erik left us forever. There was still more than a vestige of primogeniture in our area and Erik could see clearly that Gus would inherit the farm and by the time he was in his teens he had developed an abiding bitterness over the matter. It seemed unfair to me at the time and still does, an ancient unjust system that kept the farms intact but ruined so many sons who weren't first in line. So many became hapless wanderers, alcoholics, angry hired hands. The last we heard from Erik was in the early fifties and when I later traced him to Eugene, Oregon, his response was too cold to endure.

My reverie was so deep that my head began to droop. Dalva sang out a parody of a wretched country song about it being hard to be a woman and we both laughed, then continued down the hill to the pond. It was so warm for October there were still insects in the air and the remnant birds that should have headed south by now, a solitary flycatcher that perhaps was brain damaged, and a red-winged blackbird that couldn't fly very well, its left wing a bit stiff. I didn't want to think of the coming end to its story.

"You know Nelse is going to Arizona to check on his dog, then down to see Paul on the border. You think if he reads Grandpa's manuscript he might not come back. Simple as that. I waited half my life for Duane to come back though my mind told me it was out

of the question. Before that when you and Dad took trips I was always looking out the window, even at night thinking the stars on the
horizon might be distant car lights. Even when Dad died in the war
I thought he might come back with the smell of the airplane on his
clothes, the mixture of oil and gasoline and sweat. I'm sure this kind
of longing in the human race started back before we had a language."

She was slightly embarrassed by her speech and tried to change
the subject, then faltered. "What the hell will I do if I lose my job? I
have no idea. Sit by the window and wait for no one to come back.
You should know I sent Michael a check to bail him out of a drunk-
driving charge. Now he has to get an apartment nearer the university because he isn't allowed to drive for six months which is a real
public service. But you calm down. If Nelse doesn't come back I'll
track him to wherever he is. And you can give him more advice. He
said your advice was the only good advice he had gotten in this life.
That's quite a compliment. With me he said he could see where he
got some of his peculiarities."

It was my turn to be embarrassed and I suggested a long walk
which she declined. She intended to take a nap right there on the
sandbank of the pond. I needed to exhaust myself now that my fluttering sense had subsided. The whole subject of Nelse leaving had
been clarified and I inwardly cringed at the idea of approaching it
again so I set off for the northwest to a far corner of the property I
visited less than once a year because it is well beyond the last of the
windbreaks and shelterbelts and the birding is poor except for the
land immediately adjacent to the Niobrara. The terrain is rolling and
the grasses indigenous because it has never been tilled. When we were
first married I'd often go there with my husband when he was bird
hunting. There was a nearby prairie chicken lek, which is what they
call the immediate area where those splendid birds do their spring
mating dances, the males strutting in heraldic display. There are also
many sharp-tailed grouse in the area and when we were first married
my husband had a senseless old English setter named Bob whom you
couldn't stop hunting until he dropped with exhaustion, and then
my husband would carry him over to a slough off the Niobrara where

he'd revive. I'd pack us a picnic and after lunch we'd sometimes make love, quite glorious in these surroundings. The spring that the dog died, at the advanced age of thirteen for setters, he'd run off to this area and point the prairie chickens strutting on their lek from a discreet distance, never moving in his distant point. The last time it was raining and Bob had enlarged a badger hole which he had partly backed into and when we found him he appeared to be pointing, rigid and drooling from this vantage point. The birds at the lek, perhaps a hundred yards away, appeared undisturbed. Bob's hips had gone out and my husband had to carry him the nearly three miles home which took some time as the dog weighed a good eighty pounds and was ungainly to carry. I walked behind them with poor Bob regarding me mournfully from his position slung over my husband's shoulder.

I looked at Dalva from the far side of the pond and she already seemed to be dozing. I set out at a good pace wanting to return by midafternoon to make a good dinner for her and Nelse. I was so preoccupied that I'd sincerely forgotten to go to church today, the only time I've missed this year except for an early March ice storm. I was going to ask Dalva to go but then she's only been once since coming home, not liking our new minister transferred here by the Luther synod. Like me he's at the end of the road before retirement though I'm giving school my heart rather than droning through the motions like this poor nearly dead soul.

On the far side of the marsh there was a buck snort, the deer bursting from willows. How do they make this harsh nasal wheeze? Remnant blackbirds were flocking like airborne minnows. Good-bye. After this year I'd obey Paul and go places, mostly to see birds, like Mexico and Central America. My Amazon boat ride was a bit of a flop as I couldn't walk. The same reason the Everglades fell short for me. A friend says that Costa Rica is the place for birds. When Lena, Marjorie and I went to Brazil we had two days in Rio before we flew north and we laughed relentlessly, feeling so lumpish and dowdy sitting on a bench before the grand beach at Ipanema. Thousands of thonged girls, a sea of bare bottoms, and we sitting there in our flowered Nebraska summer dresses. A poor boy tried to grab Marjorie's

purse but she had come prepared with the strongest strap and she
jerked him off his feet on the sidewalk. She's certainly stronger than
most men. The best trip ever was between World War II and Korea,
1948 I think, when I went to England with my husband though old
J.W. followed us with overseas telegrams concerning land sales that
had to be attended to at the time. We took the train up to Hereford
and while he visited the Hereford Registry to talk about cattle breeding I went to this splendid cathedral. Back in London it became hot
and he bought me a sarong at which I laughed knowing he was keen
on the actress Dorothy Lamour. I wore it in our room anyway. He
also liked Claudette Colbert. I liked Robert Ryan because he reminded me of my husband. Paul too. I loved England because it further brought to life all the stories I read to my students from the *Book
House*, from nursery rhymes to "Tom Thumb" to "Una and the Red
Cross Knight." Often students love most the stories furthest from their
own background.

I was dawdling by the time I reached the side of the hillock above
the lek. The dog's hole which had been overgrown was now recently
excavated by a coyote so I moved upward to avoid the specific odor
coyotes manage. I began to think about the information advanced
cognitive ethologists are suggesting, to the effect that each bird has a
quite separate personality. I also remembered an essay Dalva had sent
in the early spring by some admittedly goofy poet she cared for that
said that reality is an accretion of the perceptions of all creatures, not
just us. The idea made my poor brain creak in expansion like a barn
roof as the morning sun heats up. I think some mystic said that we
see God with the same eye he sees us with. Despite our age I made
love with Paul this summer. We thought, Why not? I curled up there
and went to sleep dreaming of the Airedales that used to come over
from J.W.'s place to visit us and thoroughly ignored me in favor of
their playmate Dalva. She rode her horses too fast.

Unfortunately, I slept until after four, waking a little chilled and
astounded. It must have been accumulative exhaustion and I didn't
make it back to the pond until after five though I walked as fast as
possible. Nelse met me there, trotting down the hill with a worried

face. Dalva had sent him to look for me. I liked the way his face lighted up when he saw me.

Back at the house I had my first martini since our San Francisco trip in late spring, and we cooked the beef roast too fast because we were hungry. It was too rare with the potatoes, onions and carrots barely done. It was the best bad meal I could remember. The rawish meat was a contrast to Mozart's Jupiter Symphony on the old stereo. After dinner I got out the medicine kit and dressed a bad blister on Nelse's hand, a result of his fence making. Dalva watched us gravely and said, "Should I be doing that?" but then laughed. She looks more like his older sister than mother.

Nov. 29, 1986

He did come back. A few weeks ago, that is. The fact that I expected him to did not diminish the pleasure of when his truck pulled into the yard. He didn't bring back his dog, Ralph, which surprised me. He said only that Ralph had nearly doubled in weight and seemed quite happy with the old couple. It was a dog's version of retirement, with the fillip that if the couple became too infirm they'd ship him by air to Nelse.

It was evening when he arrived and he had stopped at Dalva's but there was a strange car in the yard and he hadn't wanted to interrupt if there was a boyfriend visiting. I said it was Lena's car which he should have recognized, and Dalva's visitor was her girl-hood friend Charlene who was Lena's daughter home from New York. Nelse is putting off the beginning of his phenology study until April Fools' Day when the slow and niggling spring will at least have offered an indication of it arrival. Meanwhile, he will be busy disposing of the Native artifacts and is irked that the noteworthy authority in the state is a professor he offended while in college. Of course the biggest hurdle which even seemed to narrow my peripheral vision that evening by the stress it caused was whether or not he had read the dreaded memoir.

"Did you think it would scare me away?" he teased.

"I didn't know. Perhaps it would some people."

"It's only a bit of linebreeding." And then he sensed something in my face. "I'm sure you felt very bad about it but it's thirty years ago. Besides Paul said there was an outside chance it was him. Why don't you hold onto that possibility?"

"Because Paul was probably only trying to save my feelings. Rachel, Duane's mother, seemed sure it was my husband."

"Maybe because she liked him the best of the three, or even loved him for a short while."

"The three?"

"Paul said he was sure his father was involved early on. There was a good deal of drinking. Historically, the westward movement was based on whiskey."

"Oh Jesus Christ." There I was swearing again but I was loosening inside. Think of that old bastard but then he wasn't so old at the time. I appreciated Nelse's attempt at humor until I began to cry. He leaned over my chair and put his arm around me.

"You're the one that insists my mother get rid of the ghosts in her house. You better let this one go. From what I heard you're lucky your husband and Paul were good men, compared anyway to their father who was a major league something. No, that's not right. He was in the wrong century probably. Even after Paul tried to write between the lines of what I read I admired him but then I didn't have to be his son."

We were saved when he noted coffee cups on the dining room table, and two on the table in front of us. I've always found it chilling when people are forced to talk about the deeper and most grievous things in a matter-of-fact way as if we were all undertakers for our past.

"The first two"—I pointed at the cups in front of us—"are the parents of a little girl having problems in the third grade. They're from Massachusetts and came out this way in the summer. Pulled up stakes in the Boston area. He's the cousin of the wife of a big rancher in the area. His wife is purportedly an artist but he had decided in his mid-thirties that he wanted to be a cowboy though I heard they already have him doing the ranch books. Their daughter in my school thinks we are all dumb out here. She uses the word a dozen times a day. I told them she shows signs of melting and when she gets home she probably pretends she's unhappier than she is to punish the people who moved her. The mother already wishes to move back East but the father refuses.

Nelse had quickly lost interest and I went on to the dining room. "Our Mission Group from church had their semi-annual meeting. We are partly sponsoring an orphanage in Central America."

"The Rose Bud and Pine Ridge are pretty close to the north of here. You got plenty of semi-local orphans," he said without a twinkle.

This wasn't shifting down all that far from our family's problems. The family also has a pretty good record of anonymous generosity but it was self-serving to say so to a young man with such a sharp eye for the economic brutalities.

"Maybe we prefer Central America because if we gave our money to the Sioux that would admit that our grandparents and great-grandparents shouldn't have shoved them out of here, " I parried.

This answer pleased him and a glance at the kitchen told me he was hungry. I fixed him a late supper while he almost babbled about a matter of economics dear to him to which Paul had largely agreed. A certain class of people, many with a good start in the world and largely in reaction to the Great Depression, had devoted their lives to an absorption in meaningless work and made a lot of money. These grandparents and parents then "dumped" the money on their children which has had mixed results similar, according to Paul, to the history of the gentry in Europe. It's hard for these younger people to find meaningful work, or obsessive work, because the necessity isn't quite there. Often they feel like "jerk-off amateurs," or so he said, to whom it is impossible to offer any sympathy when you think of the world at large. I mostly agreed but said any ordinary people I've known would prefer meaningful work to simply making money. And maybe ranchers and farmers tend to mythologize their supposed virtues and work to give it more meaning. It's unfortunately harder to do in an office or factory because that's more recent. I added that that's why

someone like J.M. or me, with our backgrounds, can feel a little remote from the rest of the family.

The latter made him quite melancholy for a few moments but
then he abruptly left the kitchen for the dining room phone and called
J.M. I gave an extra rattle to the dishes as I washed them to offer them
more privacy. Oh my God but reality is difficult, I thought, and if
the Christians are wrong and others right it might be pleasant to return to earth as a bird or a tree. I've always tithed and that amounts
to something given my husband's money but that scarcely buys you a
good night's sleep. The last thing someone like Nelse is looking for
is a good night's sleep.

Thanksgiving has always given me oddly mixed feelings partly, I suppose, because in my childhood the holiday actually represented the
end of harvest, the late fall butchering, and putting the farm somewhat to sleep for the winter. Neighbors would visit us and we'd visit
neighbors and the elaborate cooking was scarcely limited to the turkey, an underwhelming bird. When you teach you notice all the
wrangles centered on who is going where for Thanksgiving, what set
of parents is to be honored. It is a little comic in its ups and downs,
the raw nerves that have nothing to do with the earlier celebrations
which were communal. For instance, I felt a pang when Ruth called
and said she wasn't coming home from Tucson, but this was immediately leavened when I heard she had a new gentleman friend, a
widower, and she was cooking dinner for him and his adult children.
J.M.'s parents are coming but just for the day. Nelse's mother and her
companion will stay a single night. Nelse will drive J.M. back to Lincoln the next day as she has her studies to tend to. Dalva loathes
turkey and insists on a rib roast on the side which she will cook though
the two don't go together and I suggested a ham at which she turned
up her nose. We decided to eat at her place to avoid the family portraits at the end of my dining room.

All of which makes me have some doubts about the "bourgeois"
and the "bourgeoisie" as Dalva called them when she was at the uni-

versity, and I also have heard Nelse use the terms. He, incidentally, is taking the holiday with the stoical good manners he said he got from his adoptive father who has sounded very appealing. I asked Nelse if he'd rather roast a road kill in a cave and he said, "Why, of course." My own mixed feelings come from reading my books from my daughters' rooms which are essentially the way they left them over twenty-five years ago, or books that they have sent me to disturb my peace. Because of Ruth I've read all of these biographies of musicians, including Robert Craft's on Stravinsky and, later, Ned Rorem, and of course the older romantics. The evident scorn of middle-class flummery was startling and endearing. I also read a number of Dalva's college novels including *Lady Chatterley's Lover* which caused a lot of blushing in that my husband cherished making love out of doors and I didn't mind it a bit. I tried to read a Henry Miller novel, who was certainly what we used to call a rapscallion, but it was too much for my background, though I did care very much for his *Colossus of Maroussi* and I fully intend to go to Greece at some point after I retire. Lena also loved the book and is going with me, mostly because my dreadful father-in-law left us a travel fund and I convinced Lena that because she was the old goat's lover for a short while she certainly had earned some voyages. The all-time record for reading heartbreak was one spring vacation when Dalva was home from the university and she insisted I read *The Brothers Karamazov*. That was a long time ago and I can't say that I am over the experience yet nor should I be. Second in this line was a Christmas present from Ruth, James Agee's *Let Us Now Praise Famous Men*, which was about dire poverty in the South with copious photos by a gentleman named Walker Evans. We certainly lacked any money during the Depression but we were never short for good food on the farm. The photos of these families in the South showed the most wretched signs of malnutrition.

All of which is to say that I've been much exposed but not in real life. I doubt what I know. From this hillock I see no other human dwelling. In other words I know my own place from which you can't extrapolate the world. Dalva is three miles away and Athell Dodson's place a mile and a half. He plows me out in the winter and

on still, cold mornings I can hear his tractor start. Crow hates the
tractor and once pecked Athell on the head so I go out in my robe
and boots on blustery mornings and close up Crow in his cage.

With Thanksgiving close upon us again I've always seen the
repetitive nature of my doubts as part of the darkness of the season.
There is not quite enough sun to maintain life—I sensed this even
as a girl. I quite realize that my fascination with the natural world
has limited me and I should have traveled more in the summers, but
I always thought, How can I leave my garden and my birds. I'm
amazed at what cross-purposes we can be at with both ourselves and
others, and these emphasize themselves in November and December. My gardening magazines arrive but without savor. *Natural History* and *Audubon* can't quite hold my attention and Ruth's gift of
The New Yorker became quite irrelevant though I enjoy it during other
seasons. Dalva used to collect her *Nation* magazines and send a packet
every few months but I had her stop because as I got older the re-
counting of so many horrible problems became unbearable. On the
rare occasions that I watch television the picture becomes thin as the
screen itself, a basin of dishwater. My ordinary refuge, my religion,
becomes dry around the edges and the edges begin to penetrate the
center.

But how can this be when my religion has supposedly been my
unwobbling pivot since childhood. I believe in Jesus as the true and
only Son of God and the redemptive power of the Resurrection. There
it is. Why then does December 21st, after which the days get longer,
seize my heart's core stronger than December 25th when we feel our
Son of God was born? Of course I don't know other than during this
dark period I am more the ordinary mammal than I wish to be. I can
almost imagine one deer saying to another in the thickets along the
Niobrara, "At least it's getting lighter every day." This almost amuses
me but beyond the window there is only opaque blackness and, if I
move, my own reflection.

It is past midnight and a school night at that, an hour past my
bedtime. I pour myself a rare small glass of sherry and replay a Bach
partita, Bach because I don't want a pillow but serenity. My world

shrinks to the hundred and twenty-seven pounds I have weighed since I was nineteen. During the Korean War the voice of God seemed to be Edward R. Murrow and with Vietnam it was Walter Cronkite. I only lost one of my ex-students but a dozen were there, pleasant and eager boys. I slip to my knees and say my usual good-night prayer for my family, my inward voice hopefully penetrating a billion galaxies. A hard job indeed. I have chosen an honorable livelihood, say compared to the rapacity of the greed of my father-in-law, but right now this adds up to sore knees and the slightly beechnut taste of the sherry. Every year at this time it's as if I can taste faintly my mind's blood and it is vaguely acrid and taints my life with my elemental humanness.

I put on my coat and go out on the porch. The stars are a little dulled by a three-quarter moon which reflects off a thin skin of snow. I shiver hard though it's barely below freezing. Far behind me from the marsh I hear the delightful yelping of coyotes in chase, mindful that it is less delightful to whatever is being chased. My consolation tonight is simple enough and I can't even call it humility. I'm just Naomi, definitely an older woman looking at the moon and stars, ordinary as the earth they shine down upon. If that's not enough I have no more to offer, and to whom am I offering?

The next day I'm tired as a cowdog and I get home and there's Nelse and J.M. on the porch swing, a full day early. They're not even dressed warmly though it's in the uncommon mid-forties. I'm so pleased to see them I nearly trip getting out of the car. Nelse has let out Crow who is scolding a group of starlings at the far edge of the hedgerow. J.M. runs out to greet me, smiling widely but with the fatigue of school in her eyes. She unnerves me because Nelse has called out for her to show me how high she can jump. She bounces tentatively, then jumps a little too high for my perceptions. I am nonplussed because as a grandma I have nothing ready for dinner. They don't care and though it's only four now they say they're desperately hungry. I sense they made love in the car at some point on their trip up from Lincoln. I remember I had made and frozen some chicken soup when Lundquist brought me over a large batch of fryers. Nelse is always looking for more chunks of chicken in his soup so I'd put two in this batch. It is a Scandinavian version with rutabaga and potatoes in it and after eating two bowls each they nod off on the couch watching the six o'clock news. Nelse dislikes television but J.M. thinks of the news as an obligation.

I sit there watching them doze, thinking oddly of predestination. Is it presumptuous to think of a divine plan? All the evidence in the world seems to suggest the idea is absurd. I don't have the courage to make a decision on the matter. Her sleeping hand is on his leg and his neck is flopped over on the arm of the sofa. From memory I can imagine their nights. The phone rings and it's Dalva but they don't stir at the noise. She's pleased to hear of the early arrival. She was roasting a chicken and was going to bring it over and I tell her to go ahead, please. After so many years of camp cooking on the road Nelse seems to love everything we cook. I make a pot of coffee and J.M. wakes first with a shy smile. She puts the afghan over Nelse and we go into the kitchen. Dalva arrives and through the open door of the kitchen I see her pause, holding the roaster, and look at her son now spread out on the sofa. She adjusts the afghan, rather motherly for her, and comes toward us as if preoccupied, then nearly drops the bottle of wine she's holding under the roaster. She hugs J.M., nods at me, opens the roaster and wonders aloud if she used too much garlic. J.M. opens the wine and we sip it and for some reason the wine seems sacramental.

My Lord it's over. Nothing went really amiss though there was a brief, nervous moment when Nelse's mother's gentleman friend, Derek, asked over Thanksgiving desert, "How can you keep these paintings in an old farmhouse?" To his embarrassment Dalva helped him finish the sentence, then she said she was interested in art not the art market, quite different items. She has no idea what the paintings are worth and doesn't want to know. She emphasized that her grandfather had been a contemporary of the artists, had known a few of them, thus got them quite cheaply but likely at a price that pleased the painters. Of all people, J.M.'s father said that if you like a "picture" in your living room why should you give it up to someone else and, besides, he had a keen eye for construction and this old farmhouse would still be standing when many modern buildings were rubble. Derek joked that he was "outvoted" and let it pass though he turned pinkish.

A northern front came through and it was blustery but with not all that much snow. J.M. was worried and didn't want her parents driving home for three hours in such weather but her father, like nearly all farmers, couldn't be dissuaded from his plans. I'm always reminded in such situations of Thoreau's notion that the farm owns the farmer rather than vice versa.

The next day was quite cold, well below freezing, but clear and sunny and after seeing off his mother and her boyfriend Nelse and I took a long hike. We invited Dalva and J.M. along but they had the atlas and several other maps spread out and Dalva was showing J.M. places that she must visit. This seemed to make Nelse nervous and he waited for me out in the barnyard. On impulse he showed me his father's secret place up in the haymow and it unnerved me with its vague spiritual impact, the ungulate skull hanging from the rope twisting of its own energy, and the view through the cracks of the barn slats having a striking longitudinal effect on the landscape and the bright sunlight through the cracks casting stripes down our bundled-up bodies. Who really was Duane, anyway, I thought, with so much obvious unrest in his spirit that he had made my own religion seem abstract. He had reminded me of a boy I had found repulsively attractive (this is indeed possible!) when I was but twelve and my dad had hired a group of traveling, farm-working Lakota to help us get in the potato crop. Our family was a bit dour and the Lakotas' somewhat wild humor embarrassed us. Out my bedroom window I could see these Native men rolling their cigarettes in the evening. The whole group were bunking in the barn and of course were not allowed to smoke there. On the afternoon the harvest was finished my mother, in a rare good humor, made a venison stew out of an illegal doe my bully brother had shot. There was a fine bonfire in the barnyard so everyone kept warm while they ate. Though as I say I was only twelve at the time, one of the young Lakota with an especially hooked nose did a mock dance of a buck mule deer in rut, prancing vigorously around to the amusement of the others. He kept looking at me, recognizing in me the young woman I wasn't at the time very enthused about becoming. I must say I felt an odd tingle in my stomach. He jumped even higher than J.M. did the other day. Several of the older Lakota women looked at me and laughed. Oh how I wished my family could laugh like these poor, ragged people did, but it never would happen.

With Nelse and I exchanging leads we made a two-hour circle within the property with my thoughts only momentarily going in the unpleasant direction of the past week. We stopped to look at his cattle fences and the whole project struck me as a tad daffy. So much about the cattle business repulsed me that I didn't want to listen to his ideas about seven-part rotational grazing, though my ears perked when he said his cattle would never see a feedlot. Feedlots inevitably reminded me of the photos of prisoner-of-war camps. I said something about how in the old days the place had raised prime beef for the carriage trade and he was momentarily wistful about his amateur standing. I fretted aloud about how his plan might not work out and he drew me up short by saying I shouldn't devote the remainder of my life to worrying about my family. I said I'd try not to and laughed when I said that if you've raised enough chickens the idea of being a mother hen is not very attractive. It seemed a ghastly chore when I began feeding the chickens as a child and still does. Only Lundquist seems to enjoy raising chickens. He names them all.

The sun wasn't warm enough to melt the inch or two of snow and when we passed through a dense shelterbelt into a hundred or so acres of open prairie the effect was quite overwhelming. It was a portion of the property that had never been tilled and the indigenous grasses emerging from the thin snow cover were splendid indeed. I teased Nelse that he could build a fine sod house against the west shelterbelt border for protection against the prevailing winds and was startled when he said he had thought about it. There were fine bunches of prairie dropseed, switchgrass, buffalo grass and redtop which was especially striking against the snow. I didn't come here often because for birding reasons I prefer thickets. I recalled with painful clarity when I had walked out here with Paul after a nasty argument I had had with my husband over some stunt flying he had done at the county fair. Dalva had just recently been born and Paul was freshly home from Brazil. That's why we captiously named her Dalva, after a samba record Paul brought home called "Estrella Dalva." I believe I was crying on the porch and Frieda was holding baby Dalva when Paul suggested a walk and when we arrived in this field I was amazed at how he could identify all the different indigenous forbs and grasses and wildflowers many of which had become quite rare except in areas that hadn't been tilled or overgrazed.

I came out of my reverie when I saw Nelse crawling around in the snow and cutting small thatches and bouquets of the wild grasses with a penknife and then tying them up with binder twine from his pocket. He said he intended to hang them from the rafters of his bunkhouse for decoration. He gazed at these bouquets as if they were great art and they probably were. At such rare moments men seem glorious creatures, as if magical personages in those ancient tales in the *Book House*, rather than the oafs and louts that have made the world such a problematical place.

One warm evening in August when we were sitting on the porch swing actually holding hands Paul said, "My family never quite joined the world." I didn't say so at the time because I was waiting for what he might add but in my opinion his family never joined the world except strictly on their terms. I also could have said that included Paul himself, sitting there next to me with his mind seeing only his own ideas as if they were colored landscapes. My husband, John

Wesley, volunteered for Korea in order to fly more technically adven-turesome planes. To flout death on such a whim when you had two daughters seemed unforgivable at the time and still does.

When we got back to her house Dalva and J.M. were still look-ing at maps though there was now an empty wine bottle on the table and J.M. was telling a story about a trip she made at fourteen to a big 4-H convention in Washington, D.C. Their local leader had man-aged to get himself arrested for consorting with a prostitute but had been widely forgiven back home because that was simply the kind of thing that could happen in Washington. However, jokes of all sorts would continue to follow this man, mostly out of his earshot except the subtler ones from his peers, so that he finally moved to Kansas.

I went into the kitchen where Lundquist was fixing a clogged-up sink trap. His little dog growled and I gave him my customary piece of cheese, which caused him, as always, to twirl his slight body in pleasure. Lundquist, nearly invisible under the sink, recognized my shoes and began speaking his odd thoughts. For reasons best known to him but possibly not, the subject was my absent daughter, Ruth, whom he saw as "born" a music person the same way a young cousin of his over in Fergus Falls, Minnesota, had taken up the concertina when he was seven and never put it down. This cousin eventually became rich and famous playing for the large Polish communities in Milwaukee and Chicago, so much so that he was able to buy a new Plymouth every four years.

I reflected on this a moment and readily agreed that Ruth was a music person remembering that when Lundquist had had free time and the weather was a little less than horrible he would sit on the porch and listen to her practice, even if it was only the metronomic torture of scales. It was his contention that in heaven we will only speak in music because of the hundreds of unmanageable languages on earth. Lundquist had long since wandered beyond faith into the arena of permanent certainty which was somewhat enviable to me.

J.M. came into the kitchen and began deftly making tortillas, a talent she had learned from her Mexican-born mother. I smelled the pot of pork and green chile stew she had begun in the morning and it definitely cleared the sinuses. In fact while we ate dinner everyone sweated until their hair was quite damp except for J.M. She was embarrassed that she may have made the dish too hot but everyone loved it. Lundquist ate a small bowl before he left and did a spry little dance around the table. Nelse told a few engaging but I imagine bowdlerized stories of his adventures in the Southwest and Mexico including helping an old couple butcher a steer so spavined that there was scarcely any meat on its bones.

After dinner we sat before the fireplace in the den and listened to Glenn Gould who was Ruth's hero. The music didn't quite seem possible, whatever he played. Ruth had a photo of him in her bedroom playing with his gloves on. J.M. and Nelse had looks of blank affection on their faces and repaired to the bunkhouse early. Dalva and I talked desultorily about Nelse's nomadic existence and whether or not he'd be able to settle down but our hearts were not in an attempt to predict his future. I felt an unworded quiver of doubt over whether my own hopes and prayers should be offered up to try to influence or control someone else's destiny. I dismissed this theological question as being too onerous for my sleepy, after-dinner brain. Dalva's eyes were drooping and I thought of her own nomadic life and though it lacked the concentrated amplitude of Nelse's it had been pretty steady. I remembered some of our phone quarrels about her predilection for ramshackle cars when she could readily afford reliable ones. Of course I worried to no effect. Even now she was wearing a chamois shirt and old boots from her teens. It occurred to me yet again that our trajectories begin in childhood and are somewhat less movable than we wish to think. When tracing her life I've often thought that her grandfather had more influence on her than I did. There wasn't a single normally male prerogative she hadn't taken when the will had moved her. But then I cautioned this thought with my own plans for some wandering after the coming June when I retired. J.M. hoped to spend the summer here and had offered to take care of the garden whenever I was absent.

Dalva wouldn't wake up on the sofa so I found an old army blanket she cherished and covered her. I drove home in a white, glistening moonlight and saw Athell Dodson's old shaggy male dog trotting down the road as if he had a purpose. I sat on the edge of my bed for a short while studying the moonlight without a single thought but of the crisp shadows the moon was casting. I said good night to my long-absent husband and he bid me good night with the soft voice of one nearly asleep.

PAUL

Christmas Eve 1986

It is quite late and Naomi has gone to bed with no sense of an invitation for me to join her. How Christian in an odd sense. I had an errant feeling I might propose late this evening but then she made so much of her intentions of becoming a solitary traveler the impulse drifted away. I've always cared for birds but the interest never became an obsession to the point that I favored them over other species, including the botanical and human.

I could easily blame myself as I made a list this summer of a dozen or so places she might enjoy and when I came back for a prolonged holiday stay I noted that her shelf of travel books had expanded. Dalva looked at me strangely for a short moment when I so willingly gave up my boyhood room to J.M. who seems much taken by it. J.M. teased me about the many misidentifications in a large stone collection but then I told her I was only seven when I began gathering it. I tried to give her my arrowhead collection but she refused, saying that it was much too valuable. This was a nervous moment but then she said that Nelse was surprised by how simply I lived down on the border. She was looking at my boyhood bookcase, most of the titles quite absurd, including Horatio Alger (*Sink or Swim, Tom the Bootblack Boy*), the Hardy Boys, the Tom Swift Series (*Tom Swift and His Electric Rifle*) and the unpleasantly influential Richard Halliburton who never stopped wandering the world until he disappeared (*Seven League Boots*).

J.M. is what we used to call "fetching" rather than the more banal "pretty." Along with Dalva she strikes me as the least defenseless woman I've met and she's only twenty-two. I'd guess it's her mother's influence rather than her father's in that he resembles millions of

morose farmers who have begun to sense that the yeoman mythol-
ogy is fleeing the earth. Of course J.M. also had to have had his un-
qualified support just as Dalva had Naomi's and my father's. In so
many respects he was a monster but a splendid one in helping to raise
her, unlike myself and J.W. who received so much of his anger and
confusion. It's as if with J.W.'s death he was beaten into the ground
and emerged as a quite different human. It is proper to suspect con-
versions in general but this one became utterly convincing over the
years. It made me ponder what our succession of wars had done to so
many parents who sent off boys who were still half children in the
parents' own mind. I know J.W. packed his teddy bear for World War
II despite being his father's strident, male image in a way I could never
be. A teddy bear and a photo of Claudette Colbert in a bathing suit.
I once hid the photo as a joke and he was so bereft I immediately
replaced it on his dresser after he bellowed at Frieda in accusation.

My single, overwhelming regret about J.W. was a fistfight we
had when I was twenty and he nineteen and he had taken me for a
ride in his biplane and had done a series of stunts that had covered
my shirt with a big breakfast. We began fighting the moment we
landed for fuel in Grand Island and it took a number of bystanders
and a huge mechanic to break it up. I was embarrassed to overhear
an old man say, "Those Northridge boys are just like their daddy,"
the absolute last thing I wished to be. I was already a junior at Brown
(my mother's choice) and wished to be a geologist and a gentleman,
in that order.

I recall only looking at my father's art books furtively, not wanting him to confuse my idle curiosity with actual interest. I doubt at
the time that he much noted the degree to which I was at war with
him. I remember the ghastly moments at Brown when I first read
about the Oedipal complex, laying the book down carefully and fleeing the library. Oh my God, I thought, is behavior that predictable,
are my feelings really that primitive? The boy wishes to kill the father and have the lovely mother, Neena, to himself. The father has
pillaged her and there are occasional bruises on her arm, not because
he struck her she says but because his hands are far too strong. When

we were very young he'd bend nails with his fingers to amuse us, and flop a calf for branding as if it were a small bag of grain. After much begging John Wesley got a Newfoundland pup for his birthday which grew to an immense size within a year. The dog was an idiotic pest and one day the cowdogs ganged up and beat him severely. From the kitchen window I watched John Wesley howling with tears and my father sprinting toward the pick-up with this immense dog under one arm. I always felt there was something unnatural and evil about such physical strength and that during our worst times he became some mythological ogre from a children's story. Of course he could be charming for long periods of time and he never struck me but once and that was when I was sixteen and improperly baited him about abandoning his art and becoming a monster. He knocked me flat to the ground which made John Wesley very angry, then disappeared for several weeks. It seemed unforgivable but I soon forgave him, though he appeared never to forgive himself.

Before mother died when I was in my early twenties I was repelled when she told me he had been a wonderful lover. At first I attributed the statement to the amount of alcohol she drank and the breadth of medication she used to go to sleep or wake up. We were at her family's place at Wickford, Rhode Island, and I felt called upon to disagree, saying that being a wonderful lover had to be more than a physical thing. She said she had stacks of letters, many of them written long after they parted. I've always believed that what made them finally unsuited for each other was her sister, Adelle, who, long dead, was the most powerful influence in their lives. It was unfair to both of them but then one becomes puzzled over the word "unfair" in this century of relentless butchery. At Wickford there were many old photos of Adelle and she resembled a sensual version of Emily Dickinson. Of course this is after the fact but she certainly didn't look like a survivor. Her daffy cousin, a crusty Brahmin old maid, said that Adelle had nearly drowned as a child and had never fully come back to life except in a distorted sense. As a geologist I am primarily a scientist and I certainly didn't know what to make of this idea so simply stated over a glass of cheapish sherry.

* * *

A few days after New Year's on the day that I intended to leave, Naomi knocked at my door at five A.M., well before dawn. Within a millisecond my heart moved up into my throat. She said nothing beyond, "I'm lonely." There was a hard, blustery wind against the north window and I wondered if it was the weather that brought her to me, but quickly didn't care as her creature warmth enveloped me. Afterward I told her we had made love as if conserving energy and all she did was laugh, then quickly fall asleep. I awoke when I heard her car start and her tires spinning in the snowy driveway.

On my way out I had promised to stop at the country school and talk to her students about geology. I had tried to make some notes over coffee but the structure of the house began to disturb me. I was here for a short visit, freshly back from Brazil, when it was being built. It was rather too much like the old place for my taste though I didn't let it show. My jealousy was too poignant to hand around. The year before J.W. had taken me for a ride a hundred miles west of here near Gordon so I could meet his young love, Naomi. It was a small farm but neat as a pin showing that the family owned some storybook ideals. By that time I had just graduated from Brown and thought of myself as quite the man of the world. I was addicted to sophisticated young women from the East but thought it was appropriate that John Wesley had found himself a farm girl who was being trained to teach country school. Naomi was helping her mother in the garden when we arrived. When she stood up and walked toward us I was frankly dumbstruck. Why couldn't I find a Naomi for myself? The answer is because there is just one of each of us, both the question and the answer repeated numberless times over the years.

When I reached the school the students seemed terribly happy to be back in bondage for the New Year. I couldn't blame them as it seemed the same delightful place I remembered as a child. A half-shed windbreak had been built for the horses and three wore blankets while the other two were quite shaggy. Despite my being charmed there was a smallish streak of petulance in me that wanted to burn the place down and run off with the teacher. This feeling amused me. John Wesley had been dead for over thirty-five years, we were now into our sixties and had never gotten around to it. I had always cerebrally mocked the old saying "The spirit is willing but the flesh is weak," but this might be what it actually meant. It was less my inertia than her unspoken feeling that why couldn't I just come back home? In the small foyer after I entered I first touched, then smelled her coat as a child would. So much for growing older. I looked at posters about food groups and brushing your teeth. I was carrying a small case of rock samples I'd found in Ruth's old bedroom where I had sat down for a moment to read a book about the torments of Mozart's life, put it away, and then found similar mudbaths with Brahms and Mendelssohn. All artists as a type seem to suffer a great deal, but then so do miners.

My little chat to the students seemed to go over quite well though it was an effort to divert their interest from silver and gold. I assumed this intensity came from television but didn't inquire. I've never owned one myself though my housekeeper has a TV in her room and I can catch its soft and tinny sound through the walls. I certainly don't object to this. I'm not buying her life and she's curious about the world of which I've seen too much.

Naomi let the kids out for recess. I helped her bundle up a few of the smallest and then bade her good-bye. She kissed me full on the lips, which was a pleasant surprise, and promised she would come down and see me during her Easter vacation. I couldn't help but tease her about her motives in that the area where I live near the Mexican border has an influx of bird-watchers each spring that might very well equal the number of birds migrating. She blushed and said that I have always been nearly as interesting as a meadowlark, pinching my butt at the same time. I drove south.

I have always kept what I call "field notes" on my life though I'm not prone to reread them. There is such a lure to meaningless meaning in the face of the incomprehensible. I was, however, amazed that Nelse seemed imperturbable over losing his journals when his

pick-up was stolen, but then he said he had begun to view the journals as a form of slavery. Now he appears to be mostly redirecting his
compulsions by beginning a phenology of the ranch.

I'm a poor humanist but I remember well an old Yeats scholar
way back at Brown who several times quoted us "Byzantium" from
memory and I was very much struck by the line "The fury and the
mire of human veins." It seemed more a throwaway line than a sum-
ming up. This professor, though from Missouri, spoke in an irksome
Irish brogue. He was commonly referred to as a "daffy old fruit" by
his students, but I was curious about the extent to which Yeats ruled
his life. Driving away from the country school I struggled to remember another passage from another Yeats poem from more than forty
years before, something about age making one paltry unless you're
up to forcing your soul to clap its hands and sing. Of course poetry
must be rendered precisely but I wondered how the thought behind
the line struck me so forcefully. Dalva had reminded me after dinner
the day before of the time in my casita down in Baja when late one
still night the entire secluded bay had been filled with the sound of
dolphins surfacing and breathing. That certainly had made our souls
clap hands and sing but I've always known you have to be resourceful in the matter. You can't depend on dolphins.

I pulled off the country road onto the snowy shoulder for a
moment to decide if too much of my life had been based on aversion. Driving will do that sort of thing to one. The vehicle contains
your consciousness and it speaks to you in myriad voices. This has
long since ceased to confuse me. I certainly wasn't going to become
a rancher. My mother was somewhat asthmatic so my childhood
winters were spent in Arizona, leaving John Wesley and my father
to man the ranch. Arizona is one of those places where the formation of the earth is quite transparent and I early became fascinated
with geology. There is a mystery underfoot that is largely ignored
because it is largely invisible. Ergo, I became a geologist. I didn't want
to sit around and read and drink like my mother so I became a traveling, freelance geologist after three unfortunate wartime years working for a large corporation. I specialized in uranium deposits during

that short time, a matter of some importance in the war effort so I was considered too valuable to be cannon fodder like my impulsive brother later became. My mind can't say "uranium" now without a shudder of revulsion. After the war I only worked for individuals, usually determining the value or validity of mineral rights in inherited estates, though much of this work was done in Mexico. I also did some pro bono work for several Indian tribes to see if they were being swindled. Jean Paul Getty once made the not all that funny remark, "The meek shall inherit the earth but not the mineral rights."

I had barely reached forty when botany and a number of other subjects became more interesting than geology. Oil and mineral rights, even water rights in the West are matters of relentless contentiousness among humans. It often became too exhausting to endure but then I could easily fall back on what I inherited from my mother. I have always lived relatively close to the bone and certainly in places thought undesirable to others of my background. This is not a pointless eccentricity but came from my early distaste working for the abstraction known as a corporation. I have made brief visits to friends, male and female, in expensive enclaves from Beverly Hills to Palm Beach and these places always have seemed bleakly comic. I rather like the smells of goats, sheep, chickens, cows, the cries of street vendors, even the smells of what my neighbors are cooking, the sounds of their children. Now I live rather remotely but still simply. I like to be close to life processes, from flora and fauna to people. I like both my rich and poor friends but with the former I don't care for the shields, the barriers, the distances that keep them from all but their equals in wealth. Life is short. Why not be familiar with all of it? One quite wealthy friend contends that life is really rather long, an amusing difference of opinion. He is quite peculiar but perhaps so am I. The mainstream of any culture tends to be less than admirable.

The weather became poor and I only made it to Limon, Colorado, where I had a wretched dinner but the start of a pleasant evening in my motel room thinking of the fine time I had had with Naomi. As always Dalva had been problematical, wondering aloud on a walk, "What if Nelse doesn't want this place?" I tried to be diffident about the enormity of the question but then she drew me up short by asking if I didn't much care why had I bought out Ruth's son, Bradley? Of course, she was right but I said I had used what I call "dead money," funds that there was no likely use for, and because there were so few of us I wanted the succession graceful. I couldn't really add that despite the distance I had kept I couldn't bear to see the homeplace carved up during my lifetime, or the thought of it being carved up after I fumbled my way into the void.

I fell asleep with the light on and a book of Stephen Jay Gould essays on my chest, waking at three A.M. when the book thunked to the floor and the light went off. The bathroom light wouldn't work and the wind outside was shrieking. Out the window the mercury-vapor streetlight that had irritated me earlier was also out and the parking lot cars were covered with snow and ice and resembled dead sheep in the faint moonlight. I became pissed off as if the weather should make an exception for my trip back to the border. I felt the panels of the electric baseboard heat and noted it couldn't have been off for long. There was a small trunk of emergency supplies out in my old Land Cruiser and I had spent a great deal of time in areas of faulty electricity south of the border. The prospect of being truly cold could make the mind play unpleasant games. My younger friend Douglas had left his tent to take a pee in a blizzard in the Wind River area of Wyoming and had barely refound his tent before freezing to death, a rather astounding prospect for a man who only wished to relieve his bladder.

I took a feeble penlight from my briefcase but it served only to make my other hand look old. I was going to note down an odd dream, a college test in the usual ugly classroom where I couldn't identify any of a table of botanical specimens because my mind had created flora in minute detail that didn't exist. How could this be? This dream experience quickly transliterated itself into the thought that I was as capable as my father in presenting a false picture of myself. This caused a sensation that reminded me of what Naomi must have felt when she broke through the thin pond ice. I had scorned the false gentility in my father's memoir, remembering clearly a man so volatile that when he entered a room you weren't sure if he might walk through the far wall, blasting apart plaster and timber. Maybe he simply didn't remember himself that way. Until he was sixty or so, rather than getting off a horse, he vaulted off. He drove everyone a bit crazy except his granddaughter Dalva and his son John Wesley who was so intent on his own course that he ignored nearly everything else. John Wesley acted rather than reacted.

Perhaps the mind instinctively creates a safe middle way for memory? This was thin ice indeed for one who thinks he values self-honesty above all else, as if you could look at the vast and cloudy self the way you studied a mineral specimen, say when the mind is closer to a creek. You can become as wry, laconic and bemused as you wish if you blind yourself to the peripheries. I don't see the pile of raw meat in the corner because I'm fixed on the sunset over the Patagonia mountains.

Rachel wasn't a canine with a litter so both J.W. and I couldn't be the father of Duane. I made love to her but once and then she quickly fell for J.W. the moment she met him at the cabin. She was mine for a scant few hours. There were also suspicions about my father but Rachel insisted that J.W. was Duane's father. What a vast amount of time I've spent wondering about this and whether it truly mattered. And the fact is that in a real sense Duane had no father and by the time he showed up he didn't want one. My own father tried, knowing the whole story. And when Dalva arrived in Mexico to attempt to modestly recover, to whom could I say about Duane and his suicide that my son did this to her? A man is not entitled to fuck a woman, leave town, and insist on the title of father any more than a loaned-out Hereford bull can prate about his calves.

The night-table light came back on and with it the ticking of the baseboard heat. Anger can purify your enfeebled secrets. In over forty years I've been taken with thirteen women and five of them decidedly resembled Naomi in some respects. The idea that these five were the least pleasant of the affairs doesn't speak highly for my intelligence even though the original impulse tended to be subconscious. How can the subconscious not be part of our intelligence? I'm less sure of the ancient notion that romantic love in itself is a mental disease. How comic that I'm still dealing with Rachel and Naomi nearly forty-five years after the obvious fact that my brother swept them both away. When I drove into Buffalo Gap that coolish autumn afternoon I was sick of looking after my father and brother who were well intentioned but clumsy and sloppy on our hunting trip. I bribed Rachel away from the diner where she was working, the contents of my wallet doubtless greater than her lifetime earnings. My father has a cigar box of cash in his den that we were always welcome to and that in itself repelled me into a simpler life, but then he thought his own father's Christian penury to be quite absurd. Nelse said that when he felt too comfortable he thought he was missing something.

I had been uncommonly nervous when I drove Rachel out the twenty or so miles to the cabin. The primitive road was littered with sharp rocks and I had a flat tire. Rachel helped me change it and while we squatted there together I could see well up her skirt and, always the gentleman, I tried to keep my eyes averted. She was the polar opposite of my Eastern girls, with her skin quite dark and her hair in braids. Her body was strong but exquisitely trim. I lay on the couch in the cabin, jangled with a hangover because the cabin was always an excuse to drink too much, watching her clean up the kitchen. I asked for a glass of cold water and when my fingers touched her own wrapped around the glass we dropped it on my chest. She covered her face with her hands as if in fear and I drew her down to me. All quite wonderful indeed but the memory is unfortunately mixed with another, perhaps its metaphoric equivalent. I was quail hunting down on the border with a friend from the north and when he reached down into an old coyote den to retrieve a wounded bird I yelled out but too late. He jerked his hand out with a rattler attached to it and he spent a few weeks recovering. That was also a long time ago in the mid-fifties and when he died last year up in Vermont I suspect the memory was still quite vivid to him.

Perhaps oddly, I never felt any ill will toward John Wesley. Much has been made of sibling rivalry but I doubt either of us felt this. There was simply no arena in which we competed. He met Naomi first and his love for her was total. I met Rachel first and it made no difference. I never went anywhere with John Wesley, from hotels in Chicago to parties in Omaha or Lincoln, where both women and men weren't drawn immediately to his honest charm.

I called Naomi just before I left the motel in Limon. The weather was bad enough there, the same front from the west, that she had just finished making calls to all her students to cancel the day's school. She seemed a bit distant to me but then I wondered in a millisecond what would have compensated for my half-sleepless night when like a nitwit, psychic geologist I had stared for too long at the compressed and inescapable sediment of genes. I paused overlong on the phone and then she said she wished that I was with her today. I said thank you, feeling a nearly absurd, instant sense of well-being. I then asked her if she might ever want to get married and she laughed and replied we would be much better off "living in sin" when we wished to see each other, which she thought would be often. That has to be enough, I thought, after we bade good-bye.

The weather didn't clear until well south of Raton and then the sun shone and it was glorious, cold and sharp against the Sangre de Cristos. By midafternoon I had entered the Bosque del Apache just south of Socorro, a wildlife refuge where out of a long habit I stopped to take a nap. I find it consoling and sweet to sleep within the cacophony of birds and what better place for a man with this odd predilection than to pull up his vehicle near fields full of thousands of snow geese and sandhill cranes, the latter producing a harsh prehistoric music, perhaps my favorite of all birdsongs. It calls you back to a life without history. I was kept awake awhile by a single, modestly troubling thought that I had worked over enough so that it had lost its power to jolt. A few years ago Naomi had insisted I read *The Brothers Karamazov* and had sent along Dalva's college copy. Naomi is an absolute virago when it comes to her insisting you read a book and rather than enduring a long series of "did you read it yet" I went ahead during a week of hot July evenings in the San Rafael Valley where I live. My initial resistance had come from reading the same author's *The Possessed* for a political science course back at Brown dealing with the roots of the Russian Revolution, and I can still think of no more troubling book I have ever read. The reading went along fine with the Karamazov family until Misha, I think that's his name, the bully brother, beat up and dragged little Kolya's father down the street by his beard right in front of his son. I hit this passage during a severe thunderstorm and I frankly admit that I wept because when I was seven, surely one of the most vulnerable ages, and John Wesley was six, we had gone to town with my father one Saturday during deer season. Going to town on Saturdays was quite a thrill for us because we got to stop at the tavern owned by my father's bird-hunting crony and eat a hamburger, a menu item that was out of the question at home. On Saturdays the tavern was always filled with ranchers, cowboys, farmers and hired hands who drank while their wives shopped and the kids played in the vacant lot next door. On this particular Saturday there were also several groups of deer hunters, including a group of railroad employees from over in Alliance whom my father had denied permission to hunt on his extensive, at the time, land holdings in the area. The ringleader and largest of the group, a real grain-belt monster, had stopped at our table and taunted my father, saying he had cut a fence and driven his vehicle onto the property to retrieve a wounded deer and since it was after the fact and he had mended the fence my father couldn't do a damn thing about it. His booming voice made me fearful and I remember a french fry catching in my throat. My father put down his hamburger and without getting up drove a fist so hard into the man's gut that his mouth exploded with vomit, much of which hit our table. My father then got up and walloped the man in the face two or three times with an open hand. The man dropped to his knees and my father kept booting his ass as the man scrambled frantically for the door. His friends jumped up but were told to keep their places by others in the bar.

My father came back to the table and with what I remember as merry laughter asked the waitress to clean up the table and bring us a fresh meal. Can this be true? I remember it as if seeing a movie from the front row. I wept while John Wesley beamed.

I slept until twilight when my snow geese and cranes were flying in from every direction with their voices an intermittent din. Just before he died my father told me he had dreamt that the voice of God sounded like a billion birds. Other than its content the statement was surprising as I couldn't recall his ever using the word "God" except in a curse. Since I savor such dreams I had told him he was lucky to have had it. Perhaps the reappearance of his friend Smith had been the most disturbing thing in this somewhat suspicious memoir with all the gentility I never noted while growing up. But then again, who has a better right to record our lives than ourselves? I suddenly regretted the anecdote I had told Nelse when he was down in the fall and had read the manuscript in a single day. In the winter of 1958 right after I had read the memoir I had been in New York City on business and spent an afternoon in the main branch of the splendid New York Public Library. After some effort and the help of a librarian I found items in two newspapers about the summer of 1913 incident when my father had "throttled" and "pitched" two assailants into the Hudson River. The police were searching for an "unknown man," though the drowned and recovered bodies were those of "two known criminals." At the time I tended to think of it as murder though later I was somewhat up in the air on the matter. Nelse, however, saw it as a case of clear self-defense. Both newspapers had mentioned that the man was "well dressed," though one of them quoted a bystander from Iowa relating that the man was a "huge redskin." My father never looked so to me but whenever as an experiment I showed his photo to a Native they invariably knew and tended to guess him as at least the half he was.

* * *

I had a late-evening dinner in Socorro with a love from twenty years back, the wife of a now dead mining engineer for Phelps-Dodge. We liked each other a great deal at the time but like my mother she drank far too much for me to be comfortable with her for long. She was still on what Dalva humorously refers to my "rose list." Perhaps absurdly I still send roses to a dozen ex-lovers on their birthdays. I couldn't say quite why I do so, but then why so readily discard parts of the past that had their wonderful days?

The evening wasn't that pleasant, partly because she was a poor cook who claimed to have "special touches" and good cooking requires a specific humility. She made much of her reduced drinking but it was easily perceivable that she had had quite a warm-up period before I arrived, what with a faint Judy Garland burr to her consonants. That in itself wasn't irritating compared to the drama she was attempting to create about our mutual past, especially a trip we had taken to New York City, the main thrust of which had been wretched. We simply weren't remembering the same world. The peripheries had been gilded and her shrieking at a room-service waiter covered over, also falling asleep while attending a Eugene O'Neill revival, which she denied when waking, saying that her eyes had been closed the better to listen, and this without a single comment from me. She also fell backward into the arms of a maitre d' when he was helping her with her coat. But then I still liked her and suspected her ex-husband could have driven anyone to alcoholic desuetude. Perhaps the sidebar here is my mother and father again. How many of us actually have the resilience to survive a cruel lover, even if the cruelty is slow and accretive rather than directly violent?

I begged fatigue and escaped to my motel. She insisted that she would make breakfast for me in the morning but I felt confident she wouldn't remember. When we kissed at the door there was the mildest urge to prolong the caress for reasons that aren't clear to me beyond her past innovativeness in bed. Dalva had early guessed that I had a tendency to collect wounded birds. I thought she was unbearably shrewd at the time. When a young woman sees you so transparently you're knocked off your pins.

Back at the motel I felt relieved, safe and secure. My final thought about Kolya was that it certainly wasn't my fault that I was the bully's son rather than the victim's. John Wesley had beamed with pride as he ate his fresh hamburger while I was quite naturally choked with tears and couldn't touch mine. My father didn't notice when J.W. slipped mine into his coat pocket for his dog. My father downed a large glass of whiskey, wiped his mouth and advised his miniature sons that it was often better to hit a man openhanded, especially across the ears, because that way you avoided breaking your knuckles. How could one forget such grim wisdom?

I had a verbal scuffle at dawn with an officious motel clerk who insisted I take my receipt though I paid cash. I asked, Whatever for? He acted as if I were trying to get away with something criminal. I joked that I couldn't touch a receipt for moral reasons and he treated this as an insult. I began to turn to walk away and he tried to throw the machine-extruded receipt at me but then it is hard to throw paper. I judged that he regretted entering the transaction in the ubiquitous computer as he could have pocketed a cash payment. I've often had the feeling that as I grow older the country is becoming more primitive, certainly more stupid and impolite. One certainly notes it with airlines, the government, restaurants and hotels and among doctors. You are forever dodging the invisible shrapnel of free-floating contentiousness. You are frankly suspect if you don't act appropriately dead within the market-driven mono-ethic of pay and shut up. People yap about the bottom line as if it existed anywhere but in hell.

Luckily the moment I left the motel office the landscape made the soul clap hands and sing. I love the sun-blasted, bleached and baked small mountain ranges of the Southwest, the rather foreboding sky islands, most of which I've visited on foot. Even where there are conifers they lack the convincing greenness of the better-watered north. I've often thought how this landscape must drive painters quite batty though they keep trying, tripping over the thousands of delineations of shadows in a single arroyo. Painters do succeed more apparently than photographers, most of whom seem witless to know that a camera is a crude instrument compared to the human eye. The best photographs succeed as art but it certainly isn't the way anyone sees. Now I sound like my father!

I paused on my way south to recheck the map to be sure there wasn't a road untaken in the area. No such luck. When Nelse visited in the fall we drank a good deal of fine wine one evening and I gave him a marker and had him trace his routes on a large map of the United States on the wall of my den. I fell asleep on the couch and when I awoke and went to bed a few hours later he was still at work. At dawn when I arose to walk the dogs early because it was going to be a hot day Nelse was asleep on the couch, his handiwork completed, hundreds and hundreds of thousands of miles of dark tracery. There was very little east of the Mississippi except in the far northern Midwest, an area I had difficulty with because of the density of trees, the truncation of any view. I had once tried teaching for a spring semester at Michigan Tech in Houghton which owned the specific virtue of being the hilliest area of the state but still not enough for me. And there were still patches of snow on the ground in May, my landlady beaming with tearful eyes at the appearance of a crocus. When the temperature reached fifty after six months of winter students began wearing T-shirts. A confident girl rode her bicycle through campus with her skirt blowing up to her waist with hormonal young engineers and geologists staring dully from the sidewalk, some of them blushing. On the beaches of Lake Superior I found chunks and shards of ice beneath sand and rock the day before I left on the Fourth of July.

But Nelse's map gave me a sharp pang for the unlived life. I thought I had been a wanderer, and I had been, compared to anyone I knew, but Nelse had far exceeded me in a matter of ten years. Carlos, my male Airedale who is not very bright, kept watch over him from the far end of the couch. Carlos is an anal compulsive who is upset if someone sleeps on the couch. If I have houseguests and it's late in the evening Carlos tries to herd everyone to their bedrooms, such is his rage for order. He had doubtless watched Nelse carefully during his mapwork and now looked at me to make sure nothing was amiss. I invited him out to join his female cousins on the patio all agog for their morning walk. They prefer sleeping outside while Carlos is a bit frightened of the dark and roars and bays at something as simple as the cry of the roadrunner, or a nightjar in an Emory oak. The females bully him and once when he killed a javelina they wouldn't let him share in the eating. He is far larger but they have him totally buffaloed. When they snap at him he looks hopelessly to me for defense. When I left with the dogs I looked back at Nelse, saddened that I couldn't read his stolen journals. I had put out a reward through an acquaintance in the criminal element in Nogales but thought their return to be unlikely.

Thinking about my dogs made me homesick indeed though I knew I'd reach them by early evening. There was snow on the tops of the Black Range of the Mimbres Mountains so I couldn't cut over through Silver City. When I worked there during the war I'd taken a business trip to Washington, D.C., where I was called out of a meeting and told to phone my father immediately. I did so only to find out that John Wesley had died in Korea. The meeting had been at the Pentagon and had dealt with metals critical to national security. I hung up the phone and walked out to National Airport and found a pilot at a private aviation company to fly me home to Nebraska, abandoning my luggage at the Mayflower, also my job, and vomiting in hysteria into the Potomac. I still can't hear or read the word "Washington" without a slight tinge of nausea. O my brother, I loved you so.

When I turned off in Hatch to take the shortcut over to Deming I saw a Mexican family having a picnic off the road's shoulder, eating from the tailgate of an ancient station wagon with two little girls playing a version of hopscotch in the gravel and a little boy, a perfect miniature of his father in a straw cowboy hat, merely watching them, while the father ate his sandwich looking off at the shallow and muddy Rio Grande flowing through the chile fields. Not having any children of my own except the remote chance of Duane I tend to study families closely. I've helped raise a dozen or so children, mostly at a distance, but sometimes quite closely. Several have been the rather woebegone children of ex-lovers, and at least a half dozen Mexican orphans. Because of my mother I have too much money to think of this sideline as generous. What would I save for? My most current ward, Roberto, is at a military prep school which he loves in Roswell, New Mexico. I wish he were inclined otherwise but given his suffering in Los Angeles it is understandable. As the Natives imply you have to close up the metaphoric hole in your stomach somehow. Ruth and Ted's son, Bradley, also insisted on the military background, the Air Force Academy, after his parents' divorce which came about when Ted wished to live out his own true character which was homosexual. Early last spring when Ted and I were having dinner in Los Angeles discussing Dalva's multifoliate problems, including her alcoholic historian, Michael, and her losing her job, we ended up the evening skewing Toynbee's adversary theory of history. I've had a number of gay friends in my lifetime who became improbably successful in their fields though not as preposterously as Ted, and I wondered aloud if having to keep their nature secret so many years had made them hyperalert and attentive. Given intelligence, success in any area has always struck me as a matter of the level of attention, excluding the arts, of course, which seem to be involved in a mystery known only to their practitioners, if, indeed, they know themselves. You can read a Chekhov story, a Shakespeare sonnet, or listen to a Mozart sonata a dozen times and you'll still be left twiddling your thumbs in mute admiration. Ted didn't want to agree. He said it was like simpleminded Midwesterners thinking Jews were rich, then going to Brooklyn and finding out otherwise. I called that an asinine cheap shot and he laughed. Then I said both gay men and feminists find it unbearable when straight men try to say anything about them. Mystical experiences might not be transferable but ordinary human behavior is knowable, given the time and attention. He brought up the idea that in former times lapsed Catholics made especially good writers, then compromised by saying that possibly all the early energy given to deceit was good training for the world we live in. It gave a mastery for all the attenuations of irony and made one a student of the subtlest reactions of people. You had to build yourself antennae that ordinary people are lucky to do without. Ted teased me with the idea that the best seducers of women are simply the best listeners, supposedly one of my main virtues.

We finished the evening back discussing Dalva, both fretting over her. Ted first met Ruth at the Eastman School of Music in Rochester, New York, and when he had come home with her and met Dalva he felt even that first day that he had settled on the wrong sister. Midway through the second day, and this had nothing to do with his final sexual proclivities, he had decided that Dalva was the most violently headstrong young woman he had ever met. Ted is given to the wildest overstatements possible but they're generally very colorful. He said that he'd danced with Dalva that first evening and became more aroused than he had ever been with a woman, but then had a fearful image of her as a devourer, a killer, and on looking over her shoulder and down at the floor there was an image of a kneecap and shinbone in the morning light, the only thing that would be left of him. Of course this is laughably absurd but there is a microbe of truth to it. Like her father she never had the slightest gift for irony or subduing the primacy of her emotions. The chips were always down. I frequently felt a little sympathy for any of her boyfriends I'd met who had been selected for some temporarily usable aspect, then would be discarded for reasons that I'm sure they were incapable of understanding. She was intrigued by Michael's intelligence and had been very kind, indulgent and generous with him, then couldn't wait to send him packing. I used to tease her that she was an emotional robber baron, but then she easily drilled me through the brainpan by saying that it was only that she managed to take all the prerogatives that so-called alpha males believe are their birthright. That shoe fit very well and I was embarrassed enough to put it on, mindful that my own father had helped build this creature. There were some respects in which he was quite extraordinary.

I was laughing when I stopped for gas in Lordsburg and the attendant was quizzical about the joke. I said something quite lame

about a huge motor home with a Minnesota license backing into a
cement picnic table at the last rest stop. The antics of what are locally called "snowbirds" are the subject of a lot of humor. I couldn't
very well tell him my private story about a strangely painted buffalo
skull which is now the startling feature on the fireplace mantel of
my den. Many don't care for it, finding it unpleasantly fearsome. It
had been my father's and throughout my youth I had admired it beyond anything else he owned, including the paintings, the ranch,
whatever. When I graduated from Brown he shipped it out to me
though he didn't attend my graduation. I didn't blame him for that
as I've always found such ceremonies onerous. The painted buffalo
skull had been a gift to my grandfather from William Ludlow who
had found a long line of these skulls facing east on his expedition
into the Black Hills with Custer in the 1870s. I was laughing because
I'd suspended the skull from the ceiling in the quarters I shared in
Providence with three other seniors and during a very rainy graduation we had used the skull as a test of character for all the young
women we knew who stopped by for drinks. Some merely screamed,
some were merely polite, but most were quite curious. Oddly, visiting young men fared less well making much of the "modern world"
and how such artifacts are best stored in museums, somewhat similar
to those who'd prefer that all grizzlies, cougars and wolves be confined in zoos. But then it was a rainy, somewhat melancholy week
with the prospect of entering the "real world" after graduation quite
daunting. Many of my friends and acquaintances were eager to join
up for World War II which had barely begun by then. I ultimately
lost two of these friends after the Normandy invasion. Within the
week after graduation, rather than setting sail for battles in France or
the Orient, I was ensconced in a blistering hot Quonset hut on a hill
in southern New Mexico working for a mining company that didn't
appear to have a much better sense of ethics than the Germans and
Japanese. Earlier in this century, during the infamous Bisbee strike,
this company had loaded hundreds of workers at gunpoint onto a
train, only to drop them off in a distant desert without food or water.

* * *

Just before dark I gave up on the prospect of reaching home that night. It was only a matter of two to three hours more, a trifling amount of time, but the fatigue was cumulative after the night in Limon. My sleeping habits have never really existed. Prolonged sleep is a gift I've never had much experience with, though I can nap quite pleasantly even on a horse.

I checked into a motel in the rather charmless town of Willcox which I had always liked for indefinable reasons, then drove over to a roadhouse with the unlikely name of The Regal and ate far too many beef ribs. I'm normally a finicky eater but beef ribs were a piece of sentimentality, a holdover from my youth when I'd cook them for John Wesley at our camping spot way back beside the pond and marsh. One of my father's sidelines at the time was raising the primest of prime beef which was sent off to a few carriage-trade restaurants in Omaha and Chicago. We ate vast quantities of the beef except for Neena who quite early on had her true appetite killed by alcohol, and Lundquist who was squeamish about eating cattle he felt he knew personally. Lundquist had a presumed level of communication with the creature world that would be the envy of any mystic. I never really doubted it despite my pragmatic training that ran counter to his perceptions.

I had been at this restaurant so often that I could speak easily with the waitresses about their day-care problems. My favorite was a rather sallow young woman from West Virginia who had a flat lilt to her accent and those peculiar Appalachian cheekbones. I had modestly helped her escape a husband who beat her regularly and had financed her resettlement up in Flagstaff. I hadn't slept with her though I had very much wanted to, but then with all her problems at the time it would only have been an act of kindness on her part. Her husband managed to track me down on the phone and threatened me but I asked him, "Why would you want to change your life that much for the worse?" and he never got in touch again. I'm not sure what I meant but I was prepared to go the route whatever it was.

I have been strongly questioned and teased by a number of women for such errands of mercy under the notion that all motives are suspicious and questionable. One of them, given to psychologisms, said I'm trying to save my mother over and over. She is an otherwise likable woman and doesn't try to shield her own foibles. My only reply is that if the result is good the motive is quite meaningless and utterly separated from my difficulties of so long ago. Compared to many men I know I don't add up to a garden-variety Lothario.

One of my most critical woman friends unfortunately turned up during Nelse's visit last fall. She's certainly too young for me, about thirty, and must have had an unpleasant father for which I am an ambiguous substitute. Nelse managed to conceal his amusement about my discomfort over her arrival, though not his polite cynicism about her character. She's openly scathing about my profession of geology and its relation to mining, and Nelse pointedly asked her if her Porsche was made out of plastic. She then tried to charm him though she would have had better luck with a fence post. She came up with an odd theory that amused me for a short time to the effect that women in the Southwest are more interested than those in the East in astrology because the stars are far more visible in the Southwest. With all the ambient light along the eastern seaboard it is difficult to see the stars with any clarity. Nelse momentarily thought she said "astronomy" for "astrology" and there was a minor rupture with his "Oh bullshit!" I suppose it takes age to be more interested in absurdities than being right.

There was a further dissembling when she said that as an aspiring writer she hoped to spend her life defending nature, a noble enough ambition, but then Nelse quipped that the natural world was something you had to know and study in particular. It wasn't simply a static art museum, or a beautiful collection of photographs that you guarded against the hordes of which you are a part. She was miffed and asked him for his qualifications, to which he replied, "None," that you didn't need credentials to see that most of our virgin forests had been razed, the prairies and Great Plains almost totally scalped and denuded by overgrazing and bad farming practices, not to speak of the oceans which were coming closer to irretrievable depletion, or the out-of-check population surge which in itself clearly spelled out doom. Nelse himself charmlessly spelled out "doom" in a news-caster's faux baritone. She poured herself a gigantic glass of tequila and looked to me for defense. I tried to joke that as mammals we quite naturally bore some resemblance to other mammals, say the widely spread Rodentia.

She went to the sliding doors of the patio and looked out as if she could see southward into the high desert night. When your eyes became accustomed to the dark you could always make out the Sierra San Antonio mountains of Mexico with the border, a simple fence, only a few miles away. Carlos got up from his cushion and put him-self between her and the door to prevent her from doing something stupid like going outside without his master. The other dogs were kenneled to keep them from chasing javelinas or abusing the poor souls who were trying to migrate across the border.

I glanced at Nelse who seemed to be trying to ignore her trim figure. He then asked her what her religion was and she said, "Na-ture" in the spirit of baiting him. Sometimes your company will give you a headache but people as sheer phenomena usually outweigh my simply opting out and going to bed alone. Nelse rattled on rather list-lessly about how the theology of land rape seemed to be a corner-stone of the Christian religion and she answered rather sharply that you couldn't blame that on Jesus. Nelse had the dining table spread with the paperwork involved with disposing of the Native artifacts and at least pretended to go back to work. She sat down rather dream-ily beside me on the sofa after having refilled her tequila. I wondered, as always, if such quarrels were anything more than little dances of our general unrest.

I got up before daylight and turned off in Sonoita for the Canello Hills when it was still early morning. I felt an untoward amount of unrest because invariably when the blacktop turns to gravel with thirty miles yet to go I experience a great welling of homesickness, a kind of free-floating desperation to reach my place which since 1949 has been my retreat from all I did not like about the world. Only today the

homesickness didn't arrive and I had to blame the way Naomi had
again pushed other considerations aside in my mind. On balance I'd
have preferred to be back in her farmhouse on this Saturday morning. The ghost of my brother was benign, and the other ghosts in the
area had had their energies that produced ill feelings almost completely dissipated. Sometimes a "summa cum laude" won't help a jot
or tittle in understanding yourself, and might even mitigate against
it. I have never even accepted how inevitably we are our fathers' sons,
for better or worse but mostly in the middle. On some of my long
adolescent inward journeys which now would be called "depression"
my father would chide me, saying, "Why don't you crawl out of your
butt and take a look at the world?" If you're in a precious, somewhat
Keatsian mood this will strike you as repellently vulgar. During one
of these periods he knew very well I had a disabling crush on a girl a
half dozen miles away who it would be generous to say was as dumb
as an armadillo. John Wesley would say, Why don't you just fall for
one of the brood hens? I'd ride a horse way down the road to see her
but horses didn't turn this ranch girl's head, even my splendid buckskin Felix. I was fourteen at the time, it was June and my mother was
off in Rhode Island, a trip I wouldn't take for fear of losing this girl I
didn't have. I stayed in my room for days playing the Victrola to feed
my aching heart. My dad knocked one morning and said in a level
voice that he understood what I was going through, and all I thought
was, How could this old bastard understand anything but horses, cows
and making money? Of course I said nothing because my throat was
choked with melancholy. He then said that if I'd take a day-long walk
around the property he'd go into town and get me a Ford Roadster,
not a new one but good enough to turn a girl's head away from cowboys. He did and it worked all too well. Within a few days she was a
decal you couldn't peel off and I realized for the first time in my young
life that getting what you want and not getting what you want were
somewhat similar in emotional effect.

When I came over a certain rise, almost a mountain pass with
red-stalked manzanita everywhere and alligator juniper and Mexican pinyon pine, I could see my place nearly twenty miles away. I

was sure that most of my nagging lack of homesickness came from a
long-term squabble involving a settlement of about a dozen Mexican families seven miles to the west of my place. Both of my house-
keepers, Emilia and Luisa, lived there as did my occasional handyman,
Jorge, who was a bit of a professional bad guy. I'd judged him to be
nearly as strong as my father after first meeting him when he threw a
good-sized fence post most of the way across a corral at a rank mule
who had killed his goat. The trouble at the settlement was that the
Mexican gentleman who owned the land in the area intended to
bulldoze the small adobe houses, perhaps making it more attractive
real estate, I don't know. I had tried to buy him out but he intended
to hold on after the occupants were gone. After all of my years down
in Mexico there was still something impenetrable to Latino businessmen as if they owned more emotional ties to their businesses than
their gringo cousins in greed. I had assured Emilia and Luisa that we
could build them a house on my property but that did not lessen their
grief. All of their aunts, uncles, cousins, nieces, nephews and friends
would be gone over the mountains to the north to the small village
of Patagonia, to me a wonderful place, but thirty long miles away to
Emilia and Luisa.

There was simply no way out of this quandary. I didn't have
much sympathy for myself though I had a good deal of emotional
dependence on this little community. There's not enough sympathy
in our systems to include people with sizable bank accounts and port-
folios barring, of course, their illnesses or those of their loved ones.
When I first heard the news and tried to intervene the year before, I
was forced into an admission that though I love my solitude and privacy it is changed into something distasteful if it is enforced by outside powers. Then it becomes solitude without freedom. I'd far rather
live smack dab in the middle of New York City than in enforced
solitude without Christmas tamales, guitar music, children giving me
nickels to buy them candy when I drive up to the small store in
Washington Camp, sitting under a cottonwood on a warm summer
evening cooking and eating *carne asada* and drinking cold beer with
anyone that comes along, riding arroyos in the high country helping

someone look for lost cattle, or having someone's plump citified cousin from Hermosillo dance with me and perhaps take me to bed, or driving five old ladies down to Magdalena for the Virgin of Guadalupe celebration. These women all made the hundred-mile walk across the border and mountains until they became too old to do so. Emilia's mother made the walk for the last time at seventy-nine. I was ill equipped to comprehend the power of this motivation, the visual image of a very old lady in a flowered housedress carrying a plastic milk carton of water, scrambling over the scree and shoulders of high country arroyos on a hike that would devastate physical fitness buffs.

The question, of course, is how you make your soul clap its hands and sing. My bones seemed built out of incomprehension. The road was rutted enough by winter rains so that the car drove itself. I was ringed by four mountain ranges in this valley but then natural beauty seems to offer no more than you can bring to it. There was scarcely a patch in a thousand square miles I hadn't covered on foot. Looking down you see blue and black gama, side oats gama, curly mesquite, sprangle-top, and the grassy skin of the local earth. Straight up is invariably sky. Beneath the earth's skin are the minerals I've professionally taken advantage of as surely as preachers and priests try to mechanize our souls. I was camped last spring on the east slope of Baboquivari and had the curious sensation that the moon was shining all the way through me and when I mentally stepped back I saw that it was so. When I tried to help both the T'ohono Odom and the Hopi with mineral leases I noted that they had a cultural hesitancy to take advantage of anything whereas it is the bedrock of our culture. Up in my own country it was apparently our nature to kill seventy million buffalo just as it was our nature to destroy the Native cultures. History will not help your soul clap its hands and sing but it is unconscionable to proceed without knowing it. In college I was obsessed with the beauty of studying the morphology of rivers but then all of the jobs in this area were with the enemies of rivers. I was in Glen Canyon and when they drowned it the similarity to the crucifixion was inescapable. There is also a great beauty in the study of geology but not in its use. I suppose I could have taught it in its purest form but good colleges and universities are invariably in locations I don't care to live. I noted that when Nelse visited and scanned the library in my den he passed over any titles of literary merit. When I questioned why he didn't take "advantage" of such fine work he said it usually made his brain feel too raw. This reminded me of my father giving up his ambition to be an artist which I later saw as a resistance to the utter vulnerability of that calling.

I detoured for an hour out onto Jones Mesa, skirting the fingers of several arroyos and arriving at the one I wanted. One of these days, probably not all that far in the future, I'll no longer be able to make my way down into it and climb back out. There is a spring down there, a very small one, beneath a granitic outcropping that during the driest times before the summer rains attracts an uncommon number of birds and animals. I have no urge to find the names to all the birds as Naomi does but then I have done so, after all, with rocks. A scant ten feet from the spring, a survivor of floods from previous times, is a boulder with a large indentation that serves as a curved seat. This stone chair is not very hospitable during cold weather but on most mornings by noon it is ravishingly comfortable. When you doze off in this chair your sleep seems dense, far deeper than normal, and when you are awake you seem hyperconscious. Of course the most well-trained parts of my brain tell me this is likely nonsense but I'm under no obligation to listen to them all of the time. In fact in my mid-sixties a small part of the time is more than enough. I was certainly amused when Einstein said that he had no admiration for scientists who only drilled countless holes in thin pieces of board. Phenomena are far more interesting than my reductive conclusions.

I dozed for a few minutes, then awoke after a dream vision of Naomi sitting on her porch swing in a winter coat, her obnoxious crow beside her. I wondered if that was what she was doing at that very moment, not a profitable direction of inquiry. After I had showed him the way Nelse camped here for three days instead of his announced two, saying that he had lost track of time and had forgotten to come back. I was a little irked but still didn't want to disturb him so glassed the canyon with my binoculars from the far end until I caught him on a high ridge glassing back at me.

When the wind is from the southeast you can occasionally catch a faint, feline odor from a mountain lion lair far up the canyon wall. There are often pugmarks and scat near the spring and several times I've found a dissected deer carcass in the immediate area, barely more than a hide and the larger bones. A couple of times I've noted smaller tracks which means its a female's dwelling and she lives within striking distance of her restaurant. Nelse had said jokingly that he loved sitting there by the hour because his father's last name was Stone Horse.

The dogs, who can hear my vehicle miles away, met me at the gate except for Carlos who always stood at least thirty yards back, baying and howling. There were six in all, including three Airedales, two English setters, and a Labrador retriever. The last three were from my quail-hunting habit, a sport that has waned for me in recent years. So much of my youth was spent shifting back and forth with my mother between home, Arizona and Rhode Island that I couldn't fairly keep the dogs that John Wesley did. We bird hunted since we were twelve but the day after Christmas I would bid the dogs goodbye and entrain with my mother for the Tucson area, nearly a dozen times more populated now then it was in the thirties. And in the summer I was with her often enough at Wickford so that our dogs would make it pointedly clear to me that their true master was John Wesley though they bore the most affection for Lundquist. All of our animals were drawn to him to an uncanny degree so that even our rankest horses and bulls were practically his lapdogs. I think it must have been the muttering, singsong, nonsense language he used with them, also the slow, graceful nonhostile gestures he used in their presence. I've never known a man who had less self-importance with creatures. Whatever his self-invented language it was closer to their own.

Anyway, certain resentments built in my youth and I swore that when I had my own home quarters there would be as many dogs as I wished and there always have been. In my frequent trips, some of them quite long throughout my life, my homesickness has centered on the dogs and spread out from there. The dog graveyard is fenced off from the few well-bred steers I keep for our beef meals, including one apiece for Emilia and Luisa. Long ago Emilia and I were lovers, but then she married and made sure she put her young friend Luisa in my direction. Luisa also married ten years back and now I'm godfather to a half dozen of their children. As opposed to the cliché of poorly educated women Emilia is a student of the stock market, and also handles any legal and accounting matters I have, making the trip to Tucson once a month. Lawyers and accountants prefer her company to my own because I have what psychologists call an "attention deficit disorder" in this area.

My homecoming dinner was one of my favorites though quite simple, a *posole* made from the neck and shanks of a mule deer Luisa's brother had recently shot. The cartilaginous nature of the neck naps this hominy stew so that it glistens. In Luisa's kitchen garden there are many varieties of herbs and chiles, including epazote, needed for the *posole,* and a number of rows of garlic which is wonderful when so fresh the peeled cloves stick to your fingers. Emilia is a poor cook compared to the younger Luisa, and often carps about the lengthy grocery list she is expected to take to Tucson. I will frequently act as Luisa's "sous chef," sitting at the counter on a stool and grinding away in her ancient metate, and fetching what she wishes from the garden.

That evening after dinner we tried to force a gaiety that was improbable given the settlement problems down the road. It was easy enough during dinner because of the preoccupation with the good food. There's nothing like a sensual delight to banish enervation, but when we were finished full reality struck us quite hard. We tried to watch *Marathon Man* on the VCR and it was at least mildly diverting until Emilia quipped that their present situation with their landlord was like "living in a dentist's chair." We had a somewhat quaky three-way hug, then went to our separate bedrooms.

I can't say that I was morose because I saw this change in the way I lived my life coming for nearly a year, while Emilia and Luisa had visceral responses to the change every day. Naomi and I had spoken humorously about a "half-year" living arrangement, or trial marriage, but then I had been brought up rather sharply when she'd asked why ever would I wish to finally get married at my age? But I've loved you for nearly forty-five years I said, to which she answered that marriage might ruin it. I've never had any particular interest in Orientalia but a friend in San Francisco pointed out an old Ch'an saying, "Ashes don't return to wood." I took this to mean "What are we waiting for?" though there are a number of other subtler ramifications. Perhaps "Why are you holding back?" is more accurate to the feeling. I don't know if I've ever believed in anything more strongly than the existence of Naomi and that must be partly what love is. Our hearts yawn when we try to pretend we care for someone more than we do. Love itself seems quite involuntary. I no longer put much stock in any strict ideas of rationality. Geology itself can turn the head toward eternal questions and when a young woman brought me a bowling-ball-size rock containing the broken femur bone of a Jurassic lizard I could tell her all about the "what" but not the "why." I know nearly as much about astronomy as Nelse as there's no better place to look at stars because of the absence of ambient light than the San Rafael Valley, but I'm not as intemperate as he is about the general human ignorance of the stars. It is simply too large a question mark for most to bear continuous preoccupation. One night a few years back while camped on a mountain saddle I awoke and some sort of visual distortion led me to believe that the moon and Venus were but a few feet away, and the stars that surrounded them only a few feet further. I was instantly covered with sweat, and jumped from my sleeping bag to stoke my juniper fire out of trepidation. But maybe they aren't really that far away if you think of the relative meaninglessness of distance. I think it was Heraclitus who said that the moon is the width of a woman's thigh.

It was a very long night. My bedroom faces east but this soon after the winter solstice it is vain to anticipate the rising sun with the mind's "Hurry up, please." On the wall to my left is a grand eighteenth-century map of Mexico, enough askew in its design to make it more interesting. I prefer maps to suggest rather than tell me where to go, and I could easily see that a topographer had a more pleasurable life before highways and railroads. They could concentrate on important things like mountains, valleys, rivers and oceans, villages and cities without all those lines drawn toward them to suggest the easiest way to get there. If I traced all my travels in Mexico as Nelse did of the western United States it would look like a giant, randomly constructed bird's nest.

Next to the map is a small painting by my father's friend Davis who fell to his death from a cliff near El Salto not far from Durango. I took the painting from my father's bedroom the day after he died. I liked that part of my father's memoir. Two young men from Nebraska out to paint the world with their soaring hearts. I've spent a good deal of time in Durango on mining business, a somewhat eerie place to me, far off the tourist byways, the vast wealth that has been sucked from the local earth. It has always been a city with a specific purpose. I loved the place for the famous and peculiar splendor of its clouds. It is somehow a purer form of Mexico. It was there a few years ago I read the best possible book about Mexico, Octavio Paz's *The Labyrinth of Solitude*. While I read there was music out in the garden behind the hotel, and a welter of voices arising from an outdoor Sunday buffet. When I turned the last page of the book I went down to dine and watched the most unimaginably beautiful young woman eating from a spit-roasted pig on her family's table. She was so beautiful that I instantly lost my appetite. A guitarist played and sang quite nicely directly behind her but she continued chewing away, then became embarrassed and brought her napkin to her face. Her father, a wealthy man who looked like he had murdered a thousand of the less fortunate, dismissed the guitarist with a glance. An older brother joined them and waved at me, a young mining engineer I had met several times. When they had coffee and dessert he came over and asked if it were possible for me to join them. The father was interested in American politics and I did the best I could with barely an opportunity to glance at the daughter who dozed in her chair with her large eyes wide open. I stole a foolish look and missed my lips with my coffee. The father and brother laughed very hard, saying that everyone does that when they look at her. She became fully awake at their laughter and gave me the wide-open but terrifyingly blank look that one receives from zoo animals.

The painting by Davis brought this all back rather simply though it was of a mountain wall suffering from the sun, with the rocky crags losing their edges as if melting in the shimmering heat. It took me years to comprehend this painting, not with my mind but my senses. There was the troubling idea of how many other fine paintings are out there by curious hands that are never justly comprehended. And how could I not feel a total, searing empathy with my father over the death of his friend, the talented, somewhat crazed Davis. But when I look closely at the painting the girl at the Sunday buffet also reappears. That was a number of years ago so I was in my mid-forties. Never have I felt more mortal than when I returned to my room and looked down at my coffee-stained shirt. I laughed but the laughter had a sodden, haunted edge. I went to the window and watched her leave through the garden with her family. There was an obtuse urge to call a helicopter to get me the hell out of there. I supposed that we got older, more fragilely mortal, in terms of unavailable time, time that has fatally passed away from us, and that the ultimate level of beauty had dumbfounded me into seeing mortality in the terms of those rare suicides who stand between the tracks before an oncoming train. The humor came from the idea "Of course, how could you think otherwise." It was a wonderfully cruel and sensual lesson and I am still daily absorbed in it.

Sleep came and went in the smallest of doses, and I countered raw thoughts and memories with last summer's vision of swimming with Naomi late one evening in the Niobrara. We had had a bit more dinner wine than usual and jumped around in a state of frolic as if we

were teenagers, then made love awkwardly in the car. A smart teenage boy would have brought along a blanket.

There had been a troubling sequence of thoughts of late, most
of them just over the lip of consciousness, centering themselves on
the notion that if it took a lifetime to understand yourself this certainly must adumbrate my comprehension of those I know. This is
not the less troublesome for being so obvious. For instance, I can say
I "leaned" toward my mother. I suppose many children favor one
parent over the other, and to some extent organize an imaginary war
between the two if there's not an open one going on. I then readily
assumed since I favored her I was more "like" my mother but with
age this is somewhat less apparent than I had thought for years. I had
tended to see my youth as a diorama of us protecting each other but
from what? How do you protect a moderately wealthy woman whose
only true enthusiasms seemed to be books and alcohol? She had already constructed a rather impermeable shield between herself and
the world with these two enthusiasms.

It opened my eyes more widely talking with Nelse who had similar complications with his own mother, at least on the surface. But
then he had been quite resistant and combative with his adoptive
mother, and his experience appeared to be far less melancholy. It is
a strange feeling indeed to become a little angry with your mother
only after she has been dead for over forty years. By the time I was
fourteen I was her obviously platonic gentleman friend. Like Nelse I
had accompanied my mother to France in my mid-teens. She drank
an amazing amount of wine though unlike Nelse's mother her behavior never dissembled. I could never finish a Henry James novel
because my mother was a definite throwback to his period, and James's
uncanny perceptions about such women were disturbing to me. Just
the other day I recalled the hush with which she subdued my enthusiasms, the elegant irony with which my girlfriends were dismissed.
Some women exude great power in their weaknesses. When she was
drinking too much in an evening back home John Wesley would take
his bed roll, a sack of grub, and head out on horseback if the weather

was vaguely permissible. My father would escape to the bunkhouse
which he referred to as his office. The art studio of his youth became
his land-and-cattle office! But I'd stay in the house enduring her bitter and laconic witticisms when she looked up from a book. I had to
wonder how my father's decorum excluded such difficulties, also the
girlfriends he turned to, in his memoir.

I turned on the light, got out of bed, and looked at the first
mineral collection my mother gave me one winter in Tucson when
I was about seven. It was in a fine, glass-covered mahogany case, including small samples in rows of sedimentary rock, metamorphic rock,
various crystals and native elements, sulfides, sulfosalts like the incredible proustite, oxides, including the woeful uraninite, haloids, the
improbable sulfates such as barite, and then phosphates, vanadates,
uranates, arsenates, and so on.

The problem with this little collection from a half century ago
only occurred to me in the past year. At about the same age, probably seven, my father would let me look at the large collection of art
books in his den that he had so long ignored. The only stipulation
was that I scrub my hands first. It was a preoccupation for rainy days.
What I speculated over is that there was some association in my child's
mind between the brilliantly colored and shaped collection of minerals and the hundreds and hundreds of paintings in the books. In
the den there was also a painting I loved by the certifiable Charles
Burchfield of distorted flowers that owned the colors of a conglom-
erate of minerals. It was a bit close for comfort to believe that my
attraction to geology had begun as basically aesthetic and not unlike
my father's early calling to art. Oh Christ, will it never end, I had
thought, and the transparent answer was, "No it won't," excepting
in the way it ends for everyone.

All insomniacs know that this kind of thinking isn't the kind
that induces sleep. Good sexual memories can turn you into a drowsy
mammal if you exclude the major events. For instance, when sixteen
I had accompanied my mother to France under the title of "protec-
tor." Neena spoke fluent French, and was an experienced and somewhat imperious traveler. She was educating me in matters of food and

wine though at the time I didn't care for the grogginess produced by the latter. She'd get up quite late, take a short walk and then there was lunch (too much wine) after which she'd take a long nap, another short walk and dinner (too much wine) after which she'd read herself to sleep. She'd map my own daily itinerary which included long walks, museums, the neighborhoods she had enjoyed at my age. We were staying at the Georges V and since it was June the sky stayed light until late. Her single stricture was that she hoped I wouldn't leave my adjoining room after we returned from dinner, usually just before dark. Paris at night was a dangerous place, she insisted, though I later figured she meant the "women of the night," or prostitutes who might harm her vulnerable son. I didn't really chafe at this as our dinner wine and my extremely long walks made me sleepy enough. Then one day along the Quai des Grands Augustins I bought a risqué book of photos that raised my neck hairs, popped my skull and shortened my breath. I listened to her sleeping through the door, then headed out though not all that adventurously. I had only made it to an adjacent street, Rue Marbeuf, when I was approached by an attractive women in her thirties wearing dark clothes but with sparkling eyes. Her price was quite high as it was a good neighborhood, but I used the money I had reserved for John Wesley's present. It was quite simply wonderful. When I left her room, likely only a half hour later, I shed tears of happiness. John Wesley would be thrilled by the story and I'd give him the book of photos that had urged me out into the night, but then the next day my mother had evidently entered my room while I was out because the book was gone.

This fond memory produced the wakefulness that comes after touching an electric fence so I got up, put on my glasses and studied my wall map of Mexico. I had preferred smaller cities like Durango and Zacatecas to the larger, though I did care for Guadalajara, Oaxaca, and Veracruz, the latter reminding me of a brief trip to Cuba just before their revolution. I was eighteen when I first visited the National Geological Museum in Mexico City, and caught the disease of wandering this country though it became a core part of my livelihood. Before the Mexican Revolution the American presence in

mining in that country was dominant, less so afterward. I often regretted that I hadn't had the adventures of the early exploratory
sojourners like the great gentleman Morris Parker but so far as I
know no one had ever adjusted to the age in which they live. Gem
minerals like opal and agate interested me minimally compared to
the thousands of less obvious varieties. I was a true goner when I
saw the caves of selenite crystals, some eight feet long, at the Naua
mine in Chihuahua. I was also thrilled to see the aftereffects of the
great Parícutin volcano soon after it began erupting. People in general have little knowledge of critical metals but I doubt this is very
important. Once at a dreary geological convention which I was
obligated to attend I was amused that our group, drowning in its
own obsessions, was to be followed by the Aluminum Extruders of
America, who doubtless had their own blind spots. I suppose I was
a bit of an exception for a geologist in that the human, also the flora
and fauna, landscape eventually fascinated me more than what was
to be found underground.

A friendly, somewhat overeducated twit once told me that the
reward of patience is patience. On the surface this isn't a very appealing or interesting idea. The man himself complained bitterly
when his dessert came tardily, but the thought itself was quite valuable during thousands of hours of legal proceedings and hearings
concerning whether or not a deceased person's mining claims or stock
have any value in the settlement of an estate. Of course the pleasure
was visiting the mine itself. Most swindles occur when people don't
transcend the paperwork and see the reality it supposedly represents.
I eventually learned through patience not to waste these endless hours
of legal babble. The original barrier was the ability to reduce the
plethora to the teaspoon of gruel that was the actual measure of its
content. There can be a wonderful substratum of thinking going on
beneath the banal tonnage of human behavior. Perhaps our real
uniqueness is that our minds can escape the zoos we've built but other
creatures' minds can't, though who knows what mental devices they
use to endure the suffering we visit upon them? The mind by itself
must discipline itself to open wide enough to allow the soul to clap

its hands and sing. The dark comic aspect is in our resistance to the nature of our minds, pretending we have no more freedom than a train on its predestined tracks.

Now it's four A.M. and Carlos on his dog cushion wants me to turn off the light and go to sleep. Both his father and grandfather were what Jewish folk call "kvetches" and Carlos takes it to another level. A simple tiny lizard near his water bowl out on the patio defiles and enrages his sense of order. His eyes are dark and glittery now looking at me, saying night is the time to sleep, that's why it's dark, or as they so often say in New York City, "Give me a break." I tell him that long drives don't lead to sleep but then he refuses to ride in a vehicle. His lifelong job is solely to keep an eye on the property. He has never bitten anyone but his appearance is such that he's never had to. He's baleful as a marble Gorgon.

I turn off the light and organize my memory around the best sleeps of my life: dawn on the boulder-strewn beach near Anconcito, Ecuador, when I drifted off staring upward at a great gyre of frigate birds (they fish at sea but if they fall into or inadvertently land on the water they die), or tailing a lovely but obtuse heiress from her hotel in Paris to a country house in the Morvan region of Burgundy, where Caesar had decided that Gaul was divided into three parts, finding her too drunk in the evening to sign a paper that said I had explained to her that a family mine near Lampazos in Coahuila was worthless but inhabited by countless millions of arachnids, what we call daddy longlegs spiders. We walked country lanes for hours until we were quite lost and there were no houses, and no passing cars to flag down, and we slept away the rest of the warm June night in a meadow adjacent to a forest, waking up covered with dew and surrounded by a profusion of wildflowers, a farmer driving us back to the manor with us standing awkwardly next to him on his tractor. She died the following October in a sports car going over a hundred miles per hour out in Brittany, like the death of the genius Camus. And then the best sleep of all with Naomi on her spring vacation when we flew to Mexico City, thence in a rental car to Pátzcuaro near Uruapan in Michoacan to see the forested mountainside carpeted with what they said were over twenty million monarch butterflies readying themselves for the long flight north, and the way we slept back at the simple *pensione* with the susurration of the millions of butterflies still audible in our ears, an imponderable gift like the moonlight itself.

But then I stopped just short of burying some dreams when my consciousness floated back to Loreto and my niece's late-night call from Key West saying that Duane had committed suicide. I made my way down the patio steps and across the sand to the Sea of Cortez, lit dimly by the thin slip of the new moon now as distant as my only possible son. I never admitted to Dalva that twice in the years just previous to his suicide I had had him traced, first to Cypremort, Louisiana, and then to Biloxi. I even had photos from Biloxi of Duane in a very old pick-up and a battered horse trailer, and one coming out of a convenience store with a six-pack looking like a fearful version of death itself. The private detective, also a veteran, had managed to strike up a conversation with Duane in a shrimpers' bar where Duane had said how much he had enjoyed his several tours of fighting in Vietnam and had "felt sad" when he became too shot up to continue. It is not widely known what enthusiastic and valorous soldiers the Sioux had been for this nation in the wars of this century. If you allow it, the irony here will pound on you with the subtlety of a sledgehammer.

When Dalva had arrived in Loreto I was trying to get over the worst year of my life which had included the garden-variety illnesses of a severe kidney infection, a gall-bladder operation and, by far the most painful, a severe depression. The first two I could endure like any sick dog but the last, as many know, was akin to losing your mental feet and hands. The effort of trying to prop up a madwoman for a month when I had so miserably lost my way was the most difficult thing I had ever done. Oddly, when she was somewhat recovered so was I, which comprises a not impenetrable mystery. She was a version of my beloved dead brother turned into the loveliest of young women. Several times when she came weeping to my bed and I held her, there was a primitive ambivalence that made the

brain roar so that I bit my lip until it bled to stop myself from furthering the insanity.

It was now six A.M. and this didn't bring sleep any more than a
rifle being fired outside one's bedroom window by an unknown hand.
I rechecked my addled mind for the time zone and dialed Naomi in
the dark, not to further addle poor Carlos though he growled when
I began talking. The conversation was wonderfully simple and consoling at the onset. In the Sandhills it was seven A.M., a Sunday morning, a slight thaw had arrived and she could hear water dripping from
the icicles hanging from the eaves, and her crow was calling out
from the garage. She was going to make herself potato pancakes as
she always did on Sundays, take a long walk, then go to church. She
had played a lengthy, competitive game of double solitaire with Dalva
the night before and Nelse was returning from Lincoln in time for
dinner with some fish if he managed to remember. I mentioned my
insomnia and she suggested a long walk, as always. I said that as I had
gotten older I had lost my inclination for night walking. She laughed
and said that she had always felt there were more ghosts afoot in the
daylight, another, she said, of Lundquist's convincing theories. My
breath shortened and I said that partly because of local difficulties I
was thinking of spending eight months in her neighborhood, say from
April to December. There was a mutually breathless pause, and then
she said she would be pleased to shock the whole area by having me
live with her. I could even tend her garden if she was away, but then
we better think this over. I said that I had already thought it over for
far too long. She said a schoolteacher couldn't very well "live in sin"
in her area but it would be fun to test the waters during the last two
months of her career. We agreed once again that though we were
technically older at least our brains didn't feel that way. I asked her
to meet me in Denver, our old trysting place, the following weekend
to talk it over. When we said good-bye I impulsively said, "I love you,"
and she replied after an awkward pause that she'd have to learn again
to say that to a man after so many years.

I got dressed, nudging Carlos with a foot to subdue his irritation, made coffee, bundled up and went outside for my advised walk,

with all of the dogs accompanying me, at first without much enthusiasm. The outdoor thermometer said only sixteen degrees which
is not what folks think about the Arizona-Mexico border but then
the San Rafael Valley is a mile high. I only own a few hundred acres
bordering the Coronado National Forest so we slowly walked the
fence line with the first trace of light coming over the Huachuca
Mountains to the east. The slightness of the new moon did nothing to diminish the density of the floss of bright stars above my head,
the steam from my mouth rising upward to them punily but then
we are not much in their sight. It occurred to me that it was my
very ordinariness that was leading me back home, which at least was
more comprehensible than the vast dome of the heavens above me.
I smiled, remembering when I'd asked my father what happened
when we died while he and Lundquist were butchering a steer. He
turned to me with bloody hands and said, "If it's nothing we won't
know it," while Lundquist just behind him shook his head and rolled
his eyes. I went back to the house and asked the same question of
my mother who looked up from a book and said, "I have no idea."
As the sky got lighter the dogs ranged further and I supposed the
central thing about loving someone is that it very much made you
want to continue living.

DALVA

April 18th, 1987

I awoke just before daylight to the sound of Lundquist's pick-up entering the yard. I could see over the windowsill and the lights were on in Nelse's bunkhouse, and Lundquist's silhouette was clear at the door with Roscoe over his shoulder. Ted barked from the kitchen below me and I whistled and he came trotting up the stairs and jumped onto the bed. I scratched his belly with its peculiar hair, half Airedale and half Labrador, a furry, roundish pig dog without the strong attributes of either breed. He always remained quiet if I let him up on the bed, a graceful piece of etiquette, and I fell back to sleep and I felt protected in an already threat-free local universe. As I dozed off I remembered the story of our only local murder except for a few family quarrels, some seventy years before when a hired hand got drunk and doped on spring tonic full of alcohol and tincture of cocaine, killed a ranch wife and boarded the train. The sheriff rode down the train on horseback, swung himself on and walked through the line of cars, blowing the murderer off the last car with his .44. The murderer was unarmed but that was widely considered an unimportant detail. Grandfather always told this story as if it were a joke but then his humor was a bit rough.

An hour later when it was light there was sleetish snow against the window and I was frankly pissed off because yesterday had been so beautiful, perhaps in the mid-fifties, and I had sat against a tree in the yard with my butt wet letting the sun warm my belly and my back coolish, watching the snow steam in the ditch beyond the bare lilac grove that surrounds our family cemetery. It is neither more nor less endurable in May when it is enshrouded by the heavy-scented purple and white flowers, a smell that on warm evenings is so dense as to be

almost visible. All I ever needed was the song of the local whippoorwill to make the throat thick and the temples tighten backward so
the chin lifted upward into the evening air. The sound of crickets
arrived one by one until they were a chorus, and if you walked down
the gravel road toward the Niobrara the frogs from the lower, marshy
areas were so loud as to be barely endurable.

Downstairs I could hear the scrape of Nelse and Lundquist pushing their chairs back from breakfast, and Frieda's "Eat more it's cold
outside." Outside the team of Belgian-Clydesdale crosses stood har-
nessed to the wagon. Lundquist and Nelse had driven to western Iowa
in February and bought the team off an Amish farmer for elaborately
announced reasons: to haul hay to the cattle without gouging up the
pasture with a tractor, to drag fallen trees out of the windbreaks, but
ultimately, I thought, it was Nelse's gift to Lundquist who had kept
sets of harness at the ready since the 1940s. It was easy to love these
geldings who weighed a ton apiece and were utterly docile in their
great power, though they have to be pastured separately from the
quarterhorses who seemed perpetually angered at them for private
horse reasons. I watched as Lundquist and Nelse clambered onto the
seat of the wagon full of fence posts as if they were about the true
business of the world. Lundquist at the reins turned the wagon and
Frieda came out to her truck in her baggy red Nebraska Cornhusker
hooded sweatshirt, off to the county seat supermarket for Saturday-
morning shopping, the horses' ears tilting forward at the roar of her
truck and the gravel she threw as she left the yard.

I went downstairs still slightly troubled by the remnant of a
dream based on the early sixties when I had come home from the
university for spring vacation and spent the first morning with Naomi
and the county nurse shaving the hair from most of her students and
dressing their heads against a plague of ringworm. It seemed the furthest cry from my coffeehouse existence in Minneapolis where the
cognoscenti students were making the transition from existentialism
to the homegrown beatnik movement. We had all been quite irritated by a visiting French professor straight from Paris who had found
us quite comic in the way we tried to ape postwar European despair

from the plenitude of Minneapolis. A gay friend ("homosexual" back then) had a crush on this professor and trolled with me, taking him to a steakhouse in St. Paul where the professor laughed until tears came at a huge porterhouse and said that though the steak filled him with ennui he intended to eat every bite. My beige skirt was quite ruined by the grease stains that came when he tried to fondle me under the table. There were none, certainly, on my friend's trousers. The professor comprehended the situation in a New York minute and teased around it the entire evening, even saying that the "partouze" was a nasty bourgeois invention. On translation my friend fled the restaurant and I paid the bill. On principle I nearly refused to sleep with this man but within the texture of that time the strongest moral impetus was curiosity.

In the dream I couldn't find my five-year-old son in the school yard to shave his head. I had looked down in the horse trough and my reflection in the water was mannish, looking more like Duane than myself. I poured my coffee, thought this over and came up with nothing. Beside the frying pan full of potatoes, bacon and a single pork chop was a note from Frieda saying "Eat this Miss Skinny." I had been having the mildest ache in my lower abdomen nearly a week but it had been enough to kill my appetite until evening when a glass of red wine would prod it back to life. Frieda anyway had the satisfaction of cooking for Nelse who had to eat enormously to maintain his strength, his light coming on in the bunkhouse invariably at six A.M. and never going off before midnight. Since I had a measure of my uncle Paul's insomnia I always knew. When J.M. visits they sleep down the hall in Paul's old room which J.M. loves because she thinks of it as a "time warp" of old books, collections of rocks and arrowheads, framed magazine photos of far-off places such as the Vale of Kashmir, the Rift Valley, Glen Canyon and, for some odd reason, a tacky photo of the Rue Marboeuf in Paris.

My right hand was so stiff I spilled part of my coffee and howled "Shit" to the empty kitchen. I clenched and stretched the hand, quite sore from having spent the previous day brushing most of the winter coats off the horses, watching them do their kicking and bucking

fandangos when they were released. This was an annual spring celebration I had been doing since I was a little girl and the thing I had
looked forward to the most when I came home for a week in late April
from the university. It was the ritual of brushing the winter away and
the horses appeared to enjoy it as much as I did.

Quite suddenly I recalled the disturbing aspect of the ringworm
dream. All of Naomi's students had been dressed in the clothing of
the poorest children from my considerable experience as a social
worker. In my first jobs in Minneapolis and Escanaba, in the Upper
Peninsula of Michigan, I had lied to my superiors and said that I had
an uncle who was a sock manufacturer. There are always strict rules
against direct gifts from social workers to what are euphemistically
called their "clients." The lie didn't work in Minneapolis which is
full of rather Nordic strictures but my boss in Escanaba, a warm-
hearted Finn, saw nothing wrong with my dispersal of socks. I had
always hated it when my own feet were cold and it was unendurable
to see children, mostly Natives, wearing thin socks or frequently none
at all in winter. Oddly, it wasn't the poverty that ground against the
sensibilities so hard that depressed me the most but the attitude of
many of the more fortunate who weren't satisfied with having money
unless there were many who didn't have it. This was particularly true
in Santa Monica during the Reagan years when my occupation was
largely seen as laughable, if not contemptible. Even quasi-religious
people liked to quote Jesus as saying, "The poor you have with you
always," neglecting to add that he didn't say to sit on your ass and
don't do anything about it. The thought that my country accepts the
idea that a quarter of its citizens are destined to be social mutants peels
my nerves. Our compassion quotient has seemed to lower a bit more
every year of my adult life. I never much minded when my colleagues
would tease me for being a "bleeding heart" because if your heart
doesn't bleed you're dead, and you've become just another greedy little
shit factory on life's way.

In my dream some of the children didn't have socks and they
smelled of kerosene heaters. Their clothes were thin and shapeless
and there were specific signs of malnutrition. I ate the leftover pork

chop and potatoes mulling over this and how my childish disappointment with the weather, plus a harrowing dream, could affect my ability to keep my spirit afloat. When I was finally fired from my job
mid-March it was under blizzard conditions and I was happy to the
point of delirium. It's remarkable how much more cowed people can
be in a government job than in the private sector. I cleaned out my
desk and walked out of the old county office building with the light-
est heart possible and into a driving snowstorm as if trying to kiss the
snow that hit my face. No one would look at me after the expected
call came. I was being replaced by no one which was quite funny in
itself. All of the money appropriated for counseling the families of
downtrodden farmers had been expended in conferences on the subject in Lincoln and Washington, D.C. I went directly over to Lena's
and had a shot from her bottle of cheap brandy she keeps for dire
events. I ended up helping her for her noon rush as the storm had
made her shorthanded. I even waited on a table of county employees
who had averted their glances a few hours before. At midafternoon
Nelse arrived in his truck, not trusting my old, low-slung Subaru to
get through the storm. He had stopped at the county building and
had been appalled to learn I was fired. We sat in the tavern for an
hour full of the pleasure of watching it snow. Heavy, wet late-winter
snow is a matter of great pleasure in a ranching, farming community.
It means more moisture for the winter wheat and soil better prepared
for corn planting. Grazing land will burst with new and thicker grass
and Naomi's soul will dance at the prospect of a better crop of wildflowers. On the way home we spoke of a possible car trip together in
late May when J.M. will be busy with her final examinations and
won't want him in her way. He had been a bit distressed over the
collapse of his plans for a phenology of local birds. Naomi had finally
and rather shyly told him the work had already been done by someone Nelse refers to as "the great Johnsgard" back in 1980 when Nelse
was off wandering the country. He gave me a copy to look at and I
was reminded again how I have sunken my life in generalities rather
than particulars. I had asked Nelse for a definition of phenology as it
kept slipping my mind and one evening I found a piece of paper taped

to the middle of my bedroom's dresser mirror. "The periodic recurrence of natural phenomena such as bird nesting and migrating as
related to time, also mammals screwing and having their young, also
tree budding and leafing, plants coming to flower, all related to local
climate and precise time of year. Do not remove."

Despite the base work having been done he hopes to recheck
the printed data with his own observations and contribute corrections. I must admit his curiosity mystifies me and I supposed that one
had to start quite young to know the particularities of flora and fauna.
He said, "Why wouldn't you want to know everything about where
you live beyond the walls of this house?" and I was a little embarrassed despite not being a total slouch in the matter compared to those
I know. I've never quite been able to stand back and look at things
without them absorbing me in a distracting way as if every creature
and plant or tree had an emotional equivalent that could be drawn
willy-nilly out of my brain. I'm a little despairing when I leaf through
the stack of field guidebooks he bought me in Lincoln. I've owned
some of them, including different guides to western birds, even *A Field
Guide to Animal Tracks*, but have misplaced them along the way.
When Naomi would haul us children out on nature hikes Ruth could
remember the name of everything but her true interest was strictly
limited to music.

My only defense against Nelse as a stern teacher when he gets
out of hand is to deftly raise some troublesome human element. As
an instance, when he made some quip at dinner about what he'd do
with the rest of his life while J.M. taught I used the old university
catchphrase "terrible freedom" and his ears turned red and his gestures became nervous. This was from the black-turtleneck stage of
college life the professor from France found so amusing. By the next
year it had been largely supplanted by loud music, and the cheap wine
traded in for marijuana. This, however, didn't make the notion of
terrible freedom less obnoxious for me. I nearly envied my friends who
were so urgently seeking decently paying careers. I'd always been
financially prudent but was well aware I didn't need to depend on
my own money-making abilities. I can't say this detail troubled Nelse

but he is mindful of it. He finds my social work stories nearly unbearable even though he's seen much in his life on the road. Children are taught a sense of fair play and some of them spend the rest of their lives being bothered by it.

At age forty-six I can stand at the kitchen sink and look out at the barnyard where the event occurred and feel overwhelmingly blessed that I found my son. Both his parents were problematical and I suppose his mother still is. I conceived him out by the creek in a wet baptism dress at age fifteen. The father, Duane Stone Horse, was sixteen and has drifted far backward in time but is not the less vivid for being so long dead. I wonder if anyone can stand back from earth and get a clear look for more than a few moments at a time. Though we are of one body in some respects I am not fool enough to think I am his mother in the truest sense, the woman who raises and presumably nurtures you day by day. We are what is left of his father and my father except for Ruth who was too young to remember and who was frightened and distant with Duane. After seven months now I think Nelse and I are becoming the closest of friends and perhaps something else for which there is no category. When I see him out the window at dawn or twilight when the light is a bit blurred I think he could be either my father or Duane. After he drove me home on the day I lost my job and when by evening I became quite miserable with delayed rage we sat before the fireplace and he took my hand and held it. That has to be enough.

April 19th

I heard birds at daylight which meant the weather had turned. I got up and opened my south window and the breeze that lifted the curtains was soft. The smell of earth was much more convincing than the last, brief thaw. I was excited, put on my robe, and went down to have breakfast with Nelse and Lundquist though my tummy still felt a bit uncomfortable. They were surprised but seemed pleased to see me. Lundquist was animated, nearly upset over something Nelse had said which he repeated to draw me in. A noted entomologist named

Hopkins had posited that what we think of as the burgeoning of spring in terms of the activities of plants and animals advances at a rate of four days of difference for each degree of latitude which is seventy miles. I was a little stunned and excited along with Lundquist and saw it as a massive spirit slowly flowing north. At the same time Frieda at the stove was chatting about the difficulties the University of Nebraska football coach was having with the behavior of his athletes but what Nelse was pointing out was too fascinating for this to distract us. Lundquist suggested that it was exactly the sort of thing that God wanted us to know compared to the junk that tries to drown us. I hadn't advanced beyond the radical tickle in my brain. The south kitchen window was open a bit and when I turned in my chair there was a piercing call of a meadowlark, certainly not the first of the season but the most convincing in the density of its sound. Even Frieda turned from the stove for a moment. I quivered and Nelse laughed, saying that he felt the same when he had awakened in a pasture and had seen a meadowlark less than a foot away. Lundquist, who was deeply suspicious of Catholics, as many Lutherans are, wondered aloud if it were true that "this old-timey" Catholic saint walked around with birds on his shoulders, head and outstretched arms. He had seen a drawing of Saint Francis but doubted its reliability. Nelse teased that birds couldn't tell the difference between a Catholic and a Protestant, but then Lundquist announced that in his entire life he'd had only five wild birds land on him for any length of time and then only when he was napping in a pasture or within a wooded shelterbelt. He had also sat all one afternoon beside one of Naomi's bird feeders with sunflower seeds on his hat brim but had had no takers. He told us how disturbed he had been when Naomi had told him that humans were only trustworthy when asleep.

When Nelse and Lunquist left for work I took Ted for a long walk, carefully skirting the rock pile in the first pasture. Ted's first trauma as a puppy had been when he trotted up to this rock pile and nudged a largish bull snake which lashed out at him. Now he stares at the rock pile fearfully from a safe distance of a hundred yards and barks at it wildly but will go no closer. His only unfortunate aspect is that he reminds me of Sam who gave him to me. You have at my age this mistaken feeling that you can read your new lover pretty accurately but then the unpleasant surprises begin to arrive. With Sam it was his ample collection of resentments he couldn't manage to hide and I couldn't help him resolve. I had so looked forward to seeing him the week after our family picnic. We met up in Hardin, Montana, and intended to go to the Crow Fair, the grandest of the pow-wows, then visit a friend of mine, a falconer, who has a small ranch between Belle Fourche and Sturgis. We barely made it through two days. His local friends struck me as mean-minded nitwits. There is a smugness about real cowboys over being real cowboys as opposed to the ninety percent who try to simply dress the part. They naturally have their own valid touches, mannerisms absorbed from their work, but then much of their behavior seems adopted from movies and television. Of course alcohol can vastly emphasize bad behavior that is only potential without it. All of Sam's friends, including their wives and girlfriends, seemed terribly proud to have never read a book from "front to back" and became condescending racists when they heard Sam and I were headed for the Crow powwow. When Sam played chicken and said, "She's just hauling me along" as if he were a stud horse I was so pissed I wanted to brain him with a beer bottle.

By the first midnight in a Hardin bar it occurred to me that these people made Brooklyn Sicilians look like English gentlemen. I even began to cherish the memory of certain Ivy League graduates I had gone out with in New York and generally hadn't cared for. There's a terrible illusion that the grandeur of landscape contributes to grandeur of personality. The very last straw that late first night was when Sam's best friend squeezed his drunk girlfriend's arm so hard she turned pale and burst into tears. I abruptly got up and left and when Sam followed me into the parking lot he lamely said that the ugly incident was none of our "business." I only said maybe so but I didn't intend to stick around such behavior.

The real argument didn't start until late the next morning when we were in a fine mood driving in the lovely countryside down toward the Yellowtail Dam along the Bighorn River. I said it seemed odd that so many Eastern fly fishermen came here among the squalor of reservation poverty. We had been talking about my son, Nelse, and how wonderful it had been when he arrived at the picnic. The tip-off was that he mostly congratulated me on finding an "heir" to my property. When I mentioned the Eastern fishermen he said the best way to catch a fine mess of trout on the Niobrara was to throw a net in the river and some firecrackers upstream to drive the fish into the net. I knew he was baiting me because I had seen two fly rods in his trailer. I said I didn't want to see his friends again and that I felt cowboys in Nebraska were far pleasanter than in Montana. He challenged me directly by asking if I was "too good" for his friends and I said, "Absolutely." The fatal trump card was when he refused to pick up a young Crow girl who was hitchhiking despite the fact that the day was very hot. He said something nasty about the Crow being widely on welfare and since they didn't work walking was good exercise for them. People like himself had to work for a living. This burned my ears and I pointed out that in my experience as a social worker I had never seen being on welfare as an enviable position, and that nearly all farmers and ranchers were in some respects on the government dole. When he replied, "I'm just a cowboy, darling," I could see he was going to take a daily, though well-concealed, bath in self-pity, surely the most injurious human emotion. I wondered at the errancy of physiological attraction, how your body can fairly hum with desire for someone only to discover that your minds are as unsympathetic as Vermont and Nevada.

When I reached the creek and pond Sam drifted away on the southern spring breeze and I couldn't blame Ted for bad memories because he was only trying to chase a killdeer who affected injury to lead him away from her nest. I had left Sam at the motel and driven off to Crow Agency by myself with a rather light heart as if I had actually known this all would happen and only had to discover it in the filaments of reality. Ted jumped into the pond, swam across, then stood shivering and barking on the other side as if expecting me to retrieve him. I walked around the pond, pausing to study the burial mound in a thicket. Both my father and Nelse supposed it to be Ponca in origin. I also found my day pack containing a thermos and Van Bruggen's *Wildflowers, Grasses, and Other Plants of the Northern Plains*, the book swollen with moisture, that I had left there two days before. So much for me as an amateur botanist! I reminded myself that since it was Nelse's copy I better order another as the lovely book had fattened and many pages were stuck together. I felt another twinge in my stomach and then became irritated that I had come to the place again where I had conceived Nelse but not quite in the proper mood. The memory of an unpleasant love affair is unshakably similar to a root canal or a badly stubbed toe.

I retrieved Ted and headed north at a brisk pace, diverting my mind to the reunion of Naomi and Paul, and the grave but rather comic evening when she announced in late March that he was arriving and she was going to live with him. I couldn't help but tease by asking, "What will people say?" I am sure she is defying the laws and bylaws of the County School Board after forty years of teaching but then it is unlikely anyone would protest her living with her brother-in-law. Grandfather and I were always adequate for gossip fodder, and then Michael gave them a field day last summer. Nelse transcended any possible reproach by beginning to bring the ranch back to life. Circumscribed lives have tended to make gossip the central national pastime.

Naomi was slightly upset when I said I had known about their affection for each other within a few years after my father died. Children don't so much listen to specific words but the "why" of people saying something. They are also students of gestures and glances and of the invisible thing called moods. They notice this nonverbal language among themselves and it is a simple matter to apply it to adults. Ruth who was fixed on Paul as much as I was Grandfather used to ask in a querulous child's voice why Paul wouldn't become our father. And early in high school, when I was in the ninth grade and had begun to read the large collection of Native material in Grandfather's library, I would occasionally wonder why Paul and Naomi couldn't follow the Native custom of marrying the brother's widow. It certainly would have helped Ruth who had been always a little fearful of Grandfather to the same extent she adored Paul.

I wasn't being attentive but snapped alert when Ted barked and the bark had a new and feral quality to it, rising from deeper in the chest and mixed with a growl. We were walking to the north along the edge of a dense shelterbelt out of which emerged a young mixed breed bull, doubtless the neighbor's stock, and I suspected one of the shelterbelt trees had fallen across the fence, enabling the bull to cross over into our property. Though normally a relatively docile breed this bull thought he was a Miura straight out of Spain and began trotting back and forth, coming ever closer, roaring and blowing snot. Ted raised his hackles and charged, nipping the bull and driving it into a run for at least a quarter of a mile. I was breathless with surprise but also frightened that he might be kicked or hooked by a horn. After he had driven the bull into the distant shelterbelt across the pasture Ted returned at a comic gait with an occasional rumble in his chest, prancing and jumping sideways, wheeling around to make sure the bull wasn't in pursuit. I knelt and petted him, reassuring him that he had done the right thing. It was especially funny a few minutes later when I stepped on a long dark stick in the grass and this new Ted nearly jumped out of his skin to avoid this imagined snake.

We reached the Niobrara at noon and the sun was bright and dazzling off the high water of April, the river turbulent and bulging where it passed over rocks which raised the level of its roar. I found a patch of dry, brown grass and lay down propped by an elbow, as I recalled doing on the Little Bighorn at dawn with the sun rising through the dusty air like a bruised peach amid the powwow's incessant drums. After leaving Sam in Hardin I had watched the dancing throughout the hot afternoon, evening, and through the night with an occasional short nap in my car. There had been an embarrassing incident early in the evening when I took a swig of whiskey from a pint Sam left on the seat in plain view of a Crow policeman walking up behind me. He chided me strongly, saying it was a "dry" reservation. I handed him the bottle feeling tears form. He handed it back telling me that I could have one more drink before he destroyed it. I did so and then we both laughed.

I had left soon after my riverside nap, driven away by processes of memory that I couldn't control. I don't think I had a trace of self-pity which I've always considered the most loathsome of emotions but in the middle of the night while I watched hundreds dance, several breathtaking "fancy dancers" entered the open kiva, one with a body strikingly similar to Duane's. He was also an Oglala Lakota with the indented flesh of a bullet wound below his shoulder blade and beneath his rib cage on his chest, lightly colored in contrast to his darker flesh. I wondered if he had lived if Duane would have ever taken part in a powwow and thought not. To think so would have been a false balm. I very much liked the idea that such ancient enemies as the Lakota and Crow were dancing together, also a contingent of Blackfoot. These people with some grasp of the old ways, even when it was minimal, were better able to survive. All government strictures against the Native American Church, the peyote people, seemed quite corrupt as they interfered with essentially religious practices that had proved an excellent defense against the Native curse of alcohol.

My turmoil had continued through the night with the briefest dream of a favorite history professor back at the University of Minnesota, a New Yorker who had thrilled us with his brilliant and wickedly laconic view of the most unsavory parts of our history. He was from Columbia University and spoke without notes in elegant and piercing paragraphs. I was so smitten with his mind that when I first reached New York City I took a West Side subway up to 115th Street to see the locale that produced such a creature. When he spoke of Native Americans in the last century he focused on the admirable tendency of a culture or civilization to protect its citizens from themselves. Unfortunately, in dozens of cases in human history, there was an invariable tendency to exclude the true Natives in this protection policy, whether it was Thrace, Gaul, Ireland, Brazil or the United States. Whom the conquerors would destroy they first described as savage. In contrast to the emotive sloppiness of my friend Michael this man's voice was cold and calm and his words were rivets punched into his students' collective ship which is always a ship of fools.

Perhaps unfortunately this was the first time there was any public knowledge of our family papers. I had copied out several pages of my great-grandfather's journal for this professor, including a long description of Crazy Horse spending three days on the burial platform with his dead daughter, also certain events leading up to the massacre at Wounded Knee. Naturally the professor wanted to see the entire journals but my uncle Paul thought it a bad idea. I avoided saying so until after the semester was over thinking it might jeopardize my grade. On hearing the bad news the professor was no colder than usual, but did point out that my family had no right to withhold information that might correct misunderstandings of a period in our history. My dander was raised a bit and I said if he drove out to Pine Ridge he could find plenty that needed correcting here in the present. I suppose that was why I became involved in social work. You worked directly in the face of poverty rather than limiting yourself to writing a history of poverty. I had an inordinate respect for this man but not of his judgment of my family's reticence, though of course I didn't know at the time, as Paul did, that actual skeletons were involved. In any event, the existence of our papers gradually leaked out into historical circles and any notice of their existence tended to create problems, including the final shit monsoon of Michael himself whose very being made me smile and irritable at the same time.

Another not altogether pleasant event at the Crow Fair was when I ran into a Lakota couple my own age, both of whom I had known at the university. They were watchers rather than participants at the powwow and he now taught at a community college in North Dakota. They were rather threadbare and ironic about everything, nearly embittered, especially over the gradual dissolution of the American Indian Movement. In the late sixties, while home from New York City for the summer, I had joined them and several dozen others, a mixed bag of Natives and radical whites, to protest the dreadful smear of Mount Rushmore in the Black Hills, and also to punily demand the return of the Black Hills to the Lakota. We were all summarily arrested after threatening to dump blood-red paint on the massive stone head of George Washington. The others were sent to jail while I was sent packing, an unmarked government car following me all the couple of hundred miles to Naomi's house. This was clear evidence again of the persistence of my grandfather's name well after he was dead. Soon after, when I met up again with my radical friends, including the Lakota couple at the powwow, I was icily reminded by them that such people as myself, unlike themselves, always had a "return ticket." I hadn't the heart to be angry with them at the time because it was true. At the gathering what the couple still had was the questionable civility left over from ideological exhaustion. Demonstrating had been replaced by not very dramatic legal maneuvers, partly because the central firebrands had been faced with the intractability of white minds to whom the continuance of the emotional content of Manifest Destiny was as natural as morning coffee.

So I merely chatted with the Lakota couple though when we said good-bye she hugged me and called me "sister." Christ, life wears us out, I thought, watching them walk away with the studied gait of advanced retirees when they were really only my own age. I avoided a contingent of thoroughly white bliss-ninnies nearby, who are the source of much humor among Native Americans, along with the representations of them on television and in the movies. There is a false identification and wan hope of brushing against those who are falsely considered to have an almost genetic virtue, which in itself creates the additional difficulty of distance from the true problems. If you have been horribly swindled and desire reparations to survive you scarcely want to become a totem for the derelicts of the sadistic culture, however benign. If you want to help me don't fawn but go home and kick your congressman in the ass is the plaintive, mostly unvoiced request. You can't greedily suck out of another culture what you have failed to find in your own heart. You may recognize it in another culture but only if it already exists in the core of your own soul.

When I left Crow Agency very early that morning my eyes seemed to grate against their lids but my heart was buoyant. I supposed that it was because I had watched a people celebrate what they already are, come what may, with some of the dance steps doubtless more than a thousand years old, as if for a brief time they could emerge fully from the suffocation of our own culture. Rather than justifiably violent protest against us, they were ignoring us.

On the long, largely empty road east down through Lame Deer and Broadus toward Belle Fourche, I didn't cringe from any of my memories of 1972 when I'd barely noticed the newspaper accounts of AIM's occupation of Pine Ridge and the consequent deaths because Duane had committed suicide in the Florida Keys that year. I had flatly religious reasons for never using the name "Mrs. Stone Horse" that a fine reporter from the *Miami Herald* had used in his article. I certainly became quite blind to what is called "the larger world" in the ensuing year. I recovered an approximation of a sense of life, however slight, at Paul's casita on the Baja beach near Loreto, and at home with Naomi, but mostly back in New York City where it seems quite impossible to completely disappear into yourself, and where I brought my hiking boots from home and took the simple measure of walking thousands of blocks in the following months. I've always felt sorry for rural people who out of fear or scorn have never comprehended the mystery of a great city which is a fulsome extension of our nature, good or bad. Nelse is too young to be a nature curmudgeon and I forced him to admit his pleasure in walking out Paris and other French cities in the wonderful early-morning hours while his mother was sleeping off her wine.

May 3rd

J.M. and Nelse were having a modest quarrel so I made myself scarce, riding Rose in a brisk large loop and ending up north near the river. The last words I heard were, "You deserve to be a bachelor, you self-centered asshole." I didn't totally disagree with her because she had come back from school for a brief two days and he was gone most of the first buying weaned calves with Lundquist. And on the second, this morning, he was irritable because the inventory lists from a museum curator seemed to show several items missing during the artifacts passage through the hands of several academics who had helped with the dispersal. I suggested a clerical error while he was settling on light fingers. Meanwhile, J.M. felt ignored and even after he had offered her his day she was still a little cranky. I sided with her mentally in that like my father, according to Naomi, Nelse is singleminded, running on one track at a time, and though the track is usually admirable it can be enervating to others.

The real problem for me is that my tummyache had been increasing and on this, the first very warm day of the year, I felt a trace of nausea. Whether I walked, rode, sat or slept there was no getting away from the discomfort. I knew enough about human physiology to have specific fears but was intent on totally dismissing them because Nelse and I were leaving on our car trip within a week. Of course I knew that I better get down to Lincoln to see a doctor I had gone to school with before the trip rather than after. I no longer knew any doctors in this part of Nebraska and short of flying to Los Angeles and seeing an ex-boyfriend, a somewhat familiar face in Lincoln seemed the answer. I also wanted to be secretive on the long shot that something was seriously wrong. I had begun to feel that something was subtly amiss soon after Thanksgiving and now I felt quite stupid for not getting a checkup sooner.

When I reached the river I let Rose drink, tethered her loosely to a willow and then went through the obnoxious process of throwing a stick in an eddy ten times for Ted. Each time I throw I speak the number loudly and after only four training sessions Ted has learned that a loud "ten" means the game is over and he must stop pestering me. He then takes a nap and I do too, using his ample damp body as a pillow. I have noticed three different species of raptor on this ride but my bird book is in my saddlebags hanging over the top slat of the corral, along with binoculars, a sandwich and a bottle of water. I remembered when I was a little girl and my dad teased me that I'd forget my butt if it wasn't "tied on." I also remembered ignoring the lesson and mostly wondering just how my butt was tied on. Ted growled and I turned over to see Naomi's retarded friend, Rex, repairing fence up a hill on the far side of the river.

When I again thought of our home burial last October I started laughing despite the pangs in my stomach, then looked down at a burgeoning wildflower that Ted had crushed. My Van Bruggen guidebook was also back in my saddlebags so I picked the flower and put it in my vest pocket for Nelse. Luckily it was blue which dramatically limited the possibilities. Down on the border in Arizona Paul would laugh and call me "Penstemon" because that was the only flower I could readily identify, partly because I had seen it encircling a petroglyph of a figure that was half man and half lizard. I had camped beneath this petroglyph with Douglas under a big moon and its sleep-encouraging properties were nil. The next morning after the earth began to warm, quite quickly in May in the Altar Valley, a tuft of grass wiggled and we watched a rattler slowly emerge. It kept on emerging and we renamed it the "great mother of snakes," possibly the least friendly creature I have ever watched closely. Douglas reprimanded me, saying that "friend" was a limited human term.

The burial involved a rather long and nervous wait of several weeks. We were finally enabled in mid-October by a homely incident down in Lincoln. It's impossible to do anything around the ranch without Lundquist's notice, but then Frieda had gone off to a Cornhusker football game (the name of the Nebraskan team) and in the surge of the crowd after the usual victory she had punched a campus policeman who promptly arrested her for assaulting an officer. When the phone call came Lundquist was inconsolable over his failure as a parent though he was in his mid-eighties and Frieda in her late forties. His wife, also Frieda, had died a decade before and he doubted his capacity for guidance for this immense, violently opinionated woman. On the phone it was Frieda's contention that the policeman had grabbed her breasts, somewhat difficult to avoid in my opinion as they were at least size forty-five triple Ds. This was early on a Saturday evening and while I tried to calm Lundquist Nelse managed to get through to someone at the family law firm we shared.

There was no possibility of springing Frieda until Monday morning which terribly upset Lundquist who jumped up and said he was off on the long drive to Lincoln to visit his poor daughter in the "hoosegow." He refused the loan of my new pick-up because his dog Roscoe wouldn't be comfortable in it. He puttered out of the yard in his ancient Studebaker which would add several hours to the trip, then Nelse looked at me and suggested we get started while I thought Sunday would be adequate. He said he wanted the surface of the hole to have time to dry out so hopefully Lundquist wouldn't notice it.

It became a grandly comic night. We carried a flashlight and lantern down the stairs to the basement and with Nelse's mixed approval I took a magnum from Grandfather's wine cage which no longer had to be locked with Michael absent. Nelse went on ahead while I went back upstairs for a corkscrew and two glasses and when I returned I regretted having to go through the root cellar and down the steps to the sub-basement alone. It was cold enough for the black snakes to be quite dormant but while juggling the wine bottle and glasses plus the flashlight I stepped on a large one, heard its verbless hiss and felt its body whip against my boot.

When I reached the sub-basement Nelse was in the far corner with the lantern lit. This part of the house had never been wired because Grandfather thought it would be blasphemous. It was forever dark down here, darker than the night outside, and I felt a tremor to the effect that this business should have been conducted at noon. The lantern made Nelse cast a monstrous shadow as he packed the three clothed skeletons, the lieutenant, sergeant and private, all of whom had been intent on destroying my great-grandfather and his family. Their remains were to be buried in a hole yet to be dug beside the horse-manure pile behind the barn. The five warriors in full regalia would be buried together in a hole Nelse had already dug out near the pond. During their diaspora they wished to have their remains kept safe from grave robbers, a common practice then which still continues under the aegis of archeology. I always wondered why AIM hadn't simply entered Arlington on horseback with shovels in hand as a protest. I suppose if you went back far enough in time

Native remains might be a proper subject of inquiry but the gravesites of the Indian Wars hold the remains of the grandfathers of many still living.

I called out to Nelse to say something reassuring and he muttered, "It's a lovely evening." I shined the flashlight on the long oak table where most of the artifacts had been packed in cartons for a museum. The intent behind the contents was my grandfather's and his father's keeping them safe from the artifact predators of the time in that they had been given to my great-grandfather for secure storage. Nelse had already given three medicine bags of strictly religious nature back to the Lakota, Cheyenne and Paiutes. The rest was going to a museum because finding the descendants of the original owners was hopeless in that few records had been kept. These included braided sweet grass, otter-skin collars, fur bands of mountain lions, badger skins (Northridge's clan), Crow bustles of eagle and hawk feathers, a painted buffalo head, kit-fox wrist loops, grizzly-claw necklaces, turtle rattles, painted buffalo hides, a full golden eagle into which a Crow holy man's head had fit into the rib cage, buffalo-horn bonnets, ravens, otter-skin-wrapped lances, rattlesnake-skin-wrapped ceremonial bows, mountain-lion sashes, bear-skin belts, dog skins, a grizzly-bear headdress with ears and two claws, wolf and coyote skins, owl-feather headdresses, weasel skins, a knife with a grizzly-jaw handle, bone whistles, full bear dancer hides, huge buffalo-head masks, wolf-hide headdresses with teeth, snake-effigy rattles, dew-claw rattles . . .

When Nelse had finished packing the military remains we toasted them with wine, the hole in the lieutenant's forehead made by the .44 quite garish in the lantern light, a fatal mouse hole into the skull.

"Poor dentistry back then," Nelse said, tapping the three sets of teeth. "The sergeant's nose and jaw had both been broken at one time, and the private has one of the smallest cranial cavities I've ever seen in an adult."

In contrast to my great-grandfather's journal, where it was easy to hate these men who were on a journey to end the lives, for all practical purpose, of my ancestors, the skeletons themselves were utterly disarming. I raised my glass.

"If it had turned out otherwise we wouldn't be here."

"I don't think along those lines very well," Nelse said, standing and lifting the carton.

I guided him out and up through the root cellar, noting in the far corner a knot of black snakes, gathered in a tight ball for warmth. I was about to draw them to Nelse's attention but then his only phobia seems to be people in general. He does okay in particular cases, but the general swarm, especially his own class, puts him off his feed, as we used to say.

Out in the barnyard the horses ran toward the edge of the corral to see what we were up to and, I suspect, arrived at no conclusions. We walked past the stanchions and stalls of the barn and out the back door. At the far edge of the manure pile Nelse put the carton down, took the lantern from me and went to retrieve a shovel. I quickly and childishly took the flashlight from my coat pocket and turned it on. This was not a time to be in the pitch dark with only the slip of a new moon and a floss of stars to keep one company, even for a few minutes. I shook the carton and heard a muffled clack and rattle, the final sound these men would make, dead now for about ninety-five years. I saw Nelse's lantern coming and shivered, thinking that we all lose each other along the way. Everyone loses everyone, mothers, husbands, children, mere lovers, both the good and the evil.

Nelse began digging with an energy that reminded me of what it had been like to be thirty, when with my friend Charlene, some white-cross amphetamines and lots of coffee, we had driven straight through from New York City to way out here in Nebraska. Naomi had been irritated but only said, "Go look at yourself." Added to my city pallor were very red eyes.

In an hour or so of chat, mostly from me, the hole was deep enough and Nelse unceremoniously dumped in the mortal contents of the carton. It was certainly irrelevant but I thought he'd leave them in the box. He turned to me, nodded and leaned on the shovel.

"A prayer, if you please."

"What the hell can I say?" This request startled me.

"Just say something breathtakingly wise," he teased.

"Pause here, son of sorrow, remember death." I couldn't remember where it came from but it would have to do. I poured more wine but Nelse only sipped his, then dumped the rest on the skeletons in their still natty uniforms.

"Here's to us for being here," he said, then began filling in the hole. "First we're here and then we're not. That's what my dad said when I asked him about death. I took a half-dead starling away from our cat and tried to keep it alive but failed. It died right in my hand."

It was after midnight when we had finished wrapping the five warriors tightly in a tarpaulin, binding it with leather thongs, and bringing it upstairs to the den and putting it on the coffee table between the sofa and fireplace. We'd wait for first light, pack the tarp on a horse and ride out to the pond for our second burial. While Nelse built a fire he said he figured from reading the journals and what the warriors wore that all five were Oglala. He would have delivered them for proper burial but Paul had disagreed saying it would bring on unwarranted attention. I poured more wine and wasn't sure I agreed with Paul but let it pass wordlessly. Nelse was hungry so I cooked him part of a large sirloin I intended for Sunday dinner. It was fun to watch the improbable gusto with which he ate, studying each rare chunk a moment before he put it in his mouth.

By then it was after one in the morning and rather than bothering to go to bed we sat up on the soft leather sofa, probably as old as the house was, dozing now and then, and talking. The rare amount of wine had loosened his tongue a bit and he told me a wonderfully funny story about a Spanish woman he had loved near Espanola, New Mexico, whose husband had returned by surprise and sent the half-clothed Nelse sprinting down a mountainside. I told him about a brief fling with a Brazilian diplomat who had fibbed about his marriage and we agreed that some people have a desperate and understandable need to add a bit of drama to their lives. I clumsily explained my own modest theory that we can only go so far with thinking, and then our minds must be refilled by the "thinginess" of life—landscapes, creatures, any sort of travel, people we could not imagine not having existed. Even Sam who had worked out so wretchedly was worth the price of grief he offered, partly because I was led to that Crow Fair and could visually imagine again as I had as a girl reading Mari Sandoz, an entire culture within our boundaries that had run counter to the worst aspects of our own. I wasn't talking about flowers or birds here but human beings who pillaged and made war as we did, but also had a great deal of soul life that was not totally wiped out by clutter and greed. And there was another incident, I said, back when I was in New York and walking and grieving over the death of his father to the point that I had tunnel vision, however the peripheries had managed to dissolve themselves. A musicologist friend who was gay and lived in the same pleasantly slummish building down on Second Avenue took me up to St. John's, the cathedral, where a half dozen black choirs were performing. We were early and got seats well up to the front. By the end of the evening I was totally dumbfounded but could finally see well off to both sides as if the music had re-ordered my dried-up brain. In wild contrast to the droning Methodists and Lutherans of my youth I had finally heard "a joyful noise unto the Lord" and most of we rich-poor whites, several thousand of us, left the cathedral in a jouncy daze. It still struck me as mysterious that music could have made me see well again.

The latter story bothered Nelse a bit from his scientific tack but then he spoke of a "semi-dipshit Zen girl" he had once loved but had found him wanting (he couldn't stop eating hamburgers) who quoted some sage saying to the effect that "all over the body are hands and eyes." This had bothered him a great deal until he had talked to a visiting cultural anthropologist who specialized in ancient China who told him that the earliest roots of Zen "sitting" probably evolved from a hunter-gatherer stage. If hunters sat very still beside game trails a long time they were more likely to be successful. From that post-Pleistocene period evolved a practice that also stilled the mind and made it unresistant to the phenomena it observed. Nelse took it from there to mean that if you spend a great deal of time in peopleless areas you are sensing your local habitat with your whole body rather than simply your eyes. He then asked me about my grandfather's friend Smith, whom he had read about in the memoir. I said I only had met him that once when I was pregnant but the experience was memorable. There was no point in pretending people were all in the same boat when someone like Smith had obviously stepped out of the boat and been out there for quite some time. Such souls tend to be discounted among the intelligent because there haven't been enough of them for a meaningful study, assuming that they were going to be direct with an anthropologist in the first place. Nelse told me about an old Ponca who claimed he had invented hockey on the frozen Missouri but then Nelse later realized this was only a comic barrier to test him. I said I had known the daughter of such a man when I had been a social worker in Escanaba. She was quite contemporary but the father was a traditional Medwiwin Anishinabe (Chippewa) who lived deep in the woods on the Wisconsin-Michigan border. She took me to meet her father and when we walked down a long hill to where he was sitting by a pond a group of turtles scrambled off of his legs and back into the pond. Anyone knows how hard it is to sneak up and catch a turtle, but she laughed at my surprise and said that the turtles trusted her father. Nelse was as upset with this story as I had been surprised with the event itself, but despite his questioning I had nothing more to add.

We dozed then for a couple of hours before I got up to make a large pot of coffee and fill a thermos. I put on a Mozart tape to establish a more comfortable form of reality. Nelse came into the kitchen smiling at the music, then rinsed his face in the sink. We drank a cup of coffee wordlessly listening, then Nelse went back to the den and shouldered the bound tarpaulin of the five warriors. I remembered the thermos and we walked out the kitchen door and through the pumpshed, our feet crunching on the frost-stiffened barnyard. We saddled up Rose and a pretty-faced mare named Grace. Nelse bound the laden tarp to the back of his saddle, and I poured us another cup, then put the thermos in my saddlebags with my barely touched nature guidebooks which made me fear passing a test. We stood there in the dark staring at the east, shivering and waiting for the light, feeling but not seeing the steam of the coffee rising up our faces. Then there was a slight smear of light through the oaks and lilacs that surrounded our own graveyard and we could finally see each other standing beside our horses which gave off warmth. Then we left on the three-mile ride to the pond with a trace of bone clack and the first waking meadowlarks in the air, most of them soon to be gone south, the creak of leather, and the horses breathing. I felt it was a gift from God knows where to have spent this night with my son.

It was fully dawn when we reached the gravesite with a stiff wind from the northwest that teared our eyes and a late-October sun that offered light rather than heat. I had been wondering how long the men in the tarp had been dead before their remains had been brought to old Northridge. Nelse said that three of the five must have been on burial platforms for a long time as what they wore had been particularly weather-beaten. The other two could have been stored in Badlands caves as their elk-skin shirts were imbedded with a minuscule gravel substance like "caliche," and there were also many particles in their moccasins. There was a darkly comic aspect to Northridge's lifelong struggle as basically an agricultural missionary to the Lakota who had no interest in or cultural preparation for farming. The form which his Christian interest took in doing good was totally alien to these people and largely still is. The buffalo was their commissary and to defeat them you only had to destroy seventy million buffalo which was easy enough for us in that we had a bagful of additional motives. I'm sure their trust in Northridge came from his complete fluency in their language and that as a botanist he was dealing in the sources of food in the manner of a functional shaman. Botanists are welcome everywhere, and if this botanist marries one of your own, fathers a child and tries to protect you and your interests from the predations of his own people then you have the ultimate in trust, more than enough for some to offer up their dead in protection from the huge market for artifacts which still exists.

Nelse had cut a small tree, which stood upright against the side of the hole, in order to get himself out. I admired the hole's size in contrast to the hurried job on the military remains. He clambered down to the bottom and I slid the bound tarp to him. He cut the thongs and spread out the five facing east, then climbed back out with the tarp. We were at a loss for something to say over the grave so we sat down on the piles of dirt with our backs to the wind and had another cup of coffee. As I have said, you can't get anything true from another people unless it is already in your heart in a dormant form and you discover it there. All of the cross-cultural spiritual shopping you see seems quite hopeless to me but then this is scarcely my area of expertise. I can only see spirit in the flesh, not spirit in spirit. I had once joked to Nelse that I might be able to contribute to a phenology of the human heart. He looked at the ceiling, laughed, and said I should have been married to John Keats, and how could I continue such romanticism when there was an actual world of evidence to the contrary. I had delicately said, "Fuck that world."

We watched three skeins of geese fly over heading south and then Nelse began the long job of filling the hole, wishing to finish well before Naomi might arrive on her Sunday-morning hike. He asked if he could have some more of the steak for breakfast and I said of course. I walked through a thicket to the pond and looked downward into the water, seeing myself distorted on the rippling surface. When I came back he was throwing on the last of the dirt and then we gathered brush from the thicket to cover evidence of the hole. We then saddled on up and headed home.

May 13th

Yesterday when I drove down to Lincoln I bought a camper shell for my pick-up to keep our equipment dry and safe on our trip. We had spent the night before working on maps and I daresay that Nelse was as excited as I was. In Lincoln I met J.M. for lunch and she was terribly pleased to announce that the chances for a teaching job in our area looked good, probably because of Naomi's recommendation and Naomi knowing everyone on the school board. I said that it must have something to do with her academic record too, at which she blushed and agreed. I lied and said I had driven down to see the doctor because of a recurrence of migraines that often happen in late spring. For some reason I doubted that she believed me but she let it pass. When we said good-bye she wished me a wonderful trip with Nelse and said she'd be with us up home the minute she finished her finals. I had a little time to spare before the doctor so we walked a half hour or so, stopping and laughing before the strip club where she had met Nelse. "Isn't it strange when you see how badly they want you," she said. I agreed, adding that it is also strange how successfully we can conceal our wanting them. We decided there must be an anthropological reason for this but we wouldn't bother asking Nelse.

The visit to the doctor was even more unpleasant than I had expected it to be. If you have any sense you prepare for the worst, perhaps have even expected it for quite some time, but you really don't get the job done because the work has taken place in your mind, and that doesn't include all the decidedly nonsensuous realities of a doctor's office, the bad art and bad furniture and bad magazines and bad wall colors. My old friend was now a gynecologist and I guessed his office was mostly a spartan funnel for the operating room. We had known each other quite well as undergraduates at the University of Minnesota, he being the only science type in our sorry little group, but with an incredible collection of modern jazz. He had gained a good seventy pounds since then which is not all that surprising in Nebraska and was still friendly on the surface, but really quite brusque in the manner of doctors who try valiantly to protect their emotions from the nature of their practice. I had known a number of them in Santa Monica, two of them in the area of oncology, and one of them said, "I almost always lose unless they move away. Then someone else loses."

We had been lovers for a short weekend way back when and he was cheeky enough to whistle when I disrobed, much to his nurse's embarrassment. We were barely into our diagnostic talk and the beginning of the examination when he couldn't conceal his anger with me. I admitted my first little inklings had come before Christmas, maybe before that with a few unpleasant biological details. His ill-tempered question was how could I be as intelligent as he remembered me being and behave so stupidly with my own body. I was naturally close to tears and said, "I don't know." He went on with a pelvic ultrasound, then said we may as well head for the hospital. I said no and got dressed, and then in a long rush said I was going camping with my son first and after that I'd submit to whatever was possible to prolong my life.

He remembered clearly my story of giving up a baby for adoption in my early teens and was quite pleased that my son had found me. Rather than face me with a prognosis he stared out the window while we talked. I wouldn't agree to a CAT scan that afternoon because I wanted to go home, pure and simple. I rejected the idea of a local hospital or even Mayo in Rochester, Minnesota, after my camping trip because I wanted privacy which really meant secrecy. He suggested Johns Hopkins in Baltimore and I said I had learned to loathe the general area of Washington, and then he came up with Sloan-Kettering in New York City which was amenable to me. He immediately called an old friend and colleague there and set me up for June 7th. I thanked him and he gave me a hug, finally looking at me directly. He said this was the kind of moment when he wished that he had become something sensible like a mountain climber or a jazz musician. On the way out he gave me an assortment of pills to make me comfortable on our camping trip.

It rained nearly all the way home, but it was a warm gentle rain, a specific tonic to hearing terms like "bilateral salpingoophorectomy" which I had the doctor write out when my ears refused to accept such a pathetic word. Why not call the procedure "nasturtium" or something similarily sensible. Maybe "rhododendron."

I stopped to watch the Loup River rising near Dannebrog, then took an early-evening walk in the rain near the Calamus Reservoir, watched some birds I didn't, of course, recognize near Long Pine though I had the wit to know they were of the plover family. I got home in the middle of twilight and the lights were on in Nelse's bunkhouse but his truck was gone. He was probably over at Naomi's for dinner, I thought. I mixed my first martini since Santa Monica, and took one of the pills marked for general discomfort. Within a half hour I felt quite well, so much so that I danced around to a nit-wit song on the radio, heated up a can of hot chili con carne that was made in Texas and Nelse swore by. He loves good food but will eat just about anything for fuel. In the bunkhouse he has a large jar of peanut butter and a spoon, also a sack of venison jerky that Lundquist made him. While eating the chili I pondered my possible death sentence and strained to remember a Victor Hugo quote Paul had used to the effect that we are all condemned to death with an indefinite reprieve. Tricky but nice. The last time I saw my grand-mother Neena at Wickford before she died of cirrhosis she didn't seem unhappy. In fact I think she was having a martini while Paul grimaced on the sofa beside her. She gently teased Paul, saying that she had read enough to know what this was all about.

While eating my questionable chili I propped up Johnsgard's phenology, *The Birds of Nebraska and Adjacent Plains States*, and Van Bruggen's *Wildflowers*, but like a child (and many adults) I opted for the latter because of it colorful photos. Due to my tentative health I had the naive but rather poignant feeling that I should memorize the earth. At age forty-six I was starting very late and the names of every-thing were quite out of the question but not my eyes and how things look. I had always been incapable of dwelling on what religious folks call "eternal questions," the unknowable country, if any, after death, but then I could at least become more attentive to the actualities. I, of course, wasn't assuming that memory existed after the body died, but if anything did, memory would have to be it. The question of where the memory might reside was as specious as the fish swimming in air that I had seen in a Brueghel painting. When I was very young and we were camped in a meadow near the Missouri River I had wandered off on a sandbar trying to catch waterbirds, and when my father reached me and carried me back to the tent I remember his muscular neck and bristly face and, when I pushed back, his brown eyes, the small mole above an eyebrow, his breath smelling faintly of whiskey and tobacco, the damp feather of a pheasant we had plucked stuck to his soft flannel shirt. I had a heron feather I had found on

the sandbar clutched in my hand, and I still have it up in my bedroom. Is that what is left of my father? I don't know, and the soul
says, "How the hell do I know?" Wounds seem common but each cure
unique. Paul likes to quote Aristophanes, saying, "Whirl is king," but
then I've noticed he has spent years staring into his wood fires. He
also says, "Technically speaking rocks are alive," but I'll be damned
if I can remember quite what molecules are. When I was wandering
in that rain-soaked field near the Calamus I began counting, a nervous, perhaps neurotic, habit from my childhood. Seven bees. Nine
birds. Five june bugs. My dog Sonia had never let me count her teeth.
I liked to tell my activist girlfriends in Santa Monica that women
should learn from bitch Airedales. They are wary, suspicious, intelligent, improbably tough, curious to a fault, but when they make the
decision to let loose they are utterly jubilant. That's how I'd help train
the daughter I never had but dreamed of having. Ted at my feet is
half Airedale but it is generous to call him a dope like Paul's Carlos
who used to mate the garbage can. I wondered idly if my current problem was connected to the severity of my infection in Marquette that
awful winter when I was carrying Nelse in my belly. It would be too
much like original sin, with Duane as Adam full of plum wine out by
the mock tipi by the pond. Eve is fifteen but can't wait another moment. When you are young you are always seeing the world for the
first time. Anyway when I was near the Calamus I had that sensation, rare when you're older, of looking at this sea of grass closely for
the first time. It made me nervous and I began counting weeds and
grasses but stopped at seventeen when a crow flew by to check me
out. I memorized the crow, then walked back to the truck through
squishy puddles thick with grass, then went into the water above my
knees in the ditch. We certainly don't know how old we are unless
we remind ourselves. For a half hour or so I was five, lacking only my
bright red boots, and little Ruth tagging along beside me, squealing
"hundred" for how many times she wanted to be pushed in the tire
swing.

* * *

It was a good day packing up gear for the camping trip through I needed two pills to get through, trying a new one that made me feel too dull and wispy for several hours, then the reliable one for dinner with Naomi and Paul. It would have been nice to have someone to talk to about my problem but Naomi appeared happy as a newlywed with Paul. J.M. might be the best but then I couldn't interfere with her last two weeks at the university. I came close with Ruth on the phone but then she announced yet another new boyfriend, this one a naturalist. She has admitted that she tends to select boring men then wonders a few weeks later why they are so boring. She confided with a girlish trill that after dining out they had made love over a sawhorse in her garage. I said that that certainly sounded promising. I couldn't very well enter my illness into her newfound adventure. Her son, the pompous asshole Bradley, had stopped in Tucson on business, met the naturalist and pronounced him a "no-nonsense real man," certainly a questionable recommendation.

That left Nelse, and I doubted I had the heart to tell him such news. I also found my sense of language to be deeply suspect. There had simply been no sense of preparation for this, other than the wordless mulling that goes on when our bodies are askew. The first indicators suggest the old New York feelings of being trapped in an elevator. How can this possibly happen, especially to me? It's a little slower and less dramatic than when an airliner has mechanical difficulties. Once on an elevator in the Chrysler Building three of eight men began whistling when we stopped between floors. Counting again. Four women suspended with them, one giggling.

My pile of gear in the front hallway was judged much too large by Nelse who properly said I'd spend exhausting time looking for stuff. I pared it down, with him stooping beside me. He was startled when I winced and I lied and said I had overstretched my back getting off Rose. I had the urge to take Ted along but Nelse disagreed. You see less in the natural world with a dog along though they alert you by their scenting abilities to what you're not going to see. There also was the point that I had become softheaded of late and hadn't trained Ted nearly as well as my previous dogs. After we finished sorting my gear with Nelse smiling at my twenty-five-year-old unused North Face pack he out of the blue asked me why he hadn't simply been aborted and was the decision a close call? I said I didn't recall it ever coming up. Back in the late fifties the undercurrent of abortion was strenuously dark, and though I knew at the time that it happened it wasn't commonly practiced by reputable physicians. Charlene had heard of doctors in Omaha and Kansas City who performed abortions, also there was gossip of an undertaker doing so down in Lincoln. I said that the only close call had been when I was so ill up in Marquette during my fifth month. He seemed relieved as if he had spent time thinking about not existing, the most problematical of all questions. For some reason while we were sitting on the floor I told him about how after Duane died down in the Florida Keys I had received a death-benefit check of ten thousand dollars from some sort of armed services insurance group. I hadn't felt entitled to it, plus our family had ample money so I sent it back. They re-sent the check, saying that it was up to me to dispose of the funds, so I gave half of it to a group raising money in New York for the neediest families, and the rest to semi-indigent friends who were trying to paint or write, the two professions in which one is least likely to succeed. Afterward, I was struck dumb with my stupidity and got an equal amount from the trust from my grandfather and sent it to Duane's mother, Rachel.

Frieda had made a simple potato soup for lunch, something my system could easily tolerate, and while eating we continued my modest art history lessons for Nelse that we had started the week before. I had had two semesters of it at the university, admittedly because I liked to sit in the dark and look at the slides but mostly, I supposed, because of my grandfather. We were interrupted by Nelse's wondering where I got my "idealism" which in a real sense, he thought, was almost nonexistent in his generation. He rhetorically decided on Naomi and I agreed she had set the groundwork, but then my own generation had been intent on saving the world in every respect, from war and racial problems to hunger.

When we tried to return to art we were both yawning with the warm lilac-scented breeze floating in from the yard. Looking at our pile of luggage down the hall I wanted to say, "Let's go now" because I was fearful that something would stop our trip.

"What's wrong with you?" he said, his voice coming to me from afar.

"Nothing that can't be handled," I answered with a smile.

"I mean you always look like you're looking out a window even if a window is not there."

"I'm trying to decide what I should do with the rest of my life. I've always worked and now it's been three months. I have a friend who can help me get a social work job in New York. I'm thinking about it." This was a lie for my own convenience in explaining my upcoming trip after the current one with him.

"I wish you would wait until the fall," he said almost boyishly.

I nodded gravely, but felt terribly pleased he wanted me around. This grew with the decisive sense that he wanted to stay here himself. I also felt confident that Naomi could wangle J.M. a job. I wished that they would immediately get married and have a baby all in one week, a fine if irrational notion. I looked over at Nelse who was fingering a small stack of art books but clearly wanted to go outside. I knew he had barely cracked the Berenson and Gombrich I had given him but then I didn't want to hassle him or question his peculiar idea that many paintings reminded him of what you see out of the corner of your eye when you're looking directly at something else. He was an easy student not because of any particular knowledge but that his mind was quite naively open on the subject. To him the physiology of human vision was a great mystery and what could be more natural than to frame and contain it? His adoptive mother had a considerable library of art books but when he was a boy she had kept those with any nudes in a locked cabinet. He would look at paintings but rebelled at reading a single word of text. I reminded him that we were having dinner with Naomi and Paul, then I went off to a blanket that I had secreted behind the grape arbor and slept for a couple of hours. Before I dozed I turned over and beneath the lower vines I could see Nelse saddle Rose and Lundquist start the old Ford tractor with Roscoe beside him in a milk crate he had bolted to the fender. Ted glanced around, presumably for me, then followed Nelse out of the barnyard. I allowed a few tears to form while I looked upward at the undersides of the grape leaves. Later a bee stung me awake but it really wasn't that bad. In fact it was a grace note that awoke me from a sodden dream that I was being buried with those military men deep beneath the manure pile. I had looked at all those skulls and I had somehow known that none of them were Duane.

We had a fine dinner with Naomi and Paul. A second pill and a glass of wine before we went over gave me a pleasant illusion that I was fine during dinner, aided by the exuberant mood of Naomi and Paul. They were nearly startling and I was reminded again of the possible variance between the outward age and that of the interior which builds itself on thousands of factors including the sweetly irrational aspects of love. I felt a small but niggling envy of them that they could withhold themselves so many years and still arrive at this apparent vivacity of affection. I don't mean, of course, the magnetized bodies of young lovers, but the subtle way Naomi and Paul had all their antennae construed toward each other. There also was the slight angle of despair over why they had waited so long though I was now aware of their various meetings. It's not so comic the way that clocks race themselves with us in fragile tow and it's not enough to say "What are we waiting for?" or "Why are we holding back?" though that might occur to us later. We are far less capable of those radical emotional moves advocated by magazines that specialize in puddle-deep psychologisms, the usual seven steps to a victorious emotional life, as if we could put ourselves on a figurative grease rack or automated assembly line for overhaul.

No wonder that Nelse, Paul and Naomi became obsessed with the natural world, the grace of the divinely ordinary. Paul and Naomi made forays into the numinous, the metaphysical from that base, Nelse less so. Paul could take a four-hour walk, check a botanical text for certain details, then flop on his couch and read Chekhov stories, reread Steinbeck or Faulkner, or one of his newer passions, García

Márquez. Naomi watched birds but did not ignore the rigors of Emily Dickinson or Peter Matthiessen (a rare novelist who could identify more than five birds, she said, perhaps thousands, and years ago she sent me a book of his about shorebirds, also a novel set in South America which I could not finish because the doomed hero named Moon reminded me so much of Duane).

What I meant, too, by the ordinary was how Paul was laughing as he carved two of Lundquist's chickens he had roasted with garlic, tarragon and lemon. The joke was the wine Naomi tended to buy at a supermarket in the county seat which came from the bottom of the California barrel. Life was too short to drink bad wine and what Paul had had shipped, Bandol, was only a few dollars more a bottle. She pinched his ear as she defatted the sauce. Nelse was talking about a black-headed grosbeak he had seen on the way over and had pointed out to me. I couldn't see it in the windbreak but pretended I had. He had recently decided that when you're close it was impolite to look at birds directly since staring is generally unliked by other creatures. Naomi wasn't sure of this one, but then Nelse said if a black-headed grosbeak was as large as a grizzly bear you definitely wouldn't stare. Paul said that was "tautological" but I had forgotten what the word meant. I was looking at a map of the Midwest that came out of one of Naomi's *National Geographics*, though Nelse had already traced our route and there was no point in arguing with a confirmed map person. It was all so ordinary though I wanted to shoot the wall clock, over and over. Anything to make it stop or, better yet, keep backing up slowly.

When we got back home Nelse seemed vaguely cynical about putting a case of modest wine in the truck but I said it wasn't unreasonable to split a bottle per evening while we camped, though I was mostly thinking about its good effect on my tender stomach. For some reason I kept remembering a very old character actress in Santa Monica who was one of my welfare clients. She had had four husbands but had refused to accept any money from them in the divorces. She had the same infirmity as myself but seemed rather happy in her last year. She thought of her acute discomfort as if she were on a train and her pain was being left behind in the landscape she passed. She lived in a single large rented room about five blocks from the ocean. She had been childless but spent her time corresponding with young friends she had known from when she taught acting classes. She read a great deal, went to Sunday mass, and toward the end when she had become quite ill and I was terribly upset she had asked, "How could you think it would be otherwise?" I had no ready response. I tended to visit her quite often because her presence was so soothing. On Saturday her landlord, a heavy-set Italian man in his mid-sixties, would bring lunch and then they would listen to the opera on the radio. She was seventy-five and this had been going on for over twenty years. If you leaned out the window you could look down a slight hill to the ocean. Now I wondered if I had found it soothing because it was so ordinary? She was intelligent and extremely nonsentimental and her memories of the movies had none of the wishy-washy aspects of the old who insist that the present is a pale shadow of the past. She had lived in New York City in the late forties and thought that period to be "glorious" but she did not add that other periods were less glorious. She had also lived in Paris for two years in the mid-fif-ties with her third husband and thought her time there to also be quite "glorious" but left the judgment at that. These personal aspects were so simple as to be mysterious. I don't recall a single complaint though she was capable of some rather raw observations about movie studios and California Republicans. She just didn't take bad business or bad government behavior personally.

I was thinking of her when I went to sleep trying to calm myself for what I thought would be a difficult night. It didn't happen, other than a striking dream about Sunday school when I was a young girl with rather intense religious convictions, mostly I suppose centering on keeping my dead father safe and secure in heaven. The Korean War was as problematical as Vietnam would later be, but it was too early in my life for that observation or the obvious one that those who declare wars are never endangered by them. At the time I whole-heartedly believed in the Gospels and the saving power of Jesus though I couldn't make any sense out of the Old Testament. In the dream, in contrast to reality, we were all singing beautifully and somewhat operatically on a Sunday morning in the summer with the western sky yellowish black from an oncoming storm. When the dream was over and I got up to pee Ted barked out the window, perhaps hearing a coyote beyond my ability, and I shushed him. I looked out the window, pleased at the waxing half-moon and that it would become full on our trip. I began to ponder my dream and the existence of Jesus and wondered why I had never gotten around to disbelieving as many do. My efforts simply were never in that direction. Maybe I was so ordinary that I didn't think any opinion I could summons up on the matter was relevant. I tried to remember the last time I had actually prayed and came up with the day after the night Duane committed suicide and I had prayed that I would not go insane and die. A simple enough request. In this suffering world it was difficult to make a special case for yourself. If anything, prayer should help you accommodate yourself to biological inevitabilities or it should ask for more consciousness since that seems to be all we have anyway.

May 17, 1987. 6:00 A.M.
47 Fahrenheit. 42.5 Lat. 100.5 Long.

We left soon after first light with Lundquist kneeling in the driveway and restraining Ted so he wouldn't chase after us. Freida had forced upon us a large carton of ham-and-cheese sandwiches insisting that most road food had vermin in it. I often couldn't help myself in wondering how much time she spent in the toilet what with all she ate. When we drove off I mentioned this to Nelse and he said Freida seemed to be permanently "hyperphagic," the state bears enter into in the fall when they are crazed to get enough food to gain the fat they need for winter hibernation. He added that men in the north had a tendency to gain a dozen pounds in the late fall, a holdover genetic urge perhaps from the Pleistocene before we squatted in one place and filled the larder. We weren't even halfway down our gravel

road to the county blacktop before Nelse swerved to the shoulder and
grabbed his binoculars. "My first May chat," he half-yelled.

"Your what?" I asked, thinking for a millisecond that we were
stopping to talk but knowing otherwise.

"A yellow-breasted chat, the largest of the warblers," he said,
passing the binoculars. "Please write it down."

I stared through the glasses at the emerging leaves of the windbreak, seeing nothing, but nodded my head and said, "Marvelous."
This satisfied him and we were back on our way. He had an elaborate, to me, theory that even the simplest of us could raise the quality of our lives by vastly increasing our level of attention. Of course
he meant toward the natural world, not to each other or people in
general. The week before while we were out riding he had noted a
slight movement in the grass in a small thicket near the Niobrara. A
bull snake was busy swallowing an infant rabbit and Nelse said, "We're
so lucky to see this." I thought not and wouldn't get off Rose who
also didn't care for snakes. His request for me to "write it down,"
meaning the yellow-breasted chat, came from the idea that it was my
duty to keep a logbook of our entire trip similar to his ten years' worth
that had been stolen with his truck. I didn't mind since he would be
doing most of the driving out of nervous habit though I said I would
include any number of notations of the phenology of the human heart.
He had looked at me askance to make sure I wasn't joking, then agreed
my idea might make for better reading later. He also told me a brief
story about how he had let his father read a number of his travel journals and his father had figured out his code entries for sex. This was
amusing but then Nelse added that his father had also been critical
of Nelse's supposed distance as a junior anthropologist. His father had
an agreeable point here as if you could plastic-coat your life so no
living moisture could enter.

This reminded me of a right-wing doctor in Santa Monica I had
gone out with a few times. I didn't say so but I recognized the obvious symptoms of his having read Ayn Rand as a teenager wherein
preposterous greed is seen as admirable. On our second dinner date

this doctor offered to help me "demythologize" my life to rid it of sentimentality about the poor and the working class, the romantic interest in literature and art that was keeping me from being an effective person. At first I didn't quite believe he was serious as he seemed otherwise intelligent and attractive, though at a good dinner he insisted we limit ourselves to two small glasses of wine apiece for reasons he wouldn't specify. I couldn't clarify any of his aims other than to make a lot of money. I also suspected that when he had picked me up for the second dinner date he had taken a good look at my desk while I was in the bathroom as he seemed to know there was some sort of money in my background. There was also the possibility that he had called a friend in Nebraska. Anyway, by the third date I had a clearer sense of what an asshole he was. It had been a tough late afternoon trying to help a welfare client get a toilet fixed that had been broken three full days. There were several young children and the wife had been terribly embarrassed about the smell in the apartment. I told the doctor this little story while I fixed him a drink with too much vodka in it. The full force of his creepiness came to me when he said in reference to my welfare family that he didn't want to hear any "bleeding heart" stories. I felt trapped but then also relieved because I was taking him to a large dinner party given by my ex-brother-in-law, Ted, a music producer who lived in a cold modern palace out at the end of Malibu where there were armed guards at the compound's gate. I was betting that this doctor would fawn all over the featured guests, a dope-spavined rock group that recently had an enormously successful national tour. And I was right. He fixed himself onto these sleepy-eyed musicians as if he were a decal. In the kitchen Ted asked me where I had gotten the "cute jerk" and I said, "He's yours" and had Ted's all-around butler, Andrew, give me a ride home. The whole experience was but a week's duration and I never took a call from him again, though I kept on thinking about what might be left over if you demythologized your life of its dreams and visions, its aesthetic passions, its poignant memories of landscapes and animals, its obsessions with human parity. This doctor could have easily replaced his clumsy philosophical system with heroin and gotten the same results if you left out the money he wanted.

By midmorning we had finished covering my favorite stretch of road in America, Route 12 across the top of central Nebraska, at least until you get past Crofton and head north toward Yankton, or further east toward Sioux City. I had wanted to go the former way in order to visit Pipestone again in southwestern Minnesota, but then we had promised Lundquist we would pass through New Ulm, his place of birth, though it was considerably out of our way. New Ulm was the only thing about which I had ever had a quarrel with Lundquist. President Lincoln had cooperated with the execution of a number of Santee Sioux here for killing settlers and I had viewed it as the same thing as executing enemy soldiers after a battle, though to his credit Lincoln had lessened the number to be hanged. Lundquist claimed that the death of a great-great-aunt gave him bad dreams though he was born sixty-five years after the event. I didn't doubt Lundquist's dreams about the event as it was unthinkable for him to fib, though I wondered at the power of family stories that could cause bad dreams throughout a life.

   Earlier in the morning we had stopped for a late breakfast sandwich on a high hilltop near the village of Niobrara where both my parents and grandparents had camped, mostly because there was a clear, dramatic view of the confluence of the Niobrara and the Missouri Rivers, the colors of their intermixing waters varying with the seasons and depending on the runoff of rain and snow. Nelse had been there several times before, and I had always stopped there on the way home from the University of Minnesota to sit for a while and cleanse heart and mind of the jingle-jangle, raw nerves and lint of college life.

   I could only manage a few bites of Frieda's gargantuan sandwiches and went partway down the hill into the bushes, ostensibly to pee but really to take a pill in private while Nelse crawled around trying to sneak up on one bird or another. I was counting again and in the first few hours we had slid to a halt to watch eight different birds which I had noted in the margin of our logbook. The one I liked best, partly because it was clearly visible, was the scarlet tanager which Nelse said was rare in the area. I did wonder how he managed to note these birds in the first place while soaring along the road at sixty miles an hour or more, but then he said he had had a decade of practice. This led to the question of how much he missed the road and he said not nearly as much as expected except for the first month or two. He said it was almost Newtonian in regard to an object of motion staying in motion unless met with an unbalanced force and the force had been J.M. It's easiest to keep doing something because you are already doing it. You've patterned yourself, like enduring a bad job because you've accustomed yourself to all the little rituals surrounding it which are comfortable compared to searching for a new job.

The trouble down in the bushes was that I tried to swallow the pill without water and began choking when it caught in my throat. It simply stuck there and wouldn't go down or come up. The world was becoming pink-tinged from lack of oxygen but I managed to crawl partway up the hill on my hands and knees and groan weirdly and Nelse came running and slapped my back. Luckily the pill dropped down into my stomach. I blamed it on Frieda's sandwich but he didn't look like he quite believed me. As we walked back to the truck it occurred to me that my time might become foreshortened at a rate that was less than bearable, and that I shouldn't be counting possible years, but months, and singular days themselves might be a better idea. The fact that this was also applicable to perfectly healthy people did not miss my thoughts. I supposed that most of us drifted, floated, even happily bobbed along and it was not within our capabilities to have a clear view of when and where the river emptied into the ocean. There was not a single metaphor to placate the end of the story except for the utter commonality of the experience, the slow walk through the paradise we are witless to notice sufficiently. I imagined that there were many who wished to stay alive despite great suffering for fear of what, if anything, came after death. When we got back in the truck I had to laugh at the banality of my thinking. I had had a great deal of practice thinking of the deaths of others, my father and then my beloved Duane and then my grandfather, but then his death had been so relatively natural compared to the others in that he had had the time to gracefully prepare himself.

After cresting the hill in the village of Niobrara we "hauled ass," Nelse's term for relentless, nonstop driving, more than a bit over the speed limit. He wanted to get out of the cultivated areas and he spoke of "mono-crop mega-agriculture" and its dependence on fertilizers. It might be necessary for a hungry world but he didn't like to look at it. My own mind was allowed to drift and doze now that the pill had begun to take effect, and I didn't pay attention to Nelse's diatribe because I had heard it all before. Thank Jesus or whomever for drugs! Once while living in New York I had a severe sinus infection and I asked the doctor what they did with such an infection before anti-biotics. He said that the infection would often enter the brain and people would die "eating the rug." The homely expression stuck with me and I had resolved at the time to get help when something began to go wrong with my body rather than wait until it was out of con-trol. There was an ounce of comic stupidity here in the way I had ignored my first specific signs of physical unrest early in the winter. It had been too rankly ordinary to be tolerated.

After New Ulm we cut straight north toward St. Cloud, mostly because Nelse figured that we would otherwise be caught up in the Minneapolis afternoon rush hour. I had been caught up in quite enough of them in the Los Angeles area, and had depended on my tape deck for sanity as many do. When brought to full stops I had read entire books on the Santa Monica Freeway over a period of weeks. As a student I had had so many fine spring dawns and eve-nings in Minneapolis particularly when I had a small apartment on the hill behind the Walker Art Center and could see the city in the soft diffuse light, the pale greens growing greener in spring after the brutally cold winter. Of course cities are innocent of our moods. On a certain day New York can be as ugly as the word the doctor in Lincoln had used, "metastasis," but on the next, say after a cooling rain during a summer heat wave, it can be truly wonderful. The same with Los Angeles though the mood has to struggle harder with the sprawl because an outsider is never quite sure of where its citiness resides. But then this is just an initial step and one is ultimately in a state of surprise over how many amenities the citizens offer themselves except, of course, for the very poor on whom all backs are turned.

May 18, 87.
Duluth. Temp. 43. Long 92.5 LAT. 46.8
Time 6:30 A.M.

I'm going to have to give certain aspects of this job up to Nelse. I feel absurd writing down the latitude and longitude though absurdity is nothing new in my life. Latitude and longitude don't offer me a frame of reference when I've never thought about them except when I learned the terms in grade school geography. There is also the dim memory from college when I found out the term "horse latitudes" came from when sailing ships became becalmed and horses, dying of thirst, were forced overboard in the southern Pacific. True or not, the story outraged me at the time. Jesus Christ, the frantic horses plummeting into the salt water in blasting subtropical heat! The men watching from the rail without comment. Maybe they did it at night so they wouldn't have to see the horses' heads trailing off in the ship's foamy wake.

Much to Nelse's irritation we are staying in the same hotel I stayed with Naomi when we were driving eastward toward Marquette late in my fifteenth year and I was plump with Nelse. What accidental symmetry though I don't think of this as a death trip. He had hoped that we could camp southwest of here in the Fond du Lac State Forest, but when we reached the site he favored it was in waning twilight and rain was falling in sheets, the thunder reverberating through the dense forest greenery. We were looking out over a small lake through the whacking windshield wipers when a splintered lightning bolt seemed to hit the water and the pick-up cab buzzed. I felt much better an hour and a half later when we were having a mediocre room-service dinner in our rooms and Nelse went to the window and watched a freighter dock in the darkness. The rain had let up, the storm passing on to the northeast with lightning still visible far out on Lake Superior which has always struck me as a freshwater ocean. Behind the storm bright stars appeared, clearly visible despite the city's ambient light. New York had always overpowered the stars and one grew to miss them especially in the summer when in my youth we had lain on blankets struggling to identify the constellations though I mostly counted shooting stars. Now I hear through the wall Nelse receiving his room-service breakfast I had ordered for him in his adjoining room. I don't want to be caught not eating except for a pill, three saltine crackers I found in my purse and a glass of water. Last evening when we said good night Nelse glanced at the logbook and reminded me that I had forgotten to register two birds, a male grouse strutting behind the highway's fence and a vireo at a rest stop. I was a bit tired so was stricken by the omission. He patted my shoulder, kissed my forehead and said, "Good night, Mother." I closed the door after him and listened to him open his own. This was the first time he'd used the word "mother" since our reunion last summer. I don't think his not using the word is intentional but it was tremendously lovely to hear it. I did make the error of turning around from the door and trying to imagine Duane, a year older than myself, sitting in an easy chair watching the weather forecast on the television. It didn't work.

Earlier this morning watching the first light gather above the harbor I remembered the same harbor covered with ice so long ago. Now I feel pretty good and offer the slightest prayer to a god unknown that this infirmity will withhold itself until the end of our camping trip and I reach New York. While we sat in the truck last evening during the lakeside thunderstorm and Nelse was pissed because we weren't going to hear the tremulous call of the loon he knew lived there I could hear in my mind's ear my doctor friend droning along as he looked out the window. He seemed to be saying that if I had come to see him in early December at my first signs I would have had a fifty to eighty-five percent chance of living five years. If I had arrived in February it would have been cut to from thirty-seven to seventy-nine percent. Early April might have reduced it to between seven and eighteen percent, and when I appeared in mid-May it was only a two to eight percent chance of living five years, but probably less as I was filtering over the edge of what is called "Stage IV." These were statistics you couldn't quarrel with though in the last stage you certainly envision the ninety-two to ninety-eight percent possibility of falling off the edge of the earth. The true cruelty of the disease is that early symptoms are so vague that in seventy-five percent of the cases it has already spread beyond the ovaries at the point of diagnosis. I wished very much over my crackers and water that I hadn't taken a physiology course at the university that now enabled me to see so clearly inside myself, almost as lucidly as when I had looked at myself in the mirror a few minutes ago. I also questioned what genes had given me such a high, contemptuous pain threshold so that I ignored problems that would send any sane human to the medicine cabinet or the doctor. I was beyond questioning why ovaries, the very core of life itself, could figuratively turn their backs on life and in so doing destroy the entire body. A few minutes ago when I looked in the mirror I didn't look all that bad, a bit thinner and fatigued, a nearly effective mask for the inside in which the hopeless and tormented drama of lost cells was taking place.

Over in the corner of my room I saw a steno pad on the desk, used normally for grocery lists and errands, and rather dimly recalled that I had been up at three A.M. for the slightest of hemorrhages, had taken a pain pill and written a note and left fifty dollars for the sheet my blood had destroyed. Now I also remembered starting a list (counting again!) of what I have loved about the earth, perhaps a presumptuous idea but I thought it might help me stay fully conscious rather than falling back into confusion and hysteria. The list certainly wouldn't be an endless process because I had no intention of letting the disease run the disease's full course any more than I thought Duane should have stayed alive given his condition. Before I checked the steno pad I searched again for the small leather pouch that contained Duane's stone, passed down through the generations of his Lakota relatives, and also the tiny velvet bag that contained my grandmother Neena's engagement ring. I had tried to give it to Nelse to give to J.M. earlier in the winter but the ring had made him highly nervous and he said he would have to think it over because in his opinion "no one wears rings like that anymore." It was a three-carat blue diamond and I admitted to myself that it came from a time when there weren't all these MBAs around telling people to spend their money sensibly so they could pass on the uncertain gift of having it to their children. Now I meant to force him to take the ring.

The penmanship of the list was faulty because of the onset of the drug, the "What I Have Loved About the Earth" trailing off smaller at the end due to the narrowness of the page.

1. my mother
2. my father
3. my sister, Ruth
4. my grandfather
5. and now, Nelse
6. Lundquist
7. myself?

The "myself" had evidently been a showstopper. Nelse rapped on my door and I called out that I'd be ready in ten minutes though I was ready at the time. I had the urge to add a few items; I was certainly not thinking in order of preference.

8. horses
9. dogs. I count thirteen close dog friends since I was old enough to remember, including when I was just able to walk my father's cowdog Jack who hated cars so much he fatally collided with one head-on in our driveway. Pure male dog.
10. Birds and flowers, including also bird and flower shadows, the latter two being something I've always noted preferring to walk in early morning and late afternoon when there are flower shadows. Bird shadows are always startling.

11. The Pacific Ocean. Wherever. From tiny Puerto Escondido down in Oaxaca up to the Queen Charlotte Islands in British Columbia.
12. My dear friend Charlene
13. New York City between 3 A.M. and 7 A.M.
14. The same with Paris.

Nelse knocked again as I had drifted off into a Paris reverie where once I had been angry with a gentleman whom I couldn't get out of my room and walked from after midnight to dawn on a cool, blustery early-May night ending up looking through the fence at flowers in the Jardin des Plantes, hailed a cab finally, then asking the desk to remove the gentleman but he was already gone whereupon I had the most delicious sleep of my life with rain blowing in the tall French windows.

15. A rooster named Bob when I was five, named after a kindergarten friend who died of leukemia the next year. None of us in kindergarten, then 1st grade, all three of the remaining students could figure this out. Naomi told us he went to heaven which didn't help.

At checkout I was a bit mystified by the large phone charges but recognized a brief one to my doctor friend's office, probably an answering service, then a long one, perhaps to his home, two medium calls to J.M.'s number in Lincoln and a lengthy call to Naomi's house. Sweat quickly beaded on my forehead and I stuffed the itemized bill in my purse, not wanting Nelse to know that I knew what he was up to, but when I turned around I could see him loading our luggage out in front. I have an inane ability to remember phone numbers, including from every place I've ever lived, or I wouldn't have recognized the doctor's number. Oh Jesus I have been found out, I thought, deciding not to let on to Nelse that anything was amiss. Naomi had, of course, told me of Nelse's own silly faux secrecy when he had appeared on her front porch for the first time, assuming that she couldn't possibly recognize him.

When I got in the pick-up I quickly handed him the tiny velvet bag with Neena's engagement ring and said, "Give this to J.M.," and he said, "Of course," and we were off headed east, crossing a magnificent bridge above the harbor and driving straight into the rising sun. Nelse showed all of the transparent signs of insomnia.

> *Crystal Falls. 8 P.M. 58 degrees. Lat. 46 degrees,*
> *6 minutes North. Long. 88 degrees, 58 minutes West.*
> *(Nelse insists on these "minutes," whatever they are.)*

There is an odd-looking blackburnian warbler in a bush a dozen feet away. That's what Nelse told me when he went off to fish for brook trout. He also told me the name of the bush but I've already forgotten fifteen minutes later. The warbler has some orange feathers. Today we saw far too many evening grosbeaks dead beside the road. They come out for road salt used for icy conditions and collide with vehicles. It was quite awful to see so many in contrast to the pale green leafing hardwoods mixed with the dark conifers. We did see three loons today on separate lakes near Watersmeet and Trout Creek which are very nice names. Nelse tried too hard to be solicitous every moment of this day just short of being overwhelming. I pretended not to notice.

We're actually east of Crystal Falls and camped on the Fence River. On the narrow trail to our campsite I thought I saw cow tracks but Nelse said the tracks belonged to a moose. There are also a few wolves in the area which is a lovely idea in addition to a splendid reality. Before he left for fishing Nelse told me that if a bear happened along I should just sing the national anthem and that would scare the bear shitless. I write on my steno pad to monochromatic mosquito music, vaguely India Indian in sound.

16. Frogs and toads. The first creatures I knew after birds, dogs and cats. Naomi wouldn't allow cats because they killed birds but there were plenty in Grandfather's barn and he allowed me to befriend them.

17. Men's bodies. I have no intentions of counting them as the number could possibly be too high and embarrass me.

18. Women's bodies? The only woman's body I ever had the slightest desire for was my dear friend Charlene's. She made a pass at me when

we were teenagers but I declined. She lives alternately in Paris and New York, has been married three times to her financial advantage, and is, I suspect, a genuine bisexual. Also the mysterious roll of the baby in my stomach when I was so young.

19. Horses, horses, horses. They smell as good as they look. Looking back I see that I've already listed them under number eight.

20. Rivers. Dozens of them but especially the Niobrara.

21. My uncle Paul. Sometimes he troubles me with his high-mindedness. For a while I thought he might be Duane's father but he said he was sterile from the mumps, but then I found out he had the mumps two years after he met Rachel. I used to wonder about his improbable austerity but then I finally figured out he was no more austere sexually than I was. He has some of Nelse's tendencies of an anthropologist studying people moment by moment rather than living with them.

22. New York Jewish delicatessens. If you grew up in the Midwest or West this is obvious.

23. Add Italian and Chinese restaurants in NYC. In the Midwest bad food has long been part of our Manifest Destiny. It's horrid but it's ours so it's the best.

24. Cabeza Prieta. I always detoured here, a long one, on my way home from Santa Monica because it is immense, empty, capable of transfiguring. Cactuses, including cholla, organ-pipe, saguaro, ocotillo, immediately draw off poison. Only once did I see the night-blooming cereus but then it only blooms once and dies.

25. My grandfather's barn in winter. My true retreat, hiding place, in childhood, also later, the animal warmth, Duane's place in the haymow with the revolving buffalo skull.

26. Pond near the marsh where I made love to Duane just once. And now there is Nelse.

Who just came back from fishing with four brook trout which he fried and served with lemon, bread and salt, banishing the aftertaste of an earlier roadside meal. In the gathering dark we searched for extra wood as the night would surely come close to freezing. He was able to tear slabs from a white-pine stump which also made a good smudge for mosquitoes and offered up a fine smell to the air. I snuck in an extra pill wondering if I would have enough to get by. Beyond the circular glow of the fire there were pale green sheets of northern lights shimmering, rising and falling, which I had intended to add to my list. Naomi keeps a "life list" of her birds. That's what they call it. It always reminded me of the winter count Natives used to make to keep track of the events that truly constitute time. We were both in our sleeping bags and Nelse wore a miner's flashlight on his forehead while he checked out a guidebook on trees. He turned it off before he spoke to me.

"I know everything. I've moved up your appointments. In a few days we can drive from here."

"No we won't. I'm not in that kind of hurry. Charlene's going to meet me in New York." The last was a lie of course.

"Mother, goddammit!" That word again but not so pleasantly this time. I couldn't help myself and began to cry which I never do. He got out of his sleeping bag and sat on the bare ground beside me in his skivvies, rubbing my neck and shoulders and stroking my hair without saying another word. After a short time I could sense the shivering in his voice. It was the clarity of the stars above and his hands that stopped my weeping. I had him name the constellations above and it became a chant. The sky above and the earth below, the stars so gracefully allowing me to locate myself on earth deep in the forest beside a river, the murmuring of which put me into the deepest of sleeps before Nelse finished the constellations.

Escanaba. May 5:30 a.m.
Latitude 45 degrees, 49 minutes North,
Longitude 87 degrees, 4 minutes West.
Thermometer (stuck out window of Hotel Ludington)
says a mere 39 degrees.

Yesterday afternoon coming toward town it was warm inland but when we drove down to the fine park on the water the weather turned blustery and a big thunderstorm, rare for this time of year, really an immense line squall, was driving up Lake Michigan and far out above the whitecaps we could see its glowering approach. The air couldn't have smelled better. Nelse, however, was a bit irritated as he wanted to camp well north of here near Trenary where he knows of a spring holding brook trout. He reluctantly checked the weather on the truck radio and the forecast was foreboding indeed. "Shit," he said, over and over, and then we took rooms at an old restored hotel. His spirits lightened when we walked up the street and had an early dinner of steaks and spaghetti at an Italian restaurant. He had never had this combination before and I told him he should get "out and around," which made him laugh. It is hard to imagine a young man who knows more about wild areas and less about what the civilized world has to offer. I am bold enough to suggest that this imbalance should be corrected and he admits he may have to do some "culture travel" to keep J.M. happy.

On our way here yesterday afternoon we passed the gravel-road turnoff that led a number of miles down toward the shack of the medicine man, my Chippewa friend's father. I was surprised that I remembered the turnoff so clearly and brought the item to Nelse's attention. He had me repeat the story of the incident and we minutely examined it, though I couldn't think of anything truly extraordinary except the turtles flipping and scrambling off the old man's legs when we walked down the path to where he sat by the miniature lake. Afterward he had made us a light dinner of bowls of wild rice with onions and morel mushrooms. His shack was clean and spare with a large collection of different bird feathers tied in neat bundles and hanging from a rafter. The small dwelling lacked insulation and I had asked him if he wasn't a little cold during the fierce winters. He thought this over for quite some time then said he had never been cold in his life. His daughter teased him that everyone in the area knew that he was part bear and they both laughed loudly over this. He had asked about my job and I explained rather too elaborately about my welfare work with poor people. He told me that I should probably help rich people too and I didn't know what to make of this.

Nelse was a little disturbed over this last item and we pondered what the man might have meant. We were talking so intensely that we pulled off at a rest stop and sat down at a picnic table. Nelse observed that the quantity of misery didn't necessarily depend on economic position and I had to disagree based on my experience, though the degree of difference wasn't as great as widely supposed. Everyone knows about the miserable experiences of lottery winners, but then poverty is fairly called "grinding" because it can quite literally grind people down. Nelse, typically, thought that this might be more true of urban areas. I mentioned that I had always felt odd when I passed cemeteries and observed the pathetic vanity in the enormous gravestones to the rich. We paused then as the notion of gravestones was striking a little closer to home. We gradually admitted that the "bottom line" was, simply enough, the fact of the turtles basking on the man's legs. We were both cynical about the lambent vulgarity of New Age crap or any charlatan's claim to secret powers. But then this wasn't New Age but "old age." I had met Frank Fool's Crow twice and if pinned in a corner I would have to say he was a man with a superior secret. To say he was just like us would be unpardonable vanity. Nelse took it further and said that in the total scheme of things we don't have more than a few clues. Maybe this man was some sort of Mozart of the natural world and his relationship with turtles was forever inaccessible to the rest of us. At one point I wished I hadn't seen the turtles basking in the sunlight on the man's legs. It certainly threatened my world order which was already crumbling with my illness. Nelse threw up his hands and said that we all were desperately full of shit and that you could spend a lifetime studying birds and ultimately couldn't come up with the answer of why there were birds.

I got up early because I was in pain. I watched the first light filtering through the white curtains of my eastern-facing window through which I could hear the waves pounding in from Lake Michigan. A gust of wind would lift the curtains and my fevered body would be bathed by the flow of cool, sweet air. There had been a thankfully brief, unpleasant dream of my friend Michael. Before we had left home Naomi said she had gotten a note from Michael's daughter saying that he was off at some sort of "ashram" getting detoxed again. In my dream his body had become wildly out of proportion which was accurate enough. I hadn't been up to answering any of his letters which had all coiled down into the same repetitive sequence of knots. For some reason it reminded me of Nelse's statement that all four thousand mammal species had seven cervical vertebrae. I probably have this wrong. He also said that sixteen billion years ago the entire universe was only a pinhead-sized piece of inconceivable energy. What am I to make of this when I am flummoxed by the existence of monarch butterflies?

When I checked us out I again noticed on the bill a half dozen calls Nelse had made from his room, including J.M. and Naomi, also one to Paris to Charlene which meant my fib about her meeting me in New York had been found out. Oh well, there are vast limitations to honesty. Over my breakfast of tea and saltines I had even questioned the honesty of my list because I had made additions in a drugged-out state in the middle of the night.

27. Gulfstream waves beneath which Duane understandably slipped
28. Lundquist's voice with animals
29. A mountain ram seen in the Cabeza
30. The first glass of red wine after several days of abstinence
31. The time I saw lightning strike a tree
32. Floating naked in the Niobrara's current on a hot afternoon in August
33. The strange looks of animals making love
34. The presence of underground rivers
35. Duane riding a horse at a gallop
36. Beethoven, Bach, Mozart, Stravinsky
37. Lorca the poet at Paul's cottage on Baja
38. Riding at dawn and twilight, getting back to the barn at moonrise

Really quite ordinary and not too goofy. Everyone can't be exceptional though we are taught that we can. I had the true potential to do what I've already done.

* * *

We drove northeast toward Grand Marais on Lake Superior north of Seney, partly because I had been there on a summer job during college working with my mother's cousin on a lamprey-control project. These marvelously ugly creatures attach themselves and suck the blood out of lake trout. There were all sorts of efforts to trap lampreys and to poison them when they entered creeks and rivers to spawn. Like the noxious alewives the lampreys had entered the Great Lakes due to government ineptitude during the expansion of the St. Lawrence Seaway. I also wanted to go to Grand Marais because quite by accident three in my family had been there: myself, Nelse on the trail of goshawks, and my grandfather way back when he was a student at the Chicago Art Institute. I thought this was odd but Nelse said that if you write down your favorite places the list isn't very long. This led me to take out my steno pad and add a few items.

39. Spices including ginger, fennel, also the flavor of garlic and cilantro, hot chiles
40. Mexican music of all sorts
41. Erotic dreams of people you don't know
42. Diving down and touching the bottom of a river
43. The first morning after school was out for the year, sleeping in
44. Working with Naomi in her garden

It occurred to me quite suddenly that I couldn't say I was unhappy. I was well beyond that sort of consideration. In a specific sense I had never felt more alive and I wondered what else beside the pain had brought me to this place. You could glibly postulate that everyone is on death row but when the date becomes imminent the nature of reality becomes much more vivid.

45. Dreams of Indians and animals that seem to emerge from the landscape where I've lived much of my life but that follow me elsewhere.

I could sense that Nelse was feeling awkward so I said that I knew he had been making plans for me. He then almost blurted out that I was flying out of Marquette tomorrow afternoon and Charlene would be meeting me in New York to keep me company during my "appointments." I readily acceded and he was relieved to the point that the truck swerved when he stretched on his seat. I decided to tease him a bit and asked what he thought of a Rilke line Charlene had pointed out to me in a letter, something on the order of "don't think that fate is more than the density of childhood." He said, "Jesus Christ" loudly, then paused a few minutes before adding that the line gave his stomach a thump in the same way that a book of Edward Hopper paintings in my grandfather's library had done. I didn't quite see the connection but could feel it. The whole subject became quite anxious in the following silence as if our own humble words couldn't track Rilke and Hopper into the world in which they created. We were witnesses rather than participants. If I could have remembered a single joke I would have told it at that moment. We were saved by the sight of three sandhill cranes in the ditch of a side road. Nelse slowed down but decided not to disturb them.

I fell asleep then and when I awoke we were taking a back road out of Munising that I remembered traveled fifty of fifty miles through the forest to Grand Marais with some of the road abutting Lake Superior. There had been a brief erotic dream about Charlene but I felt it was a little late to be disturbed about such things. From the time we became close friends in our early teens Charlene had been that very rare female who was steadfastly proud of her body. I knew that in her twenties in New York she had had concurrent affairs with both a reasonably well-known actor and a quite well-known actress and had supposed at the time that they both felt fortunate though a little jealous. We'd have a sleepy Saturday morning breakfast at Ratner's and I'd ask such silly questions as "Both in the same day?" Once when we were swimming out on Fire Island even gay men seemed to give her a studied but appraising look, maybe because her face was a little androgynous. I laughed awkwardly at the notion that a thousand orgasms do not make you less interested in the next one.

My mind was diverted by thousands of trilliums in a well-shaded forest glade and I wondered how many patches of the wildflower I had missed in the sexual trance. I could say good-bye to that forever. We stopped and I walked among the profusion of flowers which raised my neck hairs with perfumed delight. Meanwhile Nelse was craning his neck to look at the clouds up beyond the pale pastel green of the trees whose leafing had been further slowed by their nearness to the very cold Lake Superior.

Further on we drove off on a side road to a promontory high above Lake Superior in the Grand Sable Dunes. It was a stunning view though I had difficulty getting Nelse out of his sodden-weather mood. He very much wanted to camp in a favorite spot and said a night in a motel would "break his heart." He then apologized and made us wretched Spam sandwiches on the tailgate of the truck. On impulse I opened the first bottle of wine of the trip and we sat on one of the largest sandpiles in the world staring down at Lake Superior. Lucky for us within a half an hour the wind clocked around to the northwest, lost its mugginess, and we watched as the blue sky approached us across the lake. He ignored it when I took another pill from my jacket and washed it down with delicious gulps of wine. We held hands waiting for the moment which was near when the sun would break through as the clouds passed to the southeast, and then we could see the sunlight racing toward us across the water. We held our breath and then it hit us. I looked down at the sunlight on my hands, and on the hole in the knee of my Levi's, and through the plastic wine glass half full of red wine, and far below at Lake Superior which now had become azure. I blinked my eyes several times as if taking a photo and wondered how all of this could just go away.

46. Goshawks!

There is a female goshawk near where we are camping. Nelse had watched the nest while camped here ten years before and was delighted that it was still what he calls "active," though the female was likely a descendent of the one he watched. I must say its voice and behavior added to my sense of the feminine, the voice almost archetypal as if it slipped into the air from prehistory, and though she didn't weigh more than a few pounds she looked much larger as she flashed close by, trying to drive us away as if she were the toughest bitch in the world.

It was still a couple of hours before dark this close to the solstice. I felt fine because of the extra pill and the wine, though there was the thought that this might be my last night of actual and total freedom. This was less intuition than a sense of reality. We wandered around the area and Nelse said if we were there in another week or so the dogwoods and sugar-plum trees would be blooming. I broke open a few buds scenting their intensely sweet odor, remembering that my grandfather, quite sick of Chicago, had come north and had been here when the area was white with these blooming trees.

Nelse was looking down a steep, sandy bank into the Sucker River and thinking about trying his luck at fishing when I said I wanted a fried beefsteak so we drove a half dozen miles to the grocery store in the village of Grand Marais. The beef wasn't attractive by Nebraska terms so I bought a bottle of steak sauce to help it out. When Ruth was seven or eight Grandfather had told her that she could make her fingers strong for playing the piano by squeezing a rubber ball a thousand times a day and also eating a steak every day. This advice drove Naomi quite batty as Ruth took it religiously and it was nearly sickening to watch this little girl devour her daily beef, though soon enough the sound of the piano grew louder, and the little boys in the country school yard avoided her strong grip.

When I came out of the grocery store Nelse had the truck started, anxious to get back to camp. I waved and headed for a bar just down the street called the Dunes Saloon for a martini, a questionable move but then I felt entitled. There was a very large bartender, even by Nebraska terms, with a scant amount of red hair though I guessed him to be in his thirties. When I ordered a martini he stared at me as if I were a zoo animal and announced that this would be the first martini made this year which meant the tourist season might be start-ing. He also asked what I figured I should pay for it since it had been so long he had forgotten what to charge, and then Nelse came in and they talked about brook trout fishing. The man drew a hasty map, saying it was his "fifty-seventh best place" to fish. Nelse took a sip of my drink and squinched up his face as if it were gasoline. I impul-sively hugged him and the bartender warned us that if a man forces his wife to go camping during mosquito and blackfly season it can endanger the marriage. "He's my son," I said, and the man laughed and said, "You don't say."

47. The night itself, or perhaps herself
48. The sound of the whippoorwill

It was nearly dark before the fire was ready and I set my grand-father's old Wagner skillet directly on the coals, putting what looked like too much salt in the skillet, and letting it heat until it was nearly red-hot. Nelse watched this somewhat cynically and I said his own camp cookery was doubtless mostly opening cans. I had rubbed the meat with raw garlic and covered it with black pepper, and when I dropped it in the pan the meat smoked and hissed and took only a few minutes on each side. I ate perhaps a half pound and Nelse easily fin-ished the other two. We drank a full bottle of Gigondas and I slipped in an extra pill when he walked beyond the circle of fire to pee.

What a night we had, with a quarter moon not really disturbing the clarity of the stars. Nelse had set up the tent in case the weather changed its mind but we laid out our pads and sleeping bags in the open. I requested another constellation chant, the music I wished to hear. We talked about love which is easier in the dark before a small fire. I told him about my absurd summer before I went off to college when I worked as a waitress at Lena's Cafe on the breakfast and lunch shift so I'd have to leave the ranch by 5:00 A.M. for the long drive. I'd take a nap on the hot afternoons and read about love since his father had only been gone for a little more than two years and I was still mortally possessed. Of all the books I read that summer only *Romeo and Juliet* and *Wuthering Heights* seemed close. After reading as long as I could bear I'd go out riding with the dogs in tow and if it was still very warm I'd swim in the Niobrara with my animals watching and sometimes joining in for reasons of their own. Nelse nervously changed the mood by admitting he hadn't read either of the love texts and I laughed and made him promise, which he did. I then reconsidered and had him take back his promise as what was the point in urging him to become more like me?

He admitted to worrying about J.M.'s volatility but suspected they would have, all in all, a fine time with their life together. He wished his adopted father had lived longer, and he wished from all he had heard about Duane that he had gotten to know him but he wasn't disposed to question what he called their "disappearances from earth." This was an odd enough expression to give me a chill and I reached for my wine glass wishing it were full of brandy. He wished his adoptive mother didn't drink so much but then she had done so since he could remember. He thought his lesbian sister in Kansas was probably better off than the sister in Washington, D.C., who had recently told him in a letter that her marriage was so "nothing" she frequently wept with boredom. I told him he should write back and tell her to fly the coop. He liked this old-time farm expression. We decided that the very idea of "wishing" was deeply suspect.

49. The smell of the ground in the woods

I woke up well before dawn having slipped off my pad so that my face was pushed against the ground. Nelse was kneeling next to the fire adding wood and he looked like some old photo of a Lakota in the dim light. I brazenly took another pill as there was another fire smoldering within me. We began talking again and by coincidence with his image beside the fire he told me about his embarrassment over driving up to Pine Ridge when he had worked on an archeological site near Valentine. He had felt so much like a spoiled white boy that there were tears of shame and anger at himself for harboring the illusion. There was certainly a point, he thought, at which the idea of blood relatives meant nothing. I agreed to a point but said that his shame, anger and embarrassment probably meant that he wasn't just a spoiled white boy. I said I remembered when my grandfather who was half Lakota told me that his own father had decided what world he would live in. I also told Nelse that I had known a half black in New York quite well (we were lovers for a month) and the fact that he could easily pass for white caused him a great deal of torment. I sensed this was confusing for Nelse and he joked that when a Navajo rose at dawn and bowed to the six directions that was really what one needed to know about latitude and longitude. You knew where you were when you bowed to the six directions.

After that he began to snore and it was a comforting sound intermixed with another call from the whippoorwill. I wondered what kind of noise the stars made up close and this childish question led me to believe that we retain intact within ourselves each of our ages. This is probably obvious and no big deal but right now I am eleven with the ghastly feeling that I have just been thrown by a horse that Grandfather had forbidden me to ride. I am also eighteen and feel like the dying Catherine in *Wuthering Heights*. I am also forty-six, and moment by moment trembling on the lip of a very short future. The grotesque expression "bottom line" raised itself like a printed blip in a cartoon, but why ask about the rock bottom or the bottom line when the rock bottom was the earth I lay upon, with eyes that watched the stars above and a mind that thought it actually could see the quarter moon move across the sky. I felt too much the mammal but that surely was what I was. Nelse has an affection for the word "primate" and it seemed quite accurate here on the ground. I blocked out the moon with my left hand the better to see the stars. If I crooned some sort of prayer there was the doubt the prayer would rise higher than the ground mist that was coiling around the greenery in the first light. First one birdcall, then three, then a chorus from down by the river. This would be a good time to die with the bottle of pills and a water jug handy, all to the gathering density of birdsong, but then I couldn't very well leave my body up to Nelse. I had thought of a better plan but also wished to say good-bye to my family.

May ?, Marquette, High Noon.

I'm going to miss latitude and longitude a little but I sense that words are beginning to fail me, or better yet, I am beginning to fail words.

50. My first airplane ride
51. My first car, the aqua convertible

At the Marquette airport I was absurdly pleased that I got a window-seat assignment. I had felt like a cow plot when Nelse awoke me finally at nine this morning with the sun warm on my face and a mosquito bite on my lower lip. I also said, "I don't have any clothes for New York" and Nelse looked at me as if I were daft. The tent was down and everything was packed except for the angular lump I made in the sleeping bag. He brought me my tea and crackers with which I took two pills. I was running low but then Charlene had always been a pill expert and I couldn't think of anything she couldn't get ahold of—men, women, money. After the ticket desk we went back outside and I wondered if there was an inside space big enough in the whole world to defeat his claustrophobia. I bummed a cigarette off a very old Finn in a bright blue suit with a vest. When I had quit smoking ten years before and while still in the throes of the mean-minded detoxification I swore if I ever received a death sentence of any sort I'd begin smoking again. Unfortunately the cigarette tasted terrible so I pitched it after a few tentative puffs. The old Finn glared at me for wasting a cigarette and Nelse laughed. We walked back inside and to the boarding area and when we hugged good-bye Nelse looked as though he were being strangled. I couldn't think of anything to say to lift his mood.

* * *

The flight to Detroit went well though I missed some of the lavish
northern Michigan scenery when I dozed with my forehead against
the window. On the Detroit–La Guardia leg I listened to a man in a
not-very-well-cut pinstripe suit talking about his marital problems.
Social work makes you able to at least affect being a good listener. In
the beginning he was flirtatious, probably a habit he couldn't break.
He slowed down when I announced that all five of my children were
quite happy and without problems. I might have flirted back but he
kept looking critically at his fingernails, a tip-off to an anal compulsive. I don't normally fly first-class but Nelse had booked the flight.
Stan's wife didn't appreciate how hard he worked, a common enough
complaint. He lived in a place outside of Detroit called Bloomfield Hills
and when he handed his suit coat to a stewardess to hang up he asked
her not to "squash" it as if she were in the habit of doing so. He was
such an egregious prick that there was a lump of fascination in my
throat. When he told me about his elaborate plans for his daughter's
surprise eighteenth-birthday party I felt sorry for his daughter. Finally
I began to sweat with his banality and feigned sleep to get away.

    Charlene's face looked much younger and as we walked up the
concourse she quickly admitted to a face-lift and an "enhancement"
of her lips. We laughed at this and I felt dowdy indeed walking along
beside her in my Levi's and leather jacket. I felt even more homely
in the lobby of the elegant hotel on Madison in the upper Seventies
though when I said so Charlene told me I was wearing what movie
stars wore to differentiate themselves from yuppies. She had brought
along a lot of extra clothes which I looked at while she made us a
drink in our rooms. When I came out of the bedroom holding one of
her simpler dresses she handed me a whiskey and water, then fell
totally apart in a weeping fit. I put my arms around her and saw myself in the mirrored armoire that doubled as a liquor cabinet. To be
frank I didn't look all that well, but what could I expect? It was a full
hour before she was sufficiently calmed down so we could talk normally. The worst thing she said was that she wished she was sick instead of me. There's really no way to respond to such nonsense other
than to recognize the depth of friendship. Thirty years before we had

won the polka contest at the county fair with Charlene dressed as a boy and now we were here in an eighth-floor suite surrounded by Audubon first-folio prints and unlikable, expensive furniture. Finally she asked me what I was going to do and I said, "Probably drown myself, why not?" and laughed. We found some inept music on the radio and did a few polka steps like we always did when we met again, but then she slumped to the sofa weeping. I said, "Charlene, cut that shit out," and she did. We sat on the sofa holding hands and then I fell asleep for a while. When I awoke I felt badly and took a Percodan from the bottle Charlene gave me and we ordered a room-service dinner. The pill made me woozy, what we used to call "high," and I loved my seafood salad and a white wine I had never had before but which was Charlene's favorite called Meursault. I thought I might take a case of it home with me for consolation but when I asked Charlene the normal cost the price made me sweat. I said that someone from Nebraska would be ashamed to spend that much on wine and she said, "Fuck Nebraska," adding that my grandfather hadn't hesitated to do so. After dinner we got dressed up and went to a café downstairs and heard a wonderful singer and pianist. This was scarcely the New York I had known and loved but then it was too late and I was too fatigued to go downtown. None of my old friends would willingly go uptown except to a museum. There were two double beds in our bedroom but we slept together holding hands. I had to get up at four a.m. for a pill which I took with a glass of brandy. I couldn't hold it down but water worked the next time around.

When I woke again at first light to the sound of rain and faint beeping I rehearsed a very sweet dream wherein I was a whole school of lovely fish I didn't recognize. How could I be more than one I thought recalling the way the sun filtered splendidly down through the clarity of the water.

I was at Sloan-Kettering from eight in the morning until three in the afternoon. It was originally intended that I stay overnight for additional tests, and start again early the next morning, but the last doctor of the day said it wouldn't be necessary though I should come in at midmorning to talk to a doctor counselor. At first I was puzzled but then deduced that I was a rather hopeless case. While I was getting dressed the doctor friend of the one back in Lincoln came in glancing at my folder which he seemed to grasp overtightly. He reassured me that I'd hear "all my options" the next morning and I replied that I bet there weren't many. Composure is always difficult when there is even the slightest personal relationship. He said there were actually a couple and then by luck his beeper went off. Some of the tests were indeed invasive but the staff and doctors were gracious, so unlike the often wretched treatment my welfare clients received at hospitals which were really medical assembly lines. I've always been aware that smiles are available if you can write the check. This wasn't a bad reflection on places that were the best in their fields like Sloan-Kettering or Mayo but an ordinary comment on the nature of the world.

I was surprised that Charlene was waiting for me in the lobby but then suspected they must have called her. I was quite wobbly but wanted to try to walk the fairly long way back to the hotel. It was such a relief to be away from being probed or connected to machines, inserted into high-whirring metal tubes, that I was almost merry. In fact I gained a measure of strength with every step, and our only rest stop was the Frick Museum where I wanted to sit awhile by the pool and look at the portrait of the Duke of Arentino. He reminded me of my grandfather.

Back at the hotel I didn't have the energy for a drink and slept several hours hearing intermittently Charlene's voice on the phone in the living room. When I got up and showered I had a martini that seemed to scorch my innards but I held it down. While Charlene was in the shower a concierge named Dwight called to say that he had managed to get two tickets to a sold-out B. B. King concert and I was thrilled senseless. Afterward I wondered about the progress of life wherein things grow smaller then finally quite larger. Other than God I couldn't think of anyone who could make me feel better that evening than B. B. King. When Charlene came back into the room and heard the good news she pranced around in her towel whooping and singing. We would try our damnedest to avoid acting our age, not to speak of my condition.

It worked fairly well. The concert was splendid to the point that I had two hours of total forgetfulness which has be part of music's intention, the essence rather than the details. Charlene had secured a car and driver for the evening and ignored my disapproval. After dinner we went down to the SoHo-Tribeca area to what Charlene described as the "hottest" French restaurant in the city and had a mediocre dinner for five hundred dollars (Charlene paid in cash which made me wonder about her current husband's occupation as a "producer"). There was a large table of stockbrokers in a far corner who were horridly noisy including singing college songs but then a waiter told us they had ordered "thousands and thousands" of dollars' worth of wine. It all made me mournful for New York in the late sixties and early seventies when the city was far shabbier and more neighborhood oriented. We talked about this and corrected ourselves to the degree that each generation coming to this fabled city has its own New York and is intolerant of the next generation's, and each previous generation will always tell you that you should have been here years ago.

We went far over the line by having crème brûlée, a cheese course, then a bottle of Château d'Yquem which I paid for: I loved this wine though it was attached to the questionable memory of a Brazilian who had given me a bottle. All of this was far too rich for my system, mentally and physically, and I had the sudden sweet but melancholy memory of my fifth-floor walk-up on Second Avenue, eating Chinese food out of a take-out carton, listening to music and reading whatever until nearly dawn.

We took a pointlessly sentimental drive around our old neighborhoods then went back to the hotel well after midnight where Charlene had another nightcap and I passed when I suddenly wondered why I was drinking so much. What were the options given the situation? We don't get much training in how to die but then what could be more ordinary? That word kept coming back and I didn't recall using it much until the past year. Perhaps at forty-six it was the onset of the menopause that I wasn't going to have.

And then we had an unbearable quarrel, however short, that began when I rejected the nightcap and also told Charlene I didn't want her flying back toward Lincoln with me late in the afternoon the next day because she was only going to turn around when I changed planes in Omaha, fly back to New York, stay at an airport hotel and take the Concorde the next day (the idea of flying faster than the speed of sound repelled me). I called this whole plan "crazy bullshit" since she couldn't bear to go all the way "up home" as she called it. She then flipped and went into a prolonged crying jag about which I could do nothing except take a pill and go to bed. When I woke in the night to take another pill she was sprawled on the sofa in bra and panties and I covered her with a blanket. At dawn she crept into bed beside me and that was that. When we finally got up with scant time for me to reach my appointment not a single word was said about the sad end of our last evening together.

My doctor counselor was an older woman with a striking resemblance to Naomi around the eyes, nose and forehead. This was a little unnerving at first and gave her the impression that I was on the edge of my chair waiting for news while in actuality I already knew to the last, banal, subordinate clause. I was well into "Stage IV" and the ovarian cancer had spread to my liver, lungs, lymph glands, bones, wherever. My single option was radical chemo and radiation therapy that might keep me alive from six months to a year, perhaps more but that was unlikely. I told her calmly that in my social work I had known three welfare clients who had endured such therapy and had decided for myself that I'd opt out. It had been worth it for one of them who had been long estranged from a daughter and needed time to make repairs but that scarcely was my situation. This all took place in the first ten minutes and then there was the sense that we were both exhaling with relief. She tried to give me Elisabeth Kübler-Ross's *On Death and Dying* and I said I'd already read it and underlined the best parts. We both laughed at my little joke. Oddly, she then asked me about where I lived in Nebraska and I got carried away in a description of the Sandhills. Only then did I cry a bit, saying, "I'll miss it so but then maybe I won't."

Charlene was in the lobby wearing sunglasses as protection against the cloudy skies. We joked about this on our longish walk over to the Museum of Modern Art where it turned out that the lines were too long to be endured. The mild depression of a hangover, assuming that you're an occasional drinker, can be quite confusing if you're forced to be resourceful, say, take a plane, or talk to your best friend for the last time. We had, however, been friends long enough to overcome our garden-variety hangovers or at least most of the bad aspects, though when we turned up Fifth Avenue into the rush of the noon-hour sidewalk crowds Charlene pressed against a building and fairly shrieked, "I don't get it." It turned out that what she didn't get was the mystery of why we must live without the foggiest notion of what it all means. I couldn't help her out with that one. When I would ask my grandfather a hopeless question like why cows and horses didn't have six legs he had several times said that answers are always acorns while questions are the largest oaks possible. I was still mildly pissed that MOMA had been too crowded to get into for a last visit even though my old favorites of Picasso's *Guernica* and Monet's waterlily series were now elsewhere.

It was lovely to cross Fifty-ninth to the Central Park side and leave the crowds behind. Charlene had become much more animated the moment the sun made an appearance and when a very attractive Latin couple passed us going the other way she said she'd like to sleep with both of them. I felt a slight jolt when it occurred to me I'd never make love again. Once I had eaten in a Hungarian restaurant over on First Avenue where they specialized in duck and when I raised a shot of slivovitz, a plum brandy, with friends I was overcome by the smell and taste because plum wine was the taste of Duane's lips the one and only time we made love. Nelse was a pretty big accomplishment.

When we reached the Metropolitan Museum of Art it was also too crowded with buses lined up releasing kids on field trips. I really didn't mind because I had spent virtually weeks in the museum and had many of the rooms memorized. We thought of heading further up Fifth to the Guggenheim before we had our good-bye lunch but abandoned both plans for simply sitting there on the steps in the sunlight and eating two franks with sauerkraut and mustard. We amused ourselves by watching young couples mooning over each other, and we talked about our high school days without much sentiment. When the time came nearer I insisted that Charlene go back to the hotel first because I wanted us to say good-bye sitting there in the bright sunlight with schoolchildren playing tag on the steps. I looked at a dollop of mustard I had dropped on the toe of my shoe rather than watching my dear friend cross the street.

The flight home was pleasant enough. I caught myself being concerned about the number of pills required to keep me mobile but quickly let it go in favor of falling asleep, waking as the plane crossed the Mississippi. Even from a plane the twilight was wonderful. I regretted packing my steno pad rather than carrying it in my purse because I wanted to add to my list. When I changed planes in Omaha for the last, short leg into Lincoln I bought another tablet. I wasn't sure of the number but what could matter less?

52. barncats, feral but friendly
53. Duane's buffalo skull in his hideout
54. The grass dance at powwows
55. rivers from the air
56. my father leading the horse on my first ride
57. my childhood Airedale Sonia
58. red moon rising in Arizona dust
59. The Edward Curtis photo of Judith, the Mojave girl

Nelse and J.M. met me at the gate looking as if they had already been to my funeral but then airport lighting is stupidly garish. We embraced and I was so groggy I stumbled which gave them the wrong impression. We picked up my luggage and drove to their apartment

with me trying to describe New York as a wonderful time. Nelse had
a fresh collection of new pills from my Lincoln doctor who had already talked to the Sloan-Kettering people. I joked that I was becoming Elvis Presley when I looked at the pill bottles and Nelse and J.M.
tried to force a look of amusement, after which Nelse broke down
sobbing. We comforted him, then J.M. heated me a bowl of *posole*
she had made which I ate with a tortilla and some ultra-fresh radishes. My father had loved the first fresh radishes and green onions
of spring, eating them with butter, salt and a chunk of bread while I
sat on his lap deciding which one he should eat next. I was thrilled
to see that J.M. was wearing my grandmother Neena's ring and while
we talked about it Nelse sat there as if trying to catch his breath. It
occurred to me quite strongly that once the death sentence is given
and there are no possible appeals it is then up to you to comfort others. You have accepted the sentence but others whom you love have
not yet been able to internalize the fact and it keeps re-occurring to
them with fresh energy. Charlene would be fine for a while and then
there would be a sidelong glance, while I on a second-by-second basis
had the pain as a reminder, and if not the pain, the soporific effect of
the pills. Nobody gets off earth alive and it was simple bad luck that
my own leaving was to be premature. The doomed give up thinking
about actuaries and it certainly meant nothing at all that the statistics said that I should have had thirty-two more years. The "back wall"
is a more effective phrase that the "bottom line." Our bodies live a
separate life and generally speak to us in the simplest phrases of cold,
hunger, heat, desire and we are slow to accept a fatal message. Sitting there with Nelse and J.M. I had exhausted all of my sympathy
for myself and did my best to offer some to them in the diffident guise
of simply planning for a metaphoric road trip.

I felt fine when I awoke soon after dawn in Lincoln to bird sounds
every bit as loud as back on the ranch. Nelse had told me a horrid
series of facts about the immense number of birds that died running
into windows especially over at the university where the buildings

are intermixed with dense greenery. There was the sweet odor of desiccated lilacs from outside the open window and on the night table a bouquet of dried flowers and indigenous grasses from back home. In the bunkhouse in the small freezer compartment of his refrigerator Nelse kept a small collection of dead birds he had found including my favorite, a yellow-headed blackbird that if properly warmed you thought might again take flight. Long ago I'd sometimes knock on the screen door and Duane would be sitting there at his bare table with his back to me and he wouldn't turn around or answer the door. He knew that he was likely my half brother but I didn't know that I was his half sister.

We had a fine time on the long road home and as a joke I took out my steno pad to record any birds Nelse might see at sixty miles an hour or over.

60. The sound of my horse's hooves in thick grass
61. seeing a fish underwater while swimming
62. sound of horses eating oats, the crunch

J.M. said she wanted to teach because nearly everyone she had met in her life was dumb, a direct enough motive. Nelse said primates in general only learned enough to feed themselves which irritated J.M. and she asked him to go a whole month without using the word "primate." I said that one of my favorite authors, Gabriel García Márquez, wouldn't mind being called a primate but then in addition, he was also García Márquez. "The same with Mozart!" J.M. shrieked. Nelse in defense said that he had never implied that anthropology was the "be all end all" of human life to which J.M. whispered, "Bullshit." She shoved in a Carlos Montoya tape which seemed to suit the landscape between Almeria and Brewster.

There was a comic episode when we passed through our county seat. I was appalled to see that my very old Subaru was still on the car lot of the dealership where we had traded it in on the new pickup. My beloved car looked lonely behind rows of spiffier models so we stopped and I bought it back. I was even offended at the low price though the speedometer had turned over once so that the total mileage was one hundred and seventy thousand, and there was some corrosion from Santa Monica's salt-air mists. I don't think this was reverse snobbism but a simple emotional attachment. I had once overheard our high school coach refer to me as a "rich bitch" but this was the same man who had snuck into the girls' locker room when I was alone and demanded to see me naked. I still occasionally dealt with the ethical question of whether I should have tattled on him, which I didn't, but then I knew his wife and kids who were nice if not overly humble under the domination of this dickhead bully.

I felt rejuvenated driving the old car back home as if I could drive far enough into the past to be fully well again, perhaps find a new job and a new lover and we would carry each other nimbly into our old age. The latter fantasy quickly became beyond my powers of imagination but not the idea that I might retrace my path to, say, last summer when my life had reached fruition. This would include, of course, going to the doctor when I felt odd in early December when my disease was likely still at "Stage I" and after surgery I might reasonably expect to live five more years and perhaps have a grandchild or two. I suppose these collective idiocies were comprehensible and it was hard to let them go but then I saw Nelse and J.M. in the rearview mirror and returned to the present, possibly a suspicious notion in itself.

I already knew that Ruth would be at Naomi's and rather perfectly Ruth, Naomi and Paul were sitting on the broad front porch. She fairly ran out to greet me as she had done when I came home from the university and she was still in high school. She embraced me lightly as if I were fragile which I was. I asked about her current gentleman friend and she said she had had to "let him go." She was still hearing music she couldn't find on earth. I looked toward the porch where Naomi and Paul were standing and thought they looked like my parents would have if my father were still alive. This gave me a good feeling and I waved.

When we were all in the living room I said that I had no intention of dragging all of this out for more than a day or two and asked

Naomi if she could also ask Lundquist for dinner. I could see by looking at them directly that this would be the hardest part. There's really no way to minimalize your love for others and you wished terribly
you could stay with them so they wouldn't be hurt. I asked Ruth to
play the piano to dispel my nervousness. Naomi brought me a glass
of lemonade and everyone wept while Ruth played some Chopin I
had especially liked, and then Ruth took me upstairs to my old room
where we talked awhile with James Dean staring at us from his poster.

After a disturbing nap where in a dream I actually saw all the horses
and dogs of my life, I slipped out of the house, waved to Naomi, Paul
and Ruth who were standing out in the garden, then drove over to
the old place. The pick-up was parked out by the bunkhouse and I
didn't want to disturb Nelse and J.M. in whatever they were up to so
I went into the house to do a few things, stopping in the pump and
storage shed to cut an ample piece from a webbed hammock which
was harder to do than I thought with simple scissors. When I passed
through the kitchen Frieda was sitting there at the breakfast table
staring at the rose-patterned tablecloth which I didn't care for but
she thought quite beautiful. Her face was swollen with crying so I gave
her a pat and sat down for a cup of coffee and a chocolate pie with
three inches of whipped cream on top which she had made for Nelse
who had the metabolism she had always been waiting for. Frieda
lacked her father's profound religiosity and stared at me, saying, "It's
not goddamned fair." That was that except for the ticking of the clock
and a meadowlark out beyond the grape arbor.

Upstairs I packed a small suitcase with hot-weather clothes and
a ten-pound smooth stone that I had retrieved from the bottom of
the Niobrara and had always used as a doorstop. I opened my little
safe that Grandfather had kept behind books in the den with its elaborate combination, one-two-three, and took out a fair-sized thicket of
cash, but also looked long and hard at a photo of his great love, Adelle,
Neena's older sister. I then left the safe open to avoid problems for
others.

I looked out the side window and saw that Nelse and J.M. were now in the barnyard talking to Lundquist so I started out to join them. Halfway down I stopped in the stairwell where there was a small Davis landscape and pondered again this young man's falling off the cliff near Durango in Mexico. My semi-quarrel with Paul about the memoir came about when Paul wouldn't quite accept the fact that Grandfather's loss of both Davis and Adelle had left a violently deep hole in his life. When I first read about Davis my mind errantly came up with the joke about life being short but very wide. Out the back door I stopped again seeing J.M. sitting in the warm dust with her back against a fence post of the corral trying to pet both Roscoe and Ted at the same time, but Roscoe wouldn't accept democracy and kept snarling at the much larger Ted who cowered. I seemed to be in a half dozen parallel universes at once with a physical ache that the pills couldn't dispel so that there was a universe of pain, plus an image of Davis drowning a toothache with tequila, climbing up the mountain and falling off, plus the coldly abstract thought that maybe all of these questions I pose to myself about the meaning of life are simply none of my business, that God or whoever is a fascist as big as Betelgeuse and mortals aren't entitled to raise questions except for a few small gods disguised as humans. The rest of us can only bark out our ultimate puzzlement like half-human dogs. I liked dogs enough so that this concept didn't strike me as all bad.

Nelse helped me saddle up Rose while Lundquist gave a curious lecture to Roscoe about being more pleasant to Ted, but then Roscoe was such a hard case he was beyond even Lundquist's reach at the moment, staring down at the earth as if he wished to bite it. I sensed that Nelse had doubts about my going for a ride but limited himself to a single, "Are you sure?" Ted didn't want to go along because, Lundquist explained, Rose had nipped Ted when he tried to steal a bite of her oats.

Nelse's doubts were justified. I wanted to show I was right in getting on Rose so I made it through the first dense shelterbelt but halfway there both mind and body were crackling with a blue light of pain. I dropped the reins short of the big rock pile, and slid off,

falling backward on my butt. Rose acted appalled at first, then began
grazing, ignoring the human foibles of her rider flopped there in the
grass. This certainly was a hundred-percent reconfirmation of my
plan. It was clearly impossible for me to live on an earth where I
couldn't ride a horse. I lay there until my pain subsided enough for
me to lead Rose back to the corral and barn. I was thankful that no
one was there to witness my embarrassment.

I went into the house, took two of the new whopper pills and
called Naomi but no one answered. When I went back outside Ruth
drove into the yard, not seeing me yet because I had gone out the
front door and I was standing by the tire swing. I walked over and
startled her because she was listening to the end of a Stravinsky tape
and couldn't hear my footsteps. "Oh, it's you," she said and we
laughed, then drove down the narrow gravel road to the Niobrara.
We sat there on a grassy bank for nearly an hour with her arm around
my shoulder, saying virtually nothing because the sound of the red-
winged blackbirds in a nearby marsh and the sound of the river flowing were quite enough.

Our good-bye dinner was nearly unendurable but I knew it would
be. Everyone was at their gracious best but there was really nowhere
to go with any concept of behavior. They were all quite pale with
effort and I kept hearing my heart thump as you occasionally do
when you suddenly turn over in bed, and then quickly move again
to avoid the sound. Only I couldn't move beyond pouring myself
some wine and lifting a fork. I had brought over several of Grandfather's best bottles but their contents were scarcely touched except by Lundquist who normally thought of wine as a papist plot.
He sat on my left and Naomi on my right and I held his hand under
the table when he began shaking.

When we finished our scant eating I delivered a little speech I
hadn't really prepared because my mind was no longer able to focus
itself for a sufficient time. This is what I feared most, that the admix-
ture of pain, drugs and sheer mammalian desperation would reduce

my mind to a gape-mouthed howl. It was time to go and that was that so I told them my plan and the reasoning behind it. I said why should I suffer and make others suffer watching me? With my plan I was being logical rather than brave. I had received my sentence but I was still capable of dying on my own terms which I now viewed as the blessing left to me other than their presence here and that we were all able to embrace our farewells. I asked Nelse and J.M. to spend the night at Naomi's because if I saw any of them again I might fall apart. I finished by saying that I'd send back my little journal in which all of this is written or at least write a good-bye letter from where I was going. I went around the table and kissed them good-bye and it was as if we all had palsy.

I kissed my mother and my son for the last time and tried to memorize the feel of their skin on my lips. I left then without looking back, driving down the gravel road toward home with blurred eyes but a lighter heart. I got Ted in from his kennel and curled up with him on the grand leather couch in Grandfather's den. I felt a bit brain-dead from grief and didn't like it that way so I leafed through a long book on Winslow Homer before I slept.

I was up at first light, fed Ted a hearty meal and was off. When I reached the corner where our gravel road met the county blacktop Nelse stepped out from a grove of trees and crossed the ditch. We kissed good-bye again through my open car window.

St. Louis, Missouri—May? I don't know the date. Who cares?

I made it here after sixteen hours of not very skillful driving. The illusion that I could drive all the way to the Florida Keys now amuses me at midnight. It was pointlessly willful and my mind drifts enough so that I'm a bit of a menace if I don't rest every two hours or so. The Subaru has also lost some of its compression, perhaps by sitting around, so that when I floor the gas pedal the car still has difficulty reaching sixty. I am in a ghastly motel near the airport, the kind that Nelse professes to hate. It is warm and muggy so I turned on the air condi-

tioner and when I awoke in the middle of the night I turned on the
television to make sure the world was still there though this is scarcely
bona fide evidence. It is dawn now and time to get myself over to the
airport. I will leave the keys in the car and hope some unfortunate
soul swipes the car. I'll put a little money in the glove compartment
as a reward.

Lower Sugar Loaf Key, a nameless day and date in my life's history!

I am at a pleasant lodge. I love this place. Too bad I don't feel well
enough to stay longer even though it's dreadfully hot and humid. I
was feeling captious when I checked in late in the afternoon and paid
for two weeks in advance. I drove around for a little while after I
washed up but on Big Pine Key I couldn't find the little encampment
on the tidal creek where Grace and Bobby Pindar lived in a shack
and Duane in an old Airstream, and the makeshift tiny corral in back
where the buckskin stayed. The horse had looked fairly good at age
eighteen though missing a hoof. It loved to swim in the creek. But I
couldn't find the place and stopped at a diner out on the highway
after leaving the general area where I knew it had been, which now
looked like a subdivision in Lincoln if you turned away from the water.
In the diner an old commercial fisherman told me the tidal creek had
been diverted into a dredged canal for the subdivision and Bobby and
Grace Pindar had long since moved over to Louisiana.

That evening I got an envelope from the desk to mail this journal
back home. Earlier, when I had returned from Big Pine, I stopped at
a marina near the lodge but it was six and they were getting ready to
close. A young, corpulent gentleman of at least part-Cuban descent
asked me to come back in the morning after he had thought over my
request which was for a small seaworthy boat with a reliable engine,
new or used, to puddle around in for a few weeks. I also bought a

navigational chart of the immediate area. There was one on the wall in the lobby of the lodge but I needed to study it. On the way back I noted a few boats passing back and forth under the highway bridge near the lodge, and up in my room I was excited to see that Bow Channel that led out toward American Shoals on the Atlantic side of the highway was quite close. This was a stroke of luck because the authorities had figured, and a few witnesses had corroborated, that Duane had ridden the horse on the road's shoulder from Big Pine down toward Lower Sugar Loaf, rather than simply in the creek on the swift outgoing tide. Those who don't really know horses are ignorant of what massive strength their musculature offers.

When I got out of the shower I put my large stone in the hammock webbing and knotted it, then ran an old *concho* belt Paul had given me through the webbing and secured the belt around my waist. It would work. This was an undressed rehearsal! I was bold enough to look at a full-length mirror for the first time in a month or so and was idiotically surprised at how much weight I had lost. At this rate I would waste away to nothing in a few months. All I was doing was beating my body to the punch. I took off my suicide equipment, put on a robe and went out on the balcony to watch a glorious sunset over the dozens of mangrove keys to the east. There were flocks of birds flying everywhere and I thought that Naomi absolutely must visit this place. I went down and had a hamburger at the bar not wanting to sit in the brightly lit dining room. The evening news was on the television, portraying a world which I had doubts about. Was anyone familiar with this pictured world of lightning-fast tic-tac-toe over the skin of earth? The hamburger was good though I could manage only a few bites and the bar was too dark to read the only book I had brought along, an anthology of American poetry about which I now had doubts in terms of a traveling companion. I was dealing with quite enough consciousness of my own, and anyone else's at this point seemed senselessly invasive.

* * *

I was up and about early, bought my little boat in trim shape with a twenty-horse engine, a notion that has always bothered me. How could this sorry little engine be as powerful as twenty horses? I paid what was probably an unfair price, far above what a sensible man would have forked over, but then cash was scarcely a problem. A pleasant young man, a Cuban in a mechanic's outfit, took me for a trial run and his instructions were simple enough. He sternly warned me not to go out when the waves were over two feet but luckily the seas were very calm. The engine was on idle and we were drifting with the tide as he gave me instructions. I thought I saw a large shark but he said it was a tarpon. I was absurdly pleased when he flirted. I offered him a hundred-dollar bill to show me Bow Channel, saying that I used to fish out there. He refused the money saying that it wasn't very far away but I leaned over and stuffed it in his pocket. It was very hot while we were drifting but when we sped out toward the channel the breeze was delicious. We changed places at the channel entrance and he was my passenger on the way back to the marina where I dropped him off, then proceeded toward the bridge, went under it and tied off at the lodge's dock.

Up in the room I nervously addressed the envelope home, sticking all my money in the back of the journal, saving out only enough for postage. I was still somewhat exhilarated by the boat ride but dreaded the long wait until evening. But then why wait until evening? Duane's timing was surely accidental. He had to wait until I was asleep and then also he could find his way in the dark. The ocean would feel much better in the brilliantly hot noonday sun. I've quickly packed my beach bag with my Niobrara stone, the piece of hammock, and the belt I will take with me on my long voyage downward. Nothing else but my body and the fresh pill I had just taken. I send a kiss and a good-bye to those I love so much. Naomi, Paul, Lundquist, Nelse and J.M. I hope I am going to join my lover.

ACKNOWLEDGMENTS

For research help, I'd like to especially thank John Carter, Jack Turner, Lawrence Sullivan and John Harrison, also Charles Cleland, Roger Welsch, Bill Quigley, Vergil Noble and Matt and Adrian Kapsner.